THE
ERKENBLOOD

Wielders of Sessara
Book One

H. FERRY

The Erkenblood by H. Ferry

www.ferryfiction.com

Disclaimer

This is a work of fiction. Characters, cultures, religious elements, and locations introduced in this book are imaginary and DO NOT represent similar entities in our world. Any resemblance to actual entities is entirely coincidental.

This book contains themes that may not be suitable for all audiences. Contact the author for more information regarding these themes.

Editing Services

Charlie Knight, Jodi Christensen, Jodie Angell

Cover Design

Lance Buckley

ISBN 978-3-910270-00-8

Independently published.

For Audrey

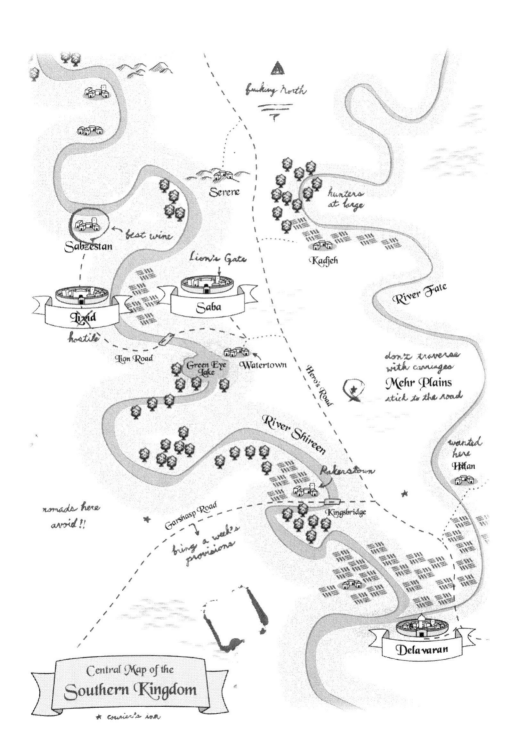

fucking North

Serene

hunters
at large

Sabzestan

← best wine

Kadjeh

Lion's Gate

River Fate

Lixid

Saba

don't traverse
with carriages

hostile

Mehr Plains
stick to the road

Lion Road

Green Eye
Lake

Watertown

Hero's Road

wanted
here
Hilan

River Shireen

nomads here
avoid !!

Garshasp Road

Pulenstown

Kingsbridge

bring a week's
provisions

Delavaran

Central Map of the
Southern Kingdom

* courier's inn

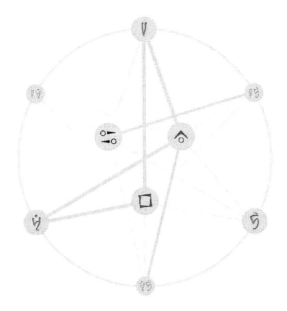

THIS BOOK EXPLORES

6 / 17

POSSIBLE MANIFESTATIONS OF THE ARCANE.

PART I

HEROES

1

I admit, she wasn't my choice at first. We had searched for centuries for the ultimate savior mentioned in the Book of Creation. The one who would bring peace to a world burning in flames of war. She did not fit the prophecy.

T HE OLD CITY SLEPT. There were no quarreling merchants, no jostling crowd. Lights had died in the derelict houses, and the streets and narrow alleyways were empty. The silence amplified the ringing in Panthea's ears, and the smell of rot in the air seemed to become more invasive every time she ventured here for the potion.

A rustle cut through the ringing, and she wheeled back. She'd made sure no one had followed her. Sapphires did not like late night exchanges between the two districts. Although they also didn't care to patrol these streets at night, there could always be that one soldier who took their job seriously enough to lose sleep over it, and all it would take for her to disappear from the face of the world was an arrest. No Erkenblood returned from that, no matter the charges.

It wasn't a Sapphire. Just a scrawny cat dragging a small carcass into the shadows. Equally startled, the cat dropped its load and gave Panthea a vexed glare through glinting eyes, adding a grating moan when she stared too long.

She pulled her hood forward and continued toward the smuggler's house before her fear took hold. If she lost control, the destruction alone would announce her as an Erkenblood, and it would no longer matter how discreet she had been.

Rassus would not be happy. He had asked her to tell him as soon as her power emerged, but she knew the result of such a conversation. He would force her to train, and she was not ready. With the way her power felt when it surfaced, with the things she had read and heard about power-lust, there was a real chance she would hurt someone or do something irreversible.

For now, she had found a temporary alternative: sapping potion.

It was what Sapphires used to capture her kind. Every time Panthea drank the concoction, her power vanished within seconds, and the effect lasted for about a day. If Rassus discovered this had been her nightly ritual for all thirteen days of the past thretnight, being arrested would be a blessing compared to what he would do.

She finally arrived in front of the misshapen clay house and its grimy wooden door, steeling herself as she knocked. Her lack of composure made for an authentic scowl well-suited to these visits.

The door opened. The smuggler's beady eyes, bloodshot with sleep, stared at her from the shadows. His wiry hair was in disarray.

She held out the usual four crowns.

The man glanced at the money, and his disheveled beard shifted with a smirk. "The price has gone up."

He seemed to recognize how desperate she was. She was too easy to read, as her friend, Ash, always liked to point out. Regardless, Panthea was in no position to haggle. She added the last of her coins—six crowns in total.

"Eight," the man pushed.

"I don't have that much," she said, her voice quavering.

"And I don't enjoy stealing from the Sapphires. Eight crowns or get out of my sight."

The sound in her ears had become unbearable, fueled by her fear of what was coming. The sweet anticipation, the power-lust, pressed under her skull. "I'll bring more coins next time," she tried through her quickening breath.

"Would you give up already?" he said with a grimace. "You're only delaying the inevitable."

The truth in those words stung. It was an exhilarating moment for most Erkenbloods to feel their power for the first time. For Panthea, it had been terrorizing. And her power grew more intense, the lust more difficult to contain, with every passing day.

"Well, then," the man dismissed, "I suppose this concludes our business."

Her vision brightened, her presence of mind drifting away as the joy of power took over. She saw the reflection of her eyes illuminating the man's face. "I'm not leaving," she muttered. "I need the potion tonight."

He recoiled, his eyes wide with fresh fear. "Wait. Just . . ." He raised a hand to gesture for her to stay. Then he scurried inside and came back with a vial of the potion. "Here. Quick."

She emptied the vial into her mouth. As the potion coursed down her throat, the ringing stopped, and the world lifted its weight from her shoulders as her power subsided. The only bitterness that remained was of the man's gaze.

"You listen to me, witch," he said, emboldened. "I hope you enjoyed your last dose. You're a menace, and you must be contained." He glanced at her hand and swiped all her coins. "Next time you show up here, everyone will learn about your little secret."

The door slammed shut, making her flinch. She took a moment to swallow the anger squeezing her heart. It wasn't like she had chosen this life. To be born a wielder, to suffer from power-lust, to live in a land where her mere existence was a crime.

Chill pierced her skin as she headed back. The neighborhood felt eerier than it had before the potion. Without the ringing, she realized how loud her footfalls were.

As she approached the sign reading Rue Square, she increased her pace, her heart racing at the thought of someone snatching her from the shadows. Lofty buildings surrounded the blind alleyway, shrouding the dark courtyard famous for some of the most vicious murder stories in Saba. Panthea hoped this night would end with her in her bed in the Upper City, not cut into pieces in this slum.

Another pair of footfalls echoed, almost matching hers in pace. *Annahid, in the name of what's dead and what's living and what's divine, protect your lesser daughter.* She wanted to walk faster. She wanted to look back. But if she had learned one thing from Evian's stories of the Old City, it was that to acknowledge a predator was to spur them into action.

"Halt."

And with that one word, none of it mattered. It could only come from a Sapphire soldier, which meant she had to stop.

The man walked to her and clapped her underarm as he commanded, "Put them up."

She complied. He flipped her hood back so abruptly it made her gasp. Then he started to frisk at her wrists. She struggled to keep her composure as he continued the search, her skin crawling as his thick hands snaked around her abdomen.

Five more Sapphires appeared ahead of her, led by an older man wearing a violet cloak. *Great Annahid, help me.*

The violet-clad man was a full head and shoulder taller than her. He had a chest-long silver beard he'd woven into a braid and an air of authority that only belonged to a politician. In fact, the lion insignia on his shirt proclaimed him as a general. Considering there was only one general in this city, this made him General Heim. The governor of Saba— the man who had killed the most powerful Erkenblood in the Southern Kingdom not so many years ago.

"What seems to be the problem here?" he asked.

The soldier brought her arms down, then held her by the wrist, so she wouldn't escape. "She was wandering the streets. She might be a rebel. Twelve out of thirteen times, they are at this time of night. I must take her in for questioning."

"But I've done nothing wrong," she protested, her wobbling legs barely holding her.

The general stepped closer and put his finger under Panthea's chin to raise her head. She recoiled, which elicited a far more aggressive response from the man. He grabbed her face, leather glove scraping against her skin.

After a long inspection, understanding spread over the man's countenance, giving birth to a satisfied smile that filled her chest with hot lead. She had forgotten to close her eyes, and he could have noticed the glimmering emerald green in them, the telltale mark of her kind. She dropped her head, even though it was too late.

He let go. "Listen, child. These are troubling times. Windhammer's rebellion has made many people nervous, and while these fellows try to keep us all safe, innocents like you could get caught in the crossfire."

The name Windhammer had become legendary. This year alone, there had been at least ten assassinations in his name in the west and even an insurrection on the Inquisition bureau in Livid. Although Sapphires had defended the bureau and arrested the perpetrators, it didn't take away from the audacity it took to plan such an attack.

She nodded, not tearing her gaze from the ground.

The general motioned for her captor to release her. Once she was free, he bent to whisper in her ear. "I know what you are. Logic says I should fear you. I say logic be damned. We all get to choose. Do not get yourself in trouble again."

His unyielding expression did not waver as he straightened. "Let her go," he said, his tone making it sound more like an order than a request. "She's no threat. I'm sure she's lost her way and ended up here."

He then spared her an inscrutable smile that left her wondering whether to feel relieved or worried. It was not like Sapphires to let someone off with a warning. Less when they knew she was an Erkenblood.

Whatever the reason, Panthea needed to use this opportunity before the governor changed his mind. She walked away, ignoring their gazes until she was out of their sight.

The walk home felt longer than it had ever been. She looked back every once in a while to see whether any of them still followed.

When she arrived in front of her house, the lights were burning. Rassus was awake, which meant a different sort of trouble.

As she opened the door, it wasn't Rassus waiting for her. To her surprise, it was Ash. The fifteen-year-old girl sat in a corner, keeping a spoon afloat in the air using her gleamstone. The white glow of the stone accentuated her dark skin and round cheeks. She whipped her head to Panthea, her curly ball of hair catching up an instant later.

Ash's brown eyes twinkled, and a grin grew on her full lips. She dropped the stone, and the spoon followed as the glow faded. This was the greatest compliment for someone who knew the girl. If she cared enough to quit wielding, she cared a great deal.

Ash ran to Panthea and pulled her into a suffocating embrace. "You're a dope, you know that?"

Panthea smiled. "I didn't expect to find *you* here this late." It was only then she registered Ash was in her white nightgown. "Are you sleeping over? It's been long since—"

"Since we thought you were dead?" Ash said, letting go of Panthea. "Master and Evian have gone looking for you."

Panthea winced. This was it. She was dying tonight.

"Yes." Ash stretched the word with a knowing nod. "You're in trouble"—she turned her voice gruff to imitate Rassus—"you reckless, imprudent brat."

"Hey!" Panthea chuckled. "Master never says brat."

Ash shrugged. "He might as well. The man's like a gleamstone without the glow."

Panthea gave her a hard look, though she couldn't keep the laughter out of her words. "Don't talk like that about your teacher."

"Oh, by the way." Ash perked up, pulling her by the hand. "Want to see my robe?"

"Your robe?"

Ash's shoulders drooped. "Don't tell me you forgot about tomorrow."

It took Panthea a moment to remember. The pilgrimage. The welcome reminder brought tonight's events to a deeper place in her mind. Come morning, the two of them would get out of this city together, and she would show Ash everything she knew about the journey. Inside the temple, with Ash at her side, power-lust stood no chance. Besides, no one in the temples cared she was an Erkenblood.

"So, you *are* sleeping over."

"No." Ash shrugged. "I'm here at midnight for laughs." The girl had a permanent curve toward the corners of her lips, which gave the impression of a smirk even when she was serious. "Of course, I'm sleeping over, Dopey. That's why I brought my robe too. I'm ready for the adventure."

"The pilgrimage is not an adventure. We're going there to pray."

"I know. I'm just excited is all." The girl's eyebrows furrowed. "Is everything okay? I didn't want to bring this up, but you've been acting weird lately."

Panthea wouldn't ruin Ash's excitement by telling her about her secret. "I'm fine. A little tired."

Ash shook her head in an exaggerated display of disappointment. "You're one. Terrible. Liar."

The door swung open.

"Uh-oh." Ash hid behind Panthea.

Rassus entered, his head almost reaching the top of the door frame. His long, ashen mustache and beard did not line up as perfectly as they normally did. Evian ran in after him. His black hair was a complete mess, his bronze skin less vibrant than usual.

Evian wasn't a wielder himself, and he rarely did anything risky. But stuck with two wielding apprentices who always got in trouble, he often ended up being the one who had to smooth things out. Now, he stood in front of the girls protectively, even though his slender form was not cut out for that kind of gesture.

Rassus touched the gleamstone tucked inside the top of his wooden staff. The glow from the stone lit the bottom of his face, and the door closed on its own.

Evian extended his arms to his sides, shielding Ash and Panthea as they stepped backward. "Master, let us all calm down and discuss this problem in a more—"

Another glow, and Evian slid out of the way, stumbling as he regained his balance.

"Look at you two," Rassus growled. "My wayward apprentices, huddling."

Ash walked away. "That's it, Panthea. You're on your own. I did—"

"Stay where you are, Ashena," Rassus commanded. "I'll have a word with you too, little Angra-spawn."

Ash's head dropped as she rejoined Panthea. "Great."

Evian didn't join them this time. When Panthea's gaze met his, he pursed his lips, the concern in his hazel eyes providing no comfort.

Rassus stared Panthea down. "What did I say about leaving the house by yourself?"

She knew better than to give an answer and enough to realize he was not looking for one.

"And you, Ashena. How many times did I tell you not to take your gleamstone outside?"

Panthea's eyes darted to Ash. Was she still doing that? If Sapphires caught her, imprisonment would be the least she could expect. One could get executed for wielding in public.

"Um, six and a half," Ash answered, too matter-of-factly for the situation. "If you count the time when—"

"It was a rhetorical question," the old man roared. "If I ask you to do something, or not to, it's for your own good. If I'm to teach you wielding, I need to be sure you won't be foolish enough to lose your heads over it."

"Sorry, Master," Panthea said.

Ash echoed her, adding, "Now, how much trouble are we in?"

"Much." Rassus walked to the shelf in the corner. "Neither of you is going on the pilgrimage this year," he said as he picked up their permits.

Ash's eyes widened in horror. "No!"

"Master," Evian stepped in. "Please. I think they've—"

Rassus tore the papers. The sound sent a shiver down Panthea's spine.

"No, no, no." Ash burst into tears.

Panthea remembered her first pilgrimage two years ago and how excited she had been. That memory made her feel Ash's pain. She tried to comfort her, but Ash shoved her away as she stomped to the door. "Leave me alone. You never wanted this anyway."

"You're not leaving, young lady," Rassus called after her.

Ash opened the door. "Stop me with your gleamstone, why don't you?"

The girl slammed the door behind her. Panthea was not any happier than her friend. Poor Ash. This would have been her very first time.

Panthea turned to Rassus. "Did you really have to do that?"

"Most certainly. I won't send you two halfway across the realm on your own, while this is the way you handle yourselves. One way or another, I'll teach you prudence."

He removed his robe and hung it on the robe rack. The wooden pendant he always wore was visible on his shirt. It was a thick disk with the Angelic word for 'light' etched on one side of it. This very word had kindled her passion for the language, and she was now fluent in it.

Rassus used to be more amiable when she was younger. He would spend day after day teaching her history and languages. He would sit with her and answer all her questions. It was hard to see him so bitter now. It wasn't fair to Ash, who had only known him for three years. And it wasn't fair to Rassus himself. Ash had never seen the kind side of her teacher.

The old man went to his room. Now that they were alone, Evian came to Panthea and held her by the shoulder, murmuring, "Are you all right?"

She drew a ragged breath. "We were so excited." Her voice cracked toward the end.

"I know," Evian said, frustration trickling from his tone. He enveloped her in his arms, pressing her head to his chest. He smelled of roses and turmeric, like he always did after a day's work as a healer.

Panthea closed her eyes and let his scent and warmth soothe her.

2

Before I tell you the story of our savior, allow me to begin with one of my own. For to know why I chose whom I chose, you must first understand why I fight.

N EXT MORNING, PANTHEA woke to the realization that the smuggler had given her a watered-down dose. The effect had worn off overnight. Her power was back with all its might, and it was up to her alone to contain it.

For the last hour, she'd been trying. Experienced Erkenbloods could use a gleamstone even without being sapped. Before her power had emerged, Panthea had thought it easy. But nothing could have prepared her for the vast difference between inborn and conductive wielding. The books could tell her how each worked, but not how they felt.

With inborn wielding, she felt everything around her. The walls, the floor, the book in front of her. It was as though they were her limbs, and she could move them as easily. It was close to impossible to draw from a gleamstone when her own blood brimmed with power.

She made another attempt to use the stone in her hand to lift the book, but the gratifying feeling resurfaced, a sign that she had once again drawn from her blood. In that one moment, she had no fear, no anxiety. Just a burning desire to continue, to let go. It was no wonder they called this power-lust.

"When it comes, you'll know it," Rassus had told her all those years ago, when she had asked how it would feel when her power manifested. "But I'll be there for you, no matter when and how it emerges."

When and how.

Matter-wielding Erkenbloods got their power at a later age than those who wielded space or time. However, most had theirs by twelve, regardless of the element. Late bloomers always faced complications. Panthea was eighteen.

If Rassus were the same person he'd been until a few years ago, maybe she would have told him everything. But he had changed. The distance between them had grown with every reproof, every punishment, every new and unbending rule. She still loved him with all her heart, but a part of her was wary around him now—a shift she could notice in Evian too.

The door opened, and Ash entered the house. Panthea got to her feet, unsure of how to start the conversation. The Ash she knew wouldn't be here while the city prepared to see the pilgrims off. She would rush to the ceremony, forgetting even to bring Panthea along. But after last night, no one could blame her for avoiding any reminder of the pilgrimage she was not going on.

Ash went to the cupboard, picked up her gleamstone, then walked in Panthea's direction with slow steps. In one unexpected moment, Ash wrapped her arms around Panthea and kept the embrace for a beat before she pulled away. Then she went to the middle of the room and sat down. Although neither talked even after that, at least Panthea knew she had been forgiven.

She sat beside Ash and got back to her futile attempts to draw from the gleamstone. It didn't take long for Ash to lift the spoon in front of her and bend it in the air, but Panthea still struggled with her target.

"Okay, now, I'm getting worried," Ash said. "What's going on with you? Since when can't you move a single book?"

Panthea sighed. She could if her blood wasn't in the way. "It's more complicated than you think."

Ash's gleamstone glowed with tendrils of white light, and the book flew away. She shrugged. "It was easy enough."

Of course, it was easy for Ash. A gleamstone was the only source of arcane power for an ordinary human like her. For Panthea, on the other hand, focusing on the faint, distant energy of her gleamstone was like whispering hopelessly to someone on the far side of the bustling main square.

She stood and went to pick up the book, but it evaded her. "Stop it," she demanded.

Ash cracked a smile.

Part of Panthea was getting impatient, while another part played along with the young wielder. Ash prevented her from reaching the book no matter how hard she tried.

"Fine." Panthea held up her own gleamstone. "I can wield too, you know."

She called the book to herself, and it proved too obedient. It flew up to her forehead and knocked her back.

Now, she would be the butt of Ash's new joke.

Except Ash didn't laugh this time. When Panthea sat up, she found the young wielder gaping.

Ash pointed at Panthea's face. "Your eyes. They . . . glowed."

Panthea had felt it. Every fiber of her body lusted for wielding now, and she chided herself for it. Her power-lust could have taken over because of a childish game.

"So, that's what you've been hiding," Ash said in understanding. "Your power's emerged. How long? Why didn't you tell me?"

Panthea shushed her, still struggling to keep the power-lust at bay. *She's Ash. She's your friend.* If she forgot to remind herself, if she disconnected from reality, disaster would follow.

Rassus entered the sitting room, carrying the bag of his healing supplies. Ash covered her mouth with the back of her hand to tell Panthea she wouldn't say a word.

The young wielder didn't greet their teacher. To make her position clear, she also turned away from him.

Rassus removed some potions and oils from the bag and replaced them with some others from the shelves. He had to have noticed Ash was theatrically ignoring him. But he seemed unaffected by her attitude. He didn't even try to apologize.

"Your parents were distraught," Rassus said in a quiet growl, "when they found out you wanted to learn wielding."

Ash looked at him over her shoulder, her expression impassive.

"They came to me," the old man continued, "and begged me to discourage you. To refuse to teach you."

He turned to face Ash, and she looked away.

"Wielding was your dream. I promised myself I'd help you realize it. And I promised your parents I'd keep you safe. I never take you two to executions. Evian has seen them; he knows the fate awaiting those who wield. I don't want that fate for any of you."

Panthea smiled—her power-lust now diminished. Ash, however, held her ground.

Evian entered the house, carrying a bucket of drinking water, his satchel hanging loosely from his shoulder by its leather strap. When he met Rassus's gaze, he looked down, biting his thin lip. The old man had that effect on people these days. Something bothered him, and it wasn't just the safety of his apprentices. Panthea wished she knew what it was, but she could not blame him for keeping secrets when she herself hid her greatest secret from him.

Evian set the bucket down and said in a jovial tone, "The ceremony's about to start. You girls want to go?"

"Not interested," Ash said.

Panthea got up and gave Evian a tight smile. "I don't think Master wants me to go."

"Master?" Evian asked. "Do you mind if I steal them from you?"

"I said," Ash enunciated her words, "I'm not going."

Evian eyeballed Rassus for a few moments, but the old man was too busy rummaging in his bag. Evian closed the door before he crouched beside the young wielder. "You know the pilgrimage is every year, don't you? Panthea didn't do it when she was your age. Tell her, Panthea."

Panthea gave the confirmation he sought with a nod.

"You two can go," Ash said. "You don't need me. I'd bring the mood down, anyway."

"What?" Evian chuckled. "Ash bringing down the mood? That's something I never thought I'd hear."

Ash shrugged. "Well, you're welcome."

Panthea put her hand on Evian's shoulder. "You can go. I'll stay here with Ash."

Evian got up and turned to her, impatience lacing his otherwise kind smile. "Come on, girls. This happens only once a year."

"Best if you all go," Rassus finally spoke. "I have to see a patient, and for obvious reasons, I'd rather have Evian keep an eye on you two."

"See, Ash?" Evian gestured toward Rassus. "Even Master agrees."

Ash shot Rassus a piercing glance. "Master also tore my paper to pieces. You need to work on your arguments, Evian."

"Ash," Panthea scolded.

"What? It's true. It's still there on the shelf."

A banging on the door turned all heads. Evian and Ash both sprang up in alarm, eyes wide.

"Open the door!" someone shouted from outside.

Rassus dropped the bag and exchanged a meaningful look with a terrified Evian before he shuffled to him. "Evian, I fear the day we've been waiting for has come a little too soon. Take care of the girls for me."

Panthea's stomach lurched. "What's happening?"

"Evian will explain everything when it's safe," Rassus said.

Ash's brow wrinkled as she glanced at the others.

Rassus went to her. "Always follow your dream, Ashena."

Ash fumbled with words for a second but said nothing coherent.

The old man turned to Panthea next and held her head between his boney hands. "Things are going to change. You need to be strong."

"Master, who are they?" she asked with a quavering voice.

"The Inquisition. They're here for me. I've been expecting this for four years now."

Panthea went cold. She knew two things about the Inquisition. First, they didn't just go around knocking. Second, Rassus wouldn't survive them. Her mind immediately went back to her encounter with the general, and the realization froze her breath. Was this why he had let her go? Had she brought the Inquisition here with her foolishness?

The man thundered again from outside, and the hinges of the door threatened to give out under the kicking. "Open this door, or we'll break it."

"You must hide," Rassus whispered. "In your room, now."

Evian tried to pull Panthea's arm, but she jerked it free. Overcome by guilt, she gave in to a sob that rendered her next words meaningless. "I'm not letting them take you, Master."

"What did I say about being strong? Don't cry like a child." The old man reached inside his robe and removed the wooden pendant from around his neck, then hung it around hers. "Here. I promise I'll come back for this. Now, go."

This time, she couldn't protest. Evian grabbed her arm and took her and Ash to the room, where he sat them on the edge of the bed before locking the door. As he joined them, the sound of the soldiers breaking through the front door shook the walls. Evian held Panthea and Ash.

Ash bit on her nails.

Panthea tried to remain quiet but couldn't stop her wheezing. Tears streamed down her face. She wished she could be as strong as Rassus wanted her to be.

"Face against the wall, wielder," a soldier shouted from the other room.

"I'm no wielder," Rassus said.

"We've heard otherwise."

The sounds grew distant. They were taking him away.

Having cried in one breath for some time, Panthea gasped reflexively. Evian clamped her mouth with his hand, but the damage was already done.

"Did you hear that?" carried one man's voice.

"Hear what?" another answered. "Let's go. We have what we want."

"I'm going to check the other rooms."

Panthea and Ash exchanged worried looks. Ash, who had kept quiet so far, seemed to be breaking. Evian curled his lips into a hushing gesture, still holding Panthea's mouth.

Shadows appeared below the door. Panthea's legs trembled. Ash took her hand and squeezed painfully as the man turned the handle. "It's locked."

"What are you doing?" said the other soldier. "Stop wasting time. You heard the Inquisitor. No side objectives on this one."

The shadow shifted, and Panthea exhaled in relief. Then, just as her heart slowed down, the loudest thump struck the door. Ash screamed.

"Told you." The soldier kicked the door open.

The man looked like he'd come out of a nightmare. Half of his face was hidden in the shadow of a raven-black hood. Layers above layers of black leather flaked over the shoulders of his suit and on top of his chest, and the same darkness covered his entire body. "What have we here? Little apprentices? Get up. You're all coming, too."

The glint of his dagger flashed in Panthea's eyes, and her vision brightened. Her fear vanished, and the lust pressed under her throat. "Evian," she rasped as she drifted into oblivion. "Take Ash out of here."

Sounds warped in her ears. The man's eyes widened, and through the indistinct jumble, she saw him mouth the word Erkenblood. She looked back at her friends' terrified faces and screamed with a voice she could not even hear, "Run!"

The earlier cacophony coalesced into a single voice in her head that called her to destroy the house, to tear the soldiers apart.

Everything around her was a part of her. It felt like her blood coursed through the walls, the floor, the soldiers. She willed the walls to detach from the ground, and they saluted her as they freed themselves of their shackles. As she walked out, people screamed and ran away. She threw a few of them off their feet, looking for her enemies to kill. Having so much power was exhilarating. *You're all my enemies.*

Before she went far, a girl appeared in front of her, bringing a distant memory. "Panthea."

Panthea. She recognized that name. It was hers.

"It's okay," the girl said.

Panthea wanted to kill the young woman. She was a threat—one of the many who would hurt her if given a chance. But there was something familiar in that voice. The joy of wielding turned into anxiety. The light faded.

"Panthea, it's me. Ash."

Ash. The memory came back. This was the same girl who had come to Rassus to learn wielding.

Rassus. He was taken.

"Do you recognize me?"

As Panthea regained her sense of reality, she said in a hoarse whisper, "What happened? What did I do?"

Evian said from behind her, "Everyone knows you're an Erkenblood is what happened. We need to go."

One arm occupied by his satchel and a pile of clothes, he used his free hand to take hers, and they all bolted toward the main square.

As more of her senses returned, a horrific thought hit her. Taking another's life was the greatest of sins, and a line an Erkenblood with power-lust could easily cross. "Did I kill anyone?"

"No," Evian said.

Relieved, she let go of her breath. There was a dull pain in her head, and she felt a little giddy—a sign that her blood had thinned because of an overuse of power. When she looked behind, the reason became clear.

The house had turned into a pile of rubble. All her books. All her childhood memories.

"Why didn't you tell us earlier?" Evian demanded as he handed her a pair of boots and her red cloak, making her realize she was on her bare feet. "We could have helped you."

"On the bright side," Ash said, "those Inquisition people did not follow us. Do we know where we're going?"

"We're going on the pilgrimage," Evian announced.

"No, we're not." Ash stopped walking. "We have no papers. You never had one to begin with."

"Those permits only take you inside the temple," Evian said. "Nobody's stopping us from leaving the city. Now, let's go. We can't stop."

They began running again. The rough ground bit into the soles of Panthea's feet, but if she tried to put on the boots now, she would fall behind and lose her friends in the crowd.

"We don't even have our robes," Ash complained.

"Neither do half of the pilgrims," Evian said between his panting. "Now, you're talking like an Upper City girl."

"I *am* an Upper City girl."

"Not today, you're not."

"Would you two just stop it?" Panthea snapped. "They just took Master. Why did he say he was expecting it? What does the Inquisition want with him?"

"I'll explain everything later," Evian said. "Right now, we have to get out of this city while we can. Master wants us to."

Panthea was not convinced. Neither of her friends understood. Neither felt the same way about Rassus as she did. She wished she could do something. She wished she were stronger.

They arrived at the main square, where the line of pilgrims slowly marched toward the Golden Gate. Evian led Ash and Panthea to the middle of the procession. Most of the pilgrims did not notice. Those who did only smiled between their silent prayers.

The slow pace of the line gave Panthea time to get into her clothes, skipping forward as she put the boots on.

"Now, listen," Evian said, only loud enough for the two of them to hear. "We're going to separate because they'd be looking for three of us. We meet outside the gates and continue from there."

"What if one of us doesn't make it?" Panthea asked. A painful, yet valid, question.

Evian had his answer ready. "Then the other two will run together.

Under no circumstances should any of us look back."

"We can decide on a meeting point," Ash suggested. "Let's say if we can't find each other on the other side, we meet in Watertown. It's close. We can get there by noon."

Panthea and Evian both agreed. Evian removed the satchel from his shoulder and handed it to Ash. "You go first."

"What's with the bag?" Ash asked, frowning.

"I have some coins in there," Evian explained. "We'll need them when we get out."

"If we get out," Panthea corrected him.

Ash had already opened the satchel and was rummaging through it. "What? You carry a knife in your bag?"

"It's useful in the Old City." Evian snatched the satchel from her and closed it before giving it back. "And not everybody here needs to know what I carry. Now, go."

And so, they separated. Ash pushed her way forward in the queue, Panthea stayed where she was, and Evian moved further back in the line. There were still no alarms.

The closer the gates got, the faster her heart beat. There were Sapphires both on top of the walls and within the gatehouse.

Those few minutes it took Panthea to go through the gate lasted forever. Once she was on the other side, Ash almost materialized in front of her. One pilgrim gave them a reproachful frown.

"Where's Evian?" Ash asked.

Panthea pointed back, still following the queue. "Behind."

"Oh, I see him," Ash said, waving at him.

Panthea pulled the girl's hand down. "What are you doing? Could you be any more conspicuous?"

The sound of horns blared from the city, and Panthea's heart dropped in her chest.

"Oh no," Ash said. "They're closing the gates. Evian's still inside. They can't close the gates."

Panthea looked back. The soldiers had made a line to keep the rest of the pilgrims from leaving the city. Ash ran out of the queue. Panthea tugged at the girl's shirt, but she slipped out of her grip, not even heeding when Evian gestured for them to move on.

"Hey," Ash called as she approached one sentry. "Excuse me? He's my brother," she lied. "Can you let him through?"

Panthea sank her head in her palms at how foolish Ash was being right now. She was about to get herself arrested.

"You either move along," said the soldier, "or stay with him. But no one else leaves this city."

"Ash, go," Evian yelled from behind the row of soldiers. "I'll join you later. Just go."

Panthea wanted to remind Ash of the plan she was about to ruin. But the last thing the three of them needed was for the Sapphires to learn they were together. Luckily, Evian alone could convince Ash, and she returned to Panthea. "Okay, I think I'm ready to panic. Why under Diva was he last?"

"What, you'd prefer I stayed behind?" Panthea said.

"Of course not, Dopey. It's just . . . you and I, we're . . ."

"What?"

"We're unworldly. How are we going to survive?"

Panthea shared that concern on top of her worry for Evian and her fear of what would happen to Rassus. But she had to stay strong for Ash. "You'd be surprised how much I know. I think I can get you to Watertown."

Ash snorted. "I can get there on my own. That's not the problem."

Panthea drew a deep breath to steady herself. In a single day, she had left behind two people she cared about. But this wasn't the time to lament. In Evian's absence, it was her job to take care of Ash. So, she forced a smile. "Let's stick to the plan. We go there, and we wait. I'm sure Evian can handle himself."

She hoped it was true. Regardless, her answer seemed to be enough for Ash. The young wielder took Panthea's hand, and they walked with the pilgrims. If they made it one mile with the procession, they could take the sideroad to Watertown.

3

*I have had three deaths. One of body, one of memory, and one
of soul. All three have made me who I am.*

THERE WAS SOMETHING about this library that drew Hilia to it. It
wasn't the old wooden beams, the thick columns, or the high-rising
shelves that made the tallest of people look small. It wasn't the plethora of
books spanning several centuries of knowledge. It wasn't even the worn
tables in the main hallway, where she spent hours at a time in the
candlelight. But there was something.

Until four years ago, if you'd asked Hilia what she'd be doing by the
age of twenty-five, serving as the queen's handmaid would be her quip at
best. But with time, you learned sacrifices were inevitable for the greater
good. And if time failed to teach you that, Windhammer would burn it
into your skull with his speeches.

It could have been the air. Not the musky smell that seeped into her
nostrils every time she entered. The air was light—free from the heavy presence
of scrutiny. Here, she could just be Hilia. Not the agent, not the maid.

The afternoon light bled in through the gaping royal entrance, which
was one of two points of entry into the library. The other opened to the

city. Both doors were five-inch-thick solid steel with locking mechanisms
that could withstand a battering ram. The design contradicted the inviting
spirit of the place. It was an addition Queen Artenus had made in the way
of fortifying the palace.

During the morning, this same library brimmed with a flock of people
from the city. Every day at noon, soldiers sealed the public entrance, and
the royal doors opened to the residents of the palace until midnight.

Hilia closed the tome, then stretched in her chair.

"Look who's here," echoed Parviz's husky voice.

Hilia smiled at the welcome arrival. He had to be what drew her here.
The library would not be the same without this man. Their conversations
were the realest she had around the palace.

She had never asked how old he was. His short hair had gone gray at
the temples, and his closely shaven face was a platter of lines. She knew he
had a son who worked in the city, but it was hard to believe the man also
had a four-year-old.

"You used to be a faster reader," he said with a half-wink.

She had never been a fast reader. But the reason she was particularly
slow these days was because she read the books more carefully, hoping
something—a line, a footnote, an annotation—would prove her theory
that the queen could die, despite what everyone seemed to believe.

"Did you find your immortals?" the librarian said as he picked up the
book. He opened the first page, then closed it, purposefully walking to a
particular shelf.

"I'm not looking for immortals," she said as she stood. "I'm looking for
what creates them in people's eyes."

Parviz snickered. "If I didn't know you, I'd say you wanted to
assassinate Queen Artenus."

Hilia almost gasped at his audacity. Even she would not utter those
words in the middle of the library in the afternoon hours. She glanced
around to see if anyone had heard them. When she was sure they were
alone, she put on a smirk and played along. "Who's to say I'm not?"

"Bah," the librarian called as he climbed a ladder. "You can play tough all you want, you can even pretend you're one of Windhammer's rebels, but deep down, you're the same innocent, kind-hearted girl who came to the palace four years ago."

Hilia had to stifle a snort. *Well, so long as I'm only pretending to be a rebel. I wonder who the innocent one is.*

Parviz put the book in place, descended from the ladder, then walked to her again. "You know what else you are? Careless. You have a habit of asking dangerous questions, and I've seen where dangerous questions lead people."

"Yeah? And where is that?"

He looked down, moistening his lips. Then, as his gaze returned to hers, a smile deepened the lines around his eyes. "Let me tell you a story. I once knew a young man who, like yourself, made me uncomfortable. He told me things I didn't want to know. Once, he came to me and said he had a secret stash of sapping potion hidden in his house."

Another anecdote. Only the army and the Inquisition had access to sapping potion, which made this story particularly unbelievable, even for a moral one.

Wearing a mischievous smile, she said, "Let me guess. He died. It always ends the same way. One might think you're inventing these stories to teach me lessons."

He swatted the air. "You always ruin my stories. And no, this really happened."

Hilia chuckled. "By the way, that book was missing the first few chapters. I swear I didn't take them."

"No, you didn't. All copies of History of the Arcane are like that."

"Hmm. Maybe there's something Sapphires don't want us to learn."

Parviz shook his head. "You go to the remotest temples of the Northern Realm and get a copy, and you'd still not find those chapters. It's known for it."

A Sapphire lieutenant entered the library, and the conversation ceased. The first time Hilia had seen one of those men in here, it had fascinated her. It made no sense for someone to be well-read and so ignorant at the same time.

"Good day," she said with her perfect, trained smile.

The man stared into her eyes as he walked past. He didn't even respond to her greeting. Or maybe he did. His head did twitch up and down ever so slightly.

Hilia left Parviz's side and pretended to browse. Minutes went by, with Hilia glossing over the books considered more fit for the queen's handmaid. Romantic stories, tales of heroes who saved damsels in distress. Even the titles were tedious. Why would anyone read something that gave them no information? What was the point?

It took half an hour—and a few years of her life—before the man finished browsing and left with a book. His irritating stare returned to her as he walked out of the library. *Guess what? The handmaid can read too. Get over it.* A hand perched on her shoulder. She flinched.

"You look fazed," Parviz said. "Did he bother you?"

She shook her head. "The way he stared. As if I'm not allowed to be literate."

Parviz spared the soldier a glance. Then, his gaze landed on Hilia's chest, and his smile returned. "Either that, or that you're wearing a dandelion pendant in the palace."

"Shit." She hadn't even noticed the unruly pendant had gotten out. It was the symbol of the Ahuraic pantheon—a hollow circle in the middle that represented Ahura, and the other twelve gods and goddesses extending outward like rays of sunlight or bristles of a dandelion seed. Wearing such a representation was especially a problem if you worked in Delavaran Palace.

Hilia wasn't even religious. The pendant had been a gift from her father for her sixteenth birthday. These days, she wore it as a reminder of a happier time—when she'd been under the illusion she'd grown up.

"That's always the start," Parviz added. "You give them something that doesn't fit their norm, and they'll keep watching you." He paused, considering the shelf in front of her. "Never took you for a fiction reader."

"I wasn't really browsing."

There was a longer pause. "Can I ask you a question, Hilia?"

It was interesting how one's own name could be so unpleasant to hear. *"Can I ask you a question?"* could be the start of a stimulating conversation, but with her name attached, it meant a rebuke was coming. She turned halfway to him, not in the least looking forward to what he was about to say.

"Why this much interest in the Dark Scepter?" he asked. "Jokes aside, I want to be sure you're not putting yourself in the way of harm. And I have a family—I need to know I'm not putting them in danger by association."

His frankness gave Hilia a jolt, even though she had expected that remark. If she lost his trust, there was nowhere she could go to escape reality and wrap her worries in the humor they shared.

"I, uh," she began. "I believe the Dark Scepter is the reason the queen doesn't age. She stopped aging around the time she acquired it. What if the immortal queen is really just a woman with a mystical artifact?" She sighed. "If only I could find some proof."

The middle-aged man's brow crinkled. "And how would that help you? Tell me you're not involved in something foolish, Hilia."

"Stop," she shot at first, but then blinked and leveled her voice. "You're making me hate my name. I'm interested in the subject, nothing more."

"Be careful. That's all I'm asking."

His eyes held genuine concern. Hilia hated lying to him. But the less he knew about who she was and whom she worked for, the less trouble he and his family would be in.

To cut the tension, she said with a lopsided smile, "You're getting old. You worry too much these days. Books don't kill people. And I won't end up like your imaginary friend."

As Hilia worked on the finishing touches of the queen's makeup, those unsettling emerald eyes stared at her through the mirror.

The woman was odd. Her hair was a darker shade of black than Hilia's own. But her skin was pale as porcelain—and not with much exaggeration. It made Hilia's dark complexion look even darker. Without the eye shadow to accentuate her eyes, without the blush to resemble some blood under her skin, the leader of the Southern Kingdom was a walking corpse. And someone looking like that giving you a lifeless, icy gaze was plain disturbing.

Most of the time, it was impossible to read the queen. This was especially a problem for Hilia, whose job required her to do just that.

None of this, however, was as strange as the queen's youthful appearance. Fifty years of age had done nothing to her perfect features and her smooth skin. It was no wonder people thought her immortal. Of course, that also had to do with the fact that no one had ever managed to kill her. And many had tried.

The palace was not exactly impenetrable. Delavaran, like any other city in the Southern Kingdom, followed the basic design principles of the Mehr dynasty. Fortified outer walls and loosely protected inner sanctums.

Anyone with a bit of knowledge of history—or an intention to harm the royals—knew Mehrian kings did not aim to protect their homes from the people but from foreign invaders. And if said invaders breached the city walls, the royals would not crawl into their holes. They would fight alongside the citizens. So, there really was no reason to build a fortified palace within a fortified city.

That was, of course, unless the royal in question was Queen Artenus. For someone who had made so many enemies over the years, a Mehrian palace was not the safest. She had spent the first few years after the king's demise building protective measures, plugging one hole at a time. And each assassination attempt revealed a new one.

The Dark Scepter, Hilia's explanation for everything odd with the queen, lay on the table in front of the woman, its length the shape of three snakes twisting together, their heads forming the top as they faced the center in a bellicose deadlock. Something looking like that could not be benign, and the fact that the queen never let it out of her sight while she was awake was a good sign that maybe her life depended on it.

The first assassin to enter the chambers was a member of the last rebellion. He came in through the library, killed a full squad of guards, then charged at the queen. As the story goes, all Queen Artenus had to do was touch him with the Dark Scepter, and he killed himself. The product of the attack were the steel doors of the library, and new rules preventing the place from being open to the public and the residents of the palace at the same time.

A mercenary was the second famous one. She even stabbed the queen before they detained her. But the queen healed within a day without a scratch remaining. That was when the rumors of her immortality began. Hilia refused to believe them. Whatever it was that made the queen invincible had to do with the scepter.

There was a spherical piece of ruby in one of the metallic snakes' mouths. The Toofanian King had gifted this gemstone to the queen four years ago, during Hilia's first days in the palace. The Bond of Second Arcane, they called it. For a long time, Hilia had thought it a cosmetic addition. Until last year when she herself witnessed an assassination attempt. By an Erkenblood.

That day, Hilia was clearing the table after breakfast when screams and shouts echoed in the hallways of the palace. The queen exited her study, eyes trained on the arched entrance. The commotion got closer by the second until a guard walked in, barring the gilded door of the chambers before running toward them. "Your Highness must hide."

The door splintered and a woman entered the room, eyes glowing white. The soldier attacked, but he didn't get far before exploding into four pieces, his insides spilling onto the carpet. Hilia yelped and fell back, bile rising in her throat. She had seen nothing like that before. She'd never watched an Erkenblood fight. Even the queen herself, who was an Erkenblood by birth, had given up her wielding before the Purge.

There was so much rage in the attacker's gait one could swear she would kill anything alive in the palace, including Hilia. But the Erkenblood beelined to the queen, the vein in her neck bulging. Hilia braced herself to watch the queen die a gruesome death.

It didn't happen.

The Erkenblood's face turned red. The white light from her eyes was almost blinding, but the queen didn't even flinch. Amidst her shock, Hilia glimpsed the Bond of Second Arcane glowing on the Dark Scepter.

Soon, the attacker held her head and dropped to her knees, screeching in agony. The queen ambled to the squirming woman. The gem glowed as brightly as the Erkenblood's eyes and as red as the blood trickling from the wretched woman's nostrils.

Soldiers poured into the chambers and restrained the woman.

The light in her eyes faded, giving way to the characteristic green color of an Erkenblood's irises. Her brow creased in fear and confusion. "How?"

The queen leaned in and whispered in her ear.

After the first few moments, the woman's eyes widened. A few more seconds and her face puckered. "No."

"It is unfortunate," the queen murmured as she pressed the scepter to the bare skin at the side of the attacker's neck. "But you've made a show of your treason, and everyone's waiting for the grand finale."

The queen borrowed a dagger from a guard and handed it to the woman. Weeping, looking in as much shock as Hilia, the woman cut her own throat. Blood gushed out of the wound as she grunted and gurgled. As the soldiers let her go, both her hands shot to her throat, holding it as if to stop the bleeding. But within seconds, she was dead.

Hilia drew a steadying breath, then focused on the queen's makeup to shake off that memory—difficult when the scepter was so close.

There was to be another attempt on the queen's life. Tonight.

Once Hilia was done, the queen rose and took a last look at her dress and its golden embroidery, then picked up the scepter. "Do not allow anyone into the chambers while I'm gone."

The queen did not wait for a response. She marched toward the exit, and Hilia almost had to run to catch up and open the door for her.

Outside, Inquisitor Kadder was already waiting with ten Sapphire soldiers, his scalp reflecting the lamplight. His well-groomed salt-and-pepper beard shifted, and the lines on his face deepened as his dark eyes smiled. An Inquisitor smiling at her was one of the benefits of working in the queen's chambers—and it was something anyone should consider themselves lucky to see.

The smile didn't last long, though. He bent in front of Queen Artenus and offered his elbow. The queen wrapped her hand around the Inquisitor's arm, and the party left.

Hilia closed the door and leaned against it. Could this be the last day she had to go through the pretense? Would the queen really die tonight? It was a sweet thought. Hilia, the handmaid who had helped rid the world of a tyrant. History would remember this. That was, of course, if Hilia was right about every single one of her speculations. If the queen wasn't immortal; if the Dark Scepter was how she defied death; and if Mehran could get the job done without being touched by the scepter.

Anxiety crept into her chest. An intrusive voice in her head said this wasn't the right time. Hilia had yet a lot to learn, a lot she needed proof of.

If they failed tonight, she would be compromised. She would become one of those nameless *heroes* whose blood watered the tree of rebellion, or however else minstrels called a nobody. A few would mourn her, deliver a eulogy, and that would be it. Her name would then go down the bottomless pit of time. Forgotten.

If she was made, the Inquisition would figure out Parviz had been helping her, and they would take the unsuspecting man too. They would find her father. They would hurt him.

Her heart thumped. *Get a grip, Hilia.*

Someone knocked, and a gasp escaped her. She covered her mouth. *You stupid girl. Do you want to be found out?* She straightened her violet dress before opening the door.

A smiling Mehran stood there. But his friendly spirit soon dissolved into a reflection of Hilia's turmoil. Hilia peeked around the corridor before she grabbed his shirt and pulled him inside. She closed the door and walked to the middle of the sitting room. "We need to call it off. It's too risky."

"What? Where is this coming from? What did you learn?"

"Nothing." She spun back to face him. "I've learned nothing, and that's the problem. I have no proof that my theory holds."

"Hilia," he said as he gingerly approached her.

"Mehran, I'm not crazy. We're going to put our lives at risk."

"Hilia." He held her arm. "I don't blame you for being uneasy. But think about this. We do this, you get to put it all behind you, and go back to your father."

"I'm not a coward." Hilia pushed his hand away. "I don't want to run. But we can't walk into this blindly."

"Windhammer wants this done tonight. But I promise you, if I get caught, I'll never admit to even knowing you. I'll take full responsibility. How about that?"

Hilia sighed. "Why would you do this?"

"Because you're our most important asset in the field."

"No, I meant, why would you go ahead with the mission with these odds? This was my idea, and if anything happens to you . . ."

He held her gaze for a few moments, then gave her a tight-lipped, almost wistful smile. "Hilia. I've known you for four years now. Whenever you've had a hunch, it hasn't failed."

She bit a hangnail off her finger. "What if my hunch says this won't work?"

He came closer and held her hands. "That is not your hunch; it's your fear. I know how much you hate uncertainty, and I know you're scared."

"I'm not—"

"Not for yourself. You're scared for everyone else. That's why you stand out from the rest of us. We're soldiers. We do what we're told. But you?" He let go. "You make it a point to protect those around you. That makes you Windhammer's second-most hated type of person."

Her nerves eased a little at the compliment, and she could not help a guilty grin. "Third. Northerners, tyrants, then heroes."

They shared a chuckle. Sometimes, Hilia forgot this man was her handler. That she had to show some manner of respect toward him, or at least not challenge his every decision. It was his own fault. He made it so easy to forget.

"By the way," Mehran said, "cover up for tonight. The new guy doesn't know you, and we should keep it that way." He squeezed her arm. "We're going to be fine."

"If you say so."

That invited a titter and a shake of his head as he left. The thud of the door reverberated in Hilia's body. *You better be right about this.*

4

*As humans, we often hold on to our beliefs, even when we have
the tools and the ability to learn. We assume our home is safe
because to think otherwise will sow the seeds of fear in our
hearts. We assume our friends won't betray us, for to admit
they might, is to question our choices.*

THE TOWN WAS LUSH for one in the Southern Kingdom, thanks to its
proximity to the Green Eye Lake, which was where the river Shireen
took a break from its long journey from the north, eyeing the kingdom.
The lake and its surrounding trees had been visible as they had walked
toward Watertown before the buildings had cut their line of sight.
Panthea had heard about the beauty of this town but seeing it with her
own eyes was a whole other story.

As they approached the town, the smell of wet leaves and damp wood
permeated the air. A stark contrast to the dead road they had taken—or
anything else Panthea had ever experienced in her life. In different
circumstances, she would have enjoyed a relaxed trip here. Then again, in
different circumstances, she would not have left Saba to begin with.

The day of walking on the rough road under the blazing sunlight had worn Panthea down, and she could see it on Ash's face too.

"Well, maybe I miscalculated a little," Ash said as she looked toward the setting Hita. "But we're here. Now what?"

"Now, we find an inn."

Ash counted the money in the satchel, and her eyes sparkled. "Evian's rich. How long can we stay at the inn for eighty crowns?"

Even left behind, Evian had still taken care of them as he always had.

After her parents' death, Panthea lived in a temple until age seven, when Rassus deemed it safe for her to leave. Moving to a large city like Saba was a frightening change. But there, amid an unknown world, Panthea found a new friend. Someone with whom she could share her fears and worries. Someone who could always comfort her, even when Rassus failed. If it had not been for Evian, the dread of the Purge alone would have killed her. *Annahid, protect him.*

She tried her best to approximate a genuine smile for Ash. "We'll only stay there until he shows up."

"All right," Ash said. "Oh, and I've brought a little something."

The girl took her gleamstone out of the satchel, and Panthea's blood chilled at the sight. She snatched the stone from Ash, her voice erupting from her throat. "Have you lost your mind? Why would you bring this? Why would you put both our lives in danger?"

"Easy, *Mom*," Ash retorted. "Nobody saw it. We're safe now."

"How can you be so foolish?" Panthea looked around to check if anyone was there to have seen the stone. "We need to get rid of this."

"Hey," Ash snapped. "You're not throwing out my gleamstone."

"Oh, I will. Somebody has to save you from yourself."

Ash made a grab for the stone, letting out an angry growl when she failed to capture it. "Now, you're acting just like Master."

"Well, maybe it's not all that bad," Panthea said, struggling to keep her voice down. "Master has done everything to protect us."

"Master is why we're here in the first place."

Before Panthea could control her fury at that comment, her hand had already slapped Ash across the face.

Ash stopped talking, her lips parted as she stroked her cheek.

"I'm sorry," Panthea said.

"That's how it's going to be, isn't it?" Ash looked stunned. "You know what's funny? Master never raised a hand to me."

The young wielder dropped the bag and walked in the lake's direction.

"Ash, wait," Panthea called after her, but she wouldn't stop. "Ash, please." Why did it have to be so hard? What would Evian do in this situation? All Panthea knew was that she couldn't separate from Ash. The girl was her responsibility.

Panthea picked up the satchel and ran after her friend. She caught Ash by the arm. "We have to stay together. Hate me all you want, but don't leave."

Ash turned with a glare. "Panthea, you're as lost as I am. What makes you think, just because Master and Evian aren't here, you're suddenly in charge?"

Panthea could only whisper through the lump in her throat, "I just want us to survive."

"And I want to die?" Ash sighed. "Go to the inn. I'll join you later. I need some air. Or is that forbidden too?"

Pushing back her worry and the sting in those words, Panthea nodded. "Just . . . be careful. Don't go too far."

Ash rolled her eyes and walked away.

Panthea tightened her grip on the gleamstone. She could not bring herself to throw it out, considering how strongly Ash felt about it. So, she put it back in Evian's satchel and headed to the town. At least it was with her now, so Ash was not a wielder so far as Sapphires were concerned.

Ash looking for trouble was not new. Panthea had known this since the day of the girl's first act of rebellion. It was back when Rassus had just taken Ash in as an apprentice.

PANTHEA WAS READING the History of the Arcane by Sinn Tiaar. The book wasn't in great shape, and the initial chapters were missing. Still, the parts about Erkenbloods and the Dark Ages seemed to be there, which were all she needed. She was engrossed in the pages when Rassus's then-new apprentice, Ashena, came and sat in front of her. At first, Panthea said nothing. She only glanced up at her without raising her head from the book. The girl's eyes were trained on Panthea, probably waiting for some form of interaction. She even smiled when their eyes met.

Panthea flipped the page and resumed reading. Ashena was everything Panthea wasn't. The girl had already made friends with Evian and was trying so hard to do the same with her. If only Panthea knew what to say or how to react.

Ashena picked up her gleamstone and held it out, and Panthea felt a slight panic when the young apprentice's small voice addressed her. "Can you teach me how to space-jump with this?"

She looked at the girl's expectant eyes and wide smile and returned a dim reflection of it. She closed the book on the bookmark and put it down. Then, she collected her black hair behind as she said, "You can't space-jump with a gleamstone. Only an Erkenblood whose element is space can do it. Conductive wielding only works on matter. You can move objects with a gleamstone, but within the confines of space and time."

Ashena gawked. "Uh-huh." Though her lips were parted, Panthea could swear there was a smile brewing at the corners. "I didn't understand half of what you said. And why can gleamstones only wield one element?"

"Um . . . because gleamstones are made of northern marble." Panthea forced herself to stop fidgeting with her hands. "Which is immune to arcane power. That's why you can't destroy someone's gleamstone or snatch it from their hand with matter-wielding. And if you think about it, for space-jumping to work, your gleamstone would need to jump with you. But with northern marble, it would stay behind."

Ashena's fingers had already penetrated the mass of her hair and were scratching her scalp. "Gleamstones sound boring."

"The first High Lady would be thrilled to hear that," Panthea said, chuckling nervously at her own joke, her face heating when Ash didn't.

"One thousand years ago, she and a few of her trusted Erkenbloods sacrificed all their power to create the Well of Light, which powers gleamstones."

Boredom dripped from Ashena's face. Unlike Panthea, she didn't seem to care much for history. So, Panthea picked another argument to defend gleamstones. "With a gleamstone, you can move things you're not strong enough to move with your hands."

That did the job. Ashena's eyes twinkled. "Wait, does that mean I can lift you?"

Panthea hadn't expected that, and she laughed. "Not today. I'd very much like to stay alive."

Ashena mused a little, then gasped with exuberance. "Oh! There's a statue in my backyard, twice my size. We can go there and try to lift that."

Not waiting for Panthea to swallow the anxiety following that proposition, Ashena scampered to the front door with the gleamstone in her hand.

Panthea rushed after her. "Ashena! Ashena, no." Before the young apprentice could open the door, Panthea blocked her way. "We can't do that. Didn't you listen to Master? It's dangerous."

The girl stood there, staring for a long moment with a mix of surprise and disappointment. She then sighed and walked back in. "You're no fun. I'm sure Evian would have let me."

This left Panthea indignant. "He would not. Wielding is a crime. If Sapphires catch you—"

"I know," Ashena said ruefully as she sat down, fiddling with the gleamstone in her hand. "I didn't mean to be rude. It's just . . . why learn wielding if we can't even use it?"

Panthea sat in front of her. At least her initial fear of the conversation had subsided. The young apprentice had a talent for breaking the ice. Panthea smiled. "Wielding is beautiful. Arcane power is a gift from the goddess, and we are preserving this gift."

She looked down, her childhood memories passing through her mind. Wielding was one element linking them all together.

Panthea had never been like other children her age. She had no friends—Rassus didn't even let her get out of the house. Her only companions used to be her books, her gleamstone, and Rassus himself, who made a point of being there whenever she wanted to practice, or when she had questions or was excited about a topic. He'd always had time to converse over something that was trivial to him, but that she had just discovered in a book.

"Question." Ashena's voice brought her out of her trance. "Do you think Master himself ever wields outside the house?"

That thought had never occurred to Panthea. Not because she knew he would or wouldn't. It had simply never mattered to her before. "I actually don't know."

That characteristic mischievous smile returned to Ashena's lips. "Would you like to find out?"

Panthea narrowed her eyes. "I don't like that look."

"I have a confession to make." Over her shoulder, Ashena pointed at Rassus's room. "I might have replaced the gleamstone inside Master's staff with a used-up one this morning."

Panthea gasped, making the girl sink into a cringe and say, "Is that bad?"

"Master's going to kill you if he finds out."

"Uh-uh." Ashena waved her finger. "He promised my parents I'd be safe. He'll break his promise if he kills me."

"Then, he'll do worse than killing."

Ashena grimaced. "What's worse than killing?" She didn't let Panthea answer that question. "Never mind. All he has to do is give me that fiery look he gave you the other day. I'll do the dying on my own."

"Or he can stop teaching you. Would you like that?"

"Of course not." Worry found its way to her dark brown eyes. "What do I do now?"

"Pray he won't find out what you did. There are things you shouldn't do. Master, as you'll learn, doesn't have a sense of humor."

"No kidding," Ashena said, then she paused. All her features suddenly gave in to a smile. "No pun intended."

As much as Panthea wanted to stifle her laughter, she couldn't. It didn't help that Ashena was laughing at her own joke.

"Don't worry," Panthea said. "I'll talk to him. He might be a little grumpy, but he's a kind man."

Ashena did not seem convinced.

"Hey." Panthea put a hand on the girl's shoulder to reassure her. "Let's make a deal. If you survive tonight, I'll teach you how to behave around here, and you promise to listen to everything I say."

Ashena shook her head in amazement. "Boy, Master has really been exploiting you."

"What?"

"Is that how he makes deals with you?" Ashena wore a grin that seemed about to break into a cackle at any moment. She could barely talk with a steady voice. "I mean, you're supposed to get something out of a deal. You do know that, don't you?"

Panthea rolled her eyes. "You never stop, do you?"

"I have a better deal for you." Ashena threw her hand forward. "If I survive, you teach me manners, and I won't make fun of you anymore."

"Sounds like a good deal."

Panthea went to shake her hand, but the young apprentice retracted it, regarding Panthea inquisitively. "Can we still make fun of Evian?"

THAT NIGHT, WHEN RASSUS arrived home, he was sulkier than usual. Panthea and Ashena exchanged worried looks while the old man changed into his inside robe, and they both jumped to their feet like soldiers when he came back to the sitting room.

"How was your day, Master?" Ashena asked.

"Unexpected," Rassus said, rubbing his long mustache. "I think I might be losing my head." He glanced between the girls. "I'm positive I placed a new gleamstone in my staff. But somehow, it was empty today."

Panthea was too nervous to say anything, but Ashena leaned toward her and whispered, "I was right."

Eyes locked onto the girl's face, Rassus ambled to her, tapping his staff on the floor. "It seems somebody thought it would be funny to replace my gleamstone. I wonder who's the funniest between the two of you."

Panthea blinked in despair. Ashena had no idea what kind of trouble she was in. The old man had almost refused her apprenticeship. He had hated to be responsible for her safety. The main reason Ashena was here at all was Evian, who had convinced Rassus that the girl would be better off learning with him than on her own. Even then, it had taken the old man a great deal of consideration to come to terms with the idea. And this could be the end of it.

"I did it."

Rassus changed the target of his scolding gaze, and Ashena's head whipped to Panthea. The girl looked incredulous.

"You always taught us not to use a gleamstone outside of this house," Panthea added. "I was curious if you used it yourself."

Rassus towered over her. "And instead of asking, you decided to test the old man, to see if he followed his own rules."

"Ye—" Panthea swallowed to unlock her throat. "Yes."

Rassus looked back at Ashena. "Is this the truth?"

The girl who couldn't stop talking was now silent and fidgety. Panthea gave her a furtive nod, and Ashena finally assented. "Yes, Master."

"Very well," Rassus said, his gaze piercing through Panthea. "You'll bring me your gleamstone and your books. Then, you'll stay in your room. You won't join us for dinner tonight. You'll eat alone and spend the night thinking about your action."

"Yes, Master," Panthea mumbled, looking down. It had been one year since Rassus had become so stern. At least her punishment was worthwhile. Ashena got to stay an apprentice, and that was what mattered. One night alone wouldn't kill anyone. She only needed to tolerate a few hours. The rest she would spend sleeping, anyway.

Later that evening, it wasn't Rassus who brought her dinner. It was Ashena. She came in and held out the tray of food, her gaze not leaving

Panthea's.

As Panthea took the tray, she found something beneath it. Ashena beamed as Panthea reached for the book the girl had been hiding there.

"It was this one, right?" Ashena asked in a hushed tone. "What you were reading earlier, I mean."

Panthea shook her head, too emotional to frown at her. "So, you look for trouble every minute of every day. What do I do with you?"

"Accept the book," Ashena said, reinforcing her suggestion with a persuasive nod. She then gestured toward the door with her eyes. "Master didn't see me smuggle it here. But if I take it back now, he might notice, and I might get into trouble."

What this girl had done for her was something even Evian wouldn't. Not that he wasn't kind enough. He just knew better than to defy the old man. "Thank you."

"I should be thanking you. You're the one who took the fall for me. You must be a real dope."

"Excuse me?" Panthea said, smiling. "Is that what I get?"

"Hey, I thanked you first. But who would take the fall like that for the annoying new girl?"

"Girls ought to have each other's backs."

Rassus's voice called from outside, "Ashena?"

The girl's smile faltered. "I should go." Before she left, she gave Panthea a last look. "I like dopes. To me, it's the opposite of boring—which I never thought you were."

The memory of that day always brought a smile to Panthea. Ash had matured since then, but some things never changed. Some things, like the illegal object Panthea now carried.

People in the town gave Panthea inviting looks as she entered. Some even smiled. Friendly as they were, it made her uncomfortable. People's scrutinizing gazes were intimidating enough when she was a lawful citizen in Saba. Now, every smile seemed sinister.

The architecture had nothing in common with other towns and cities of the Southern Kingdom—of which she had only seen Saba and had heard about the rest. There was little clay or gravel or stone in the buildings. They were mostly of wooden beams and slabs.

As she looked around for an inn, her eyes caught something much bigger. A sizeable courtyard surrounded on three sides by a colonnade supporting a one-story structure of the same shape. The middle of the courtyard was open, and there, were carriages parked. She had never seen a caravanyard before, but this one fit the description. She just had not imagined a small town like this could house such a thing. But who was she to complain? She had wanted an inn, and this qualified as one.

She walked around the colonnade until she found a sign reading, *"Rooms for rent, food for the road."* Relieved, she rushed to the building. The smell of cooked meat and fried onions wafted out as soon as she pushed the door open. Some turned their heads at the creak, though most lost their interest rather quickly.

The place was lit by a multitude of candles planted in small recesses around the walls, overcompensating for the lack of windows. If not for the alcohol and food they served here, it would make a perfect venue for the Dark Fusion vigil.

Ornamental backrests lined the walls in the common room on top of colorful rags, with the addition of some tables in the middle. Table seating was a practice Queen Artenus had imported from the north. It was uncommon, even for Panthea's generation.

Sitting at a table would draw the attention of the more traditional folks, and Panthea was not planning to make herself too easy to spot while she waited for Ash. So, she went to the far edge of the room and sat on the floor. She set Evian's satchel beside her as she leaned against the comfortable backrest, stretching her legs, shutting her eyes. She needed to unwind before going to the innkeeper.

Hiding the emergence of her power had been irresponsible on her part. She should have told Rassus, or at least Evian, instead of trying to battle the problem on her own.

As Panthea opened her eyes again, two Sapphire soldiers entered, their helmets tucked under their arms. Fear gripped her chest. She thought about leaving, but her appearance would attract their attention. They were men, after all, and a pair of emerald eyes and their contrast with the darkest black hair seemed to work wonders for them. Or so she had heard.

"New here?" said a voice from her side, and Panthea gasped.

A man with short hair and a skin a shade or two brighter than hers had invited himself to sit next to her. Although no one had any claim to any portion of the wall, there was enough unoccupied space around.

She drew her brows together. "Huh?"

Judging by the man's face and the density of his trimmed beard, he was a couple of years older than her.

"Never seen you before," he said with a pompous tone, as though frequenting an inn and knowing everyone in there by their looks was something to be proud of.

"I'm ..." she fumbled, distracted by the soldiers, her mind racing to devise an escape plan. "I'm not ... not from around here. I'm from Sabzestan."

The two soldiers sat at a table closer to the entrance, talking and giggling.

"Great city, I've heard. Are all girls in Sabzestan like you?"

This drew all her attention back to the man. He had seen something different in her, and that meant an imminent discovery on his part. "Like me?"

"You're beautiful."

It wasn't until that moment she realized what this was about. Unable to keep up the conversation and think of an escape plan at the same time, she said, "I'm not that kind of girl. Can you move to another spot?"

The man's lips parted, but he said nothing. Instead, he gave her a half-nod as he stood to leave. She resumed eyeing the soldier, which she regretted when their gazes locked for a second. The soldier got up from his chair. Had he recognized her?

She had to do something, and quickly.

"Hey," she said in an urgent whisper toward the stranger. When he looked, she gestured for him to sit back down. If she was with him, it was less likely they would suspect her.

The man's brows drew into a stupefied scowl. Her chest tightened as the soldier closed in. "Sit down," she muttered. "Do I have to beg?"

With a raised eyebrow, the stranger slowly sat. "I thought you weren't that kind of girl. What kind of girl is that, by the—"

"Hold my hand," she blurted, her face warming with embarrassment.

After a few glances between the hand and her eyes, he complied, wrapping his icy fingers around her palm.

The soldier reached Panthea's spot, and she looked down lest he see her eyes. But he just walked past her to the other corner of the room, where another young woman sat. Panthea exhaled.

Her company's eyes were narrow, studying hers. "You're scared, aren't you?" He jutted his chin toward the soldier. "Of them."

She crossed her arms to cover the shaking of her hands before he could sense it. "That's none of your concern."

He gave a lopsided smile. "I think it kind of is, considering I just saved your life."

She let out a scorned chuckle at the overstatement. "All you did was sit next to me and hold my hand."

"All the same." He glanced back at the soldiers' table. "What do they want with you?"

She only shook her head, eyes zipping between the separated soldiers.

"My name is Arvin, by the way. What's yours?"

With everything that flowed and crashed in her mind, inventing a creative name was too much of an ordeal. So, she went with the first thing that came to her mind. "Hita."

"How poetic. Like the white sun." He seemed to have a response prepared for whatever she said. She didn't even glance at him this time.

The door opened again, and two more soldiers came in. This was no longer a coincidence. More than two Sapphires in the same room was bad news.

One of the newcomers went to the table where his giggly comrade sat, while his partner kept looking around, trying to locate something in particular. Someone.

Soon after the newcomer opened the conversation with the sitting soldier, his expression hardened.

Desperate for a plan, she regarded Arvin. This could be a bad idea, but the alternative was worse. "Look, I don't know you, but you're the best chance I have. You're right. They want me. And I think they're on to me."

"There's some truth," said Arvin. "Don't worry. We'll just leave together as a couple."

The plan was as good as any. Panthea picked up the satchel, then they stood. The soldier who was talking flashed a glance in their direction as he spoke, then immediately looked back in recognition. Panthea clasped Arvin's hand as her fear caught up.

The soldier gestured his friends to wait before he strutted to her and Arvin. She felt her power rising. *No. Annahid, please no.* In a crowded place like this, there was no telling how many people would get hurt if she lost it.

A grin spread over the soldier's face. "Arvin."

He had not even been looking at Panthea, which made her feel rather foolish.

"Haven't seen you in a while," Arvin responded.

They clapped each other's backs. The soldier's smile dimmed as he spoke again. "I'm here on a mission." His gaze wandered, lingering on some faces. "They've found an Erkenblood in Saba."

"Oh?" The grip of Arvin's hand tightened on Panthea's.

"It gets worse. Soldiers couldn't capture the witch, and we think she's skipped town. Seen anyone suspicious?"

Arvin shrugged. "Well, my lady friend and I have been out of town the entire day, and we didn't see anyone." He gave her an untimely nudge. "Did you?"

Panthea shook her head without looking up, struggling to keep her voice flat. "No."

The soldier put his hand under her chin, and her skin crawled. "Hey, lady. I'm Arvin's friend."

"She's a little shy," Arvin said as he removed his *friend's* hand. "Maybe you two can get acquainted later."

"Very well," said the soldier. "Come find us here if you see something. We're staying for the night in case she shows up. Oh, and I've heard there's going to be a good price on her head. So, I'd start looking to get ahead of the competition."

They laughed. At the price on her head, as though her life meant nothing. It was sickening. Finally, they bade farewell, and Panthea and Arvin left the inn.

"You could have kept me out of the conversation, you know," she said.

He chuckled. "I thought it'd be more natural. They don't think I spend time with mutes, and you were just shy of one."

She rolled her eyes and stifled a retort. Arrogant as he was, he *had* saved her life when he'd had reasons not to. "Well, thank you for not turning me in, what with the bounty and all."

"There isn't a bounty yet." He winked at her, then glanced back at the inn over his shoulder before he said, "Do you have a place for the night?"

"I was planning to rent a room here, but now . . ."

Arvin's eyes widened with an expression that was half shock, half amusement. "Well, that would have been a bad idea."

She frowned. "Why?"

"Well, for one, this is not an inn. We're in a caravanyard. People who stay here are couriers, merchants, and the occasional bounty hunter."

"Oh." Worry tingled her scalp at the mention of bounty hunters. After the Great Reform, the government had legitimized them. Considering they were expendable and needed no training or regular wage, they were a perfect tool for enforcing the law.

"And that's not the worst part. These groups all have their own carriages and sleeping arrangements, which are, in most cases, the same. Those who pay for their stay in rental rooms are mostly criminals or fugitives. It's a surefire way to flag yourself to any bounty hunter who visits. And owners have no problem giving them their rosters—and no choice but."

She felt like a fool. How could she think of protecting herself and Ash when she could not even handle their accommodation?

"All right." Arvin scratched the back of his head. "We can go to my house. There, we'll make an actual plan."

Panthea looked into his eyes, trying to discern why a stranger would take this risk for someone he had just met. Harboring a fugitive—that was what she was now—was no joke. "Why are you helping me?"

He considered her for a moment. "Because you don't seem to know much about the workings of the Southern Kingdom. You'll be eaten alive out here on your own."

That had not exactly answered her question. Nonetheless, this was the best choice she had given the circumstances. There was only one problem. Ash was expecting her to be at the inn. Even if Panthea trusted her own life with this man, she could not make this decision for her friend. "I can't stay with you. I must leave this town."

"Not in those clothes, you don't. Once the bounty comes out, this attire will be your identification. We need to give you a new look, or you'll be a bounty hunter's dream job."

Panthea wanted to scream at how quickly things had gotten out of hand. But she had to be strong and think logically. All right. She would go with him, change her clothes, then leave. It wouldn't take that long. Ash was probably still sulking at the lake, anyway.

With her assent, they left the courtyard and traveled to the very edge of the town, where Arvin finally took them to a house. As they entered, the scent of timber made her wish for a moment she lived in this town.

The orange light of setting Diva bled from the only window in the sitting room. Arvin ushered her to the table in the middle. "Wait here. I'll go see if I can find something for you to wear."

There were two doors on the wall on the far side of the room. He entered the door on the left. She wondered why a single man like him would need such a big house. "Do you live alone?"

No answer came. She stood up to explore, leaving her satchel on the table. The house seemed tidier than Rassus's. It was almost empty. There were a few pots here, a few rags there, and a clean, unused hearth. It didn't look like someone actually lived here.

A few minutes went by. She decided to go see what he was doing. But as she arrived between the two doors, her curiosity led her to the room on the right.

It was as simple as the rest of the house. There was only a bed, a chair, and a tall and thick stand in the corner covered with a white sheet. She approached the stand and lifted the sheet's corner to have a peek.

The sheet slid right off, and the sight of what was underneath it sent a surge of fear through her. It was the dark iron plate armor of the Sapphires. So, this was why those soldiers had been friendly with Arvin. And that meant one thing.

She was in the wrong house.

Just as she dashed out of the room, Arvin's hand clamped on her mouth, and he pressed her against the wall. "Don't scream. Don't do anything stupid."

Her breaths shortened, and her heart raced.

"Things will only get worse for you if you make a sound."

She bit his hand as hard as she could, and he let go with a grunt. Using the chance to shove him away, she ran for the door.

She had almost reached the handle when something hit her head from behind, and her face smacked against the hardwood. Before she could react, another strike landed behind her neck, and her world went black.

5

I was born in a land once saved from the evil of the Dark Ages—or what's assumed to have been evil, for there is no reliable history from that time. I was born in a land promised never to see violence again. An unfulfilled promise.

IT WAS NO SURPRISE every window in the queen's chambers opened to the rose garden. The magnificent blocks and archways, the beautiful colors, and the intoxicating fragrance created the closest worldly approximation of the Garden of Virtue.

Hilia sighed as she turned away from the garden and walked toward the far less attractive rendezvous point: a simple recess on the side of the residence building. The crew was already there waiting for her. She adjusted the scarf over her nose and pulled the hood of her cloak forward before she stepped into the lamplight.

"There you are," Mehran said as he rose with the other two men.

His companions were burly. They wore everything that went with being palace guards. Steel plates, leather gloves, thick leather boots, and an unrelenting expression, without which the act wouldn't sell.

"Well," Hilia said, "you weren't lying. You brought the best for the job.

For a moment there, I thought they were here to arrest me."

The men shared smiles before Mehran addressed them. "Let's go over the plan. The two of you go up there, knock out the guards outside the chambers, and take their place."

"Every corridor in the residence building," Hilia added, "is patrolled once an hour. Wait for the patrol to pass before you engage. Once you're done, there's a room across from the queen's chambers, one door to the right. That's where you dump the guards. Look for a cross on the bottom right corner of the door. Do not mistake the room."

"I'll give you half an hour before I join you," Mehran said. "While I'm in the chambers, you stand guard and knock twice if anyone shows up. Questions?"

His companions shared a glance, then both shook their heads.

"Good. Now, go."

Mehran himself went and sat on a bench as the men headed to the building.

Hilia called after them, "Remember the cross."

She joined Mehran on the bench, removed her hood and let the scarf hang over her shoulders, then took a deep breath. "Are they reliable? They're not going to stash two unconscious soldiers in my room, are they? That'd be an image."

He chuckled. "It would, wouldn't it?" There was a silence—one Hilia didn't recognize until his hand perched on her shoulder. "Are you all right?"

"No, yes, I'm good." She gave a smirk to mask her unease. "What about you? Don't tell me you're not a little worried."

"Maybe a little." His smile dimmed. "Do you want to go over the plan one more time?"

"Good idea." She got to her feet, grabbed his wrist, and pulled him to the front side of the building. Pointing in the direction of the queen's bedchamber window on the top floor, she said, "That's the one. I'm going to stand here right below. The scepter will be on the nightstand. Grab it, throw it out, and I'll catch."

When she looked at him again, he was peering into her eyes with vague admiration.

"What?" she said.

"Nothing." His gaze dropped for a moment. "You know you don't have to take this risk. Windhammer will not be happy if anything happens to you."

She snorted. "First of all, I'm not lying in my bed while you all do my dirty work. Second." She pointed at the window. "Are you kidding me? You're going to the chambers to assassinate the ruler of this realm, and *I'm* the one taking a risk?"

He tried again to speak, but she spoke over him. "Third, you don't need to use Windhammer if you're worried about me. Here, I'll show you." She took his hand. "I'm worried about you. So, try not to die. Will you do that for me?"

He gave a tight smile as he closed the little distance between them, his hands moving up Hilia's arms. "Now, let me try," he murmured. "If I don't want you to get involved, it's because I want you safe. This place won't be the same without you."

Hilia reflected his smile. Friends were scarce for her in the palace. Rebels were often too hardened and unsympathetic, Sapphires were discovery waiting to happen, and Parviz didn't know the real Hilia. It was rare to find someone who knew who she was—all she was—and chose to stick around outside of their duty.

The stare lasted a little longer than usual. He enveloped her in his arms, and Hilia became aware of the situation when he leaned in to kiss her. She dodged and wiggled out of his embrace. "What under Diva are you doing?"

Flustered, he raised both hands. "Sorry, I . . . I thought—"

"Oh, gods." Hilia grimaced. "You thought it was an invitation? Gods, no. No. That was . . . no. Look what you made me do before you go risk your life. I'm sorry, but no. Uh-uh."

"All right, I get it," he said with a shaky smile, his face flushed.

"Listen, you're a wonderful man, but I'm not the girl for you." She squeezed her eyes closed. "Ahura's throne. I feel terrible now. Why did you have to go ahead and do that?"

"It's all good. It's on me. I shouldn't have assumed. Let's move on."

She sighed. "I don't court rebels. It really isn't you, all right?"

"Relax. I'm not a child." Mehran looked up at the window, an almost masked disappointment in his features. "I think I'll wait inside. Best if they don't see us together. Windhammer *will* kill me if you're discovered."

"Yeah, you do that."

When he left, she returned to the bench and sank her head into her palms. *Well, that happened.*

Hilia had a lot of time to kill. The first few minutes she spent wondering how she'd led the man on, concluding this was only him trying to be audacious before what could be his last mission. At least they were on the same page now.

Next, came the thought of failure. Windhammer had put her in the palace and never used her. She'd joined the rebellion to mean something, to make a difference. But at the end, it seemed, she was just a handmaiden inside and out. Tonight could change that—for the better or worse.

When the time came close, she got up and walked under the queen's window, her chest constricted with worry. The longer it took Mehran to get in position, the more difficult the wait became. And he was in no rush, it seemed. In fact, he waited so long that, when he finally threw the scepter, she was not looking. It hit the ground with a clank, making her cringe. The one job she'd had.

Luckily, it didn't break. Even the ruby didn't snap out of the snake's mouth.

Hilia darted to the scepter. As she touched the handle, someone whispered behind her. She gasped as she scrambled up, almost falling back. There was no one in sight, let alone someone so close she'd hear them. There were, however, footfalls tapping from the far wall, and a guard would be here any minute.

Scanning the garden, she snatched the scepter and ran before her mind could stop her. The whispers became thrice as loud, and this time she realized they were coming from the scepter itself. "Oh, gods," burst out of her mouth as those voices swarmed in her head.

"You are not the Watcher . . . will be your undoing."

"Your friend shall betray you."

Hilia barreled to the recess. Her breaths rasping, her heart thumping, her shaking hand dropped the scepter before she reached the destination. The whispers dissipated.

What under Diva was that? Hilia approached the scepter again, one step at a time. On her way, she removed her scarf from around her neck to use it to grab the object, hoping it would block out those whispers.

Before she could execute her plan, a voice echoed, "It came from there. Let's check it out."

Shit, shit. She had but a moment to wonder whether she could grab the scepter before the soldiers arrived, and she decided she couldn't. Even if the scarf did work, she needed time to pick up the damned thing properly. A luxury she didn't have. "Shit!"

The bench was close, so she kicked the scepter under it and left. If she were lucky, nobody would find it until tomorrow, when she would bring proper tools to wrap the thing up and have it shipped to Windhammer. In the meantime, there was no reason to risk her cover and her life.

Hilia entered the building to go back to her room, hoping unlike her, Mehran had done his job right. As she walked up the stairs, he was coming down. She stopped, giving him an inquisitive look. "Did you do it?"

Mehran pursed his lips, heaving a deep sigh. "I'm sorry, Hilia."

A total failure, then. At least that was what she thought at first. But a heartbeat later, she understood the real reason he was apologizing when he swung a dagger her way. Hilia had to flatten herself against the wall to avoid the stab. "What are you doing?"

He attacked her again. Hilia evaded him, but her foot slipped, and her heart rose in her chest as the rest of her fell. She tumbled all the way to the bottom. Her shoulders, her legs, her back, they all took a good beating, and although she tried her best to protect her head, she couldn't prevent the sharp edge of the last step from knocking against her brow.

She sprawled there, dizzy, shaken, sore, and could only watch as Mehran descended, his hands gripping the blade. *Hell, no. This can't be how I die.*

"Wait," Hilia demanded with as much of her voice as she could muster. "Please don't."

It seemed like he did not even hear her. With an unfeeling expression, he crouched in front of her and put the blade on her neck.

A group of soldiers ran down the stairs. "There he is. Get him."

Hilia could hardly breathe. She could not comprehend what was happening. Those bastards had saved her. From her friend.

"In the name of Queen Artenus," one soldier said as they seized Mehran, "you're under arrest for high treason."

As they dragged him away, one of the remaining Sapphires approached Hilia. "Need a hand, ma'am?"

Hilia groaned. "I . . . think I'm going to need more than that."

A half-hour later, help arrived—the kind of help Hilia could really live without. Inquisitor Kadder himself loomed over her, a stern expression on his face.

Four blackhoods accompanied the old man, who inspected Hilia's injuries before they got her to her feet. Now that the initial shock was over, she retraced the events of the night. Her failure, Mehran's betrayal. The whispers. "*You are not the Watcher,*" and "*Your friend shall betray you.*" Whatever under Diva any of it meant. Well, the latter one had just come true. But why? How?

She could think all she wanted, but there was no making sense of all this. Had the scepter known the future? Had she received a premonition? Why had Mehran decided to kill her? He had no motive. They were good friends. And turning down his romantic gesture didn't warrant murder.

Kadder studied her eyes as he moistened his lips. "You want to tell me what happened here? What were you doing in the hallways this late?"

His gaze was unyielding, and Hilia was not in the right frame of mind to be interrogated. "Is this an interview?"

One of the blackhoods gave her a violent shake, sending a twinge of pain down her shoulder. "Answer the Inquisitor's question."

Hilia groaned at the pain.

"Hey," Kadder barked, backhanding the blackhood's chest. "She's injured, for Annahid's sake."

Per his instruction, the blackhoods let her go, and Kadder himself helped her walk to a safe distance from them. For an old man, he was quite strong too. Hilia could almost put her entire weight on him.

Once they were out of earshot, Kadder offered her a napkin, pointing at her forehead. "For the blood."

Until this moment, Hilia had not even realized she was bleeding. Now, she also registered her blood-stained hands.

"Those idiots," Kadder growled, a faint smile on his lips. "The only thing they know how to do is interrogate." He glanced back at the stairs. "You know what's going on?"

Hilia genuinely didn't. A lot was happening in her head, but what was happening in this place was beyond her.

"Bastard tried to kill the queen," Kadder explained. "And he and his accomplices have displaced her scepter. He also killed four palace guards." *What under the fuck of Diva! He killed friendlies?* "Over the coming days, we're going to investigate the attack and find the accomplices." *Accomplice. Singular.* "So, make sure we can reach you in case we have questions."

She only nodded.

"In fact, I would really like to know what happened."

I assisted Mehran in an assassination attempt. "I was coming back from the rose garden when he attacked me."

"And what were you doing in the rose garden?"

"I, uh . . ." She shrugged. "I couldn't sleep. Thought it would help."

Kadder held her gaze—even after she was finished—probably looking for non-verbal cues. Hilia knew averting her eyes would make her look like a suspect. But the stare lasted so long it would have been more suspicious if she didn't look away.

"All right," he said at last, a foreign kindness touching his eyes. "I think

I'll stop bothering you with these questions for now and let you get some rest." His expression softened. "How's your father, by the way? Do you have news from him?"

This reminded her she had not written to her father for quite some time. "I, uh. I haven't heard anything. From him."

He patted her shoulder. "He should be proud to have a daughter like you. Few can handle life in the palace."

A daughter who associates with the queen who destroyed his entire life. What more can a father ask for?

"Be safe. And write to your father more often. We old folks tend not to stick around forever."

He left her side. As those last words sank in, an ugly realization came to Hilia. *Why did he say that?*

6

I spent my youth researching religion and the building blocks of our world. I found the path to peace by breathing smoke and dust and straining my eyes, reading page after page, tome after tome. I do not simply claim mine to be the righteous path. I have tangible proof of my claim.

A SPLASH OF COLD WATER woke Panthea, and she found herself tied to a chair in a warm room with timber walls. *What under Diva!* The room was almost empty, with only a bed and a nightstand.

The man from the inn, Arvin, towered over her, the bottom of his face lit under the light of the low-hanging lamps. A sudden rush pulsed through her entire body as she remembered everything. This was the house she had willingly—foolishly—walked into.

"This could have gone so much easier," Arvin said.

She squirmed in a futile attempt to free herself. But she was practically one with the chair.

"Don't waste your energy. It won't work."

She blew the strand of hair that blocked her eye and glared at him as she wriggled her wrists. "What are you going to do to me?"

Not caring to answer, he walked behind her. On his way, he inserted his hand into her hair. The touch of his fingers on her scalp felt like a hundred worms traversing her upper body. He moved all her hair to one side and let it flow over her shoulder, exposing the side of her neck.

There were clinks and clatters.

"Are you going to kill me?" she said, her voice shaking.

Something stung the back of her neck, and she funneled her pain, surprise, and frustration through a piercing yelp. Anyone else would have at least paused. But not him. Pushing her head to the side, he applied a few drops of some liquid to the cut.

"They call this the nightmare potion," Arvin intoned. "When ingested, it takes a few hours to take effect, but we don't have that much time. You probably won't like this." He walked in front of her again with a dim smile. "If you don't resist, this will be over soon."

As Arvin left the room, a single drop of something fell on her head. Then another, and another. The liquid tickled its way down her scalp. It was not raining outside. They were not even close to the Dark Fusion, which made the dripping unexpected. Unless ... it was not rainwater. When she looked up, it was not water at all. It was blood, dripping in trickles now.

"Panthea," someone whispered in her ear. She turned in panic but found no one beside her. "Panthea." This time, Ash stood in front of her. "Do you recognize me?"

What is happening? "Ash, you can't be here," Panthea said. "You need to run."

"Panthea, it's me."

Her growing fear brought forth the familiar feeling of power-lust, and the room brightened. The floorboards broke off and rose into the air. *She's your friend. She's your friend.* Even as she reminded herself that, she felt a rush, and Ash's eyes popped open. Panthea looked down to find a sharp, jagged end of broken timber jutting out of her friend's stomach. Blood trickled from the corner of Ash's mouth.

"No. Annahid, no. Ash!"

Tears clouded her vision. She blinked a few times, and when she opened her eyes again, Ash was no longer there, dead or alive. Panthea's heart was beating so fast, she thought it would punch a hole through her chest and burst out.

A lamp fell, and the floor caught fire. The flames spread so quickly, she gasped. They engulfed the room in a single breath. "Somebody help!"

"My daughter's in there," echoed the screeching of a female voice. "Let me save my daughter."

The entire room was ablaze. The floor, the ceiling, the bed—all burning in hot flames.

As Panthea saw her death approaching, Ash appeared again. "You'll kill me, like you killed your mother."

Panthea cried, "I didn't kill my mother!"

"If she hadn't come back to save you, she'd be alive now. Death and misery follow you everywhere you go."

"Stop!"

The flames crawled up her chair, and an excruciating pain coursed through her body as fire devoured her flesh.

Another splash of water slapped her face, and it all vanished.

"It's all right," said Arvin. "It wasn't real." He rubbed the corner of her lips and wiped his hand on his shirt. "It's worse than I thought. You were foaming."

Panthea looked around frantically. There was no fire, no blood. "What did you do to me?" Her heart still pounded, and the water on her face reminded her of the blood.

"This potion brings you your darkest fears. Now, listen carefully. While you were out, I gave you a little something. You're not powerful enough to do anything significant, but you should be able to move small objects. What I want you to do"—he pointed at the nightstand, where a silver chalice flickered in the lamplight—"is to pull that off the edge. You do that, you go free."

"No." She gave her wrists another jerk, her teeth grinding together. This level of stress could trigger her power-lust. "This is madness. You have no idea what I'm capable of."

"Maybe. But I know what I'm doing." He jutted his head toward the chalice. "And that's your way out."

She glanced between the nightstand and his expectant eyes. *Annahid, help me. Protect me from sin.* She focused on the chalice and tried to move it, but as soon as her will kicked in, so did the consuming desire for destruction.

Her lungs locked in panic, and she rasped, "I can't." Her voice resonated with the tremor in her body. "Please don't make me do this. I don't want to hurt you." Struggling to control her shattering grip on her power, she pleaded, "Please let me get out. I need air."

"Not happening," he said, heading out. "I'm going to run a few errands. We'll continue this when I'm back."

"You can't leave me here," she said, though Arvin was already out of the room. "You're making a big mistake, you hear me?" The front door thudded closed before she finished that sentence.

She screeched in frustration. Her lust for power was growing too quickly, and she needed a distraction before she made another spectacle of herself and alarmed everyone in town. *Think. What would Evian say?*

Panthea was no stranger to fear. She had felt it with all her existence at thirteen. It was during the peak of the Purge. Her power was late, and Sapphires went from door to door, dragging Erkenbloods out of their homes. She spent her days and most nights wondering when they would come for her. Her screams as she woke from nightmares had become the new norm. So had her cries that went on for hours. Rassus and Evian would try to calm her, but nothing worked.

Until Evian's lullaby came about. It was a nursery song from Delavaran. One sleepless night, he came to her room unannounced and sat beside her bed, singing the lullaby. Not to help her sleep, but to show her he would do just about anything for his friend. Even something as embarrassing as singing.

That was the perfect opener to a night-long conversation. They laughed together at Rassus, at the tiny house, even at Queen Artenus. The song became a reminder of a night she had spent without fear during the Purge.

As the memories passed, she found herself murmuring the lullaby once again. "To fight the cold of fusing suns, my dolly, shut your eyes. To feel the warmth of morning light, my dolly, shut your eyes. A hundred birds who sing with you, a hundred men at your command, to reach your greatest, wildest dreams, my dolly, shut your eyes."

Panthea closed her eyes and took a deep breath. The fear was almost gone. She barely felt the grip of the ropes around her wrists and the bite of power-lust on her senses. She was going to make it. Yes. This was what Evian would tell her if he were here.

PANTHEA SCREAMED AS she woke. Her body was drenched in sweat, her face covered in cold tears. She did not even remember going to sleep, though she had seen those images again. This time, she had not only watched Ash die, but all of them. Evian, Rassus.

She wanted it to stop, wanted to get out of here, to go home. She wanted to reverse everything that had happened.

"Hello, Hita." Arvin stood in the doorframe. "You were sleeping so peacefully when I came back. But it was time for your dose."

Warm tears traced over dried ones, but she didn't find the will to talk. He came to her and leaned in so close, the stench of alcohol slapped her as he spoke. "You're making this really hard on yourself. These nightmares—"

She spat at him, which she regretted when she saw his flushing face. He raised a hand to her, and she shut her eyes and yelped in anticipation of the strike. But the hand never landed. When she opened her eyes again, he had already brought his arm down, regarding her with what she could only describe as pity.

"Why are you doing this to me?" If her shaking arms and thighs, teary eyes, and wet cheeks were not enough, the tremor in her voice that made her question sound more like begging was proof of her defeat.

He cocked an eyebrow. "What do you think I'm doing?"

"I don't know," she cried.

Arvin's lips parted momentarily, but he bit his words back. He then left the room and returned with a bowl and a spoon. Crouching in front of her, he said, "You need to eat."

It was vegetable soup. The appetizing smell of turmeric and fried garlic in it made her stomach growl. But she would not let this monster feed her. He brought a spoonful to her mouth, but she pressed her lips together in protest.

He let out a heavy sigh. "Do you have to be so difficult?"

"I'm not hungry."

He dropped the spoon back in the bowl, and the splash sent a few drops of hot soup shooting at her face. "Fine. Starve. But you're not getting out of here." He didn't waste time to go behind her. The clatters began. "Ready for another dose?"

Panthea could not bear another bout of those nightmares. She could not bear the fear anymore. She tried to shift the chair, to no avail.

"No. Get away from me." She retreated to screaming.

The small blade stung, and the liquid found its way to her neck. Her sobs started anew as she braced herself for the nightmares.

7

I used to trust the stories of the Dark Ages. I believed Erkenbloods had been power hungry and determined to wipe out what they considered lesser humans.

PANTHEA HAD LOST track of time. Days and nights were just randomly occurring backdrops in the few moments of reality between her nightmares. She only hoped Ash and Evian had found each other and were safe.

Arvin entered with a loaf of bread and a cup of water.

She had already decided starving would do nothing other than impair her logical thinking, which she needed if she wanted to plan her escape. And plan she had.

With her eyes, she gestured toward the bowl beside the bed. "I need to go."

Arvin frowned. "What?"

"If you don't want me to soil the floor, I need to go."

He sighed. "But you went less than an hour ago." His gaze dropped to the glass. "You know what? I think I'm giving you too much water." He put the glass on the floor before he went to untie her legs. "You know the drill. Try anything, and you sleep with an empty stomach."

Blood flowed through her ankles as the ropes came loose. Once he removed them, he stood her up and took her to the bowl. He waited at three paces away, arms crossed.

Panthea glared at him. "Are you going to watch?"

Arvin rolled his eyes as he turned around. "Make it quick."

She made all the appropriate sounds with her trousers to make him believe she was getting ready, her gaze trained on the gaping door behind him. This was her moment.

She slowly picked up the bowl.

"I'm not hearing anything," Arvin said. "If you've lied, save yourself the embarrass—"

Her heart pumping fire, Panthea threw the bowl at his head, then ran through the door as fast as her legs could carry her. She charged into the sitting room where her belongings lay on the table. Evian's satchel. Rassus's pendant.

Arvin caught up with her far sooner than she had anticipated and grabbed her by the waist long before she reached the table. She kicked, clawed, screamed, but Arvin carried her back to the room and hurled her on the bed. "Why do you have to be such a wildling?"

He took her ankle and tried to pull her in when she let out her loudest scream and kicked him in the face, sending him reeling. She used the chance to jump off the bed. He tried to catch her again, but she dodged his attack and stumbled to the door.

Her legs were still weak after days of being bound, but she made her way to the table in the sitting room. Despite her shaking hands, she opened the satchel and took Evian's dagger out. Arvin's footsteps rushed toward her from behind. She spun with the knife and cut across the arm he was about to grab her with. The knife flew away from her weak hand.

Grunting in pain, he stepped back, blood dribbling from his arm. He made another attempt to grab her, but she slipped out of his grasp, shuffled to a safe distance, and yelled, "Stay where you are."

"Listen." He raised both hands in a conciliatory gesture. "We have to talk." Eyes locked on hers, he inched closer. "This is not what you think.

I'm not going to hurt you."

"I said stand back." Her vision brightened and, without thinking, she willed the table to shoot at him, and he had no time to react before it hit him across the face. His head banged against the wall behind, and the table landed next to him on its long edge.

Arvin dropped to the floor, his eyes closed.

Panthea watched him for a few moments to make sure he wasn't moving, then tip-toed to him, prepared to run if he woke. A calm stream of blood still flowed from the cut on his arm, and another one ran down his nose. But his chest rose and fell just fine.

Keeping him in her line of sight, she hobbled to the door.

Fresh air brushed over her face as she walked out of the house and the smell of grass on the lawns poured over the fire inside her. It was dark outside. A sob squeezed her airways as she tried to orient herself. She would have sat there and cried her eyes out if time was not against her, but each minute she spent lamenting was one less she had for finding her friends.

Making her way back to the caravanyard, she hoped Ash had waited there. She searched the entire yard before going to the inn to ask about her and Evian.

Upon hearing their descriptions, the innkeeper said, "Haven't seen the girl. But a young man was here two days ago. Short hair, olive skin, thin build, just as you describe. He was looking for two girls. One with black hair and bright eyes. Like yourself."

Evian had come for them, which brought a little relief to her. But where was Ash? What had happened to her at the lake? Why had she not come to the inn as planned? "Where is the young man now?"

The innkeeper shrugged. "Didn't stay. Must be still looking for you and your friend."

She spent a second or two coming to terms with her current situation before she regarded the man again. "What day is today?"

He looked at her quizzically. "Erm . . . twenty-fifth?"

Twenty-fifth of Hitian. She had been in that house for four days. Ash should have shown up by now. Panthea's only other idea was to go to the lake to see if she could find her there.

When she opened the door, her gaze caught a group of Sapphires standing further away in the yard. She kept her head down, struggling to maintain her composure. Her legs wanted to run; every fiber of her body yearned to shoot out of the town. But she had to take slow, nonchalant steps lest she attract their attention. Walking had never been more difficult. As soon as she was out of sight, she ran like a loose arrow.

By the time she arrived at the lake, she barely had any breath left, but at least she was alone. There were bushes all around, some making perfect hiding spots for the night. Could Ash have been here all this time? What would she have done for food?

Panthea spent a good hour searching for her friend. And every minute filled her with more despair. Eventually, she stopped. If Ash were alive, she wouldn't have stayed by the lake. If she were dead, Panthea was not prepared to run into her bloated body. So, she picked a secluded spot to stay for the night. She would continue come morning.

She lay down, trying to focus on the sound of water, the scent of buttonbush flowers, and the beautiful night sky. The Erken constellation was right above, and the star at the bottom of the triangle, the Matter Star, shone twice as brightly as the other two. It reminded her of what Rassus used to call her when she was younger, of how different their relationship had been.

"Is my power evil?" she had once asked him when she was six, back when she still lived at the temple.

"My little Matter Star," Rassus had told her. "Arcane power is the foundation of our world. Your power is a beautiful manifestation of *what's living* at the beginning of our prayers. Power rising from life itself."

This had been her greatest revelation. "If Erkenbloods are what's living," she had concluded, "does this mean gleamstones are what's dead?"

With a fatherly smile, Rassus had taken her hand. "Indeed. What's dead refers to everything around us that doesn't live. The rocks, the water, the soil. And gleamstones are arcane power embedded in the inanimate."

"What about what's divine?"

Rassus had rubbed his mustache and beard for a while as he had pondered. He had then caressed the back of her head. "Divine is your kind heart, Matter Star. You are not evil. I know you're afraid. Fear is a mighty tool for survival, but it can also be your greatest enemy. Sometimes, our trepidations become self-fulfilling prophecies. I promise, if you follow my rules, I'll keep you from harm. I'll help you face your fears."

And now, eleven years later, she lay on the banks of the Green Eye Lake, alone, overcome by fear, with no one to help her face it. *Where are you, Master? I broke the rules. I'm sorry.*

"I'm so sorry," she wheezed as tears slid down her temples.

HITA WAS JUST EMERGING from the east. The lake lay in front of Panthea, the water rippling and sloshing with the morning breeze. Her clothes, soaked in water, pressed against her skin with a chill. The smell of flowers had given way to that of rotten meat and feces.

She rolled over, her hand plopping in a puddle beside her. The image was blurry at first, but what she could make out was more than just grass and bushes. Unease settled in her stomach.

They were people.

She pressed her hands on the ground to sit up, but a twinge shot through her right shoulder. Standing up was an ordeal.

As the image cleared, she saw a dozen Sapphires lying motionless, their blood diluted in the water around the lake. Her chest tightened.

The soldiers were not just dead. They were ripped open, guts sprawled beside them, limbs loosely clinging to their bodies, helmets crushed into their faces. Panthea's legs shivered, either from the cold or the horror of what she witnessed. She was too light-headed to know the difference.

How had she missed all this happening around her?

She cupped her hands and held her throbbing head in them. It felt like someone twisted a knife in her skull, mashing her brain. Her nostril tingled, and when she rubbed it with the back of her palm, her hand came away smeared with fresh blood. Her breath caught. Thinned blood was the result of an overuse of power by her kind. And the headache and the dizziness had already left little room for denial. Panthea did not need more proof. She did not want more proof.

She checked again to see if her nose was really bleeding. *No, no. No!* She couldn't have been the perpetrator of this massacre. Murder was the mother of sins. Every sinner deserved a chance to change, but when one took another's life, they denied them of that chance.

And this was not just one life.

Desperately, she counted. *Five, eight, ten … so many.* So many souls hastened on their paths to becoming soldiers of Angra. She could not possibly repent for this in her lifetime.

She felt nauseous. Her greatest fear, what she had been trying so hard to avoid, had been realized. *Annahid, forgive me.*

No. What was there to forgive? It was not her. It couldn't have been.

She braced her hands on her knees and took a few sharp breaths to force down the nausea. The smell surely didn't help. She needed to get away from this before she went mad.

As she stepped around the corpses, a fragment of memory flashed before her eyes. It was one of the men yelling, "There she is!"

No! Not a memory. I'm still under the effect of the nightmare potion. I'm not a killer.

She left the lakeside and started walking along the road, wincing at each painful stride. She tried to distract herself by thinking of a plan to find Ash and Evian, but the very thought of what could have happened to them aggravated her nausea.

Another piece of memory struck. A man wearing a similar outfit to those who had raided their house in Saba. But his uniform was more intricate. He was tall, had prominent cheekbones, and had his dark brown hair tied back in a ponytail. He looked so cruel, so cold.

Before she could recover from that image, another invaded her: the same man talking to someone else, whose appearance was obscured by

Panthea's fragile memory. What she remembered was the disdainful glance she received from the man with the ponytail over the other person's shoulder.

She dropped to her knees, heaving. The smell of dead bodies mixing with that of her stomach acid fueled an unending cycle of vomiting. Her insides twisted together as she gasped between her retches.

By the time she was done, her body was as cold inside as it was outside. The pain had become unbearable, stinging from her spine, stabbing in her stomach, pounding in her head. She let out a fatigued cry as she got to her feet.

The way back to the crossroads took much longer than she remembered traveling the night before. Once she arrived, she gawked at the signs, hoping something would tell her where to go. Watertown, Saba, Livid, Delavaran.

The world spun, and she opened her eyes to nothing but the blue sky.

A gentle hand snuck under her head. "Panthea."

She glanced around, disoriented. One moment she'd been on her feet, the next, she lay in the dirt with a dry mouth. "What . . . happened?"

She looked up to see who held her, and her skin prickled with relief when she saw him.

Evian smiled as he helped her sit up. "You passed out. Where were you girls? I've been searching for you for days."

"When did you get out?" Panthea asked.

"The lockdown ended the day after. I came here straight away, but I couldn't find you. Where's Ash?"

Panthea struggled not to cry as she shook her head. "I don't know."

"Hey, hey," he said as he held her tighter. "I'm sure she's fine. Now, let's get you up."

Fighting the dizziness, she got up with his help, and he didn't let go of her arm until she could stand on her own trembling feet.

"Can you tell me what happened?" he asked. "Where are your things?"

"You, first. What's going on? Why did they raid our house? Why did they take Master? Why are we running?"

"I'll tell you when you're better." He took her hand and set to walk.

She used all her strength to tug her hand free. "No, you'll tell me now."

Evian stopped, his lips thinning. "Fine. A while ago, Master told me about this artifact, this gem the queen is after." He looked into her eyes briefly before his gaze wandered around her face. Knowing him, he was probably running a visual health assessment even as he spoke. "He knew Sapphires would come looking for it."

"Master has the gem?"

"Not exactly," said Evian. "But he knows where it is. That's why the Inquisition took him."

"Why did Master not tell me about it?"

He shrugged, averting his eyes. "I, uh, thought he had."

Panthea could barely keep her eyes open. But she needed to understand. "What does this have to do with us?"

Evian was growing more and more impatient, and the concern in his eyes made her wonder just how sick she looked. "The Inquisition," he said, "may try to use us to pressure Master. And you . . . well, you have a very good reason to run after what happened in Saba. You're kind of famous now."

She shivered at the thought, but she pushed it back in her head to focus on the more urgent matter. "We need to find Ash."

"No," he said as he took her by the shoulder again. "What we need to do is get you fixed."

"But we can't leave her alone."

"Panthea," he rebuked. "I've searched that town for two days. I've looked all around the lake. She's not here. The only thing I can think of is that she's back in Saba. The lockdown is over, and it's no longer dangerous for her to go home."

"Then let's go and make sure she's there."

"Did you not hear what I said?" he replied with an air of frustration. "It's not safe."

"For me. What about you? You can go check on her."

"I can't," he mumbled. "It's dangerous for me too." His grip loosened, and only then did she realize she had not been standing on her own. He caught her before she fell, his brows creased. "You're not well, Panthea.

Let's find a safe place, so I can heal you. I'll answer your questions once you've recovered, and you can tell me about your last few days."

Her head swam. Her breaths were intentional. The image of the dead bodies strewn around the lake repeated in her mind. And that mysterious black-clad man with the ponytail. And those nightmares in Arvin's house. So much had happened in so little time. Her chin quivered, and her lungs locked her out. "I was so scared."

Evian pulled her into a warm embrace. "It's all right. You're safe now."

She nodded against his chest and clung to him. She had not had a shoulder to cry on since they had taken Rassus. Now that she did, she didn't hold back—she cried until all that was left were silent, little hiccups. Only then did Evian pull away, wiping her tears for her. "We'll not separate again. I promise."

8

If anyone had the right to question, it was I. Many an Erkenblood has been hated for her power. I was killed for mine. That is a story in and of itself. The story of the first time I died. The death of my body.

PANTHEA WOKE TO THE comfort of a bed in a warm room. Though she was still a little groggy, her nausea had settled. She did not remember when she had passed out, but it was not too hard to believe she had, considering how awful she'd felt at the lake.

The room smelled like boiling . . . metal.

"Hey, sleepyhead," Evian's voice came from her side. After the horrific few days she'd had, waking up to a familiar face was something she cherished.

Before she had time to answer, someone else's footfalls thudded on the floor. She sat up and looked over Evian's shoulder. A middle-aged woman walked to them and sat beside Evian. Silver strands laced her short, scraggly hair, and a worn tunic covered her spindly body. She didn't seem to be a threat. "Are you all right, love?"

Panthea eyeballed Evian, hoping he would explain who this stranger was. He didn't. Instead, he gave the woman a reassuring nod before he met Panthea's gaze again. "You had us worried. There were moments when I thought you wouldn't make it."

"Oh," she said absently as she scanned the simple cottage. Outside the door, there was a farm covered in yellow wheat plants. "Where are we?"

"When you passed out, we were far away from any town. This family was kind enough to help us."

The woman looked behind at the steaming pot above the hearth in the middle. "I think your potion's ready, Master Evian."

Hearing him addressed as Master felt so strange, Panthea couldn't help a giggle. People would often call healers this way, but to her, he would always be just Evian.

He went to the pot and sniffed. "Yes. It's ready."

He poured some of the dark liquid into a cup and brought it back, blowing on it on his way. "Drink this," he said as he handed it to her.

The metallic smell was coming from the same liquid that was in the cup. She grimaced. "What is this?"

"Iron extract," he said. "It might not taste like much, but you'll need it, considering how bad your condition was."

Carefully, she blew on the drink some more before taking a small sip.

It tasted like rusty scissors. She spat it out.

"Panthea," Evian said firmly. "Your blood is still thin. You need to drink this."

Letting out a sigh, she held the cup with both hands and took a deep breath. As she sipped it, her nausea threatened to come back.

The woman returned and handed another cup to Evian, which he exchanged with Panthea's. "Water. It'll wash down the iron extract."

The water eased the aftertaste as it went down. But it did not change the fact she had a full cup of iron extract left to drink. Their host got up and straightened her tunic. "Master Evian, I'll be in the barn if you two need something." She smiled at Panthea. "Feel better, love."

Evian took Panthea's hand and squeezed it as soon as the woman left. He had probably sensed her disquiet. "It'll be all right."

She didn't want to be too hard on him, especially when he was so supportive. But all this was too much to take. A thretnight ago, she would have never imagined herself in a stranger's house, so far from Saba. She had never imagined it would become such a struggle to keep her friends close. "Up to now, it's been anything but all right. We still don't know where under Diva Ash is."

"I'm worried about her the least." Evian smiled, though it hardly found its way to his eyes. "It's Ash. If you two had a fight, I'm almost sure she's gone back to Saba."

His theory was believable, and she repressed the nagging in her head for now. "So, what's the plan?"

"Survive. The people who are after the stone are dangerous. We're talking about the Inquisition."

That mention reminded her of the black-clad man with the ponytail, and the fact that Rassus was still their prisoner. "What else do you know about the stone?"

Evian scratched behind his ear. "It's called the Bond of Third Arcane. Master was the last in the line of those tasked to protect it. That's why the Inquisition took him."

"Did he tell you where it was?"

He averted his eyes, making a few false starts before he said, "It doesn't matter. Master didn't want us to get involved in this. Especially you and Ash. He said he would die before he saw you harmed."

The idea of Rassus dying for them was not something she was prepared to handle. "Evian, if you know where it is, you must tell me. If we have the stone, we can trade it for Master. That's what the Sapphires want, isn't it? They'd let him go if they have it."

"Master would never forgive us. He said he would protect it with his life."

"I don't care if he'll be mad at us." She struggled to keep her voice from shaking. "Please, Evian. We have to do this."

"Panthea—"

"We can't let him die." That last word came out painfully. She looked away, her lips quivering, her eyes warm with tears.

The weight of Evian's stare lingered, but she could not get herself to look at him. He took her hand and said in a reassuring tone, "We'll find another way."

What other way? Evian was not a risk-taker, and he was not one to disappoint Rassus or act against his will. This was probably why the old man had trusted him, and not her, with the secret. But things were different now. The man who had raised them both could lose his life. If that did not warrant breaking the rules for once, she wondered what did.

The rest of the day was a blur. When she was not drinking that disgusting medicine or telling Evian the horrific story of her few days of captivity, she sat alone in a corner, marveling at how quickly one's life could change because of a small mistake. If she had told Rassus about her power, none of this would have happened. She would not have had to sneak out at night. Those Sapphires would not have stopped her.

The guilt of having led them to their house weighed on her like a mountain, pounding on her every time Evian said it had been nobody's fault. He had no idea what had transpired that night. She could have prevented this. And now, it was her responsibility to turn it all around. But she could not do that without Evian's help—help he did not seem willing to offer.

Come evening, she finally left the cottage, where she found Evian lying on the dirt on the outer rim of the farm, looking up at the stars. Hita had already set, and Diva drew its last breaths as it shed a streak of deep red on the dark horizon. She went and lay beside him and followed his line of sight. For the first few minutes, neither spoke.

At some point, to distract her trail of negative thoughts, she pointed at the Erken constellation. "Did you see how bright Matter Star has been for the past few nights?"

Evian smiled. "Yeah. It's guarded too. Make a wish."

Panthea peered until she saw it. The Guardian. It was a planet that passed through the Erken constellation once every few years. And if that coincided with the brightening of one of the three stars, it was considered good luck. *Dear Annahid, protect Rassus. Help us reunite.*

"Did I ever tell you the story of Master and the Guardian?" Evian asked.

"What story?"

His gaze still lost high above, he said, "So, this happened a few days after Master brought you to Saba. You should have seen how protective he was of you in the beginning. I couldn't even talk to you without his permission."

"I know. He never let me get out of the house. He always took me for this fragile little girl who needed to be sheltered from the rest of the world."

His smile turned mischievous. "I mean, you *were* kind of fragile. The first time I saw you, I couldn't believe you were an Erkenblood. You were so small, so innocent, I could not connect what I'd heard about Erkenbloods to what I saw."

"Oh, yeah." She chuckled. "I remember that day. You kept staring at me. It was so uncomfortable."

"Yeah, not the proudest day of my life. Anyway, one night, Master shows it to me and says the Guardian's purpose is to watch over the Matter Star, but he can't always be there for her. When the Guardian leaves, when the Matter Star loses her luster, it is up to the other two to pick her up. Because no matter where he is, the Guardian is happiest when Matter Star shines brightly." His smile flickered away. "He made me promise to always look after you."

Tears welled in her eyes. She had always thought Rassus called her Matter Star because of her element. She had never stopped to consider how deep a meaning that simple nickname had in the old man's heart. He had done everything to protect her, and what had she done? She had foolishly put him in mortal danger by sneaking out of the house despite his advice. Unable to keep that burden any longer, she said, "Evian, there is something you should know."

He regarded her, concern knotting his eyebrows. "What is it?"

"I think I'm the reason Master is captured."

Evian's jaw clenched. "Why would you say that?"

"The last night in Saba, when I snuck out, Sapphires stopped me. They were going to send me to the Inquisition, but General Heim showed up, and he let me go. I thought I was lucky. But now I understand. He baited me." She gulped, unable to say another word without breaking into a sob.

Evian sat up and shifted to her. "Panthea, you can't think like that. It wasn't your fault."

She gave in to her tears, and collected as much of her voice as she could to say, "Then, why did they come the morning after? It fits."

"No, it doesn't." A film of tears coated his own eyes. "It wasn't the Sapphires who attacked the house. And they weren't there for you." He reached for her hand and held it between both of his. "None of us are responsible for what happened to Master. He knew what he was doing, and he was aware of the consequences."

She took a moment to contain her sob, sniffling. Did it even matter why the Inquisition had raided their house? Did it change the fact he was in danger unless they did something?

Looking up at Evian, she said, "Please tell me you'll help me get him out."

"When the time is right. For now, we need to lie low until the Inquisition stops searching for you. Please let me keep my promise."

She wished she could extinguish her emotions the way Evian did his. The Matter Star needed her Guardian, and there was no one to help her.

"Kids?" came the woman's voice from inside the house. "Dinner's ready."

Evian stood and held out his hand. "What do you say we talk more after dinner?"

Panthea accepted his offer and got up. The smell of meat had been noticeable from outside, but as they walked in, it was so intense her mouth watered.

The landlord himself entered after them, a smile growing on his weathered face. "This is why I fell in love with that woman." This was the first time Panthea had heard him speak since he'd come back from the city in the afternoon.

His wife had already spread linen on the floor. Once they all sat, she filled a bowl of stew for each and handed it to them before joining them with her own.

The husband ate a spoonful. "So. What brings you two here? Why did you leave home?"

While Panthea struggled to find a safe response, Evian was quick to say, "We have no home. We're travelers."

"Travelers, huh?" The man seemed much more interested in Panthea, and his scrutinizing gaze didn't linger on Evian for long. Pointing at her face, he said, "I know those eyes. You're one of them Erkenbloods, aren't you?"

Panthea's chest tightened. Common folk normally didn't recognize Erkenbloods by their eyes. Not in a lit room, at least, when the glimmer was not noticeable. She shared a look with an equally alarmed Evian.

"Don't be scared," their host reassured. "You've done nothing wrong, have you?"

The way the conversation was going, it wouldn't be long before she said something that alluded to her crime, even if she tried to lie—*especially* if she tried to lie.

"No," Evian saved her once again. "But that doesn't stop Sapphires from hunting her kind. That's why she's a little scared."

"I hear ya," the man said as he shoved more stew into his mouth. He wagged a finger while he chewed, then continued, "I've got to say, though. I've heard terrible stories of Erkenbloods. She seems like a good kid, but there are those of her kind that do evil. Sapphires are not monsters. They get the difference between good and bad."

She glared at the man. "So, you agree with them? You think Queen Artenus is just?"

Evian gave her a nudge, making her realize she was being too forward.

"Didn't mean no offense, girl," the man said. "I said you seem to be a good kid. I don't care about politics. All I know is I feel safe to go sell our harvest without fearing bandits or wielders now. Back in the day, I used to pray every time I stepped outside those fences. The queen gave up her own wielding for the good of this land. She protects us like King Shahbod never could. Even as Warhammer and his thugs ravage our cities." He regarded his wife. "Did I tell you there was another attack in Livid?"

It was astounding how ignorant people could be. Did they really believe the queen had given up her power? Inborn wielding was not something someone just gave up. It was like the color of one's hair or the pitch of one's voice; it wasn't a possession. But this time, Panthea took Evian's direction and didn't retort. She ate to distract herself.

"We don't agree with everything Queen Artenus does," the woman said, putting a gentle hand on Panthea's arm. "What he's saying is our lives have been fine under her rule."

A distant voice came from across the farm, "Red is the hue, the night is due. Anybody home?"

"We know you're in there, old man," said another voice.

"We have news," another said. "Good, juicy news."

Laughter followed.

The landlord clicked his tongue. "Ah, great. Piggy. What does he want this time?"

From where Panthea sat, she could not see anyone.

The woman craned her neck and peered through the window. "I thought you weren't talking to them anymore."

"I wasn't," the man said as he drew himself up and headed out.

Malaise was visible on the woman's face. When her gaze met Panthea's, she put on a smile that was far from convincing. "You should eat. It's going to get cold."

"Who are they?" Panthea asked.

The woman shook her head with a sigh. "Lowlifes. Scavengers. Back in the day, they'd do anything for a few rings. Before the Reform, they were bandits. Nowadays, they make their living from bounty hunting. With rebels rising in every corner of the land, there's never a shortage of jobs for them."

Worry wriggled in Panthea's stomach, and the same sentiment was written in Evian's parted lips and slightly drawn eyebrows.

The woman noticed. "It's all right, love. He won't tell on you. And they won't even want you without a bounty." She complemented her words with another smile, then resumed eating, encouraging them to do the same.

Panthea's bowl was empty when the man came back. His face had lost humor, and his eyes bulged with anger. He slammed the door shut, making Panthea flinch. "Travelers, are we?" he grumbled. "Just an innocent girl?"

"What's going on?" asked the woman.

The man pointed a finger at Panthea. "Why don't you ask her?"

Panthea blinked, trying to understand what was happening. "What did they say?"

"The truth. That you two are criminals."

Evian jumped to his feet. "We're not criminals."

"Then why is there a fifty-thousand-crown price on her head?"

"What?" Panthea and Evian said in harmony.

The man sneered, glancing between the two of them. "You didn't know, did you? You thought you could just run away from the Sapphires, and they wouldn't catch up?"

Panthea stood beside Evian, and he squeezed her hand, his eyes boring into the landlord's. "What are you going to do with us?"

"Surely not what I should." The man gestured to the window. "I should give you to that bunch. But unlike you, I have honor. You're my guests and have eaten my bread and salt. This means something to us. But it doesn't mean I'll keep harboring two criminals in my house. Get your things now and get out before I change my mind, hand you to Piggy's gang, and get my cut."

She had heard in Watertown that there would be a price on her head. But fifty thousand? Where would they go? Nowhere was safe with that kind of bounty.

"Now," the man snarled.

The woman, too, was sulking now. Evian shot the landlord a pointed glance as he pulled Panthea's arm. "Let's go." As he picked up his satchel, he muttered, "Honor."

9

It was after my first death that I began questioning history itself. I wondered whether the Erkenbloods of the Dark Ages were only protecting themselves.

IT WAS DARK, AND the tall trees around the sides of the narrow path blocked even the faint light coming from the stars. If it were up to Panthea, they would have never gone off the road. Where were they? If only she could place this wood on the maps she knew, she would feel a little better. A little less lost. But she trusted Evian to have a plan. He always did.

They had not spoken since they had left the farm, and she had respected his brooding. But right now, her feet hurt, her throat had dried out, and she could hardly keep her eyes open. "I'm sorry, Evian. But where are we going?"

There was an air of frustration about him, and she could swear he rolled his eyes. "Somewhere away from people," he said somberly. "If those farmers knew about the price on your head, everyone does."

"How long will we hide?"

"I don't know, Panthea," he snapped. "I don't have all the answers, all right?"

Those words shattered her confidence, her sense of safety. She had relied on his composure, on his ability to think on his feet. If someone could get them out of this plight, it could only be him. But after this outburst, she felt like the wall she had been leaning against had crumbled. And she was not strong enough to stand on her own. "Sorry."

For some time, she said nothing more. She even tried to breathe silently lest it irritate him. He had never used this tone with her. She hoped he was not losing it. She needed him.

After a while, Evian mumbled, "I shouldn't have talked like that."

Panthea gave him a furtive glance. "No, you're right to be angry. This is all my fault. If I hadn't lost control in Saba, we wouldn't be in this mess."

"It isn't your fault. Like I said, I should have kept my mouth shut. This situation is weighing on both of us. The last thing we need now is to place blames. I just . . . I'll feel better once we're safe."

She nodded. Even if he was mad at her, pressing the matter further would do no good.

A faint burbling came from the distance, releasing some of her tension. "Is that water?" she asked. "Maybe we can . . ."

"Yes. Let's do that."

The sound had seemed closer than it was. It took them what felt like another half-hour before they were at the riverbank.

As they approached the water, Panthea tried to cut the tension. She forced a smile and said, "Find life, find Shireen."

It was a famous saying in the Southern Kingdom. Southern Sessara was hot and dry, and the river Shireen was its primary source of freshwater. It flowed from the northern boundary all the way to the Black Sea in the south, and most cities and towns were in its proximity, and every patch of woods and greenery stretched along its banks.

Evian only spared her a tepid smile. "This isn't Shireen, though. I think it's Fate."

"Oh." Come to think of it, the river was too narrow to be Shireen. Nonetheless, the earthy freshness that teased her nostrils even before reaching the water was irresistible. She went head-first to the stream, drank her fill and slapped some water onto her face, letting the coolness soothe her.

Evian was more restrained about it. He cupped his hands in the running water to collect some, then drank from his hands. As he wiped his mouth, he looked around. "We can sleep here tonight. Tomorrow, we leave before midday."

But where to? She didn't dare ask. Not after how he had responded the last few times she had tried to start a conversation. But she wanted to know. She so desperately wanted to know. "Should we make a fire?"

"It's a rather warm night, don't you think? And I doubt there are any dangerous animals in these woods."

Panthea nodded.

Evian pressed a hand on her shoulder. "Get some sleep. You'll need your energy tomorrow."

He went a little further from the shore and lay down on a patch of withered leaves.

She splashed some more water on her face before she went and lay two strides away from him. Close as they were as friends, she could not imagine herself huddling with him to sleep. She turned to her side so he could not see her open eyes. She was not sure either of them would get much sleep tonight.

Dear Annahid. In the name of what's dead and what's living and what's divine, accept your lesser daughter. Help us get through this plight.

IT WAS THE FIRST light of Hita through the leaves and branches that brought Panthea out of her sleep.

Her right arm, which had been under her the entire night, was limp. She used her other hand to get up and massage her arm, sending hundreds of needles down its length as it came back to life.

Evian was nowhere to be seen. She knew he would not abandon her.

Would he? After all, he had not been himself. She stood up. "Evian?"

There was no sign of him. The only sounds were the chirping of birds and the flutters of their wings as they flew from one branch to another overhead.

She kept calling his name as she walked toward where they had come from, tendrils of worry growing in her stomach. *No, he wouldn't leave me.*

A rustle came from behind. She spun back, but there was no one. It was not like Evian to sneak up on her.

The sound repeated, and this time, she did not wait to find out who it was. Looking over her shoulder, she ran away, but it wasn't long before she slammed into something and fell back.

A tall figure towered over her, silhouetted by the dappled morning light. "Hello, Hita."

A gasp escaped her when she saw who it was.

"Or should I say," Arvin continued, resting his hand on his belt, where he had strapped a sword, "Panthea."

The images of the house and the nightmares returned. And he had learned her real name somehow. Fear coursing through her, she scrambled to her feet and bolted away. The wet leaves on the ground were too slippery for her to run as fast as he did.

In one moment of carelessness, her ankle caught against a root, and she tumbled down a slope until she came to a stop at the bottom. Her ankle screamed with pain, and she couldn't get up on it. This gave Arvin ample time to catch up.

"Get away from me," she shouted as she crawled back. The idea of him taking her again scared her to her bones.

But he just stood there, mocking her with his smile. "Panthea. Goddess of patience. Ironic."

"How do you know my real name?"

A familiar female voice came from the side. "Panthea?"

Arvin's eyes shifted to the source of the voice, and his smile widened. Panthea followed his line of sight to find Ash's small form appear from behind the branches, holding a satchel. For a moment, Panthea forgot her fear and rasped, "Ash?"

Ash ran to her, dropped beside her, and took her in her arms. "You're a dope," she said with a crying chuckle. "Have I ever told you that?"

Panthea's laughter was closer to crying than her friend's. "Only a few hundred times."

"I'm not crying," Ash said, sniffling. "I'm not crying." She pulled away and shared another shaky smile with her.

Arvin was still standing there, looking amused. Panthea held Ash tighter and looked up at the man resentfully. "If you have any humanity in you, please leave us alone."

"What are you talking about?" Ash got out of Panthea's embrace and stood beside Arvin. "Don't talk to him like that."

"What?" Panthea squeaked.

"When I lost you back in Watertown," the young wielder said, "I didn't know what to do. It's a long story, really. But I was lucky I found Arvin. He helped me track you down."

"You brought him here?" Panthea said, her voice coming out as shrill as before, if not more so. Ash's impulsiveness was endearing back in Saba. Out here, it was going to get them killed.

"No," Ash said, accentuating her words with exaggerated hand gestures. "Technically, he brought *me* here." Her voice turned jovial as she continued, "It was so fun. You two have no idea what kinds of tracks you leave behind. It was so easy to find you. For Arvin, I mean. Not that I didn't he—"

"Hold on. You know why I disappeared, don't you?" Panthea shot a finger at Arvin. "He abducted me. Tortured me."

Ash laughed. She laughed. "No, no. It's not what you think. He told me everything."

"Should we help her up?" Arvin cut in.

Ash paused, as though having lost her trail of thought, then bobbed her head. "Of course."

Arvin held out his hand, but Panthea slapped it away. When Ash saw her reaction, she helped her instead to stand.

"How can you trust this man?" Panthea didn't even care that he was right there. In fact, she wanted him to hear it. "He's a maniac. He was going to kill me."

"Now, that's taking it too far," Arvin retorted.

"Listen," Ash said. "He told me why he gave you the nightmare potion. It was for your own good."

"How?" Panthea curled her lips. "Do you have any idea what I went through in his house?"

"It was to help with your power-lust," Ash explained, glancing at Arvin in between. "Apparently, the nightmare potion cures it."

"I didn't feel anything."

"Well." Arvin cocked an eyebrow. "You did a neat job of knocking me out and running away. Could you have done that with power-lust?"

Panthea had not thought about it until now. She'd had the full presence of mind the day she had escaped from his house. But that did not explain everything. "You could have told me if you had good intentions."

"He couldn't," Ash answered for him. "If he—"

"I asked him."

"I couldn't," Arvin said with slow, calculated words. "We're not experts in the chemistry of the nightmare potion. We speculate it's the excessive fear that cures power-lust. If you knew I had good intentions, it might not have worked."

"Fear triggers something far more dangerous in me," Panthea muttered. "You could have killed us both."

The footfalls of another person came from behind Arvin.

"Evian," Ash screamed in excitement as she darted to him, leaving Panthea without aid.

Pain shot through Panthea's ankle. It was Arvin who held under her arm before she fell. She wanted to jerk free, but she couldn't let go of her only support.

"I'm sorry," Arvin said. "I know what I did was cruel. But I had to keep you scared."

Ash and Evian joined them. Panthea didn't know if she should explain that Arvin was the same monster she had talked about before. She decided to wait until she knew more about him and his intent. For now, there was enough comfort in their reunion. Ash seemed happy, and Evian had recovered from whatever mood he'd been in last night.

"I got scared when I saw you gone," Panthea told Evian.

"Sorry. Didn't want to wake you." He produced two apples. "There were apple trees back there. I brought these for you." He glanced at Ash and Arvin. "If you two want, there's a lot more where these came from."

"No need." Arvin waved his free hand. "Ash and I already ate."

"Ash?" Panthea mouthed and jutted her head toward Arvin to signal to Ash that she wasn't comfortable being held by him. So, the young wielder took his place, and they all walked back to where Panthea and Evian had spent the night. On the way, Panthea ate her apple.

The two men stopped farther away from the shore and began chatting. Panthea asked Ash to take her to the river, and they both sat on the shore.

"We thought you'd gone back to Saba," Panthea said.

"No, you didn't." Ash gave her a knowing look, the corner of her mouth rising.

Panthea rolled her eyes. "All right. Evian thought you'd gone back. I thought something terrible had happened to you."

"Now, that's more like you. You're a worrier."

"I am not," Panthea said indignantly.

"Say what you want. Truth is the truth." The girl kept the stare for a little longer, then gave Panthea a nudge, wearing the biggest grin her face could physically accommodate. "Cheer up, Dopey. We made it. We're together."

That was true, and Panthea didn't want to kill Ash's exuberance by sharing her worry about Rassus. So, she just returned her smile. "By the way, for now, don't tell Evian who Arvin is. Remember, he's only heard my side of the story."

"Oh, I love secrets." She covered her mouth with the back of her hand.

Panthea chuckled. She glanced over her shoulder to make sure Arvin was not listening. "So, what happened? I went to the inn. They told me they hadn't seen you."

"Oh, I'm sure they saw me. They just didn't remember me." She spoke faster as the story progressed. "I didn't have to be there long to know something was wrong. Knowing you, you would have stayed in the yard until I arrived and come to the lake if I was late. You weren't in the yard or the inn, or anywhere really. So, there was no point in asking anyone. I spent the first night by the lake, hoping you'd show up. Then I got hungry, and you'd taken all the money.

"So, I walked all the way back to Saba, snuck into my home, stole some money from my parents, bought something to eat, then went to look for you again. This time I asked the innkeeper. He said he'd seen you but had no idea where you were." She scrunched her nose. "Even the mention of you got him jumpy. Arvin overheard us. He came to me and . . ." She finally slowed down. "Well, you know the rest."

Panthea gaped. It was impressive how much Ash had done on her own, and it made Panthea feel silly for worrying for her at all.

Ash put on a mischievous smile. "Who knew? Little Ashena can take care of herself."

Leaves rustled, announcing Arvin's approach. That was enough to smother Panthea's smile.

"Can I borrow her for a moment?" Arvin asked.

Ash glanced between him and Panthea before she got up. "Sure. But I'm warning you," she said humorously, holding up a finger. "If you hurt her, you'll answer to me. And Evian."

Arvin nodded with a smile. Once Ash left, he sat next to Panthea, but she inched away from him. Eyes fixed on the river, he said, "That girl is a ball of energy."

Panthea scoffed. "How did you find me?"

"I find people for a living. You're lucky it was me who found you. You three should be more careful from now on."

"We should stay away from you, is what we should do."

"I beg to differ. I think you've made enough noise. It's time you started traveling with someone who knows a thing or two about this kingdom.

You're being hunted, Panthea. You need a guide."

"I have Evian. He knows what to do. He always does."

Arvin looked back at Evian, who was talking and laughing with Ash. "Does he?"

Panthea paused. Traveling with Evian had kept them alive, but Arvin had a point. After all, Evian had confessed that he did not have all the answers. Besides, Arvin had caught up with them, which meant soon Sapphires would too. But that did not make Arvin a better choice. "And why should I trust you?"

"Really? I saved you from those Sapphires in Watertown. I brought your group back together. If I meant to harm you, don't you think I've had the chance before?"

He had indeed. "And why would you want to help the most wanted people in this realm?"

Arvin humphed. "Don't give yourself too much credit. I know one person who's being hunted more rigorously than you are. Have you heard of the Windhammer?"

She frowned. "Are you with the rebellion?"

A smirk curved the corner of Arvin's mouth.

"You could say that." He looked ahead for a moment, measuring his next words. "For the past four years, Erkenbloods have been disappearing. Some say they've seen Sapphires take them away from their homes in the middle of the night. People think the Purge is over. But it's just subtler now. True, they no longer butcher Erkenbloods in the street, but there is no saying it won't happen somewhere no one is looking. They sure don't bring them to the Inquisition. We would know if they did. If I let you run around with your power-lust, your chances of survival are slim. Besides"— he winced—"you must keep taking the nightmare potion."

"Like Diva's cold, I do," she said. Did he expect her to go through all that trauma again? She looked back at the river and took a deep breath. "So, is that the rebellion's purpose? Protecting Erkenbloods?"

"What better cause than protecting the innocent?" He winked. "But we also do other things. Don't tell me you haven't heard about the attack and the assassinations."

"Oh, I have. And I don't think it's all working the way you think it is. People despise the Windhammer and everything he stands for." She made a point of looking directly at him for the next part. "And I'm coming to see why."

Arvin chortled as though she had told him a light-hearted joke. "Don't be sanctimonious. They hate you too. Does it mean you're a bad person?" His gaze returned to the running water. "People are gullible. They believe the queen's side of the story because hers is the loudest voice they hear. That's why we're trying to create a louder voice, to reveal the truth they've been denied for almost two decades."

"And I'm guessing yours is the absolute truth. Who's sanctimonious now?"

Arvin gave her a soft glance. "I don't believe in absolutes."

Before she could ask for an explanation, Ash and Evian joined them on the riverside.

"I thought you only wanted her for a minute," Ash said in mock irritation.

Arvin gave Panthea a nudge. "What can I say? She likes me."

That statement mortified Panthea. Her face heated, and her gaze flittered between Ash and Evian to see if either of them had believed this lie. She managed a snort.

"All right," Arvin said as he got up. "If you're all rested, we need to move. There's a town on top of the hills north of here called Serene. It's a safe place to stay while we devise an actual plan."

The man was assuming himself to be the de facto leader now, and Ash's trust in him made things more complicated. Evian was stuck in a half-shrug, his eyes glazed over.

"Come on," Ash complained when they took too long to respond. "Do you still doubt him? He's not with the Sapphires. I don't know about you two, but I'm taking my chances with him."

Evian put a hand on Panthea's shoulder. "I'm staying with you. If you say we go with him, we go with him. If not, we separate from them."

Panthea did not want to go with Arvin. But she would not separate from Ash again. The three of them had to stay together. Besides, something about Arvin made her curious. She wanted to learn more about him. "There are three of us," she warned, "and one of you. Don't even think about betraying us."

Arvin gave a lopsided smile. "Is that a yes?"

Panthea regarded Evian instead of him. "We go to Serene."

10

The first-ever mention of the Dark Ages was in a book titled
Stories of the Past, which was a compilation of tavern stories
gathered by a chronicler. Every other history book recounts the
events of that time verbatim. Thus, to trust history is to trust
the one chronicler and those who told them the stories.

MISSION REPORT. Two dead agents. One gone rogue and captured by the Inquisition. One handmaid who had no clue whom to report to. A queen who was very much alive, and a Dark Scepter that was still in said queen's possession. It had taken those blackhoods only two hours to find the damned thing.

After seven days of uncertainty, the only logical course of action for Hilia was to stick to her old routines and maybe learn something useful along the way. She sat alone in the library, reading Parviz's new recommendation.

It was not exactly a history book, but a juxtaposition of facts and legends. It was a historian's attempt to find the pieces of the puzzle that were lost to time. According to Parviz, if there was a trace of the contents of the missing chapters in the History of the Arcane, it would be within these pages.

The book had little relevant information. There was, however, a chapter about Watchers, which had piqued her interest. The chilling memory of touching the Dark Scepter was still fresh in her mind. "*You are not the Watcher,*" the voice had said, and now she knew what it meant.

The chapter explained how the scepter was the oldest known manifestation of the arcane in the world and even claimed it might have given birth to wielding itself.

Watchers were those who accepted the burden of keeping the Dark Scepter. If left without a Watcher, the Dark Scepter would corrupt the minds of people until the entire world was in chaos. The Watcher would slowly descend into madness, but they saved the rest of the world with their sacrifice. For that same reason, Watchers stayed on the island of Jadew in the Southern Ocean until the day they died.

It made no sense. If the queen was a Watcher, what was she doing in the heart of Southern Sessara? Why did she have her wits intact?

There was something to say about the aging, too. Apparently, Watchers often lived three or four generations, but they also withered faster than most. They spent most of their lives as frail old beings. The Dark Scepter was not a gift of life but a curse of prolonged suffering. There was nothing about immortality, and no mention of the Bonds of Arcane.

Hilia closed the book and blew out a hard breath. This was a waste of time, and too much was on her mind for her to even try to connect all the scattered pieces that led nowhere, anyway.

Mehran's betrayal still weighed on her. She refused to accept he had been himself when he had attacked her. He had touched the Dark Scepter after all. If that thing could make people slit their own throats, slitting another's would not be outside the realm of possibility.

She wanted to believe that justification, but the theory had a few holes. If she was any proof, touching the scepter alone didn't make people do things against their will. That left two possibilities, both of which required the queen to have been awake and used the scepter on Mehran. Afterward, he had either thrown the scepter out of the window of his own volition, or the scepter had made him do it.

The first scenario was unlikely. With the queen awake, Mehran would not point her to his accomplice downstairs. He would not expose Hilia like that. And if the second scenario was the case, why would the scepter then warn her about Mehran's attack?

She hated unanswered questions, and there were too many of them for a time like this when blackhoods wandered the corridors of the residence building and lives were in danger, including her very own.

Footfalls echoed from the royal entrance. She shot up and went to the fiction shelves. She stuffed the book between a few others before playing her usual game of pretend-browsing.

From the corner of her eye, she saw a palace guard approaching. He was tall and burly, and his eyes were too intelligent for her comfort.

The man beelined to her, towering at her side. "Your failure has not gone unnoticed. With Mehran arrested, I'll be your handler from now on."

"Who's Mehran?" She stepped away from him and feigned focus on a random title to hide her growing anxiety. "I think you've got me mistaken for somebody else."

"You're the queen's handmaiden, aren't you? Hilia."

She looked at him with a scowl. She was tall and not used to looking up to meet a man's eyes. So, on top of everything else, losing her benefit of height with this guard made her especially uneasy. "Well, I don't know you. And I don't know any Mehran. Now, if you'll excuse me"—she snatched the book from the shelf—"I'll go read my book."

As she returned to the table, the man sniggered. "You can drop the act. I'm friendly. I can prove it."

She sat back in the chair, put the book in front of her, and opened it. The guard came forth and rested his palm on the table, leaning over. "I know the man who recruited you. It's a pity your relationship didn't last."

A generic story. He couldn't possibly know about him. "Leave, or I'll call the other guards. You're harassing me."

The guard resigned, pursing his lips. He tapped the table twice and, as he walked away, he said, "Arvin was a lucky man to have you."

This was no longer a coincidence.

"Wait," Hilia called, and he halted.

As if her mind wasn't in enough turmoil, this man had to remind her of whom she had been trying so hard to forget. Although she'd had good reasons to leave Arvin, the part of her he had taken away would never come back, and every time someone said his name, the memory of their last conversation came to her.

When she had joined the rebellion, she'd never imagined the violence that went with it. Granted, no one could take a brutal system down without violence, but there were lines she wished she'd never seen crossed.

"I didn't mean for this to happen," Arvin had told her on that final night when she'd already made up her mind. "I wish I could have stopped it. But it happened too fast."

Arvin and his men had returned from the assassination of a Sapphire lieutenant, who was an Inquisitor's son. That alone did not bother her. But Arvin's friends had killed the lieutenant's wife and child, who shouldn't have even been there if the rebels had followed Hilia's instructions.

"I cased that house for days," she said, her eyes filling with tears. "I told you he had a wife and a toddler. I told you exactly when you had to hit. What was the point in sending me over there if you guys were to just storm the house like savages? To taunt me?"

"This had nothing to do with you, Hilia," Arvin said. "We found the perfect window, and—"

"You killed an unarmed woman and a child."

"I'm not any happier than you are about this. But look at the other side of this coin. The bastard son of that Inquisitor, who gods know how many people he himself has killed, is now dead. You know sacrifices are inevitable in our line of work."

She chuckled painfully. "Ahura's my witness, if I hear this platitude one more time, I'm going to cut my own throat."

"Hilia. We had to kill that man at any cost."

"Forget it," she said, to end the discussion before it fell into a circle.

"That's not what I wanted to tell you, anyway." She forced herself to look him in the eye, difficult as it was. "I've asked the Windhammer to reassign me. I can't do this anymore."

His brow crinkled with sympathy, and he tried to hold her, but she pushed him away.

"No. This. I can't do *this* . . . anymore."

It was the first time she saw defeat in Arvin's eyes. He'd failed missions. He'd lost friends. But the pain on his face in that moment was the most unsettling. Even so, she held his stare. She had to be strong for both of them.

"I, uh," she said as she wiped her tears with her sleeve, "I know you had to do it. You always do. But I can't stay and watch you become this. I can't watch all our fond memories be tainted by blood. I'm leaving tonight."

Since that night, they had not even written to each other. Arvin could be dead for all she knew.

Gods damn it, you had to go there. She beckoned to the stranger.

The tall man sat across from her, wearing a dim smile. "I didn't mean to broach a sensitive topic. I just needed you to believe me."

"Oh, I believe you. You just opened a box I'd been trying to keep closed for years." She took a deep breath and glanced around. "Now, tell me. Any news from Mehran? How is he?"

"I'm not here to talk about him," the man muttered. "He knew what he signed up for. I came here to warn you we might all be compromised. Per protocol, I need to give you the address to the inn where we dispatch our messages. Otherwise, if I'm caught, you'd be completely cut out."

"Wait a minute. You don't expect me to go dispatch messages, do you? The Inquisition is on my back. I can't just wander off to the city and—"

The man held up a hand. "Let's hope it doesn't come to that. But if it does, you need to go to the winehouse called Grape and Barley in Crowway and ask for Blackbeard."

Hilia shook her head in dismay. "I told him it wouldn't work. I predicted this day. No one ever listens to me."

He let out a deep sigh. It seemed like every word that came out of her mouth annoyed him. If she knew him a little better, he would have received at least two juicy comebacks by now.

"Let's not dwell on the past," he said. "The why and the how are things you and I need to discuss later. But did you understand the instructions?"

"Yeah, yeah, Grape and Barley, Blackbeard."

"It's a terrible book, by the way." He jutted his chin toward the book. "My sister hated it."

She huffed. "She sounds smart. All fiction is stupid."

"She, um," he said, wincing, "likes . . . fiction."

Hilia waved a dismissive hand. "In my defense, I've had a rough couple of days."

"Not judging," He smirked, eyeballing her for a moment before he got up to leave.

She called after him, "I didn't catch your name."

"You won't need it. We'll meet again."

"The same way I'm meeting Mehran?"

He stopped mid-step and turned halfway to her. "I knew I'd like you. All right. Come here every day. Same time." He glanced at the book. "And try actually reading some fiction. It might surprise you."

She didn't have any response, save for looking down at the book. Right now, reading was the last thing she felt like doing.

The fear of imminent death and the pain of losing friends were inevitable for a rebel. Over the two years she'd spent on the front lines with Arvin, she had seen many come and go. But some feelings never changed. A friend's arrest still pierced the same spot in her heart as it always had. And it stirred the same dread even now that the chief Inquisitor of Delavaran was a friendly acquaintance.

She'd always thought she wouldn't have to face this kind of pain as a sleeper agent. It was one of the reasons she had asked to be transferred to the palace. But now, the palace itself had become the front line when agents like Mehran attacked the queen in her sleep.

When she looked up, the unnamed handler was already gone. He had not been patient enough to watch her brood. She sighed. She needed to get out of here. This library had always been the place of serenity, and she wasn't about to make it a reminder of everything ugly that went with her job. She had the entire palace for that. Besides, she didn't want to be sulking if Parviz showed up.

She went to the bookshelf and put the fiction book back. Then, she exited the library, strolling toward the residence building.

She still had an hour left before she had to draw the queen's bath, and there were not a lot of places she could spend it beside her room. Well, except . . . the chapel appeared on her side. The building was buried within a patch of trees said to be as old as the building itself, and their branches invaded the narrow walkway leading to the entrance.

These trees were the only ones in the palace that were not regularly pruned, which created an ancient atmosphere here, complemented by the scent of wild blackberries and damp wood. This was the only part of the palace not dominated by the aroma of the rose garden.

In the four years she had lived in Delavaran, she'd never gone inside the chapel, even though she passed it almost every day. An Angelian place of worship was no place for an Ahuraic. That's what her father would say. Hilia herself? She could barely name eight out of the thirteen gods in her own religion. She could, however, use a quiet place right now that wasn't the library. *Might as well. It's not like I'm converting.*

She turned toward the building and made her way through the twisting branches and brambles over the walkway. Once at the door, she removed her slippers, as she'd seen people do.

As she entered, the wild scent of the outside gave in to that of hardwood and lacquer, laced with the inevitable stench of feet found in any temple.

Green was the dominant color in this place, in the velvet covering most of the walls and in the cold tiles flooring it. There were only two large candles, and both sat on a dais on the far side of the room, where a statue of a woman in a long, flowing dress stood a head and shoulder taller than Hilia. This was too huge for a chapel. Most Ahuraic chapels only sported tiny effigies of the gods. Maybe it was different for Angelians.

She sat alone in front of the statue, staring at the confident look in its eyes. So, this was the Great Annahid, the goddess Parviz and Queen Artenus both worshipped. The sole creator of the world, the only authority over all existence. She snorted. *You must be exhausted, doing it all by yourself. We have a whole pantheon, and they can't hold this world together. I wonder how you can . . . If you can.*

"Oh, Great Annahid," she began, mainly for amusement. She had to spend this time somehow. "We've never talked. I don't even know if I can be an Angelian. I swear by Ahuraic gods when I'm angry." She sighed. "Things have been a little chaotic. I don't know where I'm going. I don't know what's going to happen. I would appreciate if you showed me the path, the way you show it to Parviz." She looked up at the statue and rolled her eyes. "Don't give me that look. At least I can talk. You're just a statue."

"That was an interesting prayer," came Inquisitor Kadder's voice, giving her a proper start. The painful kind, where your heart beats harder than it's meant to.

"Oh, keep going," he said from a few paces away. "Didn't mean to startle you." He came and sat cross-legged beside her, and Hilia corrected her seating position to match his. The man then gave her a fatherly smile as he continued, "Why don't you try something with me? Maybe you'll get what you're looking for, even from a statue."

She glanced between the Great Annahid and the Great Torturer and decided it'd be best to oblige. *Might as well bond a little before I'm inevitably at his mercy.* She nodded her assent.

Kadder turned to the statue and murmured, "Close your eyes, place two fingers on your chest and take a deep breath." He accompanied his words with a demonstration, and she followed his lead after a moment's hesitation. "Think of the one thing you want most in this life. The one thing missing, the one thing you have no control over."

Something like getting out of this mess.

"Now, what do you need to achieve your goal? Strength? Patience?"

"Wits, I suppose." *Are you completely out of your mind, Hilia?*

"All right, now, ask the goddess in the name of what's dead and what's living and what's divine, to accept you as her daughter, to show you the gift of wisdom. You don't need to say it out loud. Just think it."

Dear Annahid, in the name of what's dead and whatnot, I'm your daughter. Get this man out of my hair.

"As for me, I'll pray to find the attacker's accomplices."

Her eyes flew open, meeting Kadder's relentless gaze. He frowned. "You look troubled. Did you know that man personally?"

Sure, I'll confess to being an accomplice. You need to try harder, old man. "I don't know half of the guards." That didn't seem to be enough, as his stare did not leave hers. "But it's chilling to think we can't feel safe even in the residence building."

"It is, indeed." He mused on the statue for a moment. "But I assure you, those bastards are trembling with fear as we speak. They know what's coming."

That obvious?

Kadder closed his eyes again and began mumbling prayers for a while, leaving her wondering if she should stay or leave. Their conversation had not exactly ended.

When Kadder finished praying, he said, "By the way, are you attending the Reunion ceremony? I remember last year, you didn't."

"I would love to be there, but I'll have to ask the queen. Last year, she said it'd be best if I stayed behind. I suppose she didn't trust me enough." She gave her stupidest chuckle in years.

Kadder returned her smile, though his expression sobered rather quickly. He made a few false starts until he finally said, "Speaking of trust. I'm telling you this as a friend. I understand you're scared, like many people in this situation. But next time someone from the Inquisition asks you a question, don't hide the truth. I've seen you with that boy, and I didn't appreciate when you said you didn't know him."

Her chest constricted. "I'm sorry, I was—"

"Save your breath." He raised his hand. "This is not an interview. Just a friendly warning. This is the kind of thing that gets you in trouble. We, at the Inquisition, are also scared. And when we're scared, people get hurt.

I want to protect those I like from the current political storm. I'd appreciate it if you didn't make it difficult for me." He groaned as he got up. "Anyway, I have to get back to my hunt. You take care of yourself."

Hilia nodded, her stomach churning. *This was too close. Girl, you have to be smarter than this.*

11

Erkenbloods had great powers, and they were greater in numbers then than they are now. It is natural to assume they were the oppressors of their time. If one looks through credible history, however, one finds the flaw in that assumption: inherent power does not seem to have ever played a discernible role in shifting the balance of political dominance.

NOT A HILL. A mountain. Panthea and her friends had been climbing all morning, and there was still no sign of the town. She could barely walk anymore. Ash shuffled along, occasionally kicking stones off the path, and Evian had stopped glancing over every few minutes, which meant neither of them was in a much better shape than she was.

"How far is it from here?" Panthea asked.

Arvin mopped his forehead with the back of his hand. "We'll be in Serene in an hour. If we keep the pace, we can—"

Ash plopped down. "I need a minute."

That was enough to disintegrate the pace. Panthea also dropped, and Evian followed suit as he worded what they had all been thinking. "We're exhausted. I think we should have a break."

Arvin clicked his tongue. "It's risky to stop. We're exposed."

"Two minutes." Ash held up two fingers. "Just until I catch my breath. Then I'm good to go."

Evian opened his satchel and handed apples to everyone.

Having lost his audience, Arvin sighed as he took his apple. He hunkered beside Panthea. "Two minutes then."

For some time, there was only the sound of chewing and crunching, until Arvin added his own voice to it. "Is it true that Erkenbloods once ruled the entire world?" He was looking at Panthea.

"Here we go again," Ash muttered. One could not talk about history without a snide remark from the girl. At least, for the moment, she was too busy munching to steer the conversation away, so Panthea found room to answer.

"Not the world. But we dominated Sessara until the end of the Dark Ages. Then, when the first High Lady won the Arcane War, she implemented marriage laws that cut the Erkenblood population to a third in one century. They call it the Great Culling."

"Interesting," Arvin said. "First, the Culling, then the Purge. History doesn't seem to give your kind a break."

She felt a shiver at the mention of the Purge, and those sleepless nights flooded her mind. "The Culling was nothing like the Purge. Although Lady Sanaz made no friends among her own kind, she had the best of intentions at heart. She wanted to end the oppression of ordinary humans. She sacrificed her inborn power to create the Well of Light."

Arvin's eyes narrowed. "The well of what?"

She gave a bashful chuckle. Why had she assumed he would know about it? "The Well of Light. It's in the Northern Realm. It's where they make gleamstones. If you infuse a piece of northern marble in the Well, you'll have a gleamstone."

There was a spark in Arvin's eyes. "Fascinating. So, that's why all arcane artifacts come from the north." Looking at her for confirmation, he concluded, "So, inborn wielding created . . . gleamstone wielding."

"Conductive wielding," she corrected for him. "And yes, that's—"

"Ugh, seriously, Arvin," Ash shot, her tone in direct contrast to the mischievous twinkle in her eyes. "Stop asking questions. Panthea loves talking about this stuff."

Arvin chuckled. "So, let her talk."

"But it's boring. Who cares who did what a thousand years ago? Obviously, they messed up. We should just move on and make a better world for ourselves."

"Or," Panthea countered, "we can learn from them and not repeat their mistakes. Something Queen Artenus is not doing that well."

Evian, who had been quiet so far, joined the conversation. "Oh, she is. Master once told me history is a lesson without an agenda. The queen is not repeating the mistakes that led to King Shahbod's demise."

"Wow," Arvin said. "You're all wiser than your average city people."

"Mm-hmm." Ash held a finger up, gesturing them to wait. Once her mouth was less full, she said, "These two have spent too much time with our teacher."

A faint grumble swelled from a distance.

Panthea's shoulders stiffened. "Do you hear that?"

Arvin dropped the rest of his apple and got up. "Yes. Riders. Let's hope they're not Sapphires."

Ash sat up as well. "Why would they be? How could they have found us? Didn't you cover our tracks?"

"Not all of them. It would have taken us much longer if I had. You girls stay behind me. Evian. Don't let them see Panthea's eyes."

The rumbling of hooves got louder until three riders appeared at the turn. Evian and Arvin formed a shield in front of Ash and Panthea, and Arvin placed his hand on the hilt of his sword.

The riders stopped a few yards away and dismounted. They seemed to be common folk. One of them, a stout man with a wispy beard and a bald head, took a few steps closer. "Hita's up high. Best time to pry." He let out a hoarse laugh at his own joke.

"Ah, shut up, Piggy," said his companion. "You'll never be a poet. Let's get this done and be on our way."

"Bah." The large man threw a rude hand at his friend. "You don't get it. I bet these friendly people here do."

Arvin's hand pulled his blade slightly out of the sheath, and Piggy stepped back. "Whoa, easy, lad. We're not hostile. We're just curious what folks like yourselves are doing on Serene hill."

"And what you might have for us," the third man completed for him.

Piggy tried to peek at Panthea, but Evian shifted his weight to block him out.

"Thievery is a grave crime," Arvin said.

"Bet your core it is," Piggy scoffed. "What would we steal from your bunch, anyway? You don't seem to have enough for yourselves. Information. That's what we want. Answers. Inquisitor Yoltan is after a certain witch, and I think she's found her way to these parts, eh? Now, the good citizen I am . . ." He shoved Evian away, and Panthea slammed her eyes shut and dropped her head. Piggy continued, "I would like to—"

There was a violent clap.

"Hands off," shot Arvin. "We're not looking for trouble here."

The rasping of weapons coming out of their scabbards carried, and Piggy's voice said, "For someone who's not looking for trouble, you're too handsy, lad."

"Evian," Ash whispered. "The bag."

Panthea opened her eyes a crack. When she made sure Arvin blocked the intruders' line of sight, she looked at Evian, who was handing the satchel to Ash.

Panthea furrowed her eyebrows. "What are you doing?"

Arvin drew his sword and took a defensive stance as the armed men approached. "It doesn't have to be like this. Just be on your way, and we'll be on ours."

"How about you let us inspect the girls, and then we'll be out of your face?"

Ash took out her gleamstone.

"No," Panthea said in an urgent whisper. "Don't be a fool."

The men attacked, and she tried to step out of the way, but she only had a moment before the bulk of Arvin's body knocked her back. She fell to her side, her head banging against the ground as Arvin's crushing weight landed on her with an audible crunch.

Panthea's ears rang. Her scalp burned as though with tendrils of hot lead, and she smelled blood in her nose. She barely registered what was happening around her. The clanks of steel were the only sounds that got through the haze, and even those were muffled by her own breathing.

Her presence of mind returned when Evian pulled her arm and dragged her out of the melee. The familiar euphoria linked to power-lust was burning in her now. *No, no, no. Not here. Not now.* Her whole body begged her to wield, and she was too shaken to fight it. *They're your friends. Ash. Evian. Arvin. Remember them.*

"It's her all right," one attacker said. "See those freaky eyes of hers? It's payday, boys."

White light flared beside her, and all the attackers' weapons flew yards up in the air.

"Oh, crap," Ash blurted before shouting, "Watch out!"

The light had come from Ash's gleamstone. Evian threw himself at Panthea, dropping them both before weapons rained down. Friend and foe scattered. A sword pierced the ground inches away from Panthea's face.

Ash winced. "Sorry." The impetuous girl had just wielded in the open.

"Those witches," Piggy roared. "Take them both."

Arvin picked up his weapon before any of them could. He whipped his sword. A moment later, blood gushed out of the lanky man's neck as he gurgled.

Panthea's breath caught in her lungs. Ash screamed, crawling backward. Panthea would have screamed too, if she had any authority over her voice.

Arvin spun just before Piggy got to him, and he ran the man through. This had to be a nightmare.

The only remaining attacker abandoned his weapon and went for his horse.

Arvin left his sword in Piggy and marched to the runner. Once he caught up, he kicked the stumbling man in the back and sent him flat on his chest.

The man turned and began crawling away, begging for his life.

Arvin picked up one of their daggers as he towered over him.

"No," Ash pleaded. "Please don't."

Evian went to Ash and crouched in front of her. "Ash, look at me."

Ash whimpered, her eyes wide in horror.

Evian took her face in his hands. "Look at me."

Panthea herself looked away. The grating of the blade cutting through bone rang in her ears, and a grunt that said it was over. Then, there was silence.

She drew a ragged breath, trying to regain control of her shaking limbs. It had all happened so fast. Arvin came back to Piggy and sat him up. As he withdrew his sword, a little squeak escaped Ash's throat at the scraping sound. The girl was no longer screaming or crying. Just staring.

Evian shook her to get her attention. "Hey. It's over. We're fine."

Ash said nothing. Panthea rushed to her and sat at her side, holding her trembling hand as she shared worried looks with Evian. There was no animation in the young wielder's countenance.

"Ash, talk to me," Panthea urged. "Are you all right?"

"They're . . . dead," Ash mumbled. "One moment . . . he was telling jokes. And then . . ."

Arvin walked up to the girl and put a hand on her shoulder. She cringed, and Arvin stepped back. "I'm sorry you had to see that. But there was no other way. They were bounty hunters." A failed smile swept across his mouth. "You fought well."

Unable to provide her own consolation, Panthea followed Arvin's. "You did. If you weren't here—"

"No," Ash finally spoke. "No. I didn't fight. Just made some weapons fly. I didn't do what Arvin did. He kill . . ." Her eyes glistened.

Arvin pursed his lips and walked away.

Panthea wished she could do something for Ash. She wished she was equipped for this kind of situation. But none of them were.

Evian took a side glance at Panthea's nose, then turned to her. "You're bleeding."

"I'm fine." She wiped the blood off her face.

Evian leaned closer and pried her left eyelid down. "Look at me?"

Panthea didn't know what he was doing, but she did as he instructed. He peered into each of her eyes, then put his finger in front of her nose. "Follow my finger with your eyes only."

He retracted it, moved it side to side. Then, he asked, "You remember what you ate?"

She frowned. "Um . . . an apple?"

He let out a sigh of relief and rubbed her shoulder. "Good."

Once that was over, Panthea turned to Ash's petrified face.

As always, Evian seemed to recognize her concern. "Don't worry, I'll take care of her. She's in shock."

Further away, Arvin was inspecting the horses.

Panthea left Ash to Evian's more capable hands and joined Arvin. "I'm sorry. You saved our lives, and we didn't thank you. It's just, Ash is . . ."

"Yeah," Arvin said. "It's hard to see someone die for the first time. In fact, I'm surprised you're taking it so well."

"I, um . . ." The image of the dead Sapphires at the lake struck her again. "It's not my first time." He gave her a knowing look, making her realize he wasn't surprised at all. "But you already knew that."

Arvin nodded and glanced back at Ash. "I didn't let her see it. Was it power-lust?"

Panthea wanted to say she didn't know what to do about the curse her power was, but through the lump in her throat and her quivering chin, the frustrated movement of her arms ought to be enough to get the message across.

Arvin took both her shoulders. "I understand why you don't trust me. But I can help. Your power doesn't need to be a curse."

She nodded but couldn't muster the will to talk.

Arvin then regarded Evian and called, "Let's get out of here. It'll take a few hours before people notice these men are missing and come looking for them. When they do, we don't want to be here."

Evian bobbed his head. "By the way, if you're hurt, I have some healing supplies. I can—"

"I'm fine." Arvin's attention turned back to Panthea. "What about you? I almost crushed you there."

"I'm all right. Evian just examined me."

Evian helped Ash up and began walking along with her. Panthea waited for Arvin, who went to loot the corpses. She looked away. She could never do anything like that.

"Can any of you ride a horse?" Arvin asked.

Without looking, Panthea said no.

"Then we might as well leave the horses here for the folks to come collect them." The scrapes and clatters continued for a while, until Arvin's hand pressed on Panthea's back. "Let's go."

They walked at a distance behind Ash and Evian. It was for the best, considering what the young wielder had just witnessed. Panthea wondered why she didn't feel the same way as Ash did. She hoped the events of the past few days had not robbed her of her compassion.

"Oh," Arvin said from her side. "Almost forgot. I've been meaning to give you this. You left it behind at the house."

He was holding out Rassus's pendant. Her heart leaped at the sight, and she needed a moment to collect her emotions and take the pendant. "Oh, dear Annahid. Thank you. I thought I'd lost it."

"Sentimental value?"

Hanging it around her neck, she nodded. "It belongs to someone I know. Someone . . . I miss."

"Is it your teacher? Do you want to talk about it?"

She opened her mouth to say no, but the sight of Evian in front of her made her pause. He would never agree to use the stone to free Rassus.

She stopped walking, and so did Arvin.

Tentatively, she asked, "How hard is it for the rebels to rescue a prisoner from the Inquisition?"

He smiled. "You want us to rescue your teacher?"

She looked down. It was too much to ask of someone she barely knew. Or of anyone. "I, um ... I heard about your attack on the Inquisition bureau in Livid. I thought maybe ..."

"Then, I suppose you know how that went."

He was right. It had been a foolish idea. "Yeah. I'm sorry. Forget what I said."

She resumed walking, but Arvin grabbed her shoulder. Although she stopped without protest, she did not speak.

"Let's try this again," Arvin said. "I would be more than happy to do this for you." Before Panthea could express her gratitude, Arvin held up his hand. "But. I can't do it alone. Windhammer needs to organize the operation, and he'll need more than a humanitarian reason for that. Tell me. Why did the Inquisition take your teacher?"

She was giving him too much information. But she had to. She would save Rassus no matter what. Once she made sure Evian was not looking, she said, "My teacher knows about the whereabouts of an artifact the queen is searching for."

"Is it by any chance the Bond of Third Arcane?"

Her jaw slackened. *Am I the only one who wasn't aware of this until two days ago?* "How under Diva do you know?"

Arvin looked amused by her comment, but his smile he had was not one of mockery but a sympathetic one. "Everyone in the rebellion does. The queen has tasked the entire force of her Inquisition to find the stone. And while we all speculate about the reason, we would prefer if she didn't get her hands on it."

She sighed. "You're talking just like Evian now."

"Why?" he asked. "He also knows about it?"

Why did I say that? If she told him Evian might know where the stone was, Arvin would probably try to extract that information from him. And that was not the position she wanted to put Evian in, even though it would save her the trouble of coaxing him into talking. It would not be fair. "He knows as much as I do."

He nodded. "With what you just said, we might be able to convince

Windhammer to help."

"Really?" Her voice came out higher in pitch than she had intended.

He crossed his arms, looking to the side for a second. "But it won't be easy. To the Windhammer, there are two ways of dealing with a problem like this. Save the person or sacrifice them for the good of the rest."

"Are you suggesting he would have my teacher killed?"

"That's the thing." His usual confidence did not touch those words. "He might do that normally, but we're talking about someone who's important to the Erkenblood of Saba. You're one person Windhammer would want on his side."

She did not feel comfortable with where this was going. She was in enough danger as it was. "You mean as a rebel?"

"Not necessarily in those terms. I just think, with the Inquisition scouring the land for the artifact, it's best if we band together and prevent them from getting their hands on it, and in a way that works for all of us. All I'm suggesting is that you come with me to Saba and meet with the Windhammer."

She opened her mouth to express her concern, but she could not formulate a single sentence. Not even a single word.

Luckily, Arvin did not need any words to understand how she felt. "It is a tough decision. But should you choose to do it, I'll make sure you won't be in danger."

Evian would be furious if she went through with this plan. "Can I think it over?"

"Of course," Arvin said. "You can even talk to your friends about it."

"No," she blurted. "Please don't say anything to Evian. I have to decide for myself first. If you tell him, he'll—"

"It's all right. You don't need to explain yourself. Although I strongly believe you should tell your friends, I won't speak a word of this in front of them until you're ready."

She nodded her gratitude. Arvin was giving her as much space as she needed, as much freedom as she requested to decide. Still, she felt guilty for even discussing this with him. Why should he be privy to a secret her friends were not? She tried to justify it. After all, she had sought help from a stranger only because Evian would not offer his. Right?

Come to think of it, this was exactly how she had handled her power-lust. She had not even asked Rassus or Evian for help. It was becoming a pattern—a pattern of distrust toward the people she loved the most.

Arvin held out his hand, but she refused to take it. She didn't trust him. She wouldn't. No one was worthier of her trust than her friends. She walked along the path without waiting for him. Arvin followed, probably bemused by her reaction.

12

*I do not claim my version of history to be the absolute truth.
No one can make such a claim about events that happened
more than a millennium ago. I want only to highlight how
such ancient history has been used to demonize my kind.*

B Y THE TIME THEY ARRIVED in Serene, Hita was already below the horizon, and Diva painted the stone walls of the buildings in red.

Looking from the edge of the hill, it felt like the entire kingdom lay beneath Panthea's feet. She could see the road, the villages, the farms along Shireen as it meandered its way across the kingdom until it disappeared behind some rocky hills deep in the violet haze. If this was the view from Serene Hill, she wondered what it would be like atop the Zarrin mountains. One could probably see the whole world from up there.

The town itself was an almost unsettling change for someone who had grown up in Saba, who was used to the hustle and bustle of the main square and the suffocating crowd in the Old City. There were no gates, no walls, no sentries.

Ash and Evian had arrived first and were chatting on the main street when Panthea and Arvin walked through the open entrance to the town.

Evian seemed to have lifted the girl's spirits after the horror she had seen.

Evian was so good at comforting others. Panthea herself was lucky to have him in her life. He had delivered her from the darkest of places. But sometimes, she wished she had a sliver of that talent. She loved him and Ash, and she enjoyed nothing more than their company. But she could never help them the way she wanted.

She tucked the pendant under her shirt as she joined her friends. If they saw it, they would want to know how she had gotten it back, which would lead to a bigger conversation Panthea was not ready for. Not until she made her decision about Arvin's proposal.

"What are you two smiling about?" she said. "I see Evian is less grumpy when he's with you."

Ash elbowed Evian. "You hear that?" Her voice was not as jovial as usual. Still, she gave Panthea a good-humored smile as she said, "We were discussing which one of us is your best friend. See, I brought you back from," she leaned in for the words, "power-lust," and then drew away as she continued, "and Evian saved your life with his healing skills. Now, this makes us equal. But you just admitted that he's meaner to you."

This made Panthea feel a little better about herself. If they competed over being her best friend, that meant at least her friendship had some appeal. She tried to play along, cocking an eyebrow. "What about Watertown?"

"Not fair," Ash said petulantly. "You hit me first." Her gaze shifted to Arvin, who was keeping his distance, and her smile dimmed. "He can join us, you know. I understand he had to do it. I was just scared, is all." She waved at Arvin. "Come over here, you. You're one of us now."

"One of us?" Panthea grinned. "Should we include him in the best friend competition, then?"

"Of course not, Dopey. He has to earn his place."

Arvin joined them, his gaze connecting with Ash's. "How are you holding up?"

"Still breathing, thanks to you." Her smile returned. A purposeful smile. "You're good, Arvin."

"So, what's the plan?" Panthea asked once she was sure the conversation was over.

"There's an inn near the main square." Arvin pointed down the street. "We can spend the night there."

"Is it safe?"

Arvin patted her shoulder. "We're not in Watertown, Panthea."

What did that even mean? She wanted to retort, but everyone else in the group seemed content with the proposal, and she didn't want to be the only one to object.

They followed Arvin to the inn, and he rented a room for the four of them.

Once they got the key, Arvin said, "Anyone care for a drink? I know a great winehouse in town."

Although he did glance at the others, Panthea was the one his gaze lingered on. Of their own accord, her lips twitched into a smile. His presence provoked a strange sense of comfort. The kind Panthea used to receive from Evian.

"No," Ash responded. "I'm exhausted. I think I'll go straight to the room. You enjoy."

Evian looked just as tired, but he seemed to feel obligated to stay with Panthea.

"You can go too," she reassured him. "I'll join you later."

Evian gave a hesitant nod, glancing between her and Arvin for a few moments before he said, "Um, all right. Goodnight, then."

Panthea stared after him as he left, then turned to Arvin. "About your offer. I think it might help my decision if . . ."

Arvin was not paying attention. She followed his gaze to find a few Sapphires sitting around a table.

"Hold that thought," he said, a lopsided smile playing on his lips. He abandoned the counter and pulled her along. "Come with me."

"What are you doing?" she muttered, while trying to free herself from his grasp. "They're Sapphires."

"They're my friends."

"Just how many Sapphire friends do you have?"

Before Arvin could, or would, answer that question, they were already at the table, in front of four Sapphires and one of those damned black-clad men for what's divine! Panthea wished she were invisible. It was too late to turn back, too hard to act normal. The only comfort was that they did not seem hostile toward her as they greeted the two of them. One of them even got out of his seat and came forth. "Well, look who's here."

The man had a thin mustache, a defined chin, and unusually small eyes. He and Arvin hugged and clapped each other's back before he invited Arvin and Panthea to join them. Reluctantly, Panthea sat next to Arvin.

"So, you're the Erkenblood," the mustached man remarked, making her the center of attention. "You know, a lot of people are dying to see . . ." His smile wavered as he shared a glance with Arvin, who seemed to have given him a gesture. The man cleared his throat. "I believe I'm getting ahead of myself." He extended his arm. "I'm Mart."

Panthea regarded Arvin and waited for his nod before she shook Mart's hand. "Panthea."

"Fair warning," Arvin said. "You should consider yourself lucky if he remembers your name tomorrow. I bet he already has a nickname for you."

"Hey." Mart pointed a finger at his face in mock indignation. "Way to ruin my first impression. I call *you* by your real name."

"That's because you know better," Arvin quipped.

"Ooh." Mart pretended to shake in fear.

Next to Mart, the black-clad man was scrutinizing her. It was the same outfit the people who had raided her house had worn, and his dark skin almost matched his clothing. His gaze was intent. Unyielding. He was not a small man, which would have at least helped Panthea's unease. Alone, he was the size of two of those raiders combined.

She looked down, if only to slow her heart. What was she doing here?

"Don't let his appearance fool you," Mart said. "He's fluffy inside." He then smacked the giant in the chest. "Don't stare like that. You want to give her a heart attack or something?"

The man cracked a smile that was, indeed, kind, though dim. Just a curt hint of acceptance. "Gvosh," he introduced himself, his deep voice almost shaking the ground.

The name wasn't Sessaran. It sounded Seshek, which was strange because the creatures living beyond the Sessaran plateau were not even human. Not only was this one human, but also his dark skin placed him on the border with Toofan, which was on the opposite side of the continent.

"I see you two have reunited," Arvin said to Mart, glancing at Gvosh in between.

Mart patted Gvosh's arm. "Not on purpose. We're on different missions. I'd never associate with a blackhood."

"Watch yourself," Gvosh said as he gave Mart a jostle, which almost sent him toppling over together with his chair, though he managed to hold himself.

"Fucking shit, Cousin," Mart said, though somehow his eyes were still smiling. "You've got to get those muscles checked. What do they feed you at the Inquisition? Cow horn?"

"At least they don't feed us day-old horseshit."

A smile forced its way onto Panthea's lips despite her trepidation, and her nerves eased. More so when Mart added a wink to the mix. He then regarded Arvin to continue the conversation. "So, what brought you two here? Lost your way?"

Arvin glanced at Panthea. "We faced a few problems."

"Problems?" Mart cocked an eyebrow. "Problem problems, or girl-ran-off-because-I-was-too-creepy problems?"

Panthea broke into laughter.

"There you go." Mart snapped his fingers in her direction, though his eyes were still on Arvin. "When will you ever learn, Arvin?" He leaned toward Panthea. "See? I said the bastard's name. Don't trust anything this weasel says about me, or about anything else, for that matter."

"All right, all right," Arvin said, smiling. "Gang up on me. But for your information, we ran into a couple of bounty hunters. And guess whose name came up?"

Mart shrugged. "I want to say, Panthea, but that'd be too easy."

"Yoltan."

Mart slowly put his drink down, amused. "Cousin, why don't you tell my man why you're here?"

Gvosh brought up his hand and pointed his finger at Panthea. "For her." That alone undid what Mart had achieved earlier, and fear found its way back. "Yoltan's using the entire force of the bureau to find her."

"I don't get it," Arvin said, pressing a comforting hand on Panthea's forearm. "Why use Inquisition resources when he can let bounty hunters do the work?"

Gvosh snorted. "Depends how you want the work done. Yoltan leaves nothing to chance. Right now, there are more blackhoods in the field than there are bounty hunters in the entire Southern Kingdom. The prize is just to put pressure on the Erkenblood and force her to make mistakes."

Panthea's head was spinning. One mistake, and every blackhood in Saba and every bounty hunter in the kingdom was after her.

Arvin leaned back. "That's a whole lot of resources for one Erkenblood. Are you sure there isn't more to this?"

"There sure is," Gvosh growled. "But it's need-to-know basis."

"Well, we need to know," said Mart. "That's the whole point of your ass being in that bureau."

"It's need-to-know, meaning I don't know. What I *can* tell you is she's top priority." He gave Panthea narrow eyes. "Do you have any idea why they want you so badly?"

"No," she barely said, which was impossible for any of them to hear. So, she complemented that with a shake of her head. She gathered enough of her voice to add, "I lost control in Watertown."

"No, that's not it. Wielders go berserk all around the kingdom, and we don't even bother with a bounty to capture them. There's more to you. So, I'd think long and hard. Because your survival depends on the answer."

She nodded, taking a shuddering breath.

"All right, here's what we're going to do," Mart suggested. "I'm leaving

Serene in three days' time. Why don't you two tag along? Saba is the last place Ponytail will look for her."

That nickname sent a pang of fear through Panthea as it reminded her of the black-clad man she had seen at the lake. "P-ponytail?"

"Mm-hmm." Mart took a swig of his drink. "The one and only Inquisitor Yoltan. Chief Inquisitor of Saba. The biggest pain in the ass you can find in Sessara."

So, he was an Inquisitor, which fit the intricate black outfit she remembered him wearing. "What does he look like?"

Mart scrunched his nose. "Let me see. Tall, rugged face. Looks like an asshole. And not the good kind, but the kind you want to punch."

Panthea was dazed, her silence prompting Arvin to ask, "Something wrong?"

It took her another moment to gather herself enough to answer. "I saw him. At the lake. He led the group that attacked me."

"Wait a fucking minute," Mart's voice came out deeper, lower, and with far less humor than before. "You and Ponytail had a run-in at the lake, and you both just walked away?"

"Yes . . . Is that impossible?"

Gvosh gave a mirthless chuckle. "Is Hita white? Is Diva red? Kid, there are two ways such an encounter can go. He dies, or he takes you. He's alive because my mission update arrived today. So, either you're not telling me something, or you saw someone else."

Panthea had nothing to say. She did not have the faintest idea what was happening, and none of these questions even made sense to her. Less did she know the answers.

Or maybe she did. The other person she had seen with the Inquisitor. Maybe they had convinced him to walk away. But she had no clear memory of it and mentioning it would open another line of questioning.

Arvin glanced at the rest of his comrades before he leaned toward Mart. "By the way, any news from Delavaran?"

"Oh, yeah," said Mart, his voice dropping to almost a whisper. "The mission failed."

Arvin's eyes widened. "What?"

"Turns out, Grumpy's theory had a few holes."

Arvin's jaw clenched. "Is she . . ."

"Nah, she's fine. Grumpy's as resilient as they come. But the rumor is our boy attacked her."

Every muscle on Arvin's face was taut now. "Mehran attacked Hilia?"

Mart raised his hands and said, "I'm just the messenger," before he lowered them. "Anyway, the big guy's calling it quits. Grumpy's going back to being a sleeper agent, and no one will try to assassinate the immortal queen anymore."

Immortal? Panthea knew people praised the queen. But this claim was downright absurd. "The queen is not immortal."

Mart threw his head back in a cackle. Panthea scowled, confused, and a little irritated.

"Arvin, seriously," he said between his laughter. "Don't let this girl ever wander off. She's going to get herself killed."

"Funny indeed," Gvosh growled, though there was not even a hint of a smile on his face. Quite the opposite.

"No, it's not," Arvin said sternly, perhaps for a different reason from his friend's, as his hand perched on her shoulder. "Panthea's had a rough couple of days. So, let's keep the joking to a reasonable limit."

"Am I laughing?" Gvosh pressed.

"No." Mart punched Gvosh to the side of his arm, though the man's unmoving bulk of body made it look like a friendly nudge. "But that's because of that stick up your ass. Loosen up." He looked him up and down. "Or melt. Or something."

Gvosh growled in vexation, not submitting to the humor. He gave Panthea a disapproving glance before he regarded Arvin again. "Her inexperience concerns me. Keep an eye on her."

"I will," Arvin said tersely, his response not at all matching the man's serious demand. "Anyway. Mart. Do you honestly think you can sideline Hilia? You know how she is."

Mark smirked. "Sadly, I do. But I've assigned our most seasoned agent as her handler to keep her in check. The big guy's not happy with her performance. This was the best I could do for her, considering. She'll come around."

Whoever this Hilia was, she seemed like an older version of Ash, always getting in trouble and not willing to stay put.

Arvin rubbed his mouth, then tapped the table twice as he got up. "All right, Panthea. Let's go get that drink. These two are in too good of a mood. I assure you, they're not assholes . . . once you get to know them."

"Speak for yourself," Mart countered, raising his cup.

Panthea followed Arvin out, and they went to the winehouse as he had promised. He picked a spot and sat down on the carpet, leaning against the wall.

As she sat beside Arvin, she noticed an air of malaise about him. He was staring at a corner, curling and uncurling his fingers in a harmonic pattern.

"Are you all right?" she asked.

That brought him out of his trance. "Yeah. Yes. Don't worry. It's just . . ." He looked away again. "My friend is a real pain."

Panthea put her hand on his back, but she was so stiff with embarrassment she was not sure how much comfort she provided. "I think she's brave."

"You say brave. I say daft. Anyone who thinks they can take on the queen is out of their mind."

She felt a little disheartened by her failure to console him. Besides, this was not something she had expected to hear from a rebel. What was he even fighting for, if not defeating the queen? "You can't blame her for having hope."

"Hope." He gave her a scornful, sideways glance. "I know two groups who speak of hope. Bastards who sit in their palaces and try to placate people with pretty words, and innocent city girls who live in their own shells."

Now, this had been a direct attack, and not one Panthea appreciated. "I'm assuming you mean me. I may not have lived outside of Saba, but there is no history book I haven't read. It was those with nothing but hope who ended the Dark Ages. There is a similar pattern in every oppressive regime, and they all—"

Arvin scoffed with a smile she knew too well. The kind one gave a child whose ignorance, while endearing, deepened one's sorrow. The smile she herself used to give little children who sang songs about the heroic Great Reform.

"There are things you can't learn from books," Arvin said solemnly. "Like Ash's shock when she saw those men die. My friend is in grave danger. So, please, spare me the history lesson."

A strange anger rose in Panthea's chest. One with no particular target. She did not want to believe she was as ignorant as he thought her to be, but at this moment, she did not disagree with him. Historians wrote nothing about individuals who suffered in wars and disasters. Only the collective outcome. History was as cruel, as tactless as Panthea felt right now. And Arvin was not helping her with that feeling. She could no longer sit here and take this. So, she jumped to her feet and stormed out of the winehouse.

PANTHEA SAT ALONE outside the village, looking at the evening view of the kingdom below. The land was sprinkled with patches of yellow light that looked like clusters of stars in the night sky. It was breathtaking.

There had been a time when the Temple of the Ancients had been her entire world. Then, she had moved to Saba, the largest city in the Southern Kingdom. And now, sitting atop this hill, she saw just how grand the world was. Books, maps, languages. None could have prepared her for this. From up here, it felt so egocentric to assume her hopes, her fears, her concerns mattered at all.

The crunching of footsteps on grit put an end to her moment of solitude. It was Arvin, who came and sat beside her. "Beautiful, isn't it?"

She didn't respond.

"Listen, I'm sorry," he said. "What I said to you back there was uncalled for."

"It was." Though she tried, she couldn't put much emotion into her voice. It wasn't exactly a pleasant conversation to have. "I know I'm naïve, and I can't say the right things when I have to. But I was trying to help."

"I know. I was just mad at my friend, and I dumped it on you. This is on me."

To change the topic, she jutted her chin toward the view. "Do you know which way Saba is?"

Arvin perked up, seemingly appreciating the new thread of conversation. He pointed somewhere in front of them. "If you go straight in that direction, you'll reach Saba. And Delavaran," he moved his finger to the right, "is that way."

Panthea nodded. "So, Livid should be"—she used her knowledge of maps to point in the general direction—"there."

Arvin's eyes widened in surprise. "That's quite accurate, actually. Impressive."

Her chest tingled with a vague sense of pride, and she could not help smiling; a smile he reflected before they both returned their gazes to the view.

"It's hard to believe those two cities used to be a whole other country," Arvin said.

She had read about this, so she nodded. Before the annexation of those cities by the first Mehrian king, the region was called Shiran, and it had its own ruler, its own military. And Saba was its capital. Now, after over three centuries, no one talked about Shiran anymore.

"Almost forgot why I came here," Arvin said. "I promised you a drink, and I think we both need one." He extended his hand. "And it's on me. My way of apologizing for my behavior."

She raised an eyebrow. "You promise you won't be a jerk?"

"Promise."

With that, she accepted his offer. A drink did not seem like a bad idea, anyway. It had been a rough day, and a cup of wine would help calm her nerves.

Together they returned to the winehouse and sat where they had earlier. When the maid came to them, before Panthea could order, Arvin was quick to say, "Two *searing gulps*."

She grimaced. The drink was known for its high alcohol and spice content, and she had never tried it because she knew it would not be a pleasant experience. "Searing gulp? That's too strong. I wanted to order red wine."

Arvin smiled. "No problem. We'll get wine next."

Once the liquor arrived, Arvin raised his cup and waited for her to do the same. "Let's make it a game. Each round, we tell one piece of truth about ourselves."

She clinked her cup against his. "You first."

"Very well." They both drank a sip before Arvin started. "I was born in Livid and lived there until . . ." He paused, his humor faltering. "Until I was eight."

Livid. The birthplace of the first resistance against Queen Artenus. Vetrieca, the Erkenblood of Livid, seized that city for a short while before Admiral Heim defeated her. Her failed rebellion became the pretext for the Purge. "So, you were there when Vetrieca was alive."

"I was there for everything." Arvin let out a sigh and cleared his throat before he clinked her cup. "Your turn, Princess."

Panthea rolled her eyes. "Not a princess. Stop calling me that."

"You're the one who called herself Hita. Like the daughter of the late king."

"So, you do like history."

"Maybe." He smiled. "Anyway, what's your truth?"

Rassus would be thrilled to know I'm playing a game like this. "I just said it. I'm not a princess."

"Hey, that's cheating. Tell me something real. I want to know more about you."

She stood her ground. "Still, the truth."

"Fine. But this time, you go first."

She grabbed a strand of her hair and played with it while she pondered what she could share with someone she barely knew. They took another sip. "I'm an Angelian."

"Huh. I thought I'd heard wrong when you said Annahid's name before." His eyebrows furrowed, and he blinked in puzzlement. "Then, why is your name Panthea? Was either of your parents Ahuraic?"

"No." She shrugged and repeated Rassus's answer to this same question. "They wanted to choose a unique name. It was before the Reform. Before it somehow became a crime to be Ahuraic."

"I see." He looked her up and down. "Man, you're too good to be an Angelian."

Those words pierced right through her heart. Calling her a child was one thing. But insulting her beliefs? "Excuse me? What's that supposed to mean?"

"Sorry. I've never read your Book of Creation. What I see is what the queen's doing in the name of religion. They treat us Ahuraics like scum. They desecrate our temples, arrest us for the pettiest of crimes."

"The queen doesn't represent us," Panthea spat. Arvin motioned her to lower her voice. Angered even more, she continued through her teeth, "Our Book of Creation teaches us nothing but love and compassion. I'm not sorry to be an Angelian. The queen should be sorry she's ruined our image."

"You're right," Arvin said, "I overstepped."

She inched away from him, waiting for her breathing to slow down.

"Let's start over," he murmured. "For what it's worth, I think if anyone could sell Angelian to me, it'd be you." He held out his hand. "Friends?"

She took a moment to come to terms with his peace offering. But she could not let him off too easily. As she shook his hand, she said, "How about you? Aren't you supposed to hate me? Doesn't your religion teach you to hate Erkenbloods? See? It's easy to judge. I just choose not to."

"Well, our old doctrine considers wielding a sin. But that's messed up because it means people like you are born sinners. I don't buy that."

"So, a born sinner meets a born hater."

"I suppose I deserved that." He rose his cup. "To hatred and sin."

They took the next sip, the liquor burning all the way down. For someone who only drank wine on occasion, drinking searing gulp like this was excruciating. Before she could word her displeasure, Arvin ordered another round—this time, wine for Panthea.

"You're not trying to get me drunk, are you?" she said.

"What if I am?" He grinned. "Now, you'll enjoy this one. My father was a new-doctrine Ahuraic priest."

"Oh." His resentment suddenly made sense. "I suppose Sapphires haven't been kind to your family."

Arvin took an extra sip. "My father was a peaceful man. He never even preached against the queen like other Ahuraic priests did back in the day. But Sapphires did to him what they did to all the others. And one morning, they set his temple on fire. The devout Ahuraic my father was, he couldn't stand the sacrilege. He went and locked himself inside the temple as a protest, hoping that would stop them. But he had underestimated the cruelty of those bastards. They burned the building down with him still inside."

Panthea couldn't even imagine how that must feel. "I'm sorry."

"It's all right. It's a long time ago now." He brought the cup close to his lips but stopped as though he had remembered they were playing. "Your turn."

The alcohol was kicking in, and she had to think longer before giving him another piece of information that didn't reveal much. "My mother was an Erkenblood."

Arvin clicked his tongue. "You're cheating again. You're an Erkenblood, so of course your mother was too. I just gave you such a personal story. Say something useful before I make you drink three searing gulps."

She found herself smiling. Arvin's game was working, and the alcohol had eased her anxiety. "All right. My mother was the Minister of the Arcane in the Mehr dynasty."

"Ahura's throne." Eyes wide, he let out a quiet whistle of disbelief. "I never knew you were that important. If I did, I wouldn't have tied you to a chair."

She gave a brittle chuckle as she tried to repress the memory of his house. "Well, very few know about that. When the queen murdered King Shahbod and her own daughter, she sent her people to assassinate all members of the court who would oppose the takeover. My mother had already escaped from the palace. But she came back to save . . ." Her voice caught, and she felt the sting of tears in her eyes.

He pressed a gentle hand on her shoulder. "You want to stop?"

She shook her head. "Anyway, that's why my teacher has kept my true identity a secret." That was when she realized what she was doing. "Why am I telling you all this?" She cupped her hands over her face. "I'm such a fool."

"Hey." He took her hand and gently brought it down. "I can keep your secret. And this game is not supposed to make you cry. Quite the opposite. If you cry, you must drink two searing gulps."

That comment rekindled her smile, and her gaze found his again. "Now, you're just making up rules."

"You have a problem with that?"

The way he smiled was so genuine for someone as hardened as he was. He looked at her as if he really cared. Or maybe she was too drunk to make that judgment.

"Let's get another," her mouth said before her mind caught up.

13

I do not deny the Dark Ages, but I believe they were not as desperate, and their end not as heroic as the tales go. There were Erkenbloods who assumed power and Erkenbloods who fought against them. The tale of the first High Lady is the tale of a victor and not of a hero.

PANTHEA PRACTICED WITH her gleamstone in the corner of the sitting room. Every once in a while, she would glance at Rassus to see if he was still reading. It wasn't unusual for him to spend entire days on the same book, but sometimes, when Evian was not around, she felt lonely and in need of company. Why was the old man so solemn?

"Master," she dared say. "Why can't I control my wielding? Every time I try, it's so overwhelming, so easy to be devoured by power-lust. Why do I have to suffer from such a condition? Why does it have to be me?"

Rassus glanced over at her from the corner of his eyes, his frown not faltering. Neither would his attention turn from his book. Following a long, demoralizing silence, he grumbled, "I have failed you, Matter Star. All these years, I thought I was protecting you from the world. But I have only made you weak. Now, you are my greatest regret at this old age. You are my greatest failure."

Those words burned through her chest. Tears blurred her vision as the weight of that statement sank in. When they cleared, Inquisition blackhoods had already surrounded them, two of them holding Rassus by the arms. Another one stepped in front of Panthea. As the bottom of his face lit in the lamplight, she saw before her the man she'd been dreading since the Green Eye Lake. The man of her vision, with the same tall form, the same rugged visage, and that unmistakable ponytail.

Her heart throbbed as she noticed Arvin standing in a corner. "Didn't you find it strange, Panthea? That I had so many friends in the army? You should have known something was wrong."

Ash and Evian were also on their knees next to Rassus.

Panthea turned to the black-clad man. "Please. Let them go. I'll do anything. I'll get you the stone."

"How brave of you," said the man of her nightmares. "But there is nothing you can do now. Just watch everything you hold dear slip away." He pointed at his men. "Kill them."

There was fear in Ash's eyes, grief in Evian's, and Rassus's countenance shouted utter disappointment.

Evian's captor cut his throat, and blood gushed out.

She screamed at the top of her lungs.

PANTHEA'S EYES SNAPPED open, her heart pounding. The golden Hitian morning light that bled through the crack of the window illuminated a streak on the soft blanket she lay on.

It had been a dream.

Someone groaned from a yard away. She recoiled at first, but then registered who it was and where she had been sleeping. She had never been so drunk as to forget everything.

As her mind became less fuzzy, she remembered. It had been Arvin who had invited her to drink, who had gotten her one cup after another until she had blacked out. And the nightmares. "You traitor."

Arvin rolled over to her, his words fatigued and slurred as he said, "What did you say?"

She smacked her hand flat on his chest. "You did it, didn't you?"

"Did what?"

"You put that poison in my drink."

"Hush, Panthea," Arvin mumbled. "Your friends are sleeping."

"I can't believe," she began, but he was already falling back asleep. She slapped him on the cheek. "I'm talking to you."

He grunted as he slowly sat up. "Would you stop yelling?"

"Just answer my question. Did you slip that thing into my drink?"

"Yes," he said, holding his palms up to his chest in surrender.

She sprang to her feet. "I'm so stupid." She stormed out of the room, her bare soles clapping on the cold floor. It was early in the morning, and there were only a few people sitting around the common room, most of them in the white-and-navy-blue garment of couriers. Arvin shuffled down the stairs after her.

"Stop following me," she spat. They both went out of the inn, and she hugged herself against the chill outside.

"I understand you're upset," Arvin said as he tried to take her hand. "But let's—"

"Get away from me!" The morning light intensified, reflecting her anger as she pushed Arvin with all her strength. Without touching him.

Though the light dimmed, she still felt the power boiling inside her. Arvin took another apprehensive step back. Her heart brimmed with exhilaration, but it was not power-lust as she had experienced it before. She remembered everyone. Recognized everything. She was present, and yet the hair on her skin prickled with anticipation.

As their eyes met, that initial fear left Arvin's face.

Ash ran out of the inn, most likely awoken by Panthea and Arvin's argument in the room. "Oh, no. What did you do to her?" The young wielder darted to Panthea and stood in front of her. "Panthea, it's me. Do you know me?"

Panthea took a steadying breath. "Of course, I do, Ash."

Arvin shifted his weight as he let out a relieved sigh.

Ash glanced between the two of them for a second. "Your eyes were glowing," she said, her eyebrows knotted with concern. "Were you taken by power-lust again?"

"No." Panthea still marveled at the feeling that had overcome her; a slow-burn power-lust. "Sorry I woke you."

She then took Ash's hand, and together, they headed back.

As they passed by Arvin, he said, "I had no other choice. You would not take it on your own."

"I hate you," was all Panthea could give him after his betrayal. He had ruined her day. And just as she was taking the leap of faith to trust him with her quest.

When they went inside, Evian was already out of the room. "What's going on?"

Ash rolled her eyes, pointing back at the entrance as she climbed the stairs together with Panthea. "Somebody decided to have some fun. Alone."

Once they entered the room, Evian sat on his cot, and Ash and Panthea sat on Ash's. A few moments later, Arvin also entered and closed the door.

Evian's brow had creased, and his gaze jumped between everyone present in the room. Ash was giving Arvin an unyielding glare. Panthea had never seen the girl so protective.

"All right." Evian finally lost his patience. "You're all sulking. Can somebody tell me what this is about?"

"Why don't you ask him?" Panthea said as she shot a glance at Arvin. A dull headache and a nauseating fatigue were replacing the earlier rush.

"I only wanted to help," Arvin said.

Panthea curled her lips. "Would you stop it? I don't like how your help looks. People don't get hurt when they're helped. They don't feel betrayed."

"Betrayed?" Arvin scoffed. "Did you see the control you had back there? Does that feel like betrayal?"

"I hate having those nightmares. I hate seeing my friends die over and over again."

"Wait." Evian's nostrils flared as he stood. "It was him? He was the man who abducted you in Watertown?"

So much for keeping that secret. At this point, Panthea didn't care if it was revealed, either. He was far more deserving of her trust than Arvin. "Yes."

Evian's eyes were almost popping out as he glowered at Arvin. "You realize what you put my friend through?"

"Calm down, everyone," Arvin said in a whisper. "People outside might hear you."

Evian gave Panthea a soft glance before the arrow of his gaze returned to Arvin. "We'll settle this later. You and I."

"Easy, city boy," said Arvin with a menacing edge to his voice. "Threatening others without having the strength or training to back it up will only get you killed."

"Are you threatening Evian now?" Panthea shot.

"No," Arvin stretched the word, blinking in frustration. "I'm just saying you all need to calm down." He cracked the door open and peeked outside before closing it again. Then, he came to Panthea and crouched in front of her. "In case you haven't noticed," he said in a hushed tone, "there's a fifty-thousand-crown bounty on your head. Yes, you'll have those nightmares every time you take the potion, but you'll take it if you want to survive."

True as that could be, the fear of those nightmares was a nightmare of its own. "How many more times . . ." Her voice caught.

Arvin sighed. "I don't know. You need to take it until you can control your power without it. I thought you'd had enough in the house. But then I saw what happened at the Green Eye—"

Panthea gave him a hard look, and he stopped. But the damage was already done.

Ash raised an eyebrow. "What happened at the Green Eye Lake?"

"Nothing," Panthea and Arvin said almost at the same time.

"Oh, now, I have to know," Ash said jovially.

Arvin had ruined everything. Ash could not handle three dead people on the road. How would she react when she learned Panthea had killed a dozen?

"Panthea lost control at the lake," Arvin said.

"And you 'saw'?" Ash pressed. "What did you see?"

"Drop it, Ash," Panthea shot. "We have more important things to talk about."

Ash crossed her arms and shifted away from Panthea. "Just how many secrets have we been keeping from each other? Aren't we all in this together? How can we get through this if we can't even trust each other?"

"She's right." Evian shared a brief smile with Ash. "This situation has been extreme, and none of us has been prepared for it. But this is a good point to talk about how we want to go forward. No more secrets."

Arvin looked into Panthea's eyes, and it was obvious what he was thinking. There was one more secret the two of them had. Panthea's mind raced. The time had come for her to reveal the truth, and she was not ready.

"Is there something wrong?" asked Evian. Why did he have to know her so well? "Whatever it is, you can tell me."

"Yes, Panthea," Ash agreed. "You can tell us. If you don't want to tell Evian, tell me first."

There was no escaping it now. Anxiety gripped Panthea, and she had to take a few deep breaths before she talked. "Arvin, um, has agreed to help me rescue Master." To staunch the concern that was taking over Evian's features, she added the selling point of her plan. "Without the stone."

Ash scrunched her nose. "Stone?"

Ignoring the question, Panthea braced herself as she said the next part, her confidence falling apart as the reproachful look settled on Evian's face. "But that means I need to go with him to meet with the Windhammer."

Evian's expression was half disappointment, half terror. "Panthea." His voice cut like a knife. "We talked about this. I told you we must lie low until—"

"I know we did. You know that Master—Rassus—is more than a teacher to me. I can't live with myself if I don't do whatever I can."

Evian's glare turned to Arvin. "You."

"Can somebody tell me what the stone is?" Ash demanded.

Evian gestured to Panthea to explain, and she told Ash the complete story, including how Evian felt about Panthea's plan.

Once the story was over, Evian asked, "And where is this famous Windhammer, if I may ask? Or is that a secret we should just accept and—"

"Saba," Arvin cut off his ranting.

"Oh, boy," Ash muttered under her breath.

Fury took over Evian's face. The kind Panthea had never seen. His voice shook as he said, "Are you kidding me right now? You really expect Panthea to return to the city where she's hunted? Is this your master plan to turn her in?"

"She was in my house for four damned days," Arvin spat. "All I had to do was tell the authorities. So, stop with this turn-her-in nonsense when you don't know what you're talking about. And I assure you, if she goes back with me, I'll do everything I can to ensure her safe entry. We have resources. We have legal Sapphire issue carriages."

"We don't trust you," Evian almost shouted, the vein in his forehead bulging. "Panthea doesn't trust you. You think she's foolish enough to walk into your trap?"

"Actually," Panthea interjected, a little peeved, though her voice came out quiet and tentative. In two short sentences, Evian had both made her decision for her and called her foolish if she disagreed. As much as she loved and respected him, this was the moment she had to speak up if she wanted to save Rassus. But she could not get herself to meet Evian's gaze. She was not brave enough to watch his wrath when she confessed, "I'm considering it."

She took the pendant out of her shirt and let it hang over her chest. There was no point in hiding it now.

Silence. Long, crushing silence. When she dared look up, the flush of anger on Evian's face was nothing short of what she had expected. He glanced between her eyes and the pendant for a few moments, until his gaze locked onto hers. "Ten years of friendship, and you trust some stranger over me."

That statement pierced her like an arrow to the heart, and she struggled to keep her voice from dissolving as she said, "What did you expect me to do? You weren't willing to go after the stone or even let me do it. So, of course, I talked to a stranger because I want to see Master again. Now, I've found a way to save him without giving up the stone, and you're still not happy?"

"I wanted you to be safe, and your plan is to go to Saba?"

"Then what?" Panthea snapped through her locked throat, unable to hold her anger back anymore. "I'd like to hear another plan, but I'm not getting any from you. You're not even trying to save Master. You're running from it."

Ash's hand perched on Panthea's. "I think Evian has a point. It's dangerous for you to go back. Is this what Master would want?"

Evian got up and went to the door. "Panthea, if you want to risk your life, it's your choice. But I won't be there to watch you perish. Ash? We're leaving."

No! I should have kept my mouth shut.

Evian opened the door, but Ash did not move.

To his demanding look, Ash winced and said with that same reserved voice she'd acquired, "I'm sorry, Evian. But Panthea's my friend. It might be a stupid plan, but if that's what she wants to do, we can't leave her alone. So, I'm staying with her. But you can go."

Panthea's heart fluttered at that comment, and she clasped Ash's hand. Evian dropped his head, taking some time to respond to the new development. "You know, you may be risking your life to save someone who's already dead."

"Evian!" shot Ash in reprimand, but he was no longer in the room to hear it. His words shattered the last of Panthea's composure as cold rushed through her body, and she dissolved into tears.

"Ahura's throne," Arvin muttered as he joined Ash and Panthea on the bed.

Ash rubbed Panthea's back. Arvin held her hand.

"Don't cry," Ash said. "I'm sure Master is fine."

"Ash," Arvin whispered and gave a signal that made the girl leave the room. He then wrapped his arm around Panthea. "Listen to me. The Inquisition might be scary, but they're legally required to keep prisoners alive. Besides, your teacher has information they need, and as long as Sapphires don't have the stone, he'll be safe."

It took Panthea a while to be able to speak at all. "Even if what you say is true, it doesn't mean Evian's wrong. What if Rassus doesn't survive their tortures? What if they push him too hard?"

Arvin held her closer. "One thing the Inquisition knows well is people's limits. Not to say your teacher is having a pleasant time, but they won't let him die. Don't listen to Evian. He's just scared."

"Why does he think I don't trust him? He's my best friend. I told him everything, didn't I? Why can't he understand? I can't lose my teacher."

"I'm sure he won't leave," Arvin said, his voice warm and reassuring. "He said that to dissuade you. I can see he's not lying about wanting to protect you and Ash."

After a while, Ash and Evian came back together. Panthea hastily pulled out of Arvin's embrace and wiped her tears, lest Evian think she was any closer to Arvin than to him. Arvin squeezed her shoulder one last time before he got up and stood right in front of Evian's nose.

"Please leave him be," Panthea said with a shaky voice.

After a long stare-off, Arvin got out of the way, and Evian dropped on his knees before Panthea, his own eyes filled with tears. "I'm so sorry. I didn't mean what I said."

"Then why did you say it?" Panthea cried.

Evian bit his quivering lip as he shook his head. "It wasn't supposed to be this hard. Everything's falling to pieces, and there's nothing I can do to stop it."

"But you don't have to," whined Panthea, and for the first time, she realized she no longer expected him to solve her problems. She descended from the bed and took him in her arms as she rose with him. "There's three of us. We can handle anything together."

"Um," Arvin said humorously, raising his palm. "Four?"

"Shut up, stranger," quipped Ash.

Panthea and Evian kept the hug for some time. The warmth of his embrace was as soothing as it had always been, but there was now a difference. Panthea no longer felt weak in his presence. She knew that she, too, could help him as much as he helped her.

Arvin cleared his throat. "So, does this mean we're all going?"

Panthea pulled away and met Evian's gaze. With a brittle smile on his lips, he murmured, "I suppose we are."

A grin took control of Panthea's mouth. Evian's earlier outburst no longer hurt as much. She had always taken his composure for granted, and it had not occurred to her that he, too, could break. But now, she had seen Evian's worst, and she still loved him. She felt closer to him, even.

Panthea turned to Ash and said, "I think I've decided, Ash. You're my best friend."

The vulnerability and guilt in Evian's eyes upon hearing that made Panthea more certain of what she was about to say. "Evian's my brother."

14

I am not pure of heart, but the men I killed were irredeemable. They would have murdered more of my kind if given a chance. Nonetheless, I was sent into exile. The royal scholar discarded like a withered peel. They altered my writings. They reforged my identity. Such was my second death, for I died in people's memory.

THE DAY'S WORK WAS OVER, and Hilia could not wait to spend some time in the library. If she were lucky, she could even do some more research before Handler arrived; find a book that explained the unexplainable. Like how the Dark Scepter produced those whispers, how it had told her about the future, how the queen of the Southern Kingdom defied death.

For four years, Hilia had stayed in this palace because the Windhammer claimed her position was strategically important. In reality, she had made no difference, learned few secrets, and no one even heeded her warnings. She might as well not be here at all.

"The rebellion is no place for a girl." Those had been Windhammer's exact words.

After the rebels had saved her and her father seven years ago, she had wanted to give back. One reason she'd fallen in love with Arvin was how he had always supported her decisions. Those days, he would lay down his life to keep her safe. Still, he had not batted an eye when she'd asked to join the rebellion. Concerned, yes. But try to dissuade her? That just wasn't Arvin. In fact, the day they went to Windhammer to propose the idea, Arvin was ecstatic.

She had to wait outside while Arvin talked to the man in his study. Her younger mind raced. Those moments would determine her future, and she sure as Hell didn't want to continue being the damsel in distress who froze in the face of danger. She wanted to be like Arvin. Fierce, daring.

The faint sound of the men's voices carried through the door, and she could not help but listen as Arvin defended her. Out of everything else that was said in that room, one message would stick with her for the years to come. "Arvin. Those like us cannot afford to feel. The rebellion is no place for a girl. Her emotions will always impede her better judgment."

That was the last sentence she could bear before storming out of the chambers. Arvin came out of the meeting to a proof of the old man's claim. She was a ball of emotion in that moment. A ball of raging fire. She did not even let him hold her for comfort.

And then there came something that would cut through that tension and always accompany the memory of Windhammer's blatant dismissal. "Forget what he says," Arvin said. "If he can't see the light that glares at him, we'll blind him with it. You're the toughest girl I've met, and it would have been a loss if you weren't a part of the rebellion."

Hilia couldn't help a smile; less could she help the leaping of her heart. As for that last statement . . . She frowned. "What do you mean, would have been?"

A jovial grin bloomed over his face. One that was closer to that of a child having received a birthday gift than that of a hardened warrior. "You're in."

She almost screamed with joy. Almost. She'd be damned if she actually did. She would not give the Windhammer more reason to doubt her togetherness or competence.

Six long years had now passed since that day. Windhammer's acceptance no longer mattered to her. He had recommended her to the queen and gotten her appointed here, and that was the extent of what you could expect from him. It was no longer him she needed to convince, but herself. A decade from now, when she looked back at these days, she wanted to see a change she alone had made. Her last four years had not brought her any closer to that goal.

She was on her way to the usual table in the middle of the library when something bumped into her leg and attached to it. "Hilia."

It was Parviz's four-year-old son, Tremos. A northern name—another reminder of how the Southern Kingdom's culture was being systematically erased.

The boy grew every day. With the white, buttoned shirt he had on, he resembled a tiny version of Parviz. He was probably even proud of it. To him, the world was a platter of new experiences: the first time he came to the library with his father, the first time he dressed like a man, the first time he would read a book. He was far from the age when he'd start looking back as Hilia did these days. Like the last time she'd seen her own father, the last time she'd smiled and meant it.

His exuberance made that last question easy to answer. "Who are you, and what did you do to my Tremos?"

The boy grinned. "But I am Tremos."

"Uh-uh. I don't believe you. If you're telling the truth, tell me how you grew up so fast."

"I eat a lot because my dad tells me when I'm big enough, I can get married like him."

"Is that so?" She hunkered in front of him and poked the bridge of his nose. "And who do you want to marry?"

Fidgeting, he said, "I don't know. You?"

She laughed. "Aren't you a player? Now, where's your dad? I want to meet my future father-in-law."

"Right here," came Parviz's voice as he approached from between the shelves. "Sorry about the boy. His mother couldn't keep him today, so I had to bring him here."

Hilia got up. "No, it's all good. We were having a conversation about our future."

Tittering, Parviz turned to his son. "Tremos. Why don't you go in the back and draw while Hilia and I have a grown-up talk?"

It took some convincing from both Parviz and Hilia, but Tremos finally left. Parviz then gave her an inquisitive look. "You seem a little agitated."

She shrugged. "Things have been chaotic, what with the assassination attempt and all. And seeing those Inquisition blackhoods in the residence building isn't exactly the sight I enjoy waking up to. I came here to unwind. Speaking of which, have you got any good fiction I can read?"

Parviz's eyes widened, and he seemed to suppress his laughter.

"I know, I know," she said. "But I thought I'd give this a try—distract myself from all the chaos."

The librarian grinned. "I have just the right book for you. Wait here. I'll have to find it."

She sat at the table while she waited. Parviz didn't go to the fiction section. He went to the back, which played to her advantage as her unnecessarily anonymous handler entered the library. As much as she hated to taint the positive aura of this place, it had become her and Handler's meeting location.

He sat opposite to her, giving her that fake smile of his.

She didn't waste time. "Do we have any plans to get Mehran out? I can help you with information. I've befriended Inquisitor Kadder, and soon I'll be able to—"

"I'm going to stop you right there." Handler's tone was laced with reprimand. "First of all, that was an impetuous move. You're already under scrutiny, and you try to spy on the Inquisitor? I want you to stop whatever it is you think you're doing. Second." He slid a piece of paper toward her. "That's no longer your concern."

Swallowing her irritation as best she could, she retrieved the letter and took some time to rip her gaze off him and onto the writing.

General,

With growing concerns over the well-being of our agents in the palace, I hereby request the dismissal of the Handmaiden from her current role. Her services are no longer deemed required.

She snapped her gaze back to him. "Is this a joke? You're throwing me out?"

"No," Handler said. "This is for your own safety. Mehran knows everything about you, and it's only a matter of time before he gives you away. You won't last a day at the hands of the Inquisition. They prey on young women like you."

She hadn't gone through all of this, so she could quit. The disparaging remarks, the trauma, the sacrifices. This man seemed to be of the same school of thought as the Windhammer himself. Neither believed a woman could be an effective agent.

She thumped her palm on the table. "You don't know Mehran. And you don't know me. So, let my safety be my own concern."

His stern gaze sizzled for a few seconds. Then, when she didn't waver, he clicked his tongue. "Let me be frank. We all know you were the brains behind that mission. Your theory was unfounded, and it cost us one of our best agents."

"I asked him not to do it," she retorted. "I had—"

Looking away, Handler held up a dismissive hand before his gaze returned to hers. "It doesn't matter how it happened. It did happen, and now we're in a crisis because of it. They've asked me to put you back as a sleeper agent. But you don't strike me as the kind to keep your head down, and I can't have agents I need to babysit. So, you stay put, and I'll arrange your extraction."

"I don't need babysitting. I've been an agent here for four years. I know

Windhammer's been looking for an excuse to throw me out like trash, but I've done nothing to deserve it. If Mehran couldn't do his part, it doesn't mean my theory was wrong."

"Your theory is toxic. We can't afford false hope."

"I'm. Staying."

"And if I say no?" he said in a low, menacing voice.

She didn't answer. These people had proven quite comfortable eliminating threats to the rebellion, and one didn't want to make enemies with them.

Her silence seemed to give him pleasure, which manifested as a complacent smile. "Yeah, I didn't think so."

Before he got up with his letter, she used her last chance to contest his decision. "I'll prove it." When he looked at her, she added, "I'll prove my theory. Give me until the Dark Fusion."

He stopped, then turned to her, an exasperated look in his eyes.

"What do you have to lose?" she pushed. "I'll keep a low profile. I won't spy on anyone, and I'll report my progress to you."

He glanced at his letter, then at Hilia. "Very well." That authoritative tone returned to his voice. "You have until the Dark Fusion. If you can't prove your theory by then, you can forget your extraction. I'll declare you as a burned agent."

She gulped. A burned agent was one who would no longer receive any support from the rebellion. If he declared her as such, she would stay in the palace on her own and would be eliminated if her presence posed any threat to the other agents.

With a voice that scraped its way out of her throat, she said, "Deal."

The man sealed the deal with a nod and left the library.

What have I done? She had just signed her own death sentence.

Soon Parviz came back with a book. It took her a moment to turn her thoughts from the foolish decision she had made.

"Here," the librarian said. "This one tells the story of Kyra, a warrior woman who leads a rebellion against a tyrant king. It might be a little too violent for your taste, but she reminds me of you in some ways."

Hilia wanted to laugh. *Poor man. He'd be surprised at how much violence I've had to witness.* "Thank you. I'll tell you what I think. Who knows? Maybe I'll come to like fiction."

15

Religion has always been a part of my being, but before my exile, I had never allowed it to be a part of my work. And yet, it was in the Book of Creation that I found the answer to the grandest question ever asked: The destiny of our world.

THIS VANTAGE POINT outside the town had become Panthea's favorite spot for the past two days. Back in Saba, everywhere one looked, there would be walls and buildings. Perhaps, when all of this was over, when she had saved Rassus, she would come here to spend the rest of her life, away from the stress of the city. For now, though, she had a more immediate task at hand.

Even if nightmare potion cured power-lust, the trauma of those nightmares was not something she was ready to go through again. There had to be another way. Many Erkenbloods had overcome it before her. Power-lust was not a newly discovered condition, and none of the books she had read spoke of such an extreme measure.

There was a piece of rock near the ledge that seemed to be suitable as her next target. She drew in a lungful of the crisp mid-Hitian morning air, and as she let it out, she tried to pull the rock to herself.

Power seeped into her veins, inducing a gratifying rush. Her vision brightened, and before the stone even moved, she gasped, stopping herself before she would fall into oblivion. She took deep breaths to slow her heart. The euphoria sizzled in her gut for a few seconds after her attempt.

This had been the third time this morning, and power-lust seemed to be the only way her power manifested, no matter how hard she tried. Frustrated, she kicked the stone off the ledge and plopped down, wrapping her arms around her knees.

"You're up early."

It was Arvin's voice.

She glanced over her shoulder and said preemptively, "Don't ask."

"Wasn't going to." He came over and sat next to her. "Still sure about leaving with us tomorrow? I talked with Evian last night. He doesn't say it, but I can tell he's nervous. He's afraid something might happen to you."

She met his gaze. "Can something happen to me?"

Arvin looked to the land below with an air of malaise. "I'd like to think nothing will. But we can't ignore the bounty on your head. And we're going to meet the Windhammer, of all people. I can protect you with my life, but that's as much as I can promise."

She let out a shuddering breath. The reminder of her situation's gravity made her feel colder than she already was. "Is there any other way to save my teacher?"

He rubbed his mouth as he contemplated, then shook his head. "The only other option is to find the stone and give it up, which is most likely doomed to fail. There's no guarantee those bastards at the Inquisition will hold up their end of the bargain. Besides, if that's your plan, you'll have to go through the Windhammer. He won't let that happen."

"So, you'd tell on me," she said.

"Probably. The stone could make Queen Artenus more powerful. Would you risk people's lives like that?"

She smiled ruefully. "Probably not."

"By the way, Evian tells me you're something of a scholar when it comes to the arcane."

A nervous chuckle escaped Panthea. "Not a scholar. But I've read some books."

"He also warned me you'd be humble about it."

Compliments always made her uncomfortable because she did not know how to respond to them. At the same time, she liked the idea of being known for her knowledge. "Why? You have a question?"

"Yes. Do you know if it's possible to make an ordinary human immortal?"

"Immortal? You mean—"

"So they don't die, they don't age."

"Everybody ages," she said. "Even angelkins, though slower than humans. But everything in this world eventually withers and dies."

He narrowed his eyes. "Angelkins?"

"Oh, sorry." She always forgot how little he knew about these topics. "Angelkins are divine beings appointed by the Great Annahid to watch over humans. They live much longer than we do. Normally three to four thousand years."

"Interesting. And can a human become an angelkin?"

This one was so absurd, she broke into an inappropriate laughter. "A human . . . can't become . . ." She stopped laughing when she saw him staring at her with a soft and passionate smile. With the wake of her laughter lingering, she asked, "What?"

"I've not seen you laugh like this before." His voice was warm and sincere. "It's stunning."

She felt a rush, and her face warmed. This was more than a compliment. The admiration in his eyes was foreign to her. No one had ever looked at her this way. Granted, the only people she knew were her friends and Rassus. To them, she was the vulnerable child, the history buff, the Erkenblood. But for the first time, this man saw her as something she had forgotten she was. A woman.

His comment and his gaze were both pleasant and frightening. As much as she had enjoyed hearing it, the implication was more than she was prepared for. She was not ready to have such a relationship. Not with

Arvin. Not with anyone.

She averted her eyes. "So," she said, hoping to divert his attention. "Why are you asking these questions?"

He sighed. "My friend has this idea that Queen Artenus is not immortal. Back at the inn, you said the same thing. I know my friend isn't a fool, and you're not, either. So, I'm considering this. That's why I'm looking for some kind of explanation for how the queen defies death."

"She does?" Panthea asked, glad that her attempt at changing the topic had succeeded.

Arvin nodded. "People have tried to kill her multiple times through the years, but she's always survived. That, and she doesn't seem to age."

Either this was just another rumor or Panthea's knowledge had reached its limits. She racked her brain, going through the books she had read, things she had learned from Rassus. Until she remembered something from the book *Aspects and Transformations*.

Aspects were souls that left their own body to live inside another's. The host retained both souls, inheriting the aspect's powers if there were any.

The possession of an angelkin aspect by the queen could explain what Arvin claimed, but it was far-fetched. The ritual required pure consent— one could not force another to become an aspect. And no angelkin would make such a sacrifice for a human.

"She could have received an angelkin aspect," Panthea suggested anyway.

"A what?"

"An aspect," she repeated. "The soul of an angelkin absorbed into her body. Does the queen bleed? Because if she had an angelkin aspect, she wouldn't."

"Interesting. I don't know if she does, but it's worth looking into."

His eyes focused on something down the hill, and his humor dissipated. She followed his gaze to find a procession heading in their direction. They were still a good distance away, but seemed to have rattled Arvin, nonetheless.

"Who are they?" she asked, the concern in his countenance adding to her own.

"Wait here," he said as he got to his feet. "Don't let them out of your sight."

With that, he ran toward the town. Having not received an answer for her question, she returned her gaze to the procession and the trail of dust following in its wake. As they got closer, she recognized the blue color of Sapphire surcoats and the glinting of their armors in the sunlight. Her stomach churning, she kept glancing back to check if Arvin was in sight. How could he have left her here to watch? If she could see the soldiers, they could see her too.

A few minutes later, when Arvin didn't show up, she got up to go after him. But she wasn't far when she saw him approaching, together with Mart, Evian, and that giant black-clad man, or *blackhood*, as Arvin and his friends seemed to call those people.

Gvosh wore a more comfortable outfit than before. Loose trousers and a simple, sleeveless white shirt that let his sinewy arms show, each of which she could swear was as thick as her waist.

Mart held a spyglass in one hand. With the other, he squeezed her shoulder as he passed by her, adding a wink for good measure. He then stood at the edge and looked through his spyglass. "Yep. It's them, all right. We have army soldiers; we have blackhoods. There are even fucking archers." He retracted the spyglass. "Ahura's ass, Arvin. It's a whole platoon."

Gvosh let out a low growl, scowling at Mart.

"Panthea," Arvin said, his brows drawn together. "What is it you've done, exactly?"

She swallowed hard. "I just lost control in Saba. And again, at the Green Eye Lake."

Ash also came to them running. "Where are they?"

Mart handed her the spyglass, then pointed at the procession while sharing glances with Arvin and Gvosh. "Cousin. I thought they sent *your* ass to scout. Why are they here?"

"Maybe the farmers gave us away?" Panthea said tentatively, glancing at Evian.

"Or the villagers here," Mart suggested.

"Doesn't matter who." Gvosh's gaze dropped to Panthea. "A tip from a peasant alone doesn't mobilize a platoon. What I asked you the other day? Now would be a good time to have an answer."

"I don't . . ." She was falling apart, and they kept crowding her.

Mart huffed. "Girl, you know how much the bounty was on the fucking Erkenblood of Livid? Twenty thousand. And you tell me an eighteen-year-old is worth more than the face of the last rebellion?"

They did not seem to believe she had no clue why she was such an important target. More than anyone else, she herself wanted to know the answer. More than anything, she wished she would wake up from this nightmare.

"I think I know," Evian said from her side, turning everyone's attention.

All except Ash's. "Why is it all blurry?" she asked from the edge of the hill.

Mart went to her and fixed the spyglass in her hand before he returned to the rest of the group. Panthea was dying to hear what Evian wanted to say, wondering why he had not done so before.

After a few seconds, when Panthea's patience was about to reach its limit, he said, "They're here for the Bond of Third Arcane."

That name gave Panthea a jolt. "But we don't have it."

"We do," Evian said to her consternation. He approached and gently removed the pendant from around her neck. "I was afraid you'd want to go back if you knew. But I suppose it doesn't matter now that you're going anyway."

That confession also attracted Ash's attention. She, too, joined them as Evian pressed the pendant between his palms while twisting his hands in opposite directions.

The pendant clicked, and the front of the disk came off like a lid. Inside, there was a smaller object, the same color as a gleamstone. Its shape was like the lens of a spyglass.

Evian removed it and handed it to Panthea. "The stone is in this."

Her breath was frozen, and she had to remind herself to exhale.

Eyes wide, Arvin expelled air through a closed mouth. "There you have it."

"This is horseshit," Gvosh muttered. "I've got to leave this town."

Mart curled his lips. "You're bailing on us? I knew you were a dick, but not such a huge one."

"Are you sure you're a strategist?" Gvosh retorted. "You want me to stay and tell them I was here having a chat with the Erkenblood of Saba? Things are not going your way, *Cousin*. You need me alive and in the bureau for when they bring her there, and they will. In fact, I don't think anyone else should get involved. This is his mess." He pointed at Arvin. "And he alone should deal with it. Now, if you'll excuse me, I have a journey to prepare for."

And they will. Even the idea of them taking her to the Inquisition was frightening.

"That weasel," Mart said when his cousin left. He wiggled his finger in the air for a few seconds. "That . . . weasel does have a good point."

Panthea turned to Evian. "How do they know I have the stone?"

From the look on Arvin's and Mart's faces, they, too, were interested in that answer.

Biting his lips, Evian only shrugged.

She looked the tiny box over. It was not made of normal matter. Anything she could wield, she could also feel with her matter-sensing. But she couldn't sense this one. When she closed her eyes, it was as though there was nothing in her hand.

She gave Evian an inquisitive look. "Is this northern marble?"

He nodded. "It's a special kind of box. Only a matter-wielding Erkenblood can open it."

"But I can't wield northern marble."

Mart retrieved the spyglass from Ash, then clapped Arvin's shoulder. "I'll go wake up the others and prepare the carriages. And, well, say goodbye to the giant. We must get out of here before the bastards arrive.

Make sure the kids don't go anywhere."

Mart headed to the town, and Evian resumed his explanation. "The exterior of the box is northern marble, but if you focus, the locking mechanism inside is of ordinary metal. And your matter-sensing is what you need to open it."

She closed her eyes again and focused. This time, she could sense something—a tiny strip of metal suspended just above her hand. "Yes, I can feel it. It's a latch."

"Open it, open it," Ash urged, clapping in excitement.

Panthea knew how unprepared she was to wield. She had tried it minutes ago. "Sorry. I can't."

"I understand," Evian said. "You don't have to do it."

"Like Diva's cold, clammy kiss she doesn't have to." Ash produced her gleamstone. "Okay, Panthea, tell me where the latch is, and I'll open it."

Panthea sighed. "You carry that thing everywhere now?"

"Nope. Just when I hear Sapphires are coming. Come on. Where is it?"

"That's not how it works, Ash," Evian said. "It's not made for ordinary humans."

Ash swatted the air. "I'm no ordinary human. I'm special."

Panthea wanted this back-and-forth to end so they could focus on their plan. Besides, she, too, wanted to see the Bond of Third Arcane. And they had some time before Mart would return.

"Fine," she said, sharing a glance with Evian, who did not seem at all confident in what they were doing. She indicated the exact point where the latch was. "Here. About a quarter of an inch inside. And it stretches from here to here. You need to move it to the left."

"All right." Ash shifted her weight. "Here we go."

The gleamstone glowed, but nothing happened.

Evian arched an eyebrow. "Told you."

"Shut up, Evian. Let me focus." Ash put her finger on the box. "Here?"

Panthea sighed as she moved the finger to the right place. "Here. Quarter of an inch deep."

Ash locked her gaze on that spot. Another glow. No result.

Panthea was about to retract her hand when the gleamstone glowed again. This time, the box clicked, split in the middle, then swung open.

Ash jumped, screaming in triumph. "Yes! I knew I could do it."

Arvin turned to them, startled by Ash's reaction.

There it was. A round piece of milky northern marble, but much smaller than a typical gleamstone. Etched on its surface was Pol, the third letter of the Angelian alphabet. The form of the letter was in the Old Angelian form, a script no longer in use for thousands of years, though still taught in textbooks as an alternative.

They all marveled at the sight, even Evian, whose expression maintained an undertone of apprehension. Ash grabbed the stone before anyone could stop her and darted to a safe distance.

"Ash, that's enough," Evian snapped. "That's not a toy. You put it back right now."

"He's right," Panthea agreed.

Even Arvin joined them in scolding the impetuous young wielder.

Ash examined the stone. "Hmm. It feels like a gleamstone. Do you think if—"

"No, don't use it," Panthea and Evian said together. Or maybe Evian said something else. But their combined voices gave Ash a good start.

With her lips curled and her eyes almost popping out of their sockets, Ash said, "I wasn't going to. I'm not that stupid to let something so precious bind to me."

Ash held up the Bond to show everyone she was giving it up. She then came and put it inside the box, which Panthea closed and handed back to Evian.

"Bind to you?" Arvin asked. "What does that mean?"

Glancing at the sealed pendant, Panthea let out a relieved sigh before she answered Arvin's question. "Arcane artifacts bind to their owners on first use. So, for example, I can't use Ash's gleamstone because it's bound to her. We fear the same can happen with the Bond of Third Arcane."

Arvin frowned. "So, you mean to tell me, an ancient artifact has been circulating among humans for thousands of years, and no one thought about wielding it before Queen Artenus? Knowing humanity, that's a little hard to believe."

Ash's eyes narrowed into a slit. "Oh, yeah. Good point."

"Don't get any ideas, Ash," Evian said as he sealed the pendant. "We're not going to find that out." He then handed it back to Panthea. "Here. This belongs to you. Now, you know how much Master trusts you. And so do I."

Panthea couldn't help the rising of hair on her skin. Rassus had trusted her with his most prized possession. She retrieved the pendant and wore it, hoping she could once again see her teacher, her guardian. Her father.

16

Book of Creation, fifth Visage—The Wandering Queen, verses twenty-seven and twenty-eight. "She will be banished from her home and from any place she calls home. She will be a child of the world, a friend of the road." There was a time when I thought I was the savior.

B EFORE THE SUNS reached the middle of the sky, the group was already miles away from the town, and the wobbly, loud carriage put the rough road behind them at a much higher speed than Panthea had imagined. If the hunting party arrived in Serene now, they would be disappointed.

"What's Third Arcane?" Ash's voice dragged Panthea out of her thoughts. The girl hadn't spoken since their departure. Perhaps this question had been keeping her mind occupied.

What *was* Third Arcane? The question had not even hit Panthea. To her, the stone was only a token she would use to free Rassus. "I don't know. If we have three Bonds of Arcane, they could each correspond to one of the three elements."

"That's what I thought at first too," Ash said. "But why would someone put numbers on those? What makes time one and space two? Aren't they all equal?"

Ash had indeed given it some deliberation. But Panthea was out of ideas and too perturbed for puzzles. "What do you think?"

"Well, the elements are not the only way we categorize the arcane. You and I both wield matter. So, how are we different?"

Panthea scrunched her nose as she stated the obvious, "I'm an Erkenblood."

"Exactly. Maybe this is what the three *Arcanes* are about. Inborn wielding, conductive wielding, and . . ." She trailed off, waving her arms as though she found it difficult to express herself.

"And?" Panthea urged.

"Third-kind wielding," Ash said dubiously.

"You just solved the mystery, Ash," Evian teased.

Ash rolled her eyes. "Shut up, Evian. I'm sure I'm onto something."

Having nothing to add, Panthea finished the exchange with a painted smile. This mystery could wait. Right now, there were far more important things to worry about.

Mart and Arvin sat across from them, the pair taking up as much space on their side as Panthea and her friends took on the other. The two seemed at ease despite the situation.

"Can they track us here?" Panthea asked.

"They might," Mart said with a slight shrug.

"Do we have a plan?" Evian chimed in. He did not seem worried on the surface. One had to know him well to notice the brief twitch in the corner of his lips and the compulsive brushing of his thumb across his fingers.

Mart snorted. "What's the rush, kid? We don't fix problems that don't exist. My boy Salem is already out there. Once we hear bad news, we'll deal with it. In the meantime . . ." He reached under his seat and produced a decanter and two cups. "Anyone care for a drink of wine?"

Is this a joke?

"I'll have some," Ash announced.

Panthea whipped her head to her friend. How could she even think of drinking?

"What?" Ash said. "They're not here yet."

Mart chortled. "I like this girl." He filled both cups, then handed one to Ash while regarding Panthea. "Listen, Dazzle-eyes. We're rebels. If we wanted to shit ourselves over every threat, we'd live very short lives." He raised his drink. "Very short lives."

He drank up, then refilled the cup, handing it to Arvin this time.

Ash squeezed Panthea's shoulder. "Don't worry, Panthea. Arvin and Mart aren't worried, and they're proper warriors. Don't you think we should trust them?" She held out the remainder of her drink for her to take. "Look, I'm trying really hard to keep it positive. If you worry, then I worry, and that won't help anybody."

Panthea considered taking the cup from her friend. But she really could not drink. So, she gently pushed it away. Ash leaned back, crestfallen.

An additional set of hoofbeats joined the rest of the noise, then someone knocked on the carriage walls, making Ash and Panthea both jump in their seat.

Mart pulled the curtain aside and looked out. "Oh, there you are." He grinned. "Do your worst, Salem."

"The hunting party is gaining on us," said a deep voice from outside.

That was not the news Panthea wanted to hear. Few things had gone right on this journey, and although she expected this to go wrong too, part of her wished that for once, she and her friends could have a break.

Evian slipped his hand over hers, the warmth of his palm easing her nerves a little. She glanced at Ash's concerned eyes and passed on the comfort by holding her hand.

Mart and Arvin still didn't seem fazed. Mart asked the rider, "How long have we got?"

"Less than half an hour," the rider said. "That's if they don't increase their pace."

Mart nodded as he ran two fingers along his mustache. After a few moments of contemplation, he leaned outward. "Tell the drivers to maintain speed and stand by for further instructions."

The smirk on Mart's face deepened. Unlike Arvin, his levity was not even reassuring. He looked like a deranged man who got a kick out of certain doom. "There's your bad news. We might have to engage."

Ash grimaced. "Then why are you smiling?"

"It's not a smile. It's a smirk. It's different."

"Okay, I think this guy's crazy," Ash said, looking to Panthea and Evian for approval.

Panthea was as dumbfounded by the men's calm. Well, Arvin was not smiling, but he resembled someone who had just woken up from a pleasant dream. "Salem?" he said. "Did you call that man by his real name?"

"His name's not Salem," Mart mumbled, and they both chuckled.

To elicit some action from them, Panthea said, "So, what are we going to do?"

Mart turned to Arvin. "Want to have a first stab at the plan?"

"Let's see." Arvin looked up, visibly calculating in his head. "They're traveling in squads. Three groups of thirteen, with the blackhoods in the last group, who will be the least effective."

Mart nodded. "We let the first squad merge. This way, if they're not hostile, everyone goes home happy. If they want trouble, well, the first squad will be a quick sweep. The second squad will be the real fight. Once we take them down, we stop and hunt the third group. At that point, we won't be outnumbered, and we'll kill every one of them, so they don't take the news back to Delavaran or Saba. Are you on board?"

Arvin nodded. Mart then reached out of the window again. "Hey, Salem. Bring two crossbows for me and my boy here."

"Are we going to win?" Panthea asked tentatively.

"Are you going to fight three times your numbers?" Evian added, his brow crinkled.

Mart pointed his index finger at Evian. "Yes," and then at Panthea. "I don't know."

Panthea had not been heeding her growing anxiety, and she only realized how severe it had become when the anticipation of wielding pulsed in her head. "Arvin, I need sapping potion. I'm getting really anxious. I might lose it."

"No," said Arvin with a demoralizing finality.

"What?" Panthea's voice was shaking now. "I need it, Arvin."

"No, he's right," Mart joined Arvin in denying her the potion. "There's a chance our plan goes sideways, in which case I would prefer to have something powerful on our side."

"She's not a thing," spat Evian. "She's not a weapon. You keep her out of your fight."

"Panthea?" Ash gently tugged at her sleeve. When Panthea turned to her, she continued, "What's the worst that could happen? If power-lust takes you, I can bring you out of it."

"You're not helping, Ash," Panthea snapped, making her friend flinch. "And just because it worked once, it doesn't mean it'll work again."

"But I—"

"We're not discussing this."

That silenced the girl. She sank into her seat, crossing her arms.

"You're endangering her life," Evian pushed. "She can't fight, and you know it."

Arvin clucked and blinked in exasperation. "Here's what endangers her life. Taking away her only fighting chance. Turning her into a slab of meat to be skewered by those bastards. Yes, she might lose control, and she might kill all of us, but at least she'll live."

Overwhelmed by the power that rose in her, Panthea said in a half-whimper, "I'm not killing any of you because I'm not doing this. Now"— her voice lost all restraint—"give me the cursed potion."

"You know what?" Ash spat. "Give her the potion. It's not like any of us are capable of helping. No. Panthea prefers to drug herself rather than trust her own friends."

"Why are you doing this, Ash?" Panthea pleaded.

"I'm not doing anything." She was not even looking at her. "I'm just leaving you alone to do whatever you want. You know what hurts, though? I have so much faith in you, and you have none in me. None."

"I'm trying to protect you," Panthea said.

"Stop it. If you want to escape who you are, it's your choice. But if you don't need my protection, I don't need yours. You don't get to use me as an excuse." Ash then squeezed herself in the corner to maximize her distance from Panthea.

Arvin and Mart eyeballed them with a mix of derision and bewilderment. "I get a feeling," Mart muttered, "there's so much history I need to catch up on. Does this happen often?"

Arvin gave a gentle nod. "Been happening a lot."

Before Panthea would say anything or Ash could, the wall of the carriage was knocked again, then a crossbow flew through the window, landing on the floor. Then another, then a quiver full of arrows. Mart saluted the rider and closed the curtain.

Arvin handed Panthea a vial. "I don't approve of this."

He and Mart then continued discussing their plan. Panthea unstoppered the vial. It didn't matter if he approved or not. It was not his choice to make. But before she drank, she glanced at Ash, who rested her head on the carriage wall, looking out through the slit of the curtain. She was a whole different story. She had chanced traveling across the realm with a stranger to find Panthea. And whether Panthea admitted it or not, this girl *had* brought her back from power-lust.

Taking a deep breath to calm herself, Panthea mumbled, "I have faith in you, Ash."

"Whatever." Ash only gave her a sideways look, which was enough for her to see Panthea pouring the potion on the floor. Although the young wielder tried to stay aloof after that, a sneaky smile stretched her lips. "You didn't have to waste it, Dopey."

Arvin sighed, eyes wide and eyebrows raised, probably astounded by his company of entitled city people. He retrieved the empty vial and stashed it in his satchel while he listened to Mart speak using military jargon.

She phased out, focusing on keeping her power at bay.

Soon enough, Salem—or whatever his real name was—announced

from outside, "Contact."

Mart placed an arrow in his already drawn crossbow. "All right, here we go." He gave a sweeping motion of his arm to indicate his and Evian's side of the carriage. "You kids bunch up together on this side, so when I open this curtain, they won't see you."

Evian was the first to squeeze himself against the wall, then Panthea and Ash followed. It was happening. The Sapphires were here, and all that stood between them and the group was half a plan.

Panthea closed her eyes and began whispering prayers. "Great Annahid, in the name of what's dead and what's living and what's divine, accept your lesser daughter. Give me courage to face the enemy and not cower. Give me strength to fight the curse of power-lust. Save me from sin."

It became much harder to focus on her prayer when Mart said, "There they are. Salem. Ask them to merge."

Irritated by words that directly impacted her and yet she didn't know, Panthea asked, "What does it mean, merge?"

"It's a military term," Arvin explained instead of Mart. "Normally, a search party can stop a convoy to ask questions or search the carriages. But if the convoy has important cargo or a tight timeline, they can ask the search party to conduct the interview on the move."

The hoofbeats of a galloping horse approached. Mart shifted the curtain a few inches. "What's going on, Lieutenant?"

Panthea buried her head behind Evian, continuing with her prayers to distract herself.

"Sir, I'm going to ask you to stop the convoy," the man said with confidence that left no room for contest. "We need to search all carriages leaving Serene."

"We can't," Mart said. "We have important cargo headed for Saba, and we're already late. Orders from the governor."

"I understand, sir. We won't take long."

"It doesn't matter how long you take," Mart dismissed. "Protocol dictates that you comply with our request."

"We operate under an official decree," the man's voice came out with a threatening edge, "that overrides protocol, sir. Please stop the convoy, or we will use force."

"Official decree? Whose decree is that?"

"Inquisitor Yoltan from the Queen's Inquisition, sir."

Mart exchanged a look with Arvin and cleared his throat, his composure faltering. He then looked out the window again. "And I suppose I have to take your word for it?"

"Sir, I—"

"Bring me the paper, Lieutenant," Mart commanded, "instead of wasting my time."

The hoofbeats slowed down and grew farther.

Mart let go of the curtain and sank in his seat. "Panthea's ass," he mumbled, then covered his mouth. "Shit. I meant the goddess."

"And that's better?" Arvin said, smiling.

This time, Mart did not laugh. Staring out, he said, "Ponytail is playing all his cards." After some more mumbling, he called Salem again and waited until the man arrived before he commanded, "Tell everyone to engage on my signal."

"Engage?" Salem asked, hesitation wavering in his voice. "What do you mean, engage?"

"Am I speaking Kierric, boy? Or are you a dimwit? You don't know what engage means?"

"I do, sir, but are we fighting the Inquisition? Is it safe?"

"I'll tell you what's not safe, rookie." Mart's tone had taken a complete turn from earlier. "Insubordination. Now, go relay my order."

"Yes, sir. What's the signal?"

"A dead asshole good enough?"

"Yes, sir." Salem left. Mart sighed as he examined his crossbow. "These idiots don't seem to understand the chain of command." He met Arvin's gaze. "You ready?"

Arvin only nodded.

The air stood still as they all waited for the impending disaster, and it took an eternity until the rider from the platoon came back.

Mart put his crossbow on the floor. Then he reached out and took a piece of parchment from the man and took his time reading it.

In the meantime, the sound of multiple riders carried from outside. Mart frowned. "Whoa, whoa, whoa. What under fuck are they doing?"

"They're here to ensure your compliance, sir," the rider said. "My superior would also want to see your order papers."

A crooked smile turned up the corner of his lips. "Of course. Just give me a second."

He dropped the letter, picked up the crossbow, and lifted it to the edge of the window, pointing outward. In a swift motion, he brought up the weapon and released the arrow. The grunt that followed was a sign that it had hit home. Panthea's heart stopped for a moment. Ash yelped, covering her mouth.

Mart then yanked the curtain open, revealing three other enemy riders. As Arvin stepped away from his seat with his crossbow, Panthea wrapped her arm around Ash's shoulders and pressed the girl's head on her chest as she herself shut her eyes. Ash's breaths were ragged.

Angry shouts echoed in the air, accompanied by clanks and the whinnying of horses.

"I'm scared," Ash moaned in the tiniest voice.

"It's all right," said Panthea—to both herself and her friend. "We're going to be fine."

"You take the left," Mart yelled.

Panthea could close her eyes all she wanted, but she could still hear the whipping of the curtain, feel the sunlight on her face, hear the *thunk* of Arvin's crossbow.

More shouting. More fighting. Panthea no longer knew if the trembling came from Ash's body or her own, but from how cold Ash felt on her, she knew she herself was burning with heat.

Something slammed the side of the carriage, the sound reverberating in Panthea's body. Ash let out a scream, and it turned into a whimper as she clutched Panthea more tightly.

"The archer," shouted Arvin. "Get the archer."

Soon, the cries and clanks stopped. For a time, Panthea could only hear her own breathing and Ash's until she regained enough of her senses to hear the rattling of the carriage. She opened her eyes and slid out of the curled-up position she was in with her friend. When Ash's eyes opened, she screamed and jumped onto Panthea's lap, pushing her into Evian.

There was an arrowhead jutting out of the wall.

"Let me take care of that," Arvin said as he approached. He slammed the butt of his crossbow on the arrowhead and broke it off. Ash glanced around at the others. Then she slid off Panthea's lap and into her own spot.

"Is it over?" Panthea asked.

"Not even close," Mart said. "That was just the first of three."

"There's two more of this?" Ash exclaimed.

Mart winced in response. He looked at Arvin from the corner of his eyes. "We have two options now. Stop the procession and take them on, or make another maneuver like this and only stop for the third wave." He stuck his head out and made a beckoning motion. "Come here, boy."

Salem rode in. His voice had given Panthea a false impression. He was a rather small man, almost buried in his armor.

"How many casualties on our side?" Mart inquired.

"Two, sir," Salem said. "Do we send back for them?"

"We can't. I'll send for them when we're safe." Mart then reclined, giving Arvin another sideways look. "Well, my friend. Today's the day you and I took on the Queen's Inquisition."

Someone called from behind the carriage, "Contact!"

Mart's eyes went wide. "What?"

Salem looked back, but his head took a jolt, with an arrow sticking out of his neck.

Panthea went cold, and this time she screamed with Ash as Salem tumbled off his horse, pulling it out of view.

"Fuck," Mart spat as he reloaded his crossbow. "They broke formation."

He stuck his head out and called with exaggerated gestures of his arm, "Stop the carriages."

A grumble swelled from outside. It sounded like what it was. Almost an entire platoon, ready to obliterate the procession.

Mart opened the door before the carriage even came to a halt and jumped out once it did. Arvin also stood up to go, but before he got out, he regarded Panthea and her friends. "Stay in the carriage. Don't open the door no matter what happens. If they get through us and make their way here, you're done, anyway, in which case you'll have a better chance of survival if you let them take you. Do you understand?"

None found the will to answer. Ash was weeping in the corner, and Evian's eyes were as wide as they could get, his lips parted.

"I need a nod, so I know you understand," Arvin urged.

Panthea gave just that. More, she couldn't. Arvin then jumped off the carriage and slammed the door shut.

"They won't make it," Evian rasped.

Panthea rubbed Ash's shoulder and said with her most reassuring voice, "I'm sure we're going to be fine."

"I'm not a child," Ash said. "You don't have to lie to me. It's just . . . I just realized I'll never get to go on the annual pilgrimage. We're going to die here."

No. Ash didn't deserve to die here. This could not be the end. "No, we're not," Panthea said with newfound resolve. "We won't go out without a fight. Ash. If you pull the same trick you did with the bounty hunters, we can give Arvin and his friends an edge."

"Wait a minute." Ash wiped her tears, her lips twitching with a fleeting smile. "You *want* me to use my gleamstone? On the Inquisition?"

"Don't make me change my mind."

"This is a bad idea," Evian stepped in. "You heard Arvin. These are not a bunch of bounty hunters. This is serious."

Juggling with her gleamstone, Ash said, "Oh, so am I. I'm sick, and I'm tired, and I want to show these thugs a piece of my mind."

Panthea nodded. "I'll get out too, to distract them."

Before Evian could stop them, Ash opened the door and jumped off the carriage, and Panthea followed in her wake.

Outside, it was chaos. On both sides of the procession, there were clusters of people fighting, and mounted archers circled the area.

Panthea heard a whistle in the air, and an arrow pierced the wall of the carriage. When she looked to see where it had come from, the archer had already nocked another arrow and was aiming at her. Her fear resurfaced as she ran.

Further ahead, Ash bolted toward one group, holding out her gleamstone. With a visible glow, the weapons flew into the air.

"Get that witch!" one soldier bellowed.

Panthea increased her pace to reach her friend. Judging by the way her breaths rasped and her heart thumped, power-lust was moments away. *Ash. Arvin. Mart. Remember your friends.* Although this had never worked so far, Panthea desperately hoped it would.

Another arrow passed right in front of her. The archer was hunting her, and her attempt at maintaining control was failing. *Please, Annahid. I don't want to hurt my friends.*

She remembered Rassus's advice, *"Fear is a mighty tool for survival, but it can also be your greatest enemy. Sometimes, our trepidations become self-fulfilling prophecies."*

Heeding those words, Panthea stopped focusing on her memory and instead focused on her fear. *We're going to make it. We're stronger than them.*

The joy of power-lust receded. It was working.

She looked back at the archer following her, who had already loosed another arrow. Before she could register more, the arrow ripped across her left cheek with searing pain, taking her off her feet.

As she toppled on the rough ground, the voices warbled, and it got more and more difficult to know who spoke or what they said. Her mind was empty, and the only sound she could hear was of her own breathing.

She rolled and pushed on her palms to get up, but before she could, a blackhood charged at her, raising his blade to strike her down. This was real. Nothing else was.

A wave of refreshing strength swept through her, sharpening all her senses. Before the blackhood landed that blow, she willed the weapon out of his hand, his arm off his body, his insides out of him. Another attacked. *Threat.* She made the man's sword pierce through his own throat and cut all the way up, splitting his head in two. Part of his brain oozed out as he dropped.

More surrounded her, one closing in. *Threat.* She crushed his helmet onto his face. He screamed as his skin tore, blood gushing out of every slit.

She eliminated them one after the other, stabbing them with their own swords, bludgeoning them with pieces of rock. Until one of the two remaining attackers was thrown away on their own.

The other man's weapon flew out of his hand before he reached her, giving Panthea a chance to throw him at the carriage. She then spun back to face a woman approaching from behind.

"Hey," the intruder said. "It's Shen. Snap out of it."

Panthea lifted the woman up in the air from where she was. Was she a threat? She looked rather scared. Then again, so did everyone around her. But this woman had a glowing gleamstone.

Threat.

Before Panthea could eliminate her, something struck her own head, sending her falling on her face. Panthea rolled to her back and commanded the attacker's neck to turn in an impossible arc.

A paralyzing pain radiated in her head, bringing her out of her trance. As her memory returned, the name she had heard moments ago suddenly made sense.

Panthea gasped. "No, no, no, no, no."

She scrambled to her feet and frantically looked around. Dead bodies surrounded her. It took her a few seconds to locate Ash, who lay on the ground further away.

"Ash," Panthea rasped as she tried to go to her. Her legs were too weak to carry her, and she hit the dirt face-first. Blood dripped onto the ground beneath her as she crawled to her friend. "Ash," she called with what voice she had left. Her head spun, and the image in front of her became blurry. Ash's hazy figure was not moving.

Even crawling had become an ordeal. The thought of her having harmed her best friend sucked the last of her energy out. She was far from touching Ash when darkness claimed her.

17

Once I accepted I was not the savior, that I alone was no one in the story of the Wandering Queen, I sought the aid of the two people who meant the most to me. Thus, three years after my departure from our homeland, I established the Eternal Coven. Our goal was to find the truth behind the prophecy.

RUSTLES. DISTANT CHATTERING. The smell of dust. An urgent yet gentle voice. "Panthea."

The breeze brushing over the cold sweat on her forehead. The dull pain creeping into her head. She was alive.

"Panthea."

She opened her eyes to Arvin's blood-spattered face, his creased brow, and a smile that barely even touched his lips.

Her arms proved too weak when she tried to sit up, and the slightest push made her dizzy. Arvin came to her aid, pulling her up with such power she thought he'd throw her yards away. But he eased his force just at the right time.

"What happened?" she asked.

It took him a second—and a deep sigh—to talk. "Well, I realized I messed up for one. I shouldn't have argued with you about the damned potion."

Oh, no. Cowering in anticipation of what she might hear, she asked, "What did I do?"

Before she looked back to find out, he grabbed her by the temples and turned her head to himself. "Remember. Whatever you did, it wasn't your fault. You warned us about your power. We didn't listen."

Panthea's lungs locked her out. "Please tell me."

He bit his lip. "You killed everyone. Friend and foe."

A chill ran through her. The beginning of a sob exploded from her throat, which was cut short by the searing in her cheek and the twisting headache that made even breathing impossible.

She squeezed her eyes closed until the pain let go. Then she took a few sharp breaths before she could utter, "Ash? Evian?"

"Evian stayed in the carriage, so he was safe. I pulled Mart away from you as soon as I noticed you were out of control. Ash tried to save you. You attacked her."

Panthea wished those visions had been just power-lust delirium. She covered her face, and this time, even the pain could not stop the flow of tears. Under her fingers she felt the roughness of the deep cut the arrow had left, and the sutures that held her skin together and tugged at every wrong movement of her facial muscles.

"Don't worry," Arvin said. "She's fine. One of our men went to separate you. He became your target instead."

"I'm a monster," she wheezed. She extended her hand and motioned to him to help her up. "I need to talk to Ash."

"I don't think it's a good idea," said Arvin.

"I . . . don't think I care what you think."

After another moment of hesitation, he relented and complied.

When she turned to see her work, her head grew lighter than it had been, and she almost collapsed again. There was no part of the ground that wasn't covered in blood or body parts.

Arvin took her to where Ash sat on a rock, clutching her knees. There was a cut on her forehead and a bruise on the right side of her face. She did not even notice Panthea. Her eyes stared forward, no animation in them. Panthea crouched in front of her friend to try to meet her gaze, but she looked through Panthea and far behind her.

"Ash, I'm so sorry." She took her friend's icy hand, kissed it, and squeezed it between both of hers. "I never meant to hurt you."

Nothing.

From the corner of her eyes, Panthea noticed Ash's gleamstone on the dry ground beside her feet. Forcing a smile, she picked it up, put it in Ash's hand, and wrapped the girl's fingers around it. "It's over. We all survived. We're going to go back, save Master. Everything will return to how it used to be."

As soon as she let go, Ash's hand opened, dropping the gleamstone. Ash didn't try to pick it up. Didn't even look at it. Panthea got up and left her side as her composure dissolved. Although she tried not to cry, she couldn't keep her face from contorting, the pressure painfully pulling the skin around the sutures.

"Panthea, wait," Evian said as he ran after her.

She knew a reproof was in the works. "I don't want to hear it."

"You don't even know what I want to say."

"Oh, but I do. You want to say you were right. That I'm impetuous, I'm selfish, and this quest is doomed to fail. Guess what? I know all of that already. So, just leave me alone."

The headache struck again, and she pressed her shaking hands on her temples as she waited it out. This gave Evian time to catch up with her and stop her by the arm.

"No." He took a glance back at Arvin before he whispered, "I wanted to say I don't have a good feeling about this. We don't know what those guys really want. And up to now, they've brought us nothing but trouble. What if they want the stone for themselves? What if they work for the queen?"

"They don't work ..." She stopped herself before saying something harsh, like how ridiculous that idea was. "So what? After all of this, should

I just give up? Forget Master?"

"That's not what I mean. Please hear me out. We have the stone. We don't need them. I can take it back and exchange it for Master. I'll tell everyone you died here. Once Ash is home safe, once Master is free, you and I can go somewhere no one can find us."

She looked into his glistening eyes. Nothing was left of the strong Evian she knew. He fidgeted with his hands while he waited for a response.

"And what happened to protecting the stone?" she asked.

He shook his head. "I've been the good kid my entire life, and it's high time I did something that feels right to myself."

This was awful. He was stepping on his own principles for her. "I can't ask you to go against what you stand for." She glanced at Arvin. "Besides, they won't let you exchange the stone."

"And you think it's fair? They're bullying you into bending to their will."

Her only comfort so far had been that at least Arvin and Evian wanted the same thing for the stone; that she had found a way to save Rassus without giving it up. But now, Evian was taking that away from her. "They're not wrong," she said. "Master had a reason for wanting to keep the stone safe. You were the one who told me that."

"Master has a reason for everything he does. But it doesn't mean he's right. Let me be honest. If I didn't want you to go on this quest, it wasn't so much about respecting his wishes as it was about protecting you. Even before we left Saba, I told Master to give up the stone so many times. That it wasn't worth our lives. Now, look where we are because . . ." His last word died in his throat. His chin quivering, he took a ragged breath. "Sorry. I don't mean to . . . I, uh . . . I respect your choice, whatever it is."

He left in a rush. Panthea called him with her weakened voice, but even if he heard her at all, he didn't respond.

A failure. A complete failure was what she was. Her friends were falling apart, the Inquisition still had Rassus, and she had no grip on her power no matter how hard she tried.

She sat down, facing the massacre, an empty feeling settling in the pit of her stomach. It wasn't fear. It wasn't exactly guilt, either. It was grief. A life of worship, a life of good deeds, torn into pieces before her. How she needed to speak to Annahid, to ask for her forgiveness, for strength. But she couldn't find the audacity. It was like asking Rassus for a history lesson after conducting an arcane show in the main square.

Part of her wanted to turn away, to spare herself the torment. But that part of her was the innocent Panthea of the Upper City and not worth listening to. This Panthea would stay silent, amid dark blood and disfigured corpses, to remind herself of what she had become. She would repress her tears until her heart gave out. She had already crossed the line into darkness, and it was time for her to accept her new reality. Panthea, the Erkenblood of Saba, the murderer.

Arvin sat next to her on the rough ground. "You need to cry."

Oh, how she did. "I don't deserve it," she said through the suffocating lump in her throat.

"I understand your despair. But as someone who's been where you are multiple times, I can tell you punishing yourself won't make it easier. The only way to survive pain like this is to mourn your past, learn from it"— he took her hand and put a vial of sapping potion in it—"and move on."

She stared at the vial. "I've lost count of people I've killed. Each of them had a story. Each of them had a family that is now destroyed. And to me, they're all just one inaccurate number. How can you have possibly been where I am?"

Arvin remained pensive for a few moments, which gave Panthea enough time to drink the potion.

"You're right," he finally said. "I wouldn't know what it's like to be in your shoes. To be so kind, so compassionate, to blame yourself for crimes you didn't even commit. There's something inside you; a demon that thirsts for blood. She isn't you. In fact, you're the victim she likes to kill slowly—to make suffer by letting you watch her work."

Panthea's attempt at suppressing her sob was failing. More tears ran down her face, but she scrubbed them off, gulping. He had just described how she felt every day. And while his perception was comforting, it was a painful reminder of the ugly truth.

"You want a monster?" Arvin went on. "I've killed twice, maybe three times as many people as you have. I stood there as my friends killed an entire family in the rebellion's name." He paused, and although she didn't have the will to look, she could feel the weight of that last statement. Even his voice was crushed to a bare whisper as he finally spoke again. "You're not a monster."

She took a ragged breath to try to ease her ever-growing headache. It didn't matter what part of her was the monster. She had allowed it to grow out of her control. She had let her fear impede her better judgment. *This has gone far enough.* "The demon will not see the light of day again." She met Arvin's gaze. "Do you have more nightmare potion?"

PART II

MONSTERS

18

A prophecy is a reality foretold if one does not think of time as a barrier, but an element. It is not paranormal as it is within the fundamental rules of the arcane: it is elemental as it involves time, and it is exclusive as it does not directly affect space or matter.

HILIA GASPED AS SHE WOKE. Her sleep had been agitated throughout the night, but this time, it had been something different. In her dream, she'd seen a girl sprawled below the residence building. Curdled blood had covered her face and glued strands of her black hair together.

She sat up, rubbing her eyes. Dreams were rare for her. So much so that her father used to make a point of interpreting her every dream when she was younger. The man was more religious than the typical winehouse owner. He knew all there was to know about the symbolism of the pantheon. If Hilia saw a river, it meant a message from Panthea asking her to mull over a decision. If she saw flowers, it was Varina telling her to consider a prospective man. *What about a dead kid? Interpret this, dad.*

It took her some minutes to shake that nightmare. Then she remembered what day it was. Thirty-second of Hitian. Cleaning day. She expelled air from the corner of her mouth in exasperation, blowing the curly strand of hair that had blocked her vision, then forced herself to get out of bed and go about getting ready.

Once she tamed the mass of her hair and collected it into the usual bundle above her head, it took her an hour to prepare the chambers, serve the queen's breakfast, and see her off. From there, her day took a sharp turn toward madness as a mob of clueless servants and soldiers stormed the chambers. An hour of managing this horde, and she was already drained.

"No, that doesn't belong there," Hilia called as she darted to a maid who was taking the effigy of Annahid to the bedroom. Hilia snatched it from the woman and took it back to the fireplace.

On the far side of the room, a soldier was bullying another maid. Rolling her eyes, Hilia slammed the effigy on the mantelpiece, then marched to the pair. "What under Diva are you doing?"

The soldier smirked. "She was shirking her duties."

The maid turned to Hilia and said with a pleading tone, "I wasn't. I was just—"

Hilia held up a hand at the maid while she kept her glare at the soldier. "Does she work for you? Do you pay her wage?"

"No, but I'm—"

"You're here to ensure no one plants anything dangerous here. And while I was in the other room, you were harassing this girl instead of keeping watch. The sitting room is now a death trap for all I know, so why don't you leave this one alone and go inspect this entire room for anything suspicious?"

"Whatever you say, *lady*." He gave a demeaning shake of his head as he left, that irritating smirk not leaving his big mouth.

"And something else." She grabbed his arm. There was a limit to how far one could take it with these brutes, and Hilia would damned sure take it there for this one. "If you cause any unnecessary work for these people, you and I will have a problem. And if I have a problem with you, the queen has a problem with you. Is that clear, big boy?"

That finally wiped the smirk off his face. He yanked his arm free and left. Her heart beat uncomfortably fast. *One way or another, this job is going to kill me.*

The maid took both Hilia's hands. "Thank you. He was making it so hard. This job is—"

"Just get back to work," Hilia said. "I might not look it, but I'm busier than all of you right now."

Across the room by the door to the study, somebody was stepping out the window.

"Hey," Hilia called out as she ran to the servant, and a soldier joined the chase midway.

With all her strength, she pulled the transgressor in and sent him off-balance. The soldier grabbed under his arms, looking at her for direction. "Should we arrest him?"

Hilia considered the man. With that fear plastered on his face, he looked nothing like an assassin or a dissident, just someone who didn't know how things worked around here. *Ahura's throne.* "No. He was trying to clean the windowsill. I got scared he might fall. It's all good. You can go back to your post."

The soldier nodded and left. When the servant tried to leave, Hilia stopped him by the wrist. "Uh-uh, not you. I'll have a word with you."

The man turned to her with barely any color on his face. "Forgive me, my lady. This is my first day. I didn't know I wasn't supposed to."

"I bet it's that soldier's first day too. Otherwise, he wouldn't have asked for my permission to bust your sorry self. Window-hopping can get you in serious trouble. They could charge you with treason if they wanted to. Keeping yourself alive can be tough in this palace, but you can do better than this. All right, on you go. And stay inside the walls for me, will you?"

The servant went on his way. She wiped the beads of sweat that had formed on her forehead and took a deep breath as she scanned the room. Nothing else was going wrong for now.

That was until the Handler entered the room. *Is everyone a damned child today?*

She rushed to him, not returning the smile he gave her on her approach.

"What are you doing here?" she muttered.

"You haven't been showing up at the library."

"Did it cross your mind that I might have had a reason? And that reason sure wasn't for you to come all the way up here. Now, leave before you get us both in trouble."

"You need to check in," he said firmly. "That was our deal, and this is the only way this works. If you find anything out, I need to know. If you're caught, I need to know. Because my job is cleaning up people's messes. Understand?"

"I clean up my own mess," she said. "Here's how it works for me. You go to the library every day. If I have news, you'll see me."

"You don't call the shots here. I'm your handler—and the man who can decide whether you're a burned piece."

"Are you threatening me?"

"Informing." He eyed the soldiers around the room. "How's your little research going? Have you found any proof?"

"Not yet."

"Then get busy because your time is running out. Next time we meet, I expect more than your pretty face."

She was torn between two responses. The one she preferred was punching him in the nose. But that would expose them both. So, she went with the more generous response. "Do me a favor. If your goal is to bury me, let me know so I can get my affairs in order."

He just stared at her for a few moments, then said with infuriating calm, "Incredible. Do you think I have nothing better to do than plotting against you? Sorry to break it to you, but I don't give two shits about you or your insecurities. All I want is to keep us from falling on our asses. And should I remind you we planned an operation in your name? That not enough? I'm not responsible for your incompetence."

Before she could devise a comeback, a guard came forth, eyes trained on Handler. "Is this man bothering you, ma'am? Should I kick him out?"

Hilia turned to the soldier, dumping her frustration on the

unsuspecting man. "Do I look like I can't take care of myself?" She pushed Handler away. "He was leaving."

Handler's lips curved into a smug smile as he acquiesced and walked out, which worked to de-escalate the situation.

Hilia waited for the soldier to move along before she ran after Handler and stopped him by the shoulder. "Don't you ever throw that operation in my face again. The whole point was to find out if you-know-who could die without you-know-what. And we didn't even give her a scratch. You want to talk about my incompetence? Plan a successful operation first so I have something to work with, then we'll talk."

Handler let out a deep exhale. Then he gave a single nod and left, muttering under his breath. How did this man manage to suck out every bit of her energy every time he showed up? It was moments like this when she missed Mehran the most. She wished she could live in an alternate version of this where they had not gone through with that assassination attempt. A version where Mehran was free, and Hilia had him to answer to, and not this unnamed handler.

A smashing sound came from behind, and she spun to see the pieces of a vase spread on the floor. As she stomped to the culprit, she roared, "You! Get out. You're doing more harm than good. Guard. Take this one out of here."

THE DAY WAS OVER. The servants' incompetence, Handler's threats, the soldiers' bullying. Now it was Hilia and the solitude the chapel provided. She didn't exactly pray like Kadder had taught her to. It was the quiet that soothed her chaotic mind. *I'm going to get through this.* "You'll help me, won't you, oh Great Annahid?"

Kadder came and sat beside her as usual. *Are you joking?* He chose the worst moments to show up. They seemed to have become prayer mates — if that meant anything. What would the Lord of Bad News even pray for? A bloodier day tomorrow? More prisoners? Or maybe finally catching the prey who sat next to him.

"Your prayers are always entertaining," Kadder said.

If she played into his conversation, this would soon turn into another subtle interrogation. So, she put on her most charming smile and met his gaze. "Can I make a confession?"

"A confession?" Kadder gave a dark chortle. "This is the easiest confession I'll get in some time."

Was he really comparing her to his unfortunate prisoners, whom he tortured and maimed? Did the word 'confession' only make sense to him in that narrow context? Or had this been an interview after all? Better assume the latter than be caught off-guard.

She offered a congenial laughter and only spoke once she knew he had nothing else to add. "Before I met you here the first time, I never pegged you as a religious man."

Although he seemed to be thrown off a little, he kept his good humor. "Why? Are we Inquisitors not allowed to worship?"

"No, sorry, I didn't mean that. It's—"

He held up his hand. "I know what you meant. You're wondering how I can break bones during the day and pray at night."

"Let me try this again," Hilia said. "I've been enjoying our conversations in here, and I can't imagine how someone like you could muster so much hatred in an interrogation room."

Kadder nodded with a smile. "This is what I admire about you, Hilia. Your courage. Most people would be too timid to even utter the words you just did."

I should learn to be more like them.

His expression sobered, and he averted his eyes. "This monster once had a family." He eyeballed her, assessing her reaction to that statement, but she would not reveal her surprise this time. "My wife passed away giving birth to my son, and I had to raise him on my own. The day he joined the army was the proudest day of my life."

"Where is he now?" she asked.

"Dead." The word came out crude and bitter.

She bit her lip. "Oh, I'm sorry."

The old man nodded, his features tense. "He was transferred to Livid to serve. He married there and gave me the most precious little grandson. I only got to meet the little boy once."

Livid. A Sapphire soldier. The son of an Inquisitor. A grandson. An uneasy feeling took hold of her. This was too similar to that mission four years ago.

"On a cursed Bright Fusion day, word comes from Livid that my son is dead. Those godless rebels had butchered him, butchered his wife, and even my two-year-old grandson. They left a note too: 'Guilty, by association.'"

Bright Fusion. A sickening chill coursed through Hilia's body. That was a few days after Arvin's party had killed that family. This was the last nail through her chest. The complete, undeniable proof that she was sitting here, looking at the person whose life she and her friends had destroyed. Her head felt light as Arvin's voice bounced inside it. "I'm not any happier than you are about this."

"I still fail to fathom." Kadder's words opened her old wounds. "How could a two-year-old be guilty of anything? Where else did he have to go other than the embrace of his mother? What clue did he have of the damned conflict? They could have spared him." He took an uneven breath, his lips twitching. "Yes. They could have spared him."

Nausea pressed under Hilia's throat. She wanted to show him her sympathy, but she couldn't be that hypocritical.

"Now, whenever I see one of those animals in my interrogation room, I picture a two-year-old boy in a pool of his own blood. People who created that image are beyond redemption. Every moment they live"—his dark eyes turned to her, the fiery look in them almost making her flinch—"they strengthen the spirit of Angra." He paused, moistening his lips. "As a man of faith, it's my destiny to end such darkness. That's how I do it."

If Kadder knew about Hilia's involvement in that event, he'd want to cut her throat right there, and she didn't blame him.

With the dizziness and her wrenching stomach, she could no longer stay in this place. She needed air. "I, uh, h-have to get back. The queen might need me."

She shot up and rushed out of the chapel before Kadder even responded, and she didn't make it far past the exit as bile came up her throat. She made her way to the side of the passageway and spewed on the dirt. *Girl, why do you always have to open your big mouth if you don't have the stomach to hear the truth?*

Breathing in the fresh air, she cleaned her mouth with the back of her hand. This was one of the many things she had to forget if she wanted to keep her sanity.

19

Book of Creation, fifth Visage, thirty-seventh verse. "The master of all elements shall find the Wandering Queen and show her the path."

THROUGH THE GAP between the curtain and the edge of the window, Panthea's gaze was lost on the imposing Golden Gate as they rode toward it. Ever since the incident, the spirit of the group had changed. Ash barely spoke or even reacted to humor. Something had broken in her, and Panthea wished she could help put her pieces back together. But the girl had shut her out completely.

Evian was more approachable, but Panthea could tell he was not too happy. All that came out of him were one-word responses to what everyone else said, constant reminders to Panthea to stop playing with her sutures, and the occasional attempt to convince Arvin and Mart to turn back.

As for Panthea herself, she had taken so much nightmare potion she was trapped in a tug-of-war between anxiety and fatigue. The potion no longer worked, either. Even moments after waking up from the nightmares, she felt the pull of power-lust when she tried to wield.

"Here we go," Mart's voice sliced through the silence.

The sound of wheels and hooves reverberated all around them as they entered through the gate, and it wasn't long before someone called from outside, "Halt."

Mart winked at Arvin as he descended from the carriage, to which he responded with a single nod.

Once Mart was gone, Arvin turned to Panthea and her friends and whispered, "Don't worry. This is normal procedure. Mart just has to provide his identity and state his business in the city."

Panthea gave a tight smile, and only because no one else even acknowledged Arvin.

After a while, Mart climbed back in. "Everyone's on edge around here. Fucks wanted to check inside the cabin."

"But everything is good, right?" Arvin asked, clearly on Panthea's behalf, as she was the one his eyes shifted to upon the end of that sentence.

"Yep." Mart clapped the wall behind him to signal the driver to move. "No one's inspecting my carriage."

As they rode through the main square, a strange feeling overcame Panthea. She did not feel like she belonged here anymore. Not that she was scared like Evian. She just felt detached from the city where she'd grown up.

The carriage entered the Old City and stopped in front of what Mart proclaimed as the safehouse. He was the first to get out.

Panthea eyeballed Ash, who rolled her eyes as soon as she noticed. "I'm fine."

Trying to elicit some of Ash's old humor, Panthea said, "And here I thought I was the terrible liar. You know you're not alone, don't you? You can talk to me."

"I said I'm fine. Now, drop it."

Panthea ignored the tendrils of despair creeping into her heart and went to pull her friend closer when Arvin put a hand on her shoulder. "We should get out."

Torn, Panthea followed Arvin off the carriage.

He took her out of earshot and looked back to make sure no one was listening before he said, "Ash needs some space. If you keep pushing her right now, you'll only hurt yourself and drive her away."

"It's been four days," Panthea said. "At some point, she has to talk. I'm her friend."

Arvin sighed. "Listen. Your friendship might be a little strained after what happened. You've got to be patient."

"Maybe you're right. I wonder if I even deserve to have friends."

Arvin's features drooped. "Don't say that."

Panthea pointed toward the carriage. "Did you see her, Arvin? I did this. I ruined my friend because I didn't take care of my power. Can you blame her for hating me now?"

"So, this is what you think it is," came Ash's voice from behind.

Startled, Panthea wheeled back to see the girl standing there. She had made no sound on her approach.

"You think I hate you?" Ash continued. "You think this is about you? Did it ever occur to you that maybe I'm just disappointed in myself? I pushed you to use your power. I thought I had control over your power-lust. I thought I could get us out of that situation. I thought I could amount to something. But guess what? I was wrong. Turns out, I'm the same impetuous girl everyone takes me for, who always makes things worse. There. I talked. Now, leave me alone for the rest of the night because I can't take your self-loathing anymore. I have enough of it to deal with myself."

Panthea could not decide which was more disturbing. The closed-off Ash, or the self-blaming one. "It wasn't your fault," she began, but Ash left before the first word came out.

"Panthea," Arvin whispered. When she looked at him, he shook his head in a reassuring way. "She'll come around."

Trying to fight her emotions, she only nodded. Arvin gave her arm a gentle rub before he joined Mart in unloading.

Within the hour, they were inside, around the warm hearth. Mart came from the pantry, holding a decanter. "Look what I found." With a dramatic gesture of his arms, he said, "Let's drink our problems away." His gaze turned to Panthea. "Dazzle-eyes, you're drinking with us."

Panthea frowned. "Is that searing gulp?"

"Mm-hmm." Mart held up the decanter. "The finest in the Southern Kingdom. We're going to get fucked up."

"I don't like searing gulp," she said. "Do you have anything else?"

"Nope."

Ash cleared her throat. "I'll try some."

Pleased with the request, Mart went to the far side of the room and brought back a few cups, filling one with the liquor and handing it to Ash. Even as Ash drank, Panthea winced.

As expected, the girl spat the entire thing out and began coughing. "Ugh, that's disgusting! Tastes like feet."

Mart snatched the cup from the girl. "Pfft. You two don't know what you're talking about. You don't drink searing gulp for the taste. You drink it for the kick. If you want taste, drink pressed fruit. And not in my safehouse."

"My friend, everyone," Arvin said with a grin, gesturing toward Mart with his palm. "The paragon of hospitality."

"Fuck off," Mart said. "At least I don't tie my guests to a chair."

Panthea couldn't help a chuckle, and when she looked at Ash and found her smiling too, her heart melted. It was not a gleeful smile, but it was the first time since the incident. The sight was like cold water on Panthea's fire. She almost wanted to hug Mart for making her friend smile.

Arvin sighed. "The chair thing is never going away, is it?"

"No," Panthea joined the humor. "Never."

"You sure you want to drink, Mart?" Arvin said. "These three haven't seen you drunk, and I'm not sure they'll like it."

"Oh, they'll love me. Ask Cousin when you see him next time."

And so, the night began. They talked, gossiped, played Arvin's silly drinking games. Panthea learned more about Arvin's friend Hilia and Mart's cousin Gvosh. Turned out, Gvosh was not his cousin at all, and that nickname was just an inside joke. Gvosh was originally from Toofan but was adopted and raised by deevs, who lived east of the Sessaran plateau. That explained his Seshek name. Mart also had an explanation for his size. "Whatever those deevs fed him there made him the giant he is."

That last one, Panthea took with a grain of salt, especially since Mart was quite drunk by then.

Once the conversation between Mart and Arvin devolved into meaningless banter, Panthea excused herself and went to the backyard, leaning against the wall, looking up at the Erken constellation. She was a little tipsy, but she had made sure not to drink that much while playing. After all, the last time she had, she had regretted it.

A short while later, Ash's voice joined the quiet of the outside as she exited the house as well. "Can I join you?"

It was the easiest question to answer. "Of course."

The young wielder sat next to her. "What are you looking at?"

"Nothing." Panthea met her friend's gaze. "How do you feel?"

"Eh." Ash shrugged. "A little tipsy."

"You don't want to go back to the party?"

"No, I'm bored. I prefer to stay here with you."

Panthea raised an eyebrow and said playfully, "Despite my self-loathing?"

"Shut up." Ash gave her a gentle shoulder-bump. "Even if you're a self-deprecating slug, you're still my best friend. I'm sorry for earlier."

"Don't be."

Panthea wrapped her arm around Ash, who scooted in and leaned her head on her shoulder. As unsettling as tomorrow's meeting with the Windhammer was, Panthea tried to focus on the moment. She closed her eyes and drank in the safety of Ash's embrace. And she knew from her friend's slow breathing that she felt just as safe.

"You two want company?" came from the door. It was Evian, which made Panthea realize she had not spoken to him all evening.

Come to think of it, he had not even participated in the games and most of the conversations, but she had been too concerned with herself and Ash to notice it.

"Are you all right?" she asked, perhaps a little too late.

"Yeah," he said with a warm smile, which she reflected.

Ash tapped the spot next to herself to ask him to sit. And so for the first time in a long time, it was just the three of them again.

"What will you do when this is all over?" Ash asked.

"I don't know," Panthea said. "It's unlikely Sapphires will stop looking for me. When we save Master, I'll probably leave to somewhere safe with Evian."

She extended her hand toward him, over Ash's legs, and he held it. Tension wavered in his warm fingers. She squeezed firmly, complementing it with a reassuring blink.

"Um." Ash put her hand over both of theirs. "Do you dopes have room for one more?"

Panthea renewed her smile. "Of course. But what about your parents?"

"They'll be fine. I'm fifteen. I can't live with them forever. So . . ." She glanced between Panthea and Evian, wincing. "Can I?"

Panthea put her free hand over Ash's. "I'd love that."

20

The Book of Creation is more than a compilation of lessons on morality. Many of its claims have been proven, many of its predictions realized, some within my lifetime. The Prophet foretells the future in the book, albeit with a level of ambiguity that preserves the illusion that is free will.

T HE NEXT MORNING, they woke up around noon. After lunch, Evian disinfected Panthea's arrow wound and patched it up again before he took off with Ash. The plan was for him to stay with Ash's family for the rest of the day until they found a more permanent lodging for him. Mart went about his business in the afternoon, and Panthea and Arvin went to meet with the Windhammer.

"So, how many Sapphires are with the rebellion?" she asked on the way. "Because so far, I haven't met even one who was not a Sapphire."

Arvin chuckled. "We have people on the outside too. But you're right. Most of our agents are infiltrators. It's the reason the Windhammer has been able to keep this up for so many years."

They arrived in front of Governor House, where four sentries guarded the giant gate. Panthea stopped. "What are we doing here?"

"Just act casual. This is where we're seeing the Windhammer."

She searched Arvin's eyes for a telltale sign of a joke. The smile was there, but it was the kind he put on when he revealed something surprising. "But is it safe?"

"Safer than you'd think," he said as he ushered her forward.

The sentries shared nods with Arvin as they opened the gate. Beyond was a pathway edged by half-dead, spindly trees on a bed of grass that was beaten up by the scorching light of Hita and severe lack of precipitation.

Neither she nor Arvin said anything on the way to the two-story building at the end of the path. She was too nervous, and Arvin was too busy sharing nods and salutes with the soldiers they passed by. He did smile at her now and then, but even that became less effective as they went inside and ascended the stairway to the second floor.

Upstairs, there was an arched door watched by two Sapphires. Fortunately, Arvin's arrival softened their otherwise grim expressions, and they let them through.

Panthea's stomach was almost turning from anxiety.

The inside walls of the room were covered in red velvet and edged by intricate patterns made of gold. The carpets on the stone floor were the kind she'd only heard about. She took a sweeping look at the Sapphire soldiers spread around the place. This would be her living nightmare a thretnight ago.

But then an even greater nightmare revealed itself. General Heim sat there on the floor with a few other politicians in a circle. She could not mistake that face, that braided beard. Although he had let her go in their last encounter, it didn't change who he was. The man who had killed the Erkenblood of Livid.

Before she could voice her concern to Arvin, the general saw her. There was no escape now. His eyes widened in an expression Panthea failed to process, and they turned to Arvin as he gave a subtle gesture with his arm before he returned his attention to his audience.

"Hey," Arvin whispered, putting a gentle hand on her shoulder. "We need to wait outside."

Still processing the situation—or rather figuring out a way out of it—she complied. Once they were out of the room, Arvin took her to a safe distance from the soldiers and said, "Sorry. Those politicians are not friendly. He didn't want them to see you here."

"He?" Panthea couldn't control the high pitch of her voice as it came out. She cleared her throat and whispered, "You've brought me to the Erkenblood-slayer. I've dreaded that man since I was thirteen."

"I know how it looks. But there's something you should—"

"Are you planning to turn me in? Was this your whole—"

"General Heim is the Windhammer," he said with his lowest voice, and the words alone were enough to empty her mind.

"W-what?" was all she could utter. Her wide eyes had to do the rest of the talking.

Arvin gave a brief smile, which he swallowed when she did not return it. "This resistance started eleven years ago by a group of separatists from Livid, fueled by the mistreatment Ahuraics received after the Great Reform. Many folks think of Vetrieca as the person who incited the last rebellion. In reality, she was one of the few. Another member of that group was Admiral Heim of the Third Garrison in Livid."

"I don't understand. Admiral Heim was the man who killed Vetrieca."

"Also correct," Arvin admitted. "Heim and Vetrieca were friends before they were comrades. Upon starting the resistance, they had two different strategies in mind. Heim wanted to infiltrate the ranks of the local army and weaken it before taking back Shiran through a coup. But his voice wasn't heard. Vetrieca convinced the other members that the Sapphire Order was already weak, and she amassed an army of commoners."

"Which was enough to conquer Livid," Panthea argued.

"Just about. She couldn't hold on to Livid for long. Soon after the takeover, Sapphires put Livid under siege. Twenty days into that, when people's loyalties began to shake, the other high-ranking members of the rebellion convened, and they made their toughest decision yet.

"It was unanimous. Admiral Heim was to lead an incursion and kill

Vetrieca. This would sate the aggravated Sapphire army. It would also give Heim the esteem he needed to get higher in the food chain and execute the strategy he'd tried to push for years."

Panthea could not believe what she was hearing. She evidently knew so little about contemporary history, and what she was learning now made her sick. "So, Admiral Heim killed his own friend? I'd never be able to do such a thing, no matter how important."

"Neither would most people I know. It takes a special person to suspend their feelings, their humanity, for the greater good. And whether we like it or not, that's exactly the kind of person we need to lead the opposition. Windhammer plays by the Order's rules, and those are the only rules that apply."

This had to be a joke. For so long, she had seen Heim as the man who had snuffed out the last sliver of hope. Now, she was supposed to consider him a friend of the people? The famous Windhammer, no less. "So, that's why he let me go the last time I met him."

Arvin smiled, which did not quite reach his eyes. "And a lot more will make sense to you once you talk to him."

Before she could even nod, Arvin grabbed her by the shoulders in a quick sweep and spun her against the wall, edging closer. She felt a rush at the unexpected move, but when she saw the group of people passing behind Arvin, she knew why he had done it.

"Sorry," he mouthed. Once the politicians left the floor, he looked toward the arched door and said, "Let's go."

They entered the room again, Panthea walking close to Arvin, using him to break the soldiers' line of sight where she could. Until the Erkenblood-slayer approached to greet them himself.

"Arvin, my boy," he said with a good-humored smile before his eyes dropped to Panthea. "And you. You're a difficult young woman to get a hold of." That last statement made her wonder whether—and why—he had been expecting her.

"I heard about what happened in Delavaran," Arvin said solemnly.

The old man's smile dimmed. "So, you heard how Hilia wasted our resources. She's becoming a liability."

Arvin's features tensed. This was the same friend whose mention always seemed to evoke a keen concern in him.

"But let's talk about that later," the old man said. "We're in company."

Arvin sighed and stepped out of the way. "Panthea, meet the man himself."

The general locked his hands behind him as he strutted to her, his discerning eyes making her feel exposed. "Panthea." He paused, as if tasting the word. "The young woman who's rattled the Sapphire army. Did I not ask you to stay out of trouble?"

Panthea, who had no answer to that, just gave a courteous smile.

"Do you know why you're here?" the Windhammer asked.

Up until now, she thought she did. She had come here to ask him to save Rassus. But that was something only she and Arvin had discussed.

Windhammer frowned. "Arvin hasn't told you, has he?"

Confused, Panthea gave Arvin a tentative glance. "Told me what?"

Arvin opened his mouth when the old man raised a hand. "I can explain." He kept that rigid stare for a little longer before his features softened. "The night we met, I was in the Old City to gather intelligence for an important operation. And the moment I saw your glimmering green eyes, it all came together. There and then, I knew two things."

Enumerating with his fingers, he continued, "One. You suffered from power-lust, so you needed treatment. And two. You could be the missing piece in reclaiming Shiran. So, I appointed Arvin to approach you the next day. Alas, things didn't go as planned. But now, here you are." Then he said what she had been dreading. "If you join us, we'll take back what belongs to our people."

There it was. It had not been an accident that Arvin had brought her here. Although he had promised she did not have to join the rebellion, Panthea was no longer sure how reliable that promise was.

"I'm not a hero," she said, trying to refuse that proposition without confrontation.

Windhammer swatted the air. "I hate heroes. Heroes are for tales we tell our children. The only thing real-life heroes ever achieve is to die. I believe you have heard of the Erkenblood of Livid. Have you wondered why her rebellion failed?"

You killed her. That was the correct answer. But there seemed to be something Panthea didn't fathom, and everyone in the rebellion did. This perverted notion of greater good used by Arvin to justify torturing and starving her for days and by Windhammer to make the murder of his own friend palatable.

"She underestimated the enemy," Windhammer answered his own question. "She thought a group of commoners could defeat the Sapphire Order. We, on the other hand, are destroying it from inside. We have infiltrators within ranks of the army, and we're about to take over the Inquisition too."

"And what does this have to do with me?" she asked.

The man chortled. "Everything. You're a Shiranian before everything else. This region has been trampled by kings and queens who didn't have the first clue about our faith, our culture. For centuries, our people had accepted their occupation. And then, with Queen Artenus in power, they found their motive to fight back. With Vetrieca's rebellion, they found the courage. With my leadership, they found the means. And with your help, Panthea, Shiran can once again become an independent nation.

"I have already arranged the cards so one of my trustees becomes the chief Inquisitor in Saba after Inquisitor Yoltan, and thus the city will be ours without the queen even noticing. But for that to happen, Yoltan must die."

She took a ragged breath as she understood. "You want me to kill the Inquisitor." Her mind went back to every event throughout this journey, seeing them in a new light. "And the nightmare potion was just to make me a more efficient killer."

"The nightmare potion helps you focus your power. It also makes you immune to sapping potion for a few hours after each intake. The plan was for you to be captured by the Inquisition and then kill the Inquisitor inside the bureau." He paused, assessing her. "They'd try to sap you before taking you in, but with the nightmare potion in your system, that wouldn't work."

Panthea looked at Arvin. "Is that true?"

"Yeah." Arvin wore that stupid smile, probably expecting her to be positively surprised. But her glare was enough to snuff out that smile. "You were on two doses of sapping potion when you knocked me out in Watertown."

The thought was chilling. Sapping potion was the most certain way to keep her power dormant. To think that Arvin had, even for a short time, rendered it ineffective without her consent, to think that such a thing was even possible, was terrifying.

And to think that he would do this to her for a mission.

"Evian was right," she mumbled. "You don't care about me. I was just a weapon to you. And I played right into your game."

"Don't say that," Arvin said. "You hate the Sapphires as much as we do. And now, you can make a difference. Think about all the lives the queen has ruined. Think about your mother."

"Don't bring my mother into this. This is not about her. This is about you and your mission. After all those nightmares you put me through, you've brought me here to willingly kill another human."

"Excuse me?" Windhammer scoffed. "Am I hearing this right? Is the ferocious Erkenblood of Saba hesitant to take one life?"

Panthea's face was on fire. Her palms were warm and sweaty. She had been trying to forget those deaths, to convince herself that they had not been her fault. But now, she knew those murders would forever be in her name in people's eyes.

"Sir," Arvin stepped in, "allow me." He then turned to her, his brow creasing. "I know this isn't fair. It's killing me to have to ask you to do this, but we all have to make sacrif—"

"Stop lying," she snapped. "Stop pretending you care about my feelings. This was always about my power. You people found an Erkenblood, and you thought she'd be a perfect addition to your arsenal. That's all I am to you."

"Let's not get too bitter." Windhammer raised his hands. "Child, I'm not any happier than you are that things turned out this way. I'm not asking you to fall in love with how we work. I'm asking you what I ask of everyone else who joins the cause. Let's put our differences aside and work together toward our shared goal."

Caught in the quicksand of a dozen pairs of expectant eyes, Panthea had nothing any of those people wanted to hear.

Steeling herself enough to glower at the disappointment that was the great Windhammer, she said, "I'm not a killer." Then she regarded Arvin for the next painful words. "There was a time when I thought you knew that."

She marched toward the exit when two soldiers blocked her way with crossed spears.

"Not so fast," Windhammer yelled like a father would at his unruly child. "Little girl, I've spent too many resources to get you here, and I'm not letting you prance out in a juvenile tantrum. What do you think will happen to you once you leave? You won't last a day out there on your own."

Trying not to break like the child he took her for, she turned back. "Well, I don't see any other choice. The Inquisition has my guardian. Arvin told me you could help me free him. But now that I know what you want with me, I'll have to figure it out myself."

In truth, there was nothing to figure out. Without Arvin's help, trading the pendant was her only option.

She set to leave again, but this time, to her consternation, it was Arvin who commanded, "Seize her."

The soldiers grabbed Panthea. She gaped at Arvin, no longer sure whom she was looking at. Had he really called for her arrest? His eyes were shut, and he was pinching the bridge of his nose. He was trying so hard to avoid her gaze, but she made a point of staring directly at him for as long as it took.

"Panthea." Arvin's words contorted his face as they trickled out of his mouth. "I know what you want to do, and I can't let you do it." He turned to the Windhammer. "She has the Bond of Third Arcane. It's inside the pendant around her neck."

A swarm of despair shook her like the icy winds of the Dark Fusion. He had ruined her.

"Take the pendant," snarled the Windhammer.

Two more soldiers charged at her. No matter how much she resisted, no matter how much she screamed, she was no match for four armored men, and they took her pendant away.

"Give it back," she shouted once she was free. She ran to the thief, but the soldiers restrained her again.

Windhammer received the pendant from his soldier and looked it over. "What was your plan? Hand this over to the queen, the fate of the entire realm, for one man?"

"You have no right," she cried out.

"Panthea," Arvin said, his voice reserved. "Please don't make this harder than it has to be."

He signaled her captors, and they released her. She went and stood at a safe distance from everyone, struggling not to cry.

"I need you to think carefully," Windhammer said, "before dismissing my proposal. I want a real, calculated answer. Give me that, and you can go wherever under Diva you desire."

Without a moment of hesitation, she repeated, "I'm not killing another man."

"Yoltan doesn't deserve to live, Panthea," Arvin said. "Every minute he lives, more people suffer."

"It's not my choice to make," she said through gritted teeth. "Neither is it yours. I won't be the judge and the executioner. Now, please, give me the stone, and I will be on my way. I'll not hinder your cause." She directed the next part at Arvin. "You'll never see me again."

"I can't do that, child," Windhammer said. "We don't know what happens if Queen Artenus gets her hands on this. Until we do, and until you come to your senses, the stone stays with us."

"Panthea," Arvin pressed. Did he assume repeating her name would make his betrayal hurt less? "Try not to think about being wronged and focus on the sad, ugly, urgent reality. You can't run for much longer. Soon, you'll get caught, give up the stone, and get tortured to death. Instead, you can turn yourself in, kill the bastard, and let us secure your safe return."

"And what about Rassus?" she almost cried. "What do you think will happen to him if I do something like this?"

"We'll find a way."

Panthea was sick of being lied to. "No, you won't. You don't care if he dies. For all you care, even I could get killed in there as long as I take the Inquisitor down with me. Because this is how the rebellion works. Everyone is expendable."

Windhammer clicked his tongue. "You are not expendable. I want you to calm down and—"

"I don't care about the independence of Shiran and its heritage," she said. "I'm from Delavaran, I'm an Angelian, and this is the Southern Kingdom. Now, if you want to give me nightmare potion, you can do it. If you want to turn me in, go ahead. But if you do that, I'll happily give them the stone. And the Windhammer."

The room fell into a deafening silence. Windhammer's eyes lost all emotion but rage, like two daggers ready to cut her down. Panthea's heart thumped in her chest. This had not been the smartest thing she could have said, but she had been too angry to stop herself.

"Sir," Arvin said, "she doesn't mean—"

Windhammer held up a finger. "Shh."

The towering man ambled to Panthea and stopped behind her. He put his bulky hand around her shoulder and pressed, his fingers digging painfully below her collarbone as he whispered, "Do you have a death wish, girl? Erkenblood or not, that was a serious threat and one I can't have hanging over my head."

She grunted and writhed as the pain became unbearable.

"You don't want to cooperate," the Windhammer continued, "then don't. But be careful where your mind goes. Thoughts and actions can have dire consequences."

He let go, and she gasped as she held her aching shoulder. Windhammer then stomped away as he commanded, "Remove this brat from my house now. And keep her on a leash."

The soldiers went to grab her, but she evaded them. "I'm not leaving without the stone."

Arvin rushed to her and turned her away from the others. "What are you doing? Do you want to die? Because he *will* kill you."

Overwhelmed, she spoke with a broken voice. "I'm left with nothing, and you just want me to walk away?"

"Listen to me," he whispered. "You're lucky he even let you live after what you said. I'm sorry. I'm sorry for the circumstances. But what you're doing is not helping anyone. You want to run with the stone and risk letting it fall into the queen's hands. We might not be able to save Rassus, but neither can you on your own. So, for once, think outside of your problems and about others who can suffer because of your actions."

"I've sacrificed too much. I'm not giving up. You told me you could help me protect the stone and save Rassus at the same time. But if I can't do both, then curse you, curse the stone. I'll trade it if I must, and I'll save him."

"Fine, let's talk about this later. But right now, you need to get out."

Panthea knew it was a serious situation when the normally composed Arvin was so distraught. Maybe he cared, after all, in his own twisted way. Resigned, she followed him out.

"I can't believe you did this to me," she said as they walked. "I trusted you."

Arvin huffed. "You and trust. You know, you don't need trust to get people's help."

"Right. I forgot." She gave him a scornful look. "I can manipulate them into helping me."

"Oh, don't get sanctimonious on me now. You want to talk about manipulation? You and I both know Evian is terrified of this quest, and somehow, you've dragged him along through everything."

Her chest clenched with anger, though she tried to keep her voice down as she said, "Evian's stronger than you think. And I'm not trying to manipulate him. I need his help."

"You need his affirmation, and you shut him down every time he expresses a different opinion."

She stopped. "Who are you are to judge me?"

"I'm not judging you." He grabbed her arm and got her moving again with a gentle push. "I just want you to realize our decisions are not always as simple as they seem. It's easy to put labels on people without knowing where they come from and everything that goes into their decisions."

She stared at him for a second. "You really believe what you do is right, don't you?"

"There is no right. Or wrong, or good, or evil. Only people and their self-importance. We all learn to hate each other from the moment we're born. Ahuraics hate Angelians, southerners hate northerners, peasants kings, and this cycle keeps repeating as we all twist and turn in this cesspit in an endless struggle to claim the surface for a day or two."

"While drowning others," she argued.

"Yeah, well." He squinted at the light of the fusing suns as they stepped out of the building and toward the main exit. "As vast as the world is, it never seems big enough for everyone in it. So, no. I don't think of what I do as right. I just do what I have to, so people I care about suffer a little less."

Even after they left the grounds, Arvin didn't leave her as she had thought he would.

"Where are you taking me?" she demanded.

"Back to the safehouse. I'm not dumping the Erkenblood of Saba on the main street."

He accompanied her all the way there. Once they were at the entrance, she could no longer handle his presence, and she didn't need to. She stood in the doorway, crossing her arms. "I think I'll manage from here."

Arvin took a glance inside. "Fine. Just try to stay out of trouble. I'll come back tomorrow to talk about our options." He looked down, shaking his head. His gaze didn't quite land on her again as he said, "I really did want to help you."

She rolled her eyes as she turned to enter the house, but suddenly, an idea struck her. Facing Arvin again, she said, "You really want to help?

Windhammer said he wouldn't give me the stone before he knew what kind of power it had. I might have an idea. I think Ash was onto something. In the History of the Arcane by Sinn Tiaar, there were hints of this third arcane power. The book didn't give them numbers, but it was clear inborn and conductive wielding are not the only kinds. My copy of the book had missing pages, and I believe the answer lies somewhere within those parts. Can you find me the book?"

Arvin sighed. "He won't give you the stone. Now that he knows how important it is to you, he'll keep it as collateral until you cooperate. That's how he works."

Although part of her already knew that, it did not make it any less disconcerting to hear. "You know things like this, and you still follow him?"

"Like I said. People I care about suffer a little less if the Windhammer wins. Even you, hard as it may be to imagine." His eyes lost focus as he stared at a corner. An uncomfortable pause neither of them seemed to know how to fill. Then, as if suddenly registering Panthea still standing there, he ended it with, "Get some rest. We'll talk later."

He left, and Panthea went inside, marveling at the enigma he was. One minute, he would be so kind and caring, and a minute later, utterly heartless. It was as though some good side of him yearned to reach out from beneath the product of years of ruthless fighting. She found that despite his betrayal, she did not hate him. The man was at war with himself, and Panthea was all too familiar with that feeling.

When she entered the guest room, Evian was sitting there, his face buried in his palms.

"Evian?" she said. "What are you doing here? Why aren't you with Ash?"

He looked up at her, his pale face and wet eyes filling her with worry.

"What's wrong?" she dared to ask.

A fresh tear tumbling down his cheek, he said, "I messed up."

21

The Book of Creation never uses a pronoun when referring to the master of all elements. It doesn't give a clue whether it is a single person or a group.

FOR THE FIRST FEW SECONDS, Evian did not say a word. His gaze flittered about, and he fidgeted with his hands. Panthea went and sat beside him on the bed, barely able to keep her voice steady as she said, "What do you mean, you messed up?"

"I tried so hard to avoid this," he mumbled. "I did everything I could. We shouldn't have come back."

"Evian, you're scaring me."

He looked at her, remorse bleeding from his eyes. "Please don't hate me for what I'm about to say."

"Of course, I won't. Why should I hate you?"

He let out a shuddering sigh before he began. "You remember when you asked me why Master told me about the stone and not you?"

"Yes. What about it?"

He wiped his tears, though new ones replaced them almost immediately. "Four years ago, the queen found the Bond of Second

Arcane. Master knew sooner or later, she would send after him to claim his Bond too. That's why he wanted me to succeed him as the protector if something happened to him."

Panthea frowned. "But I figured that out on my own. You're the true protector."

"I'm not. I kept telling Master the stone was trouble. It was bad enough that he was putting us in danger by not just giving it up. Now, he wanted me to do the same." His eyes shifted to her, though he didn't keep the stare for long. "I made a choice. I chose you and Ash. I . . ."

Although he didn't finish his sentence, Panthea had heard what she needed to hear.

Her breath locked in her lungs as she uttered the bitter words, "You tipped off the Inquisition." She covered her mouth as that thought sank in. All this time, she had blamed herself for the raid on the house, and she had never imagined there would be an alternative that hurt even more. She could not digest the reality that Evian had done something so unspeakable to the man who had raised him. "Please tell me I'm wrong."

Silence.

"Evian." Her voice vibrated. "Tell me I'm wrong. Why aren't you talking?"

He sank into his palms, weeping.

A laugh erupted from Panthea, more painful than any sob. "So, we're in this mess because of you?"

"It wasn't supposed to be this way," he said. "They weren't even supposed to know you existed. On the day of the festival, I was going to take you and Ash out of the house before they arrived. But I couldn't do it in time."

Panthea did not know how to react. Her mind had completely shut her out. She got up and stepped away while she collected her thoughts. "Where is Ash now?"

"We were on our way to her house when Inquisitor Yoltan caught sight of me. He took Ash as collateral."

Panthea's heart pumped ice into her veins. "Oh, Annahid, no."

"He said you must meet him in Rue Square in the Old City and bring the stone with you. If you don't show up soon . . . He also asked me to sap you, but I couldn't."

Panthea's chest was an empty space. The horror stories of Rue Square passed through her mind like a storm. She knew what awaited her there, but she had to save Ash. "How did he know I had the stone?" Before Evian had the chance to answer that, she realized it did not matter. "I don't even have it, anymore. Arvin stole it."

Pacing across the tiny room, she tried to think of a way to save her friend. "I, um . . . I'll go to the meeting," she said through her short breaths, scratching her head nervously. "You go to Governor House and find Arvin. He's on his way there. Tell him where I am and what's happened. Ask him to bring the stone." She regarded Evian, tears blurring her vision. "I know I said I wouldn't, but I really hate you right now." She scrubbed her tears off, containing a sob that was in the works.

Evian still sat there, indecisive.

"What under Diva are you waiting for?" she shouted. "I meant now for what's divine!"

That spurred Evian into action. He sprang up and went to the door, though he still didn't leave. "Wait. But if Arvin stole the stone from you, how can I get him to return it?"

"He will," she said, hoping she had judged the man right. "Because my life is on the line."

"So, maybe you should wait until he's here. You don't have to actually put your life at risk."

"We have no time. I'm not waiting for him to try to convince me to let Ash die."

"What if Yoltan kills you both before we come back?"

"I guess I'll find out," Panthea cried. "At least I won't be the one who has to live the rest of his life with our blood on his hands."

"Please don't talk like that. I don't—"

"Move!" she screeched.

He ran out like the coward he was, and she leaned against the wall, dreading her meeting with the man who had invaded her memory, her thoughts, her nightmares. She was probably going to die today—or in the coming days, crushed under the boots of the Inquisition.

Even if she survived, even if she and Ash walked away from this encounter unscathed, the stone would be gone, and with it, Panthea's hope of ever saving Rassus.

Dear Annahid, in the name of what's dead and what's living and what's divine, accept your lesser daughter. Give me courage to face my enemies. Give me the strength to save my friend. Protect me from those who mean me harm.

PANTHEA WADED HER WAY through the Old City, almost bruised by the constant shoving and jostling she received from the crowd. The suns were setting when she entered Rue Alley. It was empty. The stream of people still flowed behind her like a roaring river, but no one dared to come here.

She followed the narrow alleyway into the secluded courtyard.

Tall, abandoned buildings surrounded her, covered in soot and grime. The stench of death in the stale air foreboded the inevitable fate of whoever ended up here.

After a short while, footsteps came from the neck of the alleyway, and when she turned back, six blackhoods trickled in, followed by a man she could not mistake for anyone else. She could hardly contain the trembling of her legs as the man of her nightmares sauntered in.

"Hello, witch," Yoltan said in a melodic tone, wearing a sickening smirk. His voice was higher in pitch than she had imagined, but every bit as menacing. "You and I have come a long way. I've been told you have the stone. So, be a good girl and hand it over."

"Where's my friend?"

As if on cue, more blackhoods emerged from the alleyway, holding Ash by both arms. Panthea's heart sank. The girl had new bruises on her face, and gag in her mouth muffled her screams. Panthea ran toward her, but two blackhoods grabbed her before she could reach Ash. They slammed her on her back, leaving her breathless.

"No, no," Yoltan almost sang. "Let's not rush. First, you give me what I want, then your friend walks."

Panthea gasped for air once her lungs gave way, just before the soldiers sat her up, pulling her arms back to immobilize her.

"She's scared," Panthea cried. "Please let me talk to her. I promise I won't try anything."

Yoltan scratched his chin and, after some contemplation, stepped out of the way and motioned to his men. They removed Ash's gag. Both girls sobbed. Panthea kept begging for Ash's forgiveness, although she could not speak loud enough, making both their voices mix into a meaningless cacophony.

"Shut up," the Inquisitor barked. "Both of you."

Ash's captor pulled out a dagger and held it in front of her neck.

"No," Panthea squeaked. "Don't hurt her. I'll do anything."

"Stop crying," the Inquisitor said, "or he'll slit her throat."

Panthea held her mouth with both hands, unable to contain the crashing wave of tears.

"I said, stop crying."

Her hands shaking, Panthea gasped and held her breath. Her head felt as if it would explode. But she would do anything to save Ash.

The blackhood brought the knife closer to Ash's skin. "She's still crying."

"Ash," Panthea said with a broken voice. "It's all right. I'll give them what they want, and they'll let you go." Borrowing from Ash's humor, she added, "Don't be a dope."

A fleeting hint of a smile graced her friend's mouth, and her cry turned into a quiet snivel. "No . . . You're . . . the dope."

The man removed the knife, and Panthea drew a relieved breath. *Just hang in there, Ash. I'll get us out.*

"Now," Yoltan said. "The stone?"

Panthea looked toward the alleyway, hoping Arvin was coming. Then she met the Inquisitor's eyes. "Let her go, and I'll take you to the stone."

"Take me?" Yoltan spluttered into laughter, which turned into a baleful grin as he tramped to Panthea and struck her across the face. More than the strike itself, his twisted smile stole her breath.

He slapped her again, and she whimpered as she tried to get away from his aggression. He caught up and grabbed her by the hair. Her scalp screamed with pain as the courtyard spun around her in a blur, and her head banged against the rough ground.

Before she could register what had happened, the blackhoods surrounded her. From there, there was a flurry of kicks, some in her chest, some in her stomach. One even landed in her face, opening her wound. Through the jumbled sounds and violent strikes, she could make out Ash's pleading screams.

Panthea was numb when they stopped. She gasped and coughed as she tried to get enough air into lungs that refused to expand. The twisting pain in her stomach slowly gave way to nausea.

Two pairs of gloved hands forced her up, and through her daze, she felt the warmth of her power. The effect of the sapping potion was gone. *Please, Annahid. Give me a little longer. I don't want to hurt her again.*

The Inquisitor approached, looking pleased as he let go of a bundle of hair he had detached from her head. "Now. Tell me where the stone is, or you and your friend will both rot in here."

"Don't give them anything," Ash cried. "They'll kill you once they have what they want."

That did not bother Panthea one bit. What crushed her was that she could not give Yoltan the stone, even though she wanted to. Looking over the Inquisitor's shoulder, there was still no sign of Arvin. She had misjudged him for the last time.

Arvin had probably already convinced the faint-hearted Evian to leave her and Ash for dead, and if Panthea was going to die, she would not go a coward. She would not beg. She would not give them the pleasure.

Staring into Yoltan's eyes, she muttered, "Get damned."

"I see." The Inquisitor moistened his lips. "Have a good look around, girl, because this is the last time you'll see the light of day." He shoved her toward the blackhoods. "Let's take her to the bureau. We'll teach her how to talk there."

The fear she had been suppressing up to now came back as reality dawned on her. They were taking her to the Inquisition bureau. She was going to disappear like all other Erkenbloods.

A scream from Ash cut her thoughts short. The young wielder elbowed her captor and freed herself from his grasp, running to Panthea.

"Ash, no."

Yoltan turned to see what was happening just before Ash slammed into him and sent him off-balance.

She then yelled, "Panthea, run!"

Heart pounding, Panthea clasped Ash's hand and together they ran toward the alleyway. They were almost out of the courtyard when she felt a tug from Ash and, when she looked back, Yoltan had grabbed the girl and was drawing her to himself, rage swimming on his face.

The pull disconnected them from each other. Ash kicked and jerked in the Inquisitor's arms, and Panthea saw the glint of a dagger as Yoltan said to no one in particular, "Accept your son. Let this sacrifice strengthen" — his voice stiffened as he plunged the dagger into Ash's chest, putting an abrupt end to her screams — "your army."

Panthea went cold. The young wielder froze, her eyes wide.

Yoltan withdrew the bloody knife and dropped Ash to her knees, a self-righteous smile cutting through his anger. That monster even spat on Panthea's best friend.

Ash stared at Panthea in terror as blood bubbled out of her wound. Panthea opened her mouth to tell her she was going to be fine. That she would live through this. But there was so much blood. Ash's entire tunic was drenched, and it kept pouring out of her.

As Ash fell on her back, Panthea rushed over, dropping at her side. *They can kill me if they want.* "Ash?" she said, trying to stay strong for her, failing at it. "You're going to be fine. It's better than it looks."

She didn't know whom she comforted. Ash was not even

acknowledging her. She just convulsed on the floor while a pool of blood grew under her.

"Ash, look at me," Panthea said, placing her trembling hand on her friend's cheek to turn her to herself. "It's nothing, you're . . ."

Blood trickled out of Ash's mouth and nose.

"Oh, Annahid, no." Panthea's cry pressed under her throat, but she contained it. "Ash," she rasped, struggling to ignore the blood that now gushed out of her friend's mouth. "Do you hear me?" She looked up at the men who stood there, watching. "Please help her."

"She's already dead." Yoltan sheathed his knife. "Now, get up."

"She's not dead," Panthea said in a guttural scream. Ash couldn't die. She had survived much worse. She'd survived Panthea's power-lust. When she looked back at her, however, even her convulsions had stopped. Blood covered her face. Her eyes stared at the sky, no light in them.

"Ash?" Panthea whispered.

Nothing.

"Ash," she repeated, shaking the young wielder. She called over and over, her whispers turning into wheezing.

A sob exploded out of her, but she had to gasp for air as soon as it began. Then another, and soon, Panthea found herself in a raging battle between a sob that couldn't break free and lungs that couldn't draw enough air. Desperate, she cried out as loudly as she could, but her voice barely got out.

She gasped and repeated. Every time, a fleeting hint of relief brushed her hollow chest, and her voice became louder. Until at once, it broke through the suffocating barrier and into a scream. Cold waves swept over her body. She pulled Ash into her arms, blubbering, "Ash, tell me this is a nightmare. Tell me you're joking. What do you expect me to do now?"

Ash said nothing. She would not say anything anymore.

"Well, that's touching." Yoltan's calm, unfeeling voice ignited a fire inside Panthea. Her hands clenched as if of their own accord. "But I don't have all day. Get up. She got what she deserved."

Grief turned to rage, and Panthea bellowed as she charged at Yoltan.

But before she could reach him, a blackhood elbowed her in the chest, making her fall in the blood. Screaming again, she tried to get out, but she kept slipping, as though Ash was still too scared to let her go.

By the time Panthea was away from the body, she was soaked in blood, paralyzed by the violent tremor in her limbs. How could this have happened? *Dear Annahid ...* There was nothing she could ask the goddess, nothing she wanted. There was simply nothing left.

Her power was now strong and alive—the joy of power-lust settling in.

The blackhoods came to grab her, but as soon as they touched her shoulder, she could no longer hold it. She wielded the walls around her and made them collapse with a deafening blast, pulverizing the pieces of rubble that would otherwise crush her, letting the rest devour the blackhoods.

To her confusion, the remaining men dropped their weapons and held up their hands in surrender. Even the Inquisitor himself, though one of his hands was behind his midsection. It didn't matter. The murderers had to die. Panthea lifted all the blackhoods yards in the air and let gravity finish the job.

It was now just her and Yoltan.

Although some trepidation was visible on the Inquisitor's face, he looked composed. He even smiled as he said, "I'll be damned. You're in control."

Panthea had not had time to think about that. She'd been in full control of her power. It had not been about eliminating threats to her life. She had been hunting. She could no longer blame her actions on power-lust. And more frighteningly, she no longer felt the need.

She stood three strides away from Yoltan. Her breaths were short, her body ached, and her head spun because of her thinned blood. *This is me, not power-lust. This is me, the Erkenblood of Saba, ending you.* "Any last words, Inquisitor?"

Yoltan scoffed. "Just this. You sealed your friend's fate with your actions." He glanced at Ash's body. "You have a choice now. We have transferred your guardian to Delavaran. Come with me, and he survives.

But if I go alone, I'll make sure he dies a slow and painful death."

Panthea lifted all the daggers from the blackhoods and let them float in the air, pointed at Yoltan. "You won't hurt anyone anymore."

She willed every single blade to shoot at him. Yoltan's eyes widened, but before the blades reached him, he turned into a green plume of smoke. The weapons scattered further away as the smoke disappeared. *What under Diva?*

"I think I'm having a déjà vu," Yoltan's voice came from behind. Panthea wheeled back to find him standing there with a glowing gleamstone in his hand. "This is exactly what you did at the lake."

Defying her weakening body, she rose the remaining pieces of rubble and threw them at him, but he disappeared again, showing up at the neck of the alleyway. How under Diva could he wield space with a gleamstone?

"It's fascinating," Yoltan said. "Control or no control, you're still a wild animal, acting only on your instinct."

She sent another flurry of daggers his way, but he evaded those too. She struggled to keep her eyes open. Her legs failed to bear her weight. *I can't lose. I owe this to Ash.*

The wound on her cheek was bleeding like a waterfall.

Yoltan took notice. "Make your blood any thinner, and you'll die from that wound."

Panthea could now hear her own heaving breaths. Her face was cold. She no longer had the energy to even stand straight. Regardless, she attacked again, but Yoltan was too swift.

Her legs buckled, and she dropped on her hip, her muscles rigid as stone. It felt like dozens of serrated chains crawled up her limbs. *Ash. I'm sorry. I . . . can't.*

The blurry image of Yoltan towered over her. He picked up her limp body and began taking her out of the courtyard.

"Put her down," came from the far end of the alleyway.

A series of footfalls joined that voice, and when Panthea found the will to look, she saw Arvin and Mart running into the courtyard with a few soldiers.

"Inquisitor," Mart said firmly. "Put the girl down, or we'll be required to use force."

Yoltan clicked his tongue. "Major. This is Inquisition business, and I urge you not to interfere. Tell your men to stand down."

"This is not the Inquisition bureau," Mart countered. "This is a crime scene, and that makes it our business."

Yoltan lowered Panthea, the motion in rhythm with her swimming head. "What's the meaning of this disturbance?"

"Oh, interesting," said Mart. "I was about to ask the same question. You've entered my district, caused panic, left a bunch of dead bodies. May I remind you that your impunity is restricted to your bureau? In here, the way I see it, you're the prime suspect of the murder of a minor." He jutted his chin toward his hand. "And is that an arcane artifact you're holding?"

The Inquisitor pointed at Panthea. "It's hers." A dirty lie.

"Is that so? In that case, I'm going to ask you to drop that too, and we'll book it together with her." When the Inquisitor took too long, Mart's voice dropped to a level Panthea could barely hear. "Inquisitor Yoltan. I hate to escalate the matter to General Heim. Trust me, it'll be a headache for both of us."

"This girl," Yoltan muttered, "killed these people. She's the most wanted criminal in the Southern Kingdom."

"And we'll treat her as such. Per protocol, she'll remain in our custody until we have all our questions answered, and we'll send her to Delavaran if necessary. Feel free to appoint someone to supervise the interrogation, but you're not taking her away today because, frankly, I don't trust someone who thinks they're above the law. Now, if you please. Sir."

After a few moments, Yoltan dropped his gleamstone and said with a low, menacing grumble, "Very well. But if she gets lost while in your custody for any reason, I'll come for you. And I'll follow every protocol to make sure my face is the last you'll ever see. You pick a fight with the Inquisition, you damn well better be prepared, Major."

He then kneeled and whispered in Panthea's ear, "If you're not in Delavaran—with the stone—by the Dark Fusion, I'll send your guardian where I sent your friend."

He stood up, swept a look around, then left, jostling Mart on his way.

"By Ahura," Arvin said when the Inquisitor was gone. He rushed to Panthea and sat her up, holding her. "I'm so sorry we were late. Mart. We need . . ."

Panthea's mind drifted away from their voices. She had failed. She'd had her chance with Yoltan. Twice. Once to prevent all of this at the lake, once to make him pay for what he had done. "He defeated me. I failed Ash."

None heard her.

Mart closed Ash's eyes, then picked her up. The image sucked out what was left of Panthea's energy, and the exhaustion, the blood loss, and the pain finally won. As darkness took over, the last image she saw was of Mart taking her best friend away.

22

*It took us years until we uncovered the secrets of the arcane—
the balance between our powers. Thus, we became the master
of all elements.*

THE EVENING WAS STILL. Even the queen's quiet voice was jarring. The woman had spent her entire day in the throne room, and she now sat with the commander-in-chief of the army and the minister of trade, both of whom had business that could not wait until tomorrow.

As Hilia poured tea into the sparkling, northern glass teacups, she listened to the conversation. She was not at all interested in glass price. But the matter General Gorman had brought to the table, the execution of two hundred people linked to the rebellion, weighed on her.

High-ranking rebels were invisible. They were mostly infiltrators within the ranks of the army. She knew very well what kind of people were now arrested and faced possible execution. She herself had probably recruited some of them. They were commoners who tried to be heroes by distributing Windhammer's nightly letters or distracting a few guards during operations. They were nobodies. They had lives. Families.

"Minister," the queen said. "If you resign yourself to the Northern

Realm's every request, you will further weaken our fragile economy. They are doubling the glass price to force our hands into importing arcane artifacts again."

"I understand, Your Highness," the minister said in an ingratiating voice. "But we cannot boycott the glass import. Many of our merchants . . . goddess, two of our clans depend on it."

Hilia picked up the tray and brought it to the dining table, dreading her intrusion in the heat of the argument.

"When our economy collapses," the queen said, "clan leaders will be the least of our problems. People will revolt. I'm going to send a letter to the High Lady Sarian to challenge her invasive policy. For now, keep the clans satiated by compensating some of their losses."

As Hilia approached, the short, chubby minister turned to look at her. His crimson vest was so tight it accentuated his flabby chin, and the golden buttons threatened to burst open if he breathed too hard. The queen, who had lost her audience and her trail of thought, gawked at Hilia for a few seconds before she blinked. "Well, don't just stand there." She gestured toward her guests.

The minister's thick mustache shifted in a smile as Hilia held out the tray to him. While he picked up his tea, his saucer, and a few of the sweets, the queen turned to Gorman. "And about your proposal, General. I fear the execution of two hundred in one day will turn people against Delavaran."

"The rebellion has grown bold." Gorman slid the warrant toward the queen. "If we keep showing leniency, we won't have a kingdom to protect in a year."

The estimate was astonishingly accurate. If Windhammer's vision came to fruition, Shiran would be freed, and Delavaran would be under siege in no longer than one year. But what Gorman failed to see was that executing these commoners did nothing to stop it from happening.

The queen picked up her pen and dipped it in the inkwell. Hilia's chest clenched. The fate of two hundred people was one inch and a few drops of ink away from being sealed.

Something smacked her arm, the shock almost making her drop the tray, the sting lingering. It was Gorman. "Hey, maid, do you think I can have my tea?"

"Yes, my lord." She held out the tray for him, glad she'd lived in this palace for long enough to lose her instinct of twisting his arm.

Her *mistake* also invited a disapproving glance from the queen before she resumed perusing the document. Hilia went to her next and offered the tea, a juvenile part of her hoping it would delay the inevitable and make the queen think twice about signing that warrant.

The woman didn't acknowledge Hilia. She just sighed and muttered, "Isn't this why we have the Inquisition? To find and contain insurgencies? Perhaps I should talk to Inquisitor Kadder about this and get his insight into the situation."

Gorman had his response ready. "The Inquisitor and I have already discussed this, and we both agree this is the right course of action. We need a display of power. We need to be decisive to send these thugs scurrying back to their holes."

The queen nodded, lowered the pen, and hesitated for just another second before she signed the warrant and handed it to the general. Hilia's chest emptied. Two hundred people were going to die, and it had taken the queen a mere few seconds to decide that.

"I don't want tea." The queen gave Hilia a shooing gesture. "I'll call you again if I need you."

Hilia bowed her head and left the table with the remaining glass. As she filled the tray with the dirty dishes and the rest of the sweets to take back to the kitchens, the queen and the minister continued their lengthy discussion about trade.

Hilia picked up the glass and looked it over. This useless piece of garbage was worth more deliberation, it seemed, than two hundred lives.

The minister said, "I can suspend glass import while we negotiate with the northern High Lady, but not for long. It will be two, maybe three thretnights before clan leaders become impatient."

"Do what you must, Minister, but I will not sign this," the queen announced with an irrefutable finality. "We either import glass at the same price, or we don't import at all."

So, the woman was capable of denying decrees. As if on its own accord, Hilia's hand slammed the glass on the counter, smashing it, sending a searing pain up her arm.

"What under Diva are you doing?" the queen shot.

When Hilia turned, three pairs of stupefied eyes drilled into hers. *What under Diva indeed! Pull yourself together, girl.*

"I'm ..." Her voice shook with anger. Luckily, she knew how to channel that into playing the timid maid. "I'm sorry. Butter fingers. I'll ... I'll clean this up."

The queen grimaced as her gaze dropped to Hilia's hand. "Clean *yourself* up. You're bleeding all over my carpet."

It was then Hilia noticed the gaping wound on her palm. "I'm ..." She tried to pick up the tray.

"Leave it there," the queen said in a condescending tone, "and go tend to your wound."

Just as Hilia resigned, a soldier opened the door. She scurried to him while she pressed her thumb against the cut to stop the bleeding. "Not now," she whispered. "The queen is still in the meeting, and she's not in the mood for visitors."

The soldier sneered. "Well, neither is Inquisitor Kadder for a turndown. Go inform the queen and let her decide."

Hearing that name sent a twinge of worry up Hilia's nape. Something was afoot. She bobbed her head and returned to the queen.

"What now?" Queen Artenus said impatiently, her glare sharp and uncompromising.

"My apologies." Hilia's voice came out raspy. She cleared her throat. "Inquisitor Kadder is here. He has urgent business."

The queen shared a dubious look with her guests. "Very well. Call him in."

Hilia relayed the command, and the soldier went and opened the door of the chambers.

Accompanied by six Sapphire soldiers and five palace guards, Kadder walked in, his expression grim. He barely even spared Hilia a glance as he beelined to the table.

The queen, who'd already risen from her seat, picked up her scepter and stepped forward. "What is it, Inquisitor?"

The minister was also on his feet, spying them over the queen's shoulder.

Kadder growled, "The Bond."

Hilia could've sworn the queen paled—if that was even possible with her complexion.

Kadder looked down. "Inquisitor Yoltan's report came in today. They have reason to believe the Erkenblood of Saba is in possession of the stone."

They were most likely talking about one of those Bonds of Arcane. And who under Diva was the Erkenblood of Saba?

"And she has help," Kadder added, the queen's features tensing more and more as he went on. "A few days ago, they took down an entire platoon sent to capture her."

"Let me be," shouted the queen, dropping her scepter, which landed under Hilia's feet.

Silence ruled as people in the room tried to interpret that reaction. Kadder pursed his lips as he ushered his company to leave the chambers.

"Not you, Inquisitor," the queen mumbled.

The scepter just lay there. It was the perfect opportunity for Hilia to listen to the whispers again. She bent to pick it up.

Her hands were inches away from the scepter when the queen commanded, "Don't."

Hilia drew herself up. She'd been so close, but it was either compliance or discovery.

The queen then cracked her neck and continued in a low, raspy voice, "I'll pick that up later." She shot a hard glance at the scepter. "For now, everybody, get out. I need to talk to the Inquisitor."

Gorman waved a hand in the air, signaling his men to exit. His signal for Hilia was a little harsher. As if annoyed she hadn't understood his military gesticulation, he shoved her forward.

Outside, the general barred the door before he let out a deep sigh. "Annahid, save us all."

The minister slipped toward the stairway, but Hilia lingered. She wanted to know about the Erkenblood, but she went with the less conspicuous question. "Why was the queen so distressed?"

Gorman gave her a derisive look, his brows knotted together. "Who under fuck do you think you are to ask me questions? Fuck off before I slice you up for intrusion. This is a restricted area as of now. Shoo."

Even if there was something to learn here, she couldn't risk defying the commander-in-chief. So, she bowed and left. There was only one place she could go now to get her head straight.

HILIA SAT IN THE DARK, empty library, reading the tale Parviz had given her—the story of Kyra, the woman who was supposed to be a lot like herself. Except she wasn't. The woman in the book was valiant. She didn't have a handler; she could fight for what she believed in. Hilia was a useless pawn. She'd joined the rebellion to make a difference, and the only differences she'd made so far were the wrinkles she had to hide every morning, the regrets that kept piling up, and now a sliced, bandaged hand.

Light flickered from between the shelves, and soon, a drowsy Parviz arrived, squinting behind his candle. "Hilia. What are you doing here?" As though having answered that question in his head, he changed it to, "Can I get you something new?"

"The queen kicked me out." She answered his first question as she closed the book, trying to hide her frustration. Pressing her hand on it, she said, "Can you tell me how this one ends?"

Parviz tittered. "That's not how it works. Reading fiction is like living another life. You never know what future awaits yourself, do you?"

She sighed. "Sometimes, I wish I did. Would spare me a lot of stress."

"Would rob you of a lot of excitement. Tales teach us what it means to be alive. Things might look bleak at times, but you learn that beyond darkness, there is always light."

"Light," she mumbled to herself, the word tasting bland in her mouth. Wherever this light was, she was yet to see it. "Parviz, do you know what a Bond of Arcane is?"

"And here I thought we were going to have a heart-to-heart." He winked. Picking up a more serious tone, he continued, "I'm not familiar with a Bond of Arcane as an object. But I know what binding is in the context of the arcane."

"Oh?" She turned her chair to face him, hopeful.

"Arcane artifacts bind to wielders on first use. An artifact bound to one wielder can no longer be used by another."

She narrowed her eyes. "This wasn't in the History of the Arcane. I've read that book twice."

"No, no." He chuckled. "This is more of a fact known to wielders. You could find it in wielding textbooks, which are not allowed in this library anymore."

"Hmm." She leaned back, considering the new information.

Footsteps of another person sounded from behind. Parviz gave the newcomer a fresh smile. When the man stepped into Hilia's view, she knew beyond light, there was always darkness. Handler. With no patience left to spare, she rolled her eyes. "Parviz, is he your tenant? Does he sleep here?"

Parviz laughed. "Seems like you two know each other. I'll leave you be."

Once the librarian was out of earshot, Handler, who had been following him with his eyes, turned to Hilia, "He your friend?"

"Oh, no you don't. Leave him out of this."

Handler raised his hands in surrender. "Someone's being protective. I was just making conversation."

"It's never just a conversation."

He picked a chair, taking as much time to sit on it as he possibly could. "I was going to ask you this in our next meeting, but now you're here, so might as well. Are you going to attend the Reunion ceremony?"

"It's not final yet." She gave a curious frown. "Why?"

"Make it final. We'll want you there."

Hilia rolled her eyes. "You know, saying it as an order doesn't automatically put me in charge. I'm a maid. The queen asks me to go, I can go; she asks me to stay, I have to stay. I'm not a game piece you can move around. Besides, I thought I had to keep a low profile."

The man had been staring upward halfway through her argument, not listening. He only regarded her again when she was finished. "Are you always this difficult?"

"Oh, I'm difficult?" She pointed an incredulous finger to her chest. "You treat me like a liability. I don't think you understand all I've done for this cause. I've read every book I could find about the queen's particular ability. I've almost blown my cover spying on her."

"We want results, and you've given us none. The only thing you did was get Mehran caught."

"Is this a joke?" Hilia tried to trap her anger inside. Although she managed not to shout at the man, she couldn't help her sharp tone. "He attacked *me*. I even told him to abort."

"Yes, on the day of the mission. The mission that was based on your wild theory. Every action, every thought, has consequences. The reason I'm the one ordering you around is because I see the bigger picture, and you don't."

"Well, maybe that's the problem. I'm trying so hard to squeeze information out of the queen while you might already know what I'm risking my life to find out."

This gave him pause. "Have you found out something?"

"Who's the Erkenblood of Saba? And why do I get a feeling the Windhammer has plans with her?"

Handler sank in his chair, considering her for a few moments. Then he took a vial out of his pocket and placed it on the table. There was a brownish liquid inside. "You knew too much, even before this. We can't risk losing you to the Inquisition."

"What is that?" Her stomach dropped as the answer dawned on her. "You're not going to kill me, are you?"

He chuckled. "No. Though it would save me a lot of headache. I want you to keep this with you at all times. With everything you know, and what I'm about to tell you, you cannot be taken alive. Do you understand?"

She grimaced. "You're asking me to—"

"You know what I'm asking. Do we have an agreement?"

She took a shuddering breath. It was getting too serious too fast. She could be dead long before the Dark Fusion. "Do you also have one of these? You know more than I do."

He took out a few more vials and flourished them before pocketing them again. "I know what I signed up for. Besides, I'm trained to withstand torture. You're not."

Torture. The word was a reminder that, while she sat here talking, Mehran was going through so much pain in the bureau. She regarded Handler and asked the question she'd been too ignorant to ask. "Any news from Mehran?"

"Well, yeah." A deep sigh left his throat. "There's something you should know."

"What sh . . ." Hilia's hand leaped to her mouth. "Oh, Ahura's throne, don't say it." Her voice cracked, and her eyes filled with tears.

"He resisted for a long time. But he had reached his limit. He took his own life."

"Please stop talking," she wheezed.

"Hilia." He put his hand above hers. "I need your strength right now. You can give his death meaning."

Another cold wave at the word *death*. But this was not the time to break. She scrubbed tears off her face with her palms. "You're right. You didn't come here to watch me cry."

He waited until she contained her weeping. "So, the Erkenblood. You're not wrong. The Windhammer is planning to recruit her."

"What?" Hilia exclaimed before lowering her voice to a whisper. "Has he gone mad? You can't trust Erkenbloods."

"He's aware of the danger. But we can use any help we can get."

Hilia sighed as she organized her thoughts. "And they said she has the stone. Is this another one of those Bonds?"

Handler nodded. "The Bond of Third Arcane."

She scoffed. "This is what I'm talking about. You can't hide this information from me."

"Hil . . ." Handler closed his eyes, rubbing his forehead in frustration. "You're a sleeper agent. You're not entitled to any information. Your job is to stay put until you're needed. *If* you're needed."

She did her best to ignore that remark, which would otherwise send her to another fit of rage that helped neither of them. Her friend was dead, the fate of the world was at stake, and all Hilia had to do was attend a stupid speech by a usurper.

"I'm not assigning you to a petty task," Handler said, as if having read her mind. Or rather, her face—she was not exactly masking her emotions. "Attend the ceremony. You'll thank me later."

He got out of his chair, and as he passed by, he put a hand on her shoulder. "Sorry about your friend. He was a good man and a great soldier. I don't know what came over him that night."

She forced a smile. "You and me both."

As Handler left the library, her gaze fell on the poison lying there on the table. At one point or another, she had to take her own life like her friend had. *Mehran, you fool. I had so many questions for you.*

She picked up the vial, then took a deep breath to level her emotions. Parviz could be here any moment, and she was not in the mood to make up new lies.

23

My third death was when I was reborn as a part of three. I no longer had the luxury to have dreams of my own. I was—we were—the means to an end.

"SHE'S WAKING UP."

Panthea opened her eyes to a clay ceiling. She lay on a comfortable bed in a new room, with Arvin sitting at her bedside. She felt drained. "Was it a dream?" she whispered, hoping.

He shook his head, an air of melancholy wavering in his countenance. "Sorry, Panthea. Ash is gone."

Silent tears trickled down her temples, fueled by the onslaught of memories of a friend she no longer had, the voice she would no longer hear, the smile she could no longer look forward to.

One memory, above all, haunted her. *"You don't have to lie to me,"* Ash had said during the attack on their convoy. *"It's just . . . I just realized I'll never get to go on the annual pilgrimage."* Panthea had comforted her back then, but what a prophecy it had been.

She let out a husky cry to silence those images, though she paid the price immediately when her head pulsed with pain, and she burst into agonizing coughs.

"I know," Arvin murmured, pressing her hand in his. "I'm so sorry."

That smell.

Until this moment, Panthea had not noticed the metallic smell permeating the air. She remembered it from the day they had spent at the farmers' house, and she knew what it was and who had made it. Evian proved her assumption when he approached with a bowl. He did not even look her in the eye. "Here. For your—"

Fury coursing through her, she slapped the bowl off his hand, making everyone jump back to avoid being scalded by the liquid. "Get away from me! You have no right to be here." When he balked, she turned to Arvin. "Take him out of here. I don't want to see his face."

Arvin signaled to Mart, and he led the distraught Evian out. Even then, she didn't stop while he was still in the room. "You're a coward. We're in this mess because of you. You killed Ash. You hear me? You killed Ash."

Arvin, who had been calling her name throughout her outburst, finally found room to speak when the door closed. "Panthea, please listen. You're still weak. We'll deal with Evian later, but you need to drink . . . whatever that is, to heal."

"He's a traitor," she cried as she lay back down, the twisting headache making it even harder to breathe if her chest pain was not enough. Arvin tried to caress her hair, but the very touch of his hand filled her with disgust. He was every bit as guilty. He was the reason they had come here. And if he had not taken the stone, she would not have had to go to the meeting without it. "You, too. Get out. I don't want to see anyone."

Arvin opened his mouth to say something, but he stopped himself and left the room.

She turned away from the door, bawling. There was one person she could never be rid of, even if she pushed everyone else out of her life. One person who bore the greatest guilt. She, herself, had brought this on Ash. By losing control in Saba, by trusting Arvin when Evian had warned her about him, by going to the meeting instead of waiting for help. Panthea should have been the one to die. She was far more deserving of it.

She cried for hours, stopping only when her headache became unbearable. She did drink a few cups of iron extract to remedy the excruciating pain. Arvin entered a few times to bring her water and once to bring her something to eat. She drank the water but did not touch the food. Ash would not be eating tonight, and neither would Panthea.

PANTHEA WAS NUMB for the next few days. Mart agreed to keep her in his house until she recovered. Her head felt like cotton, and the headache had become a constant burden. She was always tired, and yet, she could hardly sleep. And whenever she did fall asleep, she would either wake up from another nightmare or into a suffocating panic attack.

On one occasion, when anxiety overwhelmed her in the middle of the night, she instinctively sang Evian's lullaby to calm herself, but when she reached the line, "my dolly, shut your eyes," the image of Mart closing Ash's eyes flashed in her mind, and her heart almost stopped beating. Then she remembered who had taught her the song and now tainted it for the rest of her life. *Curse you, Evian.*

This cycle went on until, one afternoon, she finally got out of bed. She didn't want to, but part of her anxiety was because she knew she still had Rassus to save, and her passiveness kept adding up to the ever-growing mountain of guilt.

When Arvin opened the door and found her on her feet, a genuine smile graced his face. "I see you're feeling better."

"What day is it?" she said, unable to put any life into her voice.

"Thirty-ninth."

So, the cold was not just something she felt inside. There was a mere thretnight left until the Dark Fusion. She had wasted so much time.

"Do you want to come and join us in the other room?" Arvin said. "Maybe a drink could help?"

She shook her head. "I prefer to pray."

Arvin nodded, keeping a tight smile. He had learned to leave her alone when she wanted, which had been most of the time since Ash's passing. Once he left the room, she sat cross-legged northward, placed two fingers on her chest, and closed her eyes.

"Great Annahid . . ." She no longer knew how to finish that sentence. Everything she'd prayed for had remained unanswered. Everything she'd cared about was gone. "I'm confused. I prayed to you to protect my friends. You took them both from me. I asked you to give me courage. I'm still afraid. My faith is the last piece of me that's left. Please don't take it from me. If you're listening—if you exist . . ." Her skin prickled at those last words. "Forgive my blasphemy."

She kissed the back of her hand and wrapped the blanket around herself as tightly as she could manage with her bruised ribs. Then she exited into the sitting room. The crimson light of setting Diva bled through the windows, painting the room red.

Mart and Arvin sat on their chairs around the hearth, each holding a cup. Gvosh was here too, for some reason.

Mart smirked. "That was a short prayer. I pray for longer, and I don't even believe in the gods."

"Leave her be," Gvosh growled. "And cursing doesn't count as prayer."

Panthea went to the table at the far end of the room. She picked up a chair and joined the others at the hearth.

"How do you feel?" Arvin murmured.

What a stupid question. "Take a wild guess."

The men exchanged a doleful look. Mart sipped on his drink. Gvosh kept studying Panthea in silence.

After some time, Mart pointed at Gvosh. "Don't mind him. Ponytail sent him to watch us, so we don't let you *escape*."

"I'll do it," she mumbled, never more certain of what she wanted to do. "I'll kill Yoltan."

Mart sprayed his drink out in shock and broke into a raging bout of coughing.

Meanwhile, Arvin said, "Panthea, you don't have to do this. Mart and I can help you rescue your teacher. I gave you my word, and I'm going to keep it."

"It's not about Rassus anymore. You were right. As long as Yoltan lives, more people suffer."

"Then leave it to us. We'll kill him."

Mart, whose face was now red, harrumphed. "Varina's cunt, Arvin. Can you—"

"Hey!" Gvosh smacked his chest. "Language. Some of us actually worship those gods."

"Oh, believe me, I worship Varina." Mart sniggered and jumped out of his seat as Gvosh tried to grab him.

"Asshole," Gvosh said.

"Thank you."

"It wasn't a compliment."

"Wrong." Mart walked to the table and leaned against it. "You can decide what you say to me, but you can't decide how I take it." He then regarded Arvin again. "Think, Arvin. Isn't this what we all wanted? Can you just let her do it?"

"Have some integrity, Mart," Arvin said. "She's been through enough."

"You can't kill him on your own," she interjected. "I'm not even sure I can." Her mind ran over the fight with the Inquisitor. "It doesn't make sense. He wielded space. With a gleamstone. He evaded all my attacks."

Arvin frowned in confusion. "But you said that was impossible."

"It is," she said. "It should be."

Arvin's gaze shifted to Mart. "There you have it. The Inquisition is using arcane power."

"Yeah, things are stopping to make sense." Mart cleared his throat, still recovering from his coughs.

"Stopping?" Gvosh snorted. "Have you forgotten our queen is a fucking Erkenblood? I know all that crap about her giving up her power for the good of the land, but she can use it any time she deems necessary. Now, Inquisitors are also pulling tricks. What's next? Every soldier having one of those stones? Well, at least that makes it easier to tell friend from foe. Because I don't remember ever owning one."

"Nice speech, Cousin," Mart mocked.

Arvin finished his drink and got up. He rummaged in his pocket until he produced Rassus's pendant, holding it out to Panthea. "I believe this belongs to you."

She took the pendant and did not hesitate to wear it. Her instinct was to thank him, but she found no sense in that. Things would have been so much easier if he had not taken it away to begin with.

"I'm going to talk to Heim," he said. "I haven't seen him since . . . that day, and we didn't part on the best of terms. So, are you sure you want to go through with this? Because once we leave this city, there's no turning back."

Some irritating part of her still clung to her old values. She ignored it. What was one more person when she had killed so many? She was already beyond saving. At least this way, she could become one of those lost souls mentioned in the Book of Creation who cleansed the world with their taint. "Yes. He killed Ash. There's no way I'm letting this go."

"All right." Arvin sighed with an air of melancholy. "I'll ask Heim for a convoy to take you to Delavaran."

"No convoys," Mart countered. "Ponytail is the kind of man who sends a scout, then a hunting party as contingency. I don't want to look over my shoulder. We'll take her on a civilian coach and out of Lion's Gate. If we make it to the next courier's inn, we'll be safe."

"You're the strategist." Arvin headed for the door. "So, you go get the coach, and I'll go get provisions. I'll meet you all back here."

As he opened the door, Panthea asked, "By the way, is the traitor still at the safehouse?"

Arvin paused. "Evian? Yeah, I think so. At least he was, the last time I checked."

"Can you go there and ask him to take a walk? I want to go pick up my things, and I don't want him to be there when I do."

Arvin let go of the handle and turned to face her. "It's none of my business, but you two have been friends for most of your lives. Not that I don't understand where you are right now. But is this how you want to end things?"

Panthea sighed. "You're right." She shot him a sharp glance. "It's none of your business."

He pursed his lips, and it took him a moment to rip his gaze from her and turn it to Mart. Jutting his chin toward Mart's drink, he said, "You finish that, then take her to the safehouse. I'll make sure the boy isn't there by then."

Mart showed his agreement through a half-wink, adding, "I'll have another refill for good measure."

Arvin gave Panthea a last sympathetic glance before he left.

WHEN PANTHEA ENTERED the room, Evian wasn't there. What stood out was that neither were his things. He had just left without saying goodbye, without even leaving a note. Although that was what she'd asked for, part of her expected him to defy her decision like he used to. To at least try to make amends. *Coward.*

She picked up her satchel, stuffing her hood inside it. The emptiness of the room gave her a thought. She'd had full control when she'd fought Yoltan, and this was the chance for her to see if it had been happenstance. There was no one here she could hurt if she lost control.

To test her wielding, she removed her pendant. As she began pulling on the lid, the intoxicating exuberance of power-lust spilled into her veins, but she pushed on anyway, inviting the short-lived relief from her anguish. The lid popped open. Nothing else happened.

It didn't make sense. She had felt the unholy excitement as strongly as every other time. Come to think of it, this rush had always been there when she used her inborn wielding, even when she had been under the influence of the nightmare potion. But how was it she could only wield without consequences when that poison was in her system?

No. The last day in Saba, she had pulled the book to herself using her inborn wielding, and she had not fallen into oblivion.

Her breath caught. She retraced all the instances where she had wielded. Pulling the book in Saba, knocking Arvin back in Watertown and Serene, drawing the piece of rock to herself on top of the hill, her fight in Rue Alley. She had maintained her presence of mind in all of them. The instances she had failed to do so were the raid, the attack at the Green Eye Lake, and the one on their carriages.

The nightmare potion was not the common factor in her successful attempts. It was something else. Something very simple. In all of those instances, she'd used her power voluntarily. Power-lust had always befallen her when she had refrained from wielding, delayed it, resisted it. All she'd ever had to do was let go.

She had been looking for this answer for so long. But now that she understood, it did not make her even remotely as happy as she had thought it would. What good was her power, anyway? What was left to preserve? She had gone through so many nightmares, only to end up in the middle of one she would never wake up from. She had subjected everyone to so much suffering because she had been too scared of her own nature.

She had gotten Ash killed.

Struggling to shake that thought from her mind, she picked the marble box out of the pendant, focusing on the mechanism inside the box and opening it. And for the first time, she held the Bond of Third Arcane between her fingers.

She remembered the time when Ash had held the same artifact. To the young wielder, it had felt like a gleamstone. But to Panthea, it was unlike any form of arcane she knew. Conductive wielding was felt in one's hand. Inborn wielding was felt in one's head and surroundings. This one had no specific source—a kind of ambience foreign to her.

She dropped the stone back in the box and shut the pendant over it before she would be tempted to use its power, whatever it was.

24

The Book of Creation recognizes the perpetual nature of the elements, yet it is vague about that of our own. As a scholar, reading those parts of the book raised one question in my mind: how can perpetuity give birth to transience?

D RESSING THE QUEEN for public events was one of the most tedious tasks around the palace. On a normal day, her outfit was like that of any wealthy woman in the city. She still held on to the simplistic elegance of the Northern Realm, even though she'd lived in Delavaran for almost two decades. But not on a day like this. Today, she had to be the queen of the Southern Kingdom.

Hilia had spent half of her morning collecting pieces of garment and jewelry reserved for the queen's public appearance, and the other half, she'd spent in the bathhouse. Her lunch had been a piece of bread, and for the last hour, she had been dressing the queen with the help of another maid. They were just finished with the fourth layer of garment, and the sash was the last piece . . . *Oh, I almost forgot.* "My girl, can you go pick up the silk?"

"Silk?" the maid asked, perplexed.

"Yeah, the veil. It's over there. Has a clip on either end. You won't miss it." The girl looked so lost. Hilia sighed. "You know what, I'll get that. You go get the necklace." *I still have to put makeup on this corpse. We'll never make it.*

The maid scurried away.

When Hilia got up to get the silk, the queen said, "I don't need it." She turned her head from side to side, looking at herself in the mirror. "The crown will suffice. I believe I qualify as the queen even the way it stands. I have another task for you. General Gorman has employed two new girls. I want you to go show them the ropes."

Hilia bowed slightly. "Yes, Highness." Before she left, she remembered her latest assignment from Handler. "Forgive my insolence, Highness, but can I take care of the new maids tomorrow?"

The reflection of the woman's eyes drilled into Hilia's through the mirror. "And what will you do today?"

"If you honor me, I've always wanted to attend the Reunion ceremony."

The queen cocked her head. "You reek of sweat, you have stains on your dress, and your hair looks like you just woke up. I won't have a street cat in my entourage."

Well, try handling you for a full day, and see how your hair looks afterward. "I'm sorry. I stepped out of line."

"Go get changed," the queen said, her rigid expression not wavering. "Fix your hair and put on some makeup. If you're not here in an hour, you're not attending the ceremony."

Well, that was easy enough. "Thank you, Highness."

THE SOUND OF DRUMS and horns swelled from the distance as the procession made its way to the main square, filling the only space left amongst the crowd gathered to see the spectacle. The returning pilgrims walked in their green robes, seeming oblivious to the cheers they received.

Two rows of soldiers stood in front of the stage, and an array of guards stood like pillars behind the podium. There were chairs set up there for the officials. When Hilia first arrived, she didn't know where to sit until Kadder tapped the seat next to himself, urging her to join him.

Hilia gave him her most charming smile as she obliged. As she sat down, she said, "Isn't it strange, me sitting beside you?"

The old man huffed, though his features showed good humor. "I don't think anyone minds. And it's a far better image than you standing there like a lost duckling."

On the other side of Kadder sat General Gorman, followed by a few clan leaders, before the queen herself. Then there were ministers and lesser nobles and their aides.

Hilia studied the crowd more rigorously than the blackhoods present did. Handler wouldn't have insisted on her attendance for no reason, and that was foreboding.

"Welcome home, my brothers and sisters," announced the speaker. "I, for one, envy your devotion, your purity of heart . . ."

"I bet he hasn't ever prayed in his life," Kadder whispered in Hilia's ear. When she met his eyes, he was wearing a crooked smile. "Can you tell?"

Hilia forged another grin for him. "Yes."

"I wish for once they'd choose someone who's at least opened the Book of Creation."

Still smiling, Hilia drew her brows together. "Didn't the queen sign off on the announcer?"

"Well, none of us are without fault, are we?"

He seemed to enjoy making her uncomfortable. What kind of official would question the queen in front of the handmaid if he didn't have ulterior motives? Unsure how to respond, Hilia said, "I . . . suppose?"

Kadder returned his gaze to the man, whose introduction was over and was now announcing the queen, "Let us all welcome the queen of Delavaran, the savior of the realm, the denouncer of the arcane, Queen Artenus."

The crowd roared their cheers. As the queen stood up, the entire row of officials got to their feet in unison, and it took Hilia a moment—and a nudge from Kadder—to get up and join the rest in applause.

The queen sauntered to the lectern, raising both her arms as she invited more cheers. Some even began chanting praises. Hilia had never felt smaller. The passion in the crowd was a reminder that, after more than a decade, the Windhammer and his people, herself included, had done nothing.

After a while, the chants and the applause died down. The queen waited in silence for a little longer, scanning the crowd.

"Citizens of Delavaran," she finally said. Her voice was poised as it always was, though it was now powerful at the same time. "We have gathered here to celebrate the return of our pilgrims: favored sons and daughters of the Great Annahid, touched by her light, forgiven for their sins. This day is a reminder to us all that the Angelian religion is about forgiveness and tolerance."

Tolerance. Hilia stifled a snort.

The leader of the realm pressed a hand on her own chest. "I pride myself on being the purveyor of faith in the south as I once was in the north. But more importantly, I pride myself on having a small part in the beauty that is in your hearts. We've faced hardships. We've faced intolerance from the followers of the pantheon and those who aimed to divide us. But we showed them we can coexist without . . ."

The crowd was buying this ruse. Did none of them remember what the queen's army had done to the Ahuraic temples? Were they oblivious to the fact that, while she boasted about her achievements here, people were being tortured and killed at the bureaus of the Inquisition?

Hilia got a glimpse of Kadder from the corner of her eyes, whose unwavering gaze was fixed on the queen, his lips turned up in a bright smile. He and Hilia were on opposing sides of the same conflict, both for valid reasons. She fought against a system that treated its citizens as lesser compared to northerners, their religions less valid. Kadder fought the movement that had taken everyone he'd loved from him.

She wondered which one was the greater evil. The kingdom where a northerner had more rights than its own citizens, a kingdom that snuffed out any voice of disagreement in the most gruesome manner, or a force that killed entire families to make a point?

Hilia had been part of the Windhammer's game for so long, she hadn't stood back and thought about what she'd been part of. Had it all been worth it?

"Death to the tyrant," tore through the air, and Hilia's head snapped up to see a man shouting from within the crowd. "King-slayer. You ruined our land."

The entire court seemed as stunned as Hilia.

The rows of soldiers rifted as half of them charged the crowd to get to the man. The queen stopped talking, but that was all her reaction to the situation. Her eyes dropped to the lectern as she calmly waited while the soldiers made their way to the transgressor.

Even as they beat and dragged the man out of the petrified crowd, he continued shouting, "Go back to where you came from, you northern witch! The Southern Kingdom doesn't need you."

The queen's stony face didn't falter. Four Sapphires lifted the man by his limbs and took him away.

Something whipped in the air, and the queen let out a sharp grunt as she reeled back. Another swish, and this time Hilia also heard the thud. The queen fell into Kadder and Gorman's arms with three arrows sticking out of her. The image chilled Hilia's blood.

There was silence for a few moments. Then, as realization rippled through the crowd, a roar of terror erupted. The pathway reserved for the pilgrims filled with spectators, the lines broke, the distance between the crowd and the officials shrank to a point where the soldiers and blackhoods had to use force to hold people back.

Hilia was still processing all of this when Kadder shook her. "Wake up. The queen needs your help. Get her to the physician." And to mobilize the rest of the retinue, he bellowed, "Move, move."

The world spun around Hilia's head. Enclosed in a circle of guards, she and Gorman and a few others took the queen off the stage.

"Hilia," the queen said in a broken voice. With her face even paler than usual, she did not look immortal at all. She was a dying woman, struggling for every word coming out of her mouth. "I don't have long." She gasped in pain. "Don't let them take me to the physician. I want to go to my chambers."

"Highness, we're not letting you die," Hilia said what was expected of her. "Just do what you're told."

By the time they were in the palace, the woman's face glistened with cold sweat. Gorman stopped to break the shafts, and the blood-curdling cries of pain that came out of the queen were something Hilia would remember for the rest of her life.

Gorman started toward the infirmary when Hilia said, "No. The chambers. Call the physician to the chambers."

"Shut your mouth," the general barked. "Her Highness needs immediate help."

"She won't die," Hilia insisted, digging her own grave deeper. "Trust me, General. Please."

"Do what she says," the queen herself came to her aid.

Gorman clicked his tongue and said pointedly, "All right, but if anything happens to her, it's your head, maid."

They went to the residence building, up the stairs, and into the chambers.

"Bedchamber," the queen requested. Once they arrived there, she wiggled out of their hold, then stumbled into the room. Blood dribbled from the bottom of her dress. "Now, everyone, get out."

"What?" Hilia said with a trembling voice, her heart pounding.

Gorman insisted, "Ma'am, we can't leave you. Our protocol doesn't allow—"

"I'm protocol." The leader of the realm coughed and gasped. "Get out now. Hilia will tend to my wounds."

Hilia turned to the queen, flustered, but the woman gave her a fatigued blink, sending the message across.

The governor muttered curses before he addressed his men. "You heard Her Highness. Get the fuck out of here. I'll stay here with the maid."

"No one stays," the queen said in her weakening voice. "This is an order. I'll have your . . . your heads." She almost collapsed, but Hilia held under her shoulder to keep her standing.

Agitated, Gorman took his men out. As they left, Hilia frowned in confusion, her voice shaking, her limbs a trembling mess. "Highness, I'm not a healer. I can't do—"

"Get out of this room. Stay in the chambers for the rest of the night and make sure . . . no one enters." She then pulled away and let Hilia leave before she closed the door behind. The lock turned and clicked from inside.

Now that the chaos was over, Hilia realized she was the only person attending the queen. In other words, if the woman died tonight, Hilia would be the scapegoat. She sagged down against the wall, trying to steel herself. Clatters came from the bedchamber. A sign the queen was not dead yet. Why had Handler asked her to be there for this, to go through this? *I'm going to kill that bastard.*

The clatters went on for another few minutes until they stopped.

Was it over? Had the queen finally died?

Out the window, the sky was preparing to bid farewell to the last light of Diva. A dangerous idea bloomed in her head. She drew herself up and went to the window, looking at the ledge, the bottom, and the window of the bedchamber, which was only a few yards away from this one. She would not survive the fall, but she would not fall if she could take these few steps. *What are you doing, Hilia?*

Some unknown force inside her made her climb and slide out of the window, sitting on its edge—a voice in her head that told her this was her chance to find out how the queen defied death. It was a mix of curiosity and responsibility or, more likely, just pure idiocy.

Her feet touched the ledge, and before she could stop herself, she was standing, hand clutching the window frame. Her head spun when she looked down, and her hand slipped. She yelped and flattened herself against the wall despite her shaking limbs. Closing her eyes, she took a few breaths to steady herself before she was ready.

One side step. Then two.

"Don't look down," she whispered to herself, but the closer she got, the harder that seemed to get. *Curiosity killed the cat. Curiosity killed the cat.* She was now further from the sitting-room than she was from the bedchamber. There was no turning back. "Curiosity killed Hilia."

When her fingers touched the edge of the bedchamber window, she gave a nervous chuckle of victory. Tightening her grasp, she pulled herself toward it, and peeked inside—if one could call it that. The sense of stealth that went with peeking was hard to associate with how Hilia held herself.

There was fresh blood on the floor, but there was no sign of the queen. Hilia grabbed the inner frame and climbed through. She was now officially punishable by death, and that didn't bother her as much as the queen's absence did.

The key was still in the keyhole. Even if the queen was dead, there should at least be a body. People didn't just evaporate. Hilia looked under the bed, opened the closets, inspected the ground for any secret hatch. There was nothing. The queen had outsmarted her again.

This was exactly how it had happened last time the woman had been stabbed. She'd gone to her room and come out alive and well, leaving Hilia to wonder and the rest of the rebels to think she was immortal. "Not this time. I'm solving this mystery tonight."

She crawled under the bed and hid there. It no longer mattered that she could, in fact, be executed for trespassing. The reality of her current situation was that it had taken an unrepeatable miracle for her to hop windows, and splatting on the palace ground for nothing would be a far less noble death.

This could take a few minutes, or an hour, or she might have to spend the entire night here. The floor was not as comfortable as her bed, but that was good. This way, at least she wouldn't fall asleep.

25

Book of Creation, The Wandering Queen, twenty-fifth verse.
"She will have nothing to live for but her cause, nothing to lose
but the unending war."

T HE AIR SMELLED OF URINE, and grime caked the walls and the tables. But according to Mart, a courier's inn was perfect for hiding. Outside any city, and unpopular among bounty hunters.

The travel from Saba to Delavaran was taking longer than it should, and not only because of the distance between the two major cities. Arvin insisted they take frequent breaks for Panthea's health. This had gone so far that eventually, Panthea joined Mart in his protest. They had been traveling for four days now, and they were only halfway there.

The Dark Fusion was having quite the entrance this year. The world had started its descent into madness already. It was pouring outside, making even this place a blessing.

"Psst."

Panthea looked up.

"Psst, Cousin." Mart's eyes were locked on something in front of him. "That girl over there is checking you out."

Arvin and Gvosh both followed Mart's line of sight.

"Not at the same time, you idiots," Mart hissed.

"First of all," Arvin said, "you yourself are practically devouring her with your eyes. Second, we're in company."

Mart's eyes shifted to Panthea. "Oh, how rude of me. Of course, you're the prettiest woman in the room."

Arvin slapped his own forehead at that comment.

Panthea didn't know how to react. Being pretty was the least of her concerns, next to responding to the *compliment* at all.

"Third," Gvosh said, "I don't like women."

"You don't?" Mart frowned. "Since when?"

Gvosh gave him a warning look, his lip curled. "Since always."

"Well, then go sit somewhere else. I like women, and you're stealing that one's attention from me."

Gvosh thumped his palm on the table, making both Mart and Panthea jump. Then he got off the bench and left.

Mart winced. "I actually didn't expect him to leave. You think he got upset? I was joking."

"Well," Arvin said, "you have a peculiar sense of humor." He put a hand above Panthea's, causing a whirlwind of memories to come crashing over her.

She freed her hand from his, then crossed her arms.

Arvin didn't give up. "You've been awfully quiet. Are you sure you don't want to talk?"

She shrugged. "I do want to talk. You promised we'd review the plan. I'm still waiting."

"You're right," Arvin said apologetically. "Mart, no more goofing around. Let's get to business."

"Sure." Mart quaffed the last of his drink. "So, Dazzle-eyes, here's the plan you're not supposed to ruin."

Arvin gave him a hard look, and the gesture irritated her regardless of how well he had meant it. It did not matter how fragile he thought she was. She was not his to protect.

Mart pursed his lips momentarily. "On the day of the Dark Fusion, we enter Delavaran Palace through the Royal Library. I've already sent the mission briefing to Grumpy's handler, which," he gave Arvin a mischievous look, "I think you should have sent to her yourself."

"Why would I do that?" Arvin countered.

"I don't know. There was a time when you two couldn't spend a minute away from each other."

Arvin shook his head. "That was in the past. We've both moved on. But now I see you haven't."

Mart's expression turned wistful. "Can't blame a man for missing the old times. All of us together, dreaming of a better day."

"Yeah," Arvin said somberly. "We've all grown up."

"Guys?" Panthea interjected. "Plan?"

"Right," Mart said. "Where were we?"

"We enter through the library," she said.

Mart chortled. "No, Dazzle-eyes. Arvin and I enter through the library. You and Cousin go straight through the front door. He'll take you to the bureau."

Panthea frowned. "Why? If you're sneaking into the palace, why can't I come with you?"

"Because if you're caught trespassing, you'll end up in the army's custody. From there, it can be hours before they hand you over to the Inquisition, by which time the effect of the nightmare potion will have worn off. Then they'll sap you at the door, and you're done. If you go with Cousin, they'll sap you less than half an hour before Ponytail's arrival."

She reclined in her chair, nodding.

"We would have come with you too," Mart added, "but Ponytail has seen our faces, and he'd be quite surprised to see us again in the capital. We could have sent someone else to do it." He shot Arvin a disapproving glance. "But my boy here wouldn't trust this mission with anyone."

Panthea missed a gesture Arvin showed Mart, but whatever it was, it made him sigh. "Anyway. Your old man will be in that bureau. You'll have an hour to take out Yoltan, find your guardian, and fight your way out.

Outside, we'll retrieve you both. I've already asked a few of our agents to join us, so it looks like a proper ..." His eyes changed focus. "I knew it. That lying weasel is talking to the girl."

This time, Panthea followed their gazes to see Gvosh sitting with that woman, though he soon got up and rejoined the group.

Mart sneered on his approach. "You have a strange way of not being into women. How was your lover?"

"Room four," Gvosh said.

Mart scrunched his nose. "What?"

"She's staying in room four. She'll have a chat with you when you're done here."

Mart jumped to his feet. "Oh, I'm done here."

"Sit your ass down," Arvin chided. "Let's have another drink first."

There were three girls sitting at the next table. One of them was making the others laugh. Panthea couldn't help but think about Ash, whose silly jokes had always lifted her mood. How she missed her.

The touch of Arvin's hand on her shoulder ripped through her thoughts. "Are you all right?"

"I told you I'm fine." She shoved his hand away. "Get off my back, Arvin. I mean it."

Pursing his lips, he raised his cup to ask Mart if he cared for another drink. Mart showed two with his hand.

When Arvin left, Mart rested his elbows on the table and leaned forward. Panthea looked down, playing patterns with her fingers to fill the silence.

"You've got to cut him some slack," Mart mumbled.

She wanted to throw him a retort, but she didn't feel close enough to him to do that. Instead, she glared into his eyes, hoping it would get the message across.

It didn't. Keeping that unyielding stare, he said, "I know you want to say it's none of my business, but I have a habit of not doing what I'm told. So, let me tell you something, Dazzle-eyes. I've known that asshole for ten years. He lost both his parents when he was a kid, and Windhammer took—"

"I also lost my parents, but I don't—"

"Don't interrupt me," Mart said pointedly, pausing to reinforce his request. "Windhammer raised Arvin. Sometimes, I bend the big man's rules when I see fit, but in all the years I've known Arvin, he only ever defied Windhammer's direct orders once." Another brief pause. "Once. And it was when he went to that alley to save your tan ass. Now, I'm not asking you to fall in love with him. Just stop giving him shit for me, will you? Because he's taking it, and it's pissing me off." He sighed and got up. "I'll go talk to Room Four. Tell Arvin to enjoy my drink."

He left the table. Panthea looked over at Gvosh, who shrugged. "Don't look at me. I've never seen him like that."

Soon, Arvin came and put the drinks on the table. Two cups of searing gulp in front of Mart's seat, one in front of his own, and a cup of wine in front of Panthea. She hadn't asked for a drink and almost pushed it away, but at the last moment, she thought of what Mart had said. So, she grabbed the cup and slid it closer.

"Where did Mart run off to?" Arvin asked, glancing around until he found his answer. He chuckled. "That fucker."

Gvosh also smiled. "He said you could help yourself to his searing gulp."

Arvin snorted as he sat. While he and Gvosh moved on to small talk, Panthea looked around, observing people to pass the time. She'd go to the room and sleep if she weren't so alert.

Although it was called a courier's inn, there seemed to be all kinds of people here. Young, old, courier, farmer. Suddenly, among all the faces, an unmistakable one in the far corner caught her eye, and her stomach lurched. Evian. He sat alone, leaning against a backrest. Memories of the past two thretnights crashed on her. Rassus's capture. Ash's death.

"Ahura's throne," Arvin said, having followed Panthea's line of sight. "What under Diva is he doing here? Do you want to go to the room?"

"No." Panthea would not run from Evian. He did not deserve to control her. Steeling herself, she got out of her seat, then went to confront the man she had once called her brother.

Evian had two tankards in front of him. His eyes had dark circles around them, and his eyelids had swollen. Panthea sat down next to him.

"I don't want company," Evian said at first, but as soon as he saw her, he paled. "Panthea—"

"Don't say my name."

Evian rubbed his face with one trembling hand, his eyes glistening. "I . . . never meant to hurt you. I was weak. I was scared. I thought I was saving us by giving them Rassus."

"Saving us?" She let out a pained chuckle, which almost turned into a sob. How did he have the audacity? Pointing at her face, which still hosted that ugly gash and the bruises that had not yet fully healed, she said, "Do I look saved to you? Was Ash saved from her horrible fate? The only person you saved was yourself."

"I was there." Evian took a moment to meet her gaze again. "At the Green Eye Lake. Yoltan wanted to take you, but I stopped him. I told him I could use you to get to the stone and bring it back. It was the perfect excuse. We could have disappeared together. But you had to go back to Saba, no matter how much I begged you not to."

She could not believe what she was hearing. She had to repress her tears. "How dare you blame this on me? We were fine in Saba. It was you who brought those brutes into our home, who put us all in danger. It was you who turned Master in. It was you who got Ash killed. You. Not me."

"You're right." His chin quivered. "Will you ever forgive me?"

"No."

He cradled his face in his palms, weeping.

She waited for a time in case he had more to say. But then she decided she no longer needed to listen to him sob. This was the end of the conversation. The end of their friendship. She got up to leave. "Do me a favor. Never let me see you again. If you see me coming, walk the other way."

With that, she headed back toward her own table, where Arvin was on his feet, watching with a crease of concern between his brows. Her chest hollowed as she left the last piece of her past behind. The sudden surge of emotion was both painful and liberating. Painful, for she couldn't let herself cry, to look as weak as Evian was. Liberating, for she knew her feelings were one thing Evian hadn't taken from her.

26

When you possess the power to crumble entire kingdoms, your decisions shape the world, and your mistakes can bring it to ruin. That was why I had to be certain of my choice before I approached her.

IT WAS THE USUAL sound of morning. The distant chattering of people in the bazaar, the tapping of footsteps across the hallways, and those sharper ones of patrols on the palace grounds. And, of course, the sporadic chirping of birds with the apparent delusion that if they loitered around a stone tower long enough it would turn into a damned tree.

Hilia's mind was still foggy. Her eyes refused to open. She forced herself up, and something banged against her head, making her grunt as she went right back down. This time, her eyes snapped open to an array of wooden bars. "What under . . ."

Then she remembered. She clamped her mouth with both hands as if that would undo the unmistakable announcement of her presence. *For what it's worth, waking up is out of the way.*

The room was quiet and, from what she could see from under the bed, the door was closed. Could the queen really be dead? Did immortals just vaporize when they died?

Everything hurt. Her neck, her back, her shoulders. Wincing, she crawled to the edge, then hauled herself to her feet.

The place hadn't changed since last night, and even the key was still in the keyhole, which meant Hilia was stuck here. She couldn't unlock the door and leave without being found out. She was also too sore and rigid to climb out of the window again. In fact, she could live without having to do that again for the rest of her life.

She rubbed her face, trying to devise a way out of this predicament. While she thought, she opened the top drawer of the nightstand. There was nothing but a few pieces of paper.

Might as well. She flipped through them. The language was not Sessaran. Not even close. Was it northern script? Didn't northerners speak Sessaran? And why did the queen keep these in her bedchamber?

Hilia could worry about this later once she had accomplished the task at hand: staying alive. She closed the top drawer. As she opened the next one, the sight of what was inside sent a pulse of fear through her body. The Dark Scepter. This must be the reason the queen had locked the door—or at least a huge part of it.

She looked around to see if she was alone. Her heart raced. The scepter was there for the taking, and she could finally examine it the way she had wanted to since her last mission.

She moistened her lips as she sat down and reached for it. "This is a bad idea."

Closing her eyes, she grabbed the scepter. The voices erupted in her head, making her gasp, but she pushed on. Through all the jumbled whispers, through all the threats, she singled out, "*The Watcher must live on,*" and, "*Don't let the girl die.*"

She let go of the scepter and fell back. The last sentence brought forth the image of the dead girl she had seen in her dream. *Don't let the girl die.* This could no longer be a coincidence. There had to be more to that dream.

Collecting herself, she got up, straightened her tunic, then closed the drawer.

As she turned to the door, a green plume materialized in front of her, and a moment later, the queen of the Southern Kingdom was standing right there. *Well, shit.*

The queen's eyes bore into Hilia's, her brows drawn together in a mix of shock and anger. "What are you doing here?"

"Highness, y-you were out all night, and I-I got worried. I thought I'd come here to—"

"Enough," the queen spat, putting an end to Hilia's blabbering. She went to the door and inspected the key before her eyes turned to the window. "Did you window-hop?"

Hilia only managed a nod.

Eyes bulging, the queen rushed to the drawer. As she opened it, a little relief spilled into her countenance as she picked up the scepter. Then, without turning her piercing gaze away from Hilia, she went and opened the door. "I could hand you over to Inquisitor Kadder."

"Please, Highness," Hilia said with as steady of a voice as she could muster. "I had your well-being at heart."

"Get out. I'll deal with you later."

Hilia scurried into the sitting room like a spooked cockroach. Could she have been any more stupid? This could be the end of her. Then again, she'd known this while hopping windows.

The queen also emerged from the bedchamber, muttering, "I'll have these windows barred. Clearly, I can't trust my own servants."

Now that Hilia was over her initial shock, she registered what she was seeing. Although the queen's dress bore the holes and the blood from yesterday, her face had as much life in it as always—which wasn't much. Hilia still had no clue how the woman defied death, but at least now she knew it involved disappearing.

"How's your wound, Highness?"

"Don't concern yourself. Get out of here before I decide to act on your transgression. I don't want to see you today."

"Thank you," Hilia said, meaning it.

When she opened the door of the chambers, a mob of agitated guards, accompanied by Kadder and some of his blackhoods, surrounded her, giving her inquisitive looks.

"She's inside," she managed.

The guards poured in, and Kadder gave her a curt smile as he followed. It was over. Hilia had survived the night. The question was, could she survive the day too?

She spent the morning in her bed, thinking. The queen had renewed. The wounded queen had evaporated, and a new, healthy queen had been born—into the same clothes. This was not arcane. If it were, one of those books would have mentioned something about it.

Noon took its time to arrive. As soon as the bells rang, Hilia shot out of her room and headed to the library. There she could try to find a book that would give her an answer.

"Parviz?" she called as she walked in and kept calling until he emerged from between the shelves, his eyes wide with concern.

"Hilia, are you all right? I heard about what happened yesterday."

She ignored his inquiry. "Queen Artenus used to be the High Lady of Sepead before she moved to the Southern Kingdom, yes? Do northerners have an analog to our Book of Kings?"

"They do. In fact, I might have a copy." He gave a wry smile. "Let me guess. The queen survived, and now you're even more curious."

"Something like that. I want to know what kind of power she has. It's not any form of arcane I've read about, and it's not the scepter. I thought maybe a northern book could help me find out what it is."

"You're as stubborn as they come," he said. "You'll make an excellent scholar, you know. Wait here. I'll be right back."

As he walked away, guilt rose in Hilia's chest. She was involving the man in her mess, possibly putting him in danger.

After a while, the librarian came back with a book. "Here. Let's have a look together."

"You don't have to." She tried to take the book.

He kept his grip on it. "Nonsense. You're not the only seeker of knowledge around here."

He put the book on a table, and they began perusing it. It contained the history of Sepead, the capital of the Northern Realm, including information about all the High Ladies.

He flipped toward the end of the book, then halted when they found Lady Artenus. Born 1058. Appointed 1080. Exiled 1090. There was a bunch about her childhood and her brother who was in the High Council, whatever that was. And then there was it. Erkenblood with power over the element of space.

"That's it," Hilia exclaimed.

The librarian looked closer. "That's what?"

"Last night, the queen disappeared. I thought it was death and rebirth. But now I believe she just space-jumped . . . somewhere."

Parviz drew his brows together. "But it doesn't explain how she survived."

"No, but if we could stop her from . . ." she trailed off. She'd almost forgotten whom she was talking to.

"Right." The look in Parviz's eyes meant the damage was done. "It makes sense now. When were you planning to tell me you were a rebel?"

"Please don't judge me. I did what I had to."

"What you had to?" He huffed. "You knew you were endangering me and my family, and you decided it to be your choice and not mine."

Gods damn it. "I didn't want to lose our friendship. My time in this library, our conversations . . . those were the closest things I had to a normal life. You were my only real friend."

"And yet somehow, I was the one whom you lied to. I was the one you hid your true self from."

"My true self is a mess," she confessed. "I'm a pawn, stuck in a war I never wanted to be a part of. I didn't want you to get to know that pawn. I wanted you to know me. Hilia."

"And who is Hilia?"

She sighed. "Can we start over?"

"Let's." Parviz sat down. "Why did you join the rebellion?"

If that was his first question, she was in for a rough ride. She looked around to make sure they were alone, then sat next to him and braced her head in her palms. *I don't need this right now.*

"It's up to you to decide which Hilia you want to be," urged Parviz. "Because the only version of this where we'll remain friends is the one where you tell me the truth."

Hilia released the air trapped in her lungs. She had stayed hidden from the Inquisition for so long, yet she'd just given herself away to this librarian, and his piercing glare was proving more effective than any method the Inquisition would use.

After a long struggle, she complied. "I was eighteen. My father had a popular winehouse in Livid, and I worked there with him. Business was good. We weren't rich, but we lived a comfortable life. Do you know about the Impunity Law?"

He narrowed his eyes, which made for an even deeper frown. "It concerns citizens of the Northern Realm, doesn't it?"

She nodded. "They're immune to prosecution and harm in the Southern Kingdom. That means they can do whatever they want. You get used to the bullying over time, but one day, one of those bastards had had too much to drink and started vandalizing the winehouse. A fight broke out, and the northerner died."

As the memories refreshed in her mind, she struggled to keep her composure from breaking. "The next day, Sapphires poured into the place and were about to arrest me and my father. We hadn't even been involved in the fighting, but they wanted to take us to the Inquisition. To protect me, my father picked up his cleaver and charged at the Sapphires." She took a heavy breath. "The scariest day of my life. The thought of it still gives me shivers. Thinking this is it, my father is going to die in front of me."

She cleared her throat to mask the tremor in her voice. "But then that boy showed up with his friends. He was about my age, but he was fiercer than I'd ever wished to be. They fought the soldiers, and they won. They took me and my father to a safehouse and asked us to stay there. Sapphires searched every house in the neighborhood. They burned my father's winehouse to the ground. They destroyed our life. My father was not the same after that."

Parviz nodded. "Then that man, your savior, recruited you. Said you could make it right."

"He was my hero," Hilia admitted, remembering how close she and Arvin had once been. "I fell in love with him. He helped us get through it all. He helped my father get back on his feet. So, when the opportunity presented itself, I wanted nothing more than to join his cause. I thought they were making the land a better place, and I wanted to be part of it."

"And then?"

"And then . . ." She tried to find a suitable answer, but there were so many things that had happened, so much that had changed. "And then I grew up."

Parviz considered her for a time, then gave a tepid nod as he got to his feet. "That's enough for today. I believe your friend is waiting for you."

That was when she noticed Handler sitting at the next table, waving at her. She got up, bracing herself for another argument.

"This conversation isn't over," Parviz said.

She responded with a tight smile, trying to keep the pain out of it. Then she picked up the book and went to the other table.

As she sat, Handler said, "I thought we were keeping him out of this."

She rolled her eyes and blew out a breath in frustration. "I've had a really bad day, so don't start with this again. He's safe. He's my friend."

"You don't have friends." He was pushing it. "Except for me."

She thumped her palm on the table. "You know what friends don't do? They don't set you up. Why did you ask me to be with the queen for an assassination?"

"You yourself asked for it," he said.

"Uh-uh. I think I'd remember if I had."

"Cleaning day. I came to the chambers to look for you. You asked me to plan a successful assassination if I wanted results. Now, what do you have for me?"

"Wh . . ." For the next few seconds, Hilia could not even utter one coherent word. "You sent a man to his death for an angry comment I made?"

"I didn't think you'd perform as well as you did if you expected it. I withheld that information for your protection."

"Hey!" She pointed her index finger at him. "I've been performing well. I was keeping out of trouble on my own. In fact, all my troubles began when you came into the picture."

He snorted. "I was always in the picture. The only reason I have to deal with your big mouth right now is that our mutual friend is no longer among us."

"Yes, keep bringing it up. Keep rubbing it in, in case I'm not in enough pain. It's good for my morale. For my performance."

He sighed, rocking his head in frustration. "We have to stop doing this, Hilia. You and I both know we don't like each other. But we have to work together. So, let's get back to the point. The Inquisition has the attacker. I'm going to figure out a way to keep us out of trouble, but you must prepare for anything."

"And by anything, you mean killing myself."

"Yes. As cruel as it sounds." He paused. "I hope at least you put this opportunity to good use."

Opportunity. "I may have a lead toward how the queen survives. I think it might involve a space-jump."

He narrowed his eyes. "A space what?"

"She, uh, she instantly travels to a certain location." She made a fist and opened it. "Poof."

"Poof," Handler imitated. "So, you're telling me, if we can stop her from *jumping*, she won't be able to heal. And she'll die."

"Yes, in theory. I'm close to figuring it out, but I need a little more time. And I think I've earned the right to demand it."

"You're close enough," Handler said. "I have eyewitnesses who saw the queen collapse. Everyone knows she's not invincible. In fact, there are rumors the event has emboldened smaller resistance groups, and the Inquisition is working overtime to prevent an uprising."

He gave a lopsided smile. "I do hope they can contain the situation because the last thing we need is a premature insurgence by a bunch of hotheads with no allegiances. Anyway, the moral of the story is you've delivered on your promise. Now, I want you to stop your research because I have a new assignment for you."

"I can't stop now," Hilia said. "If I can get to the bottom of this, those insurgents won't be a problem. We can eliminate the queen before the Dark Fusion."

"We're not," Handler shot, clenching his fist over the table before he lowered his voice to a bare whisper, "killing the queen." Hilia opened her mouth to protest, but he shut her down with, "And I don't want to hear about this anymore."

What was the point of proving the queen was mortal if they were not doing anything about it? If only Hilia had the energy to argue further. *One problem at a time.* "Fine." She leaned back and crossed her arms. "What's the assignment?"

Handler kept the glare for a little longer before he said, "Your old friends, Arvin, Mart. They're coming to Delavaran on the Dark Fusion."

Hilia felt a jolt. After so long, this was not at all how she'd imagined seeing Arvin again. On another mission. "For what?"

"To lead a special operation. The chief Inquisitor of Saba is visiting the capital. It's our best chance to eliminate him without drawing too much attention to Shiran."

Hilia curled her lips. "And how are they going to kill an Inquisitor exactly?"

"That's where the Erkenblood comes in. Our friends will turn her in, and she'll kill him at the bureau. That's all you need to know for now."

Oh, of course. The Erkenblood. Gods, this is going to be another mess. "Not all of it. You still haven't told me what my part is in this."

"Well, someone has to get them inside the palace without notice."

"Don't tell me. I'm getting them in through this library."

Handler gave a toothy grin. "I suppose your wits were why the Windhammer recruited you. Because it couldn't have been your attitude."

"How flattering," she said with a sardonic smile.

He also chuckled with the same humor—or lack thereof. "So, you think you're up to the task?"

"Is there another way? I don't want to put the librarian in danger."

He shook his head. "This library is the best point of entry into the palace. If you do it right, no harm will come to him. So, what do you say? Because if your answer is no, I'll have to call abort."

"Isn't it too late for that? What if our mutual friends have already left Saba?"

"Hence why I expect you to accept this assignment," Handler said. "But if you think, for any reason, this plan can fail, I have my ways of handling the situation. I can plug a sentry at the gates to warn them and ask them to turn around."

Hilia rested her head on the back of the seat, looking up at the high beams of the ceiling as she pondered. If this mission succeeded, it would mark the beginning of the end for the Sapphire Order. For six years, Hilia had wanted to be a part of something of this magnitude, and turning this mission down felt strange. To convince herself, she considered the fact that Mart had planned this mission. He was always thorough. The only thing stopping her was the thought of Parviz. Involving him in this mess would not be fair. He had a family.

A few soldiers and blackhoods entered the library. She opened the book and pretended to read. Handler got up and went to the shelves.

One of the blackhoods approached Hilia. "Were you speaking with that man?"

"Um, yes. He asked me about a book. I told him where he could find it."

A thunk came from the direction Handler had gone, and when Hilia looked, the Sapphires were grabbing him. Worry clenching her stomach, she asked the blackhood near her, "What's happening?"

"You don't need to concern yourself. He's with the rebellion, and we're taking him in for questioning."

Before Hilia's eyes, Handler reached into his pocket and took out his poison. Hilia's heart stopped as he threw the whole vial into his mouth.

Oh, gods, no. She covered her mouth, trying to contain the shock. Handler spat out, first the cork, then the empty vial. *No.*

They dragged the man away, but before they got to the exit, he began shaking, then foaming, then his weight fell on the soldiers who were carrying him.

They set Handler down, confused. He convulsed on the floor, frothy blood pouring out of his mouth, and after a long struggle, it all ended. His hands fell limp, his eyes stared at the ceiling. Hilia could not process what had transpired. A minute ago, they were bickering.

"I'll ask you again," the blackhood ripped her out of her trance. "Did you know that man?"

Hilia shook her spinning head. "Is he . . . dead?"

"No, he's not, because he never existed. This never happened. Understood?"

She nodded. Was she allowed to break? Would they suspect her? The sneaky tear that slid down her cheek decided it didn't matter. As she watched in disbelief, they carried Handler out, and thus he ceased to exist.

Hilia sat there, staring at the blood on the floor. This was the last of the man she'd met in this place, the man she'd gotten used to arguing with, the man who had . . . As though she was not frightened enough, more of her new reality gripped her mind. Handler was supposed to organize this operation. With him gone, this mission was doomed to fail, and everyone was going to die. Arvin, Mart, Hilia herself. She had to find a way to call off the whole thing before it was too late.

The memory of her first conversation with Handler passed through her mind, and she seized it. *Grape and Barley.* Handler had told her the rebels dispatched and received their messages in that winehouse. Maybe someone there could organize an emergency abort. *Shit. Shit.*

27

I have lived many lifetimes. I have seen kingdoms rise and fall. I have seen benevolent kings and savage slaughterers. I know the shape of a world in balance, and I know when the world needs a savior.

As Hilia walked down the stairs into Grape and Barley, the women in the winehouse gave her dubious looks, and the men stared at her with hungry eyes. Although she'd tried her best to dress like a commoner, she was far from inconspicuous here. The memory of her winehouse days seemed to have evaded her. Either that, or this place was the most dilapidated one in the Southern Kingdom.

The rugs and backrests were in desperate need of replacement, and the floor was sticky with dried beer and wine. The only thing matching her expectation was the stench.

She waited at the bar area until a man with a shiny head and a mass of dark, fuzzy beard arrived behind the counter as he cleaned a tankard with a piece of cloth. "You better run, lassie. Pretty girl like you gets devoured here."

Hilia rolled her eyes. "Are you Blackbeard?"

"What makes you say that?"

She pointed at his face and wiggled her finger as she said dubiously, "Well, you, uh, have a black beard?"

The man sneered. "Well, look over there. He could be Blackbeard. Or that one. That man can definitely be Blackbeard. In fact, we got a whole bunch of them here. Now, bounce. This is no place for your type."

Hilia glanced at all his references, then turned back to him. "Listen, twitwad," she said in a tone that was half playful, half intimidating, just the way one talked to a drunk who harassed a maid, the intonation and all. She put on her thickest Shiranian accent for the best dramatic effect, even though it was not how people in Livid talked. "You can't scare a winehouse girl out of a winehouse."

The man cocked an eyebrow, considering her for a moment. "You sure talk the talk. What do you want with Blackbeard?"

"Depends," she said. "Are you him?"

"Let's say I am." He scanned the place before he leaned forward. "Who are you? And what is it you want?"

"The handmaiden." She picked out the note she'd written and placed it on the counter.

The man went to grab the letter, but Hilia kept her grip on it. "How do I know you're the right man?"

He snorted. "How do I know you're the handmaiden? You're not even supposed to be here. Where's your handler?"

"Gone."

Blackbeard curled his lips. "Dead?"

"No, he went on a road trip."

It took the man a second to read her sarcasm and show the first signs of fear. "Fucking shit. That's why he disappeared all of a sudden. Wait here."

She let go of the letter, and he left with it. Meanwhile, she looked around at everyone who had a black beard, and she couldn't help a smile. Soon, the man came back with her letter still in his hand. "Can't do this. It's too late to abort the operation."

"What do you care?" she said. "You're just a messenger."

"I'm also a brother to the agents who will be left bare-ass under Diva because of a technicality."

Hilia blinked in frustration. "Since when do Windhammer's men have a conscience?"

"Since when don't his women?"

She snatched her letter from his hand and slammed it on the bar. "Listen, Blackbeard, or whatever your real name is. I've had a bad couple of days, and I'm in no mood to argue. If we don't call off this mission, two of our top agents die, including the big guy's right-hand man. And so will your brothers, you, and me. There's a chance I can turn this around or at least mitigate the damage, but I need your help. Before my handler died, he told me we can plug someone at the gates to warn our comrades. Can you do that?"

He scoffed. "Who do you think I am? I'm not authorized to take such actions without a signature from a high-ranking agent."

"Right now, my signature is the best you're going to get."

"Your signature is worth shit. You're a sleeper agent, for gods' sake. I need your handler's signature."

She blew her breath out in a huff of frustration. Maintaining her accent, she spat, "Keep up with me here. I told you my handler's dead. Do you want everyone else to die too?"

"I got an idea. Why don't you stay at the gates and warn them?" He smirked at his own stupid joke. A smile that vanished when he noticed Hilia's icy glare. "There's nothing I can do for you. I'm not spitting on the chain of command. If you want to, be my guest, but keep me out of it."

Hilia grabbed the back of his neck and slammed his head to the counter, pressing it there as she muttered in his ear, "Now, listen to me, Blackshit. You're going to help me get this situation under control. I have friends in high places, and I'm not afraid of answering to the Windhammer. So, set this up, or Windhammer will be the least of your problems."

A few had turned to look. *I suppose my winehouse days are not all forgotten.* Hilia let go and put on her signature charming smile to pacify the onlookers.

Blackbeard straightened his jacket and cracked his neck, groaning.

"You really are a winehouse girl, aren't you?" He sighed. "Fine. I'll send out the orders, but if anyone asks, I'll tell them you sent them yourself. If you have a problem with that, go ahead and waste me now, because that's the extent of the shit I give about you and your orders. Now, get the fuck out of my winehouse."

She taunted him with a smirk as she set to leave.

The front door opened, and her prayer mate, Inquisitor Kadder, walked down the stairs, accompanied by two blackhoods and at least two units of soldiers. *Is he kidding me?* "All right, this winehouse is closed. Get out."

Before Hilia could even think about hiding or running, Kadder's discerning gaze caught her.

Blackbeard produced a crossbow from under the counter and yelled, "Get fucked," as he loosed the arrow in it, striking a blackhood.

Weapons were drawn, and a fight broke out as Hilia watched in horror. Dark memories flashed before her eyes. The sickening sound of steel cutting through bone, the sight of blood splashing over the walls. Shouts. Screams. It was Livid all over again, and she was the same eighteen-year-old weakling, dead frozen.

The voice of her younger self echoed in her ears. *"Dad, please!"*

Every man who died, every man who charged at the soldiers, was her father. Every woman who had curled in a corner was an ugly reflection of herself.

Out there, at the other end of the winehouse, stood a young woman, pale, face slick with tears—an almost perfect window into Hilia's own past. Their eyes met for a fleeting moment, an unfortunate connection between a woman who'd seen this one too many times and one who had trouble digesting it.

The sharp edge of a sword ended that fickle moment as it cut across the girl's throat. Her eyes grew wide, her hands shot to her throat as blood gushed out of it. Hilia's ears rang as she watched reality take hold of the petrified woman as she collapsed.

Hilia stumbled backward until the counter helped her stand upright, and she turned away from the massacre. She was now a small prop in a dance of steel and blood, at the mercy of two opposing hordes that killed for the thrill of it, waiting for a sword to cut her life short.

It all ended when the last man dropped at her feet. The letter was scrunched to a ball in her fist as she waited for the right moment to destroy it. Pressing her free hand on the counter, she turned to the pile of corpses. There were barely any survivors, save for the officials.

The soldiers brought Blackbeard to Kadder. The man spat on the Inquisitor's face.

Wiping the spittle off with the back of his hand, Kadder growled, "Delivering messages for the rebellion? I'll deliver you to the afterlife. Take him away."

Delavaran was now a slaughterhouse for the rebels, cut out from the rest of the kingdom, with at least two agents taken to the Inquisition, among them Blackbeard, the man who knew almost every rebel in the city.

There was murder in Kadder's eyes. He gave Hilia a sharp glance as he went behind the bar and picked out a decanter of wine. "Let's have a drink, shall we?"

The soldiers were inspecting the bodies, slitting the throats of those who still breathed. Hilia joined Kadder. Not that she had a choice. Kadder slammed two cups on the counter and poured wine into them. Hilia covertly shoved the letter under her girdle. The Inquisitor lifted one cup and slid the other toward her. It was hard to even look at the bloody color of the wine, but she had to. She was lucky to be alive. She took the cup with a trembling hand and drank half of it in one gulp, staring at it as she put it back down.

Kadder poured her more. "You know what I hate most about my profession?"

The weight of his stare was crushing, and Hilia didn't have enough courage to return it. Less to answer.

"Here's a hint." He swept an arm across the room. "It's not this. It's not the violence and death."

They both took a sip. Wine had never been so nauseating.

"It's not seeing people pushed to their limits," he continued, "seeing their bodies give out under torture. Those who die are the lucky ones."

To ease the anxiety that kept building up, Hilia bottomed her second cup, but Kadder immediately gave her another refill.

"It's the ones who live. Seeing headstrong kids like you, with dreams, with promise, come to the bureau and turn into nothing. Shells turning days into nights, wishing they'd not survived." He pointed at the front door. "You go to the bureau, you won't come out the same person." He finished his drink and motioned his men to leave. Before he himself joined them, he clapped Hilia's shoulder and muttered, "Something to think about."

She fought every muscle in her face to keep it from contorting. It was hard enough to stay out of trouble when she wasn't a suspect. Now, it would only be a matter of days. Tears budding in her eyes, she only nodded.

Kadder left the winehouse. Hilia turned away from the counter and sagged against it, looking up at the shelves of liquor. What would she do now? How under the fuck of Diva was she supposed to cancel the operation? She had two options before her. Call off the mission by contacting people in a non-existent roster, or make sure everything went according to an unknown plan.

A bubble of laughter pressed under her throat, and soon enough, her jaw and lungs chose option number three. Laughing. The kind she had no control over. The kind that hurt. Physically. She barely had time to breathe between her cackles. It was infuriating. The fate of the rebellion and everyone in it was at stake, and she was laughing. Or crying. Or whatever this was.

Let it go, girl. It's not your problem. You've done enough. You can't do more. That only made her laughter worse. Her inability to accept it. With eyes that had teared up, with an anger that grew by the second, she kept going as if she had heard the most amusing joke. Come to think of it, this *was* a joke. This was the perfect punchline to a life of always being in the wrong place at the wrong time with the wrong plan.

Hilia was sick of being responsible for people's deaths. She was tired of living in fear, tired of being a pawn. She just wanted to get out of this mess. Was it so impossible for the world to give her a break? If gods existed, they were mocking her right now because that's what gods did.

She jumped to her feet and stomped to the shelves. Laughing turned to growling. Growling turned to screaming as she swept all bottles and decanters off the shelves. Those that survived the fall, she grabbed and threw at the walls. She screamed until her voice caught, and she began coughing.

Once her rage settled, once her coughing stopped, she leaned over the counter, panting through her sore throat, clenching her shaking, bloodied fist, and forced herself to think. She took the letter out and held it over a candle until it burned out, flicking the last bit of it away.

What now?

28

She was wise beyond my expectations. She was determined to help her people. And above all—and this is not something many of my candidates had in common—she was ambitious.

THE SAME NIGHTMARE—the girl's body sprawled under the bedchamber window. This time, it had been more lucid too. Whatever the Dark Scepter had done to Hilia, it seemed to be here to stay. She didn't know if these were premonitions or if she was descending into madness as Watchers did. Her outburst at the winehouse strengthened the latter argument.

She sat up and looked out the window. The Dark Fusion was only a few days away, and a deep red tint on the horizon was the only sign of dawn. That, and the damned cold. She shivered as she removed her blankets to get out of bed.

Hair fixed, outfit on, covered in the woolen Dark Fusion robe, it was time for her to begin the day.

She fetched the queen's breakfast from the kitchens. As she carried the tray up the stairs, she could hardly maintain her smile. Not with the foreboding in her heart. Not with her mind racing to prevent an impending disaster.

When she arrived at the door, she heard Queen Artenus talking to someone. Hilia waited outside and listened.

The person, whose voice she didn't recognize, spoke with long, exaggerated intonation. "The Erkenblood has already lost her friend. She's fragile. I can break her within the day."

"No, Inquisitor," the queen said.

Inquisitor. Perhaps this was whom Handler had talked about. The one the Erkenblood was going to kill.

"You have done enough damage in Saba," the queen continued. "When the Erkenblood shows up, I want to be the first to meet her."

Hilia didn't know how the operation was supposed to go. But meeting with the queen herself was never good news.

"I agree." *Shit.* It was Kadder's voice. Hilia had hoped she would not run into him after their last encounter. "Inquisitor Yoltan. As someone who has lived longer than you and who cares deeply about our values, I must tell you this. What your men did in Saba, killing a fifteen-year-old girl in the middle of the street, isn't the image we want for the Inquisition."

Those words painted an ugly picture in Hilia's head, and one she could not shake off. A fifteen-year-old.

Yoltan tittered. "I live in the Shiranian region, Inquisitor. The only reason Windhammer's thugs have not overrun Saba is that I know how to maintain a clean image. No one will link then girl's death to the Inquisition. She was never booked, the army has been given proper instructions, and the family has been silenced."

"Very thorough," Kadder said in a low growl, "but that's not the kind of answer I was looking for."

"With all due respect, you don't suggest we show compassion toward those criminals, do you?"

"Let us not argue over this matter," the queen interrupted the conversation. "The Bond is more important than our reputation. We can repair what's broken once we have it."

Hilia finally walked in. The queen frowned. "How much did you hear?"

"N-not much, Highness. I just brought your breakfast. I can leave."

Yoltan didn't seem to find Hilia worthy of his attention. Kadder, however, beckoned to her, showing no sign of tension from last time, which was unsettling on its own. "No, come on in. We're done talking about business, anyway."

"What are you waiting for, then?" the queen shot. "Put the tray on the table."

There was so much to be learned here, but Hilia could not linger too long. They all seemed too stingy with information around her, and if she stayed longer than she should, it would raise suspicion. So, she did as commanded, curtsied, and left.

The day went by with Hilia struggling to keep the conversation between the Inquisitors out of her mind. What was the world coming to? Old men and women churned politics from the safety of their homes, and children had to bleed for them?

Luckily, she had enough work to keep her distracted for the most part. All day, disgruntled clan leaders came to visit the queen, and Hilia had to carry their belongings around.

By night, her neck throbbed from a day of carrying heavy trunks. Once she was done clearing the table after the last guest, she stretched and rubbed her nape to release some of the pain.

When the queen approached, Hilia quickly removed her hand to stand upright. On its way, her finger got caught in the chain and made it snap.

Shit! The pendant flew down her dress, landing on the carpet. Hilia bent and snatched it from the floor, but by the time she straightened again, the queen stood right in front of her, giving her a knowing look. To eliminate the element of doubt, the woman's gaze fell to the dandelion pendant—the undeniable symbol of the pantheon—then back up to Hilia's eyes.

There was no way to salvage this. Hope felt like the best strategy. The queen stole another glance at her hand before she said, "Sit down, Hilia. I would like to talk."

"I don't think I should linger, Highness. You must be—"

"It wasn't a request."

The expectant look in the queen's eyes took all manner of choice away. Hilia stifled a sigh as she picked the chair in front of her. Even after they both sat, the queen kept staring at her with her characteristic icy gaze.

To change the energy—and perhaps get something out of the woman—Hilia said, "Should I go introduce myself to the prisons?"

The queen smiled, though her voice was in her usual calm, deceptive melody when she answered, "Why? Because you have a different faith than mine?" She looked away, shaking her head wistfully. "I never wanted this war. I had nothing against those who followed the pantheon. But long before the Great Reform, even when King Shahbod was still alive, the old-doctrine Ahuraics never recognized me as their queen.

"Those priests preached their hatred toward the northern Erkenblood, who had become the queen in the south, and my husband did nothing to stop them. I didn't mind while he lived. I had his protection, and he had their respect. But when I became the sole leader of this realm, my status changed from an error in judgment to a usurper. I had to show strength and authority, or the kingdom would fall, taking with it more than just me."

Hilia wanted to laugh at the irony. The queen pretended to care for the kingdom when she herself had brought it to ruin. She *had* started this war when she'd killed the king—and her own daughter—to take the throne. That was the definition of a usurper. And showing strength was a far cry from what Sapphires had done to Ahuraic temples.

When the queen's eyes found hers again, Hilia only nodded. It wasn't like she could argue with her about this. Not if she wanted to stay alive and keep her position in the palace. She'd made enough mistakes for an agent of the Windhammer.

"You're very hard to read, Hilia." *That makes two of us.* "But today, it was easy to notice something bothered you. As someone who holds many secrets, I understand the burden, and I do not enjoy prying. However, something that can cut through the air of mystery around you cannot be a small matter. Some questions are dangerous to ask; others are dangerous if they remain unanswered. Doubt leads to fear. Fear leads to treason. If there is anything on your mind, I want you to tell me now."

Hilia was too tired to lie that well. Apparently, she was not hiding her emotions well, either. So, she sprinkled some truth over the mountain of secrets she'd built in the palace, hoping that would sate the queen's untimely interest in her feelings. "Forgive me, Highness, but I overheard what that Inquisitor did to the girl. Maybe I expected you to do something about it."

"I knew you were listening." The queen's eyes narrowed slightly, the expression so subtle Hilia couldn't tell if it was disdain or incredulity. "I cannot go around punishing Inquisitors for every mistake they make. The job Yoltan has been doing is of utmost importance. There will come a time when he answers for his crimes. But it isn't now."

Hilia held back a sigh. "While you give him more time, a family mourns their daughter. What about them? Do they mean nothing?"

"You're not asking the right questions. Here's one I want you to think about. What if killing one child could lead to saving the lives of many more? What if I could create a world where there would be no more mothers who mourned their children? Would that justify that one death?"

Was this how she slept at night? And this rhetoric, this old platitude, was what Windhammer had nailed into his follower's heads, Hilia's included. Fighting for the greater good. Sacrificing one to save many. It was what had kept Hilia in this palace for four long years. Politics was the most disgusting game of hypocrisy.

"No," Hilia said. "Nothing justifies willingly taking an innocent life."

The queen smiled, though there was not even a hint of joy in it. There was not a hint of anything. Pain, maybe. "Tell that to the Mehr Guard who let my daughter," her voice rose to a shout, "burn alive." This was the second time in four years Hilia had heard her this loud.

The queen took a moment to breathe, then continued in almost a whisper. "I can still hear my own screams. 'Let me save my daughter. She's in there.' 'You have to listen to me.'" She bit her lip, seeming to struggle with every word now. "Those idiots probably thought they were the heroes, averting the threat of the queen who had breached the terms of her exile. I don't even want to imagine the pain my little Hita went through as those flames consumed her."

The woman stopped speaking altogether. And Hilia saw in her eyes something she had never seen in them before: tears. They were not enough to leave her eyes, but it still seemed strange that those eyes could produce tears at all. And this version of the story was different from the one Hilia had heard, where the queen herself had killed her daughter.

After a long pause, a fresh smile played on the queen's lips. It was in such a contrast to her still glistening eyes, it almost looked psychotic. "We are all monsters in someone's story. Far too often, saving one person means letting another fall. And those moments are what define you as a hero. The decision, not of whom you save, but whom you let fall. I know where I stand. I know where I draw the line. I know the sacrifices I'm willing to make, and I've accepted the monster within me. A freeing thought that I hope one day you, too, come to experience."

Hilia let out a small puff of breath. If the queen wanted to be a monster, if she wanted to be the judge of whom to sacrifice, it was her choice. But Hilia would neither be, nor aid, a monster.

If the Erkenblood faced the queen alone, she would die. If she was to survive, she could use any help she could get. *That witch better be worth what I'm going to risk.*

29

According to the Book of Creation, the Wandering Queen must herself be touched by "the divine" or what we scholars refer to as First Arcane. That was my first clue. But what made me choose her was her willingness to sacrifice everything she had for what she believed in.

THIS LIBRARY WAS NO LONGER a sanctuary. The table where Hilia used to sit and read had become the spot from where she had watched Handler die. And here she was, about to snuff out the last part of what made this place her refuge.

Parviz was still talking to another patron. While Hilia waited, she pretended to browse. It was the greatest skill she had gained. Her greatest achievement as a rebel: being a proficient liar. Even the word rebel was an overstatement. She was a separatist. Windhammer's movement had never been about justice. Justice was only a shiny banner he flourished before new recruits.

Suddenly, a barreling Tremos shot at her and clung to her leg, almost making her yelp.

"Look who's here every day now." She cocked her eyebrow. "Are you planning to steal your dad's job?"

He laughed.

"Tremos?" came Parviz's stern voice. "Go back to the study."

"But daddy, Hilia's here."

Parviz gave her a piercing glance that emptied her chest, and said with an edge of irritation, "Hilia's busy. You can talk with her next time."

Tremos tried to argue, but Parviz ended it with a resounding, "Now, Tremos."

The boy pouted as he shuffled away. The librarian waited until his son was out of earshot before he said, "Here to continue our conversation?"

"I'm here about one of your stories."

Parviz snorted, then walked to a shelf on the far side of the main hallway. He spent some time counting and scrutinizing the books and writing things down, ignoring her presence. "My stories," he said impassively after a while, "were for a woman whose passion was learning. A woman who had dreams."

"I have dreams."

"What you have is no dream. I always admired your curiosity. I thought knowledge was the reward you sought. But now, I see everything you did had one purpose. You're on a mission."

Hilia could no longer handle his reproof. She went and stood beside him. "Just because I have a mission, it doesn't mean I don't value knowledge. You can't reduce me to this only because I hid certain aspects of my life from you to protect us both."

"Protect *you*," Parviz said, drilling his finger into her chest. "You didn't protect me or my family. Look around you, Hilia. Everyone who's talked to you more than twice is already dead. You brought death onto my sacred ground."

"Now, you're being insensitive." She had to force herself to speak with a level voice. "I have a heart. I've always cared about you, about Tremos."

Parviz stopped what he was doing and regarded her. "Inquisitor Kadder was here earlier today. I had to sit through an hour of questioning. This is not the kind of thing I expected to experience when I became a librarian."

Her head pulsed with fear. "Did he ask about me?"

Instead of answering that, Parviz shook his head with disdain and asked, "Why are you here?"

Hilia hesitated. This was not exactly the perfect timing to make her request, but she had no energy left to dance around the subject. "There's something I need to know. In one of your stories, you mentioned sapping potion."

He threw a derisive hand in the air as he walked back to the shelf.

Shaking with frustration, she called after him, "If I do nothing, people will die, an innocent eighteen-year-old girl among them." The more Parviz ignored her, the louder she spoke. "I'm saving lives here. You have no idea what's going on in this kingdom. You call me selfish? At least I don't have my head in the dirt. At least I do something. I'm risking my life to—"

"Stop." He heaved a deep sigh before coming back. "You know why I gave you that specific fiction book?"

She narrowed her eyes at the unrelated question. "You said Kyra was like me."

"Yes, but do you know what part of her? This"—with his hands, he drew an invisible contour around Hilia—"isn't about saving lives. This isn't about helping your father. I'm a father. If I were in the same circumstances as yours, I wouldn't want my son to pick up a sword and fight my fight. I want my kids to live well. I would give my life for them to be safe. Your father doesn't want to be alone in some remote corner of this world, counting days until one day, maybe he can see his daughter again."

The image of her father watching the door every day, having no one to talk to, no one to keep him company, while Hilia toyed with her own life in here, tore her apart.

"Your father doesn't need justice," Parviz continued. "He needs a daughter. I bet he stays awake so many nights with the fear of losing you. And one of these days, you're going to realize his nightmare because being a hero is so damned important to you. You want to be Kyra, and you're oblivious to all the hurt you're leaving in your wake. It's not my place to tell you what to do. But do me a favor. Keep me and my family out of it."

He gave her some time for his words to sink in before he leaned into a more conspiratorial distance. "Hitian street, third house after Grape and Barley. It's abandoned." He scoffed. "Figures. The stash is inside the fireplace. Do with this information what you want. And never ask me about any of my stories again."

Hilia nodded. She was not ready to let him go. This wasn't how she wanted him to remember her. "I can't let them die. You understand that, don't you?"

He raised his eyebrows as he shook his head. "I don't think you need my approval. Being a hero is a lonely job. This decision, you have to make on your own. Do what you believe is right but do your damned best to survive. No parent deserves to outlive their child."

And yet, the fifteen-year-old girl's parents . . .

Parviz was leaving already, reminding Hilia of the true meaning of loneliness. Would things have come to this if she'd never left Livid? Would she be in a position to choose whose life to protect? On one hand, there was one life, her life, and on the other, a long line of sacrifices and a roster of people who would die if she did nothing. She took a deep breath. "Sorry, Dad," she mumbled to herself, "but you didn't raise a coward."

Hilia marched out of the library and toward the residence building. She could go nowhere near Grape and Barley tonight. Even now, days after the raid, there were still blackhoods lurking around the place. Hopefully, she would have a better chance tomorrow.

THE INQUISITION HAD finally left the street. What was left of Grape and Barley were a few beams still standing inside a deep, charred hole. Hilia picked up her pace to get past before the whirlwind of memories would sweep her away. Her father. His winehouse. The day her life had changed forever. *Get a grip, Hilia.*

She arrived at the address Parviz had given her. It fit the description.

An abandoned house. The windows had no drapes to cover them, and the worn door was half-open. As she entered, the smell of rot filled her nostrils, almost making her gag. Grime caked the floor. Looters hadn't left a single spoon.

She located the fireplace and went to do what she'd come here to do. There was no point spending a second longer here than she had to. She removed the charcoal and threw the pieces on the already blackened floor. She hauled the grate out and carefully let it rest against the wall.

There was nothing that even looked like a stash. Just a years-old mix of ash and dust. *Come on, brother, talk to me. Where did you hide your stash?*

With both hands, she felt about under the layers of ash until she touched something like a lid. She cleared up that specific spot to reveal the hatch she had found. Then she removed the lid and began probing. It wasn't long before her fingers caught a pouch.

Excited, she took it out and unstrapped it. "Yes!" More than a dozen vials.

Hilia was not going to be greedy. She grabbed three of them and was about to put the bag back inside when a voice stopped her. "Get up."

Kadder's sight sent ice through her veins. There was the kind of fire in his eyes that only his prisoners got to see. He held out his hand. "Let's see what you have there."

There was no defying him. She handed him the vials.

It didn't take him long to recognize what they were. And by the look in his eyes, she knew it was over. She put her hand on her belt, where she'd hidden the poison. The image of Handler's gruesome death flashed in her mind. *Be strong, girl. If you have to do it, you have to do it.* Her father's nightmare was moments away.

Kadder flourished one of the vials. "Sapping potion, huh?" He huffed. "You know how I knew to follow you here? I was coming to your room to talk, to give you one last chance to repent, when I saw you leave the palace. Talking wouldn't have worked, anyway, would it?"

Hilia curled her thumb and grabbed the poison as she got up. "I can explain."

"There's nothing to explain. If I let you off for so long, it was because

I thought you were just a silly girl, deceived into doing the rebellion's dirty work. But now, you've hit me with the real surprise: you're more than a pawn in this game. I bet if I squeeze you hard enough, Windhammer himself will pop out of you. So, here are your options. Come with me, tell me everything you know, and have a clean execution. Or resist, I call the guards, they break a few of your bones, and I'll make sure horror is the last look on your face when you die."

Her legs wobbled as she stepped backwards. "Please don't do this. You know me. I'm not a bad person. We prayed together."

Kadder followed her along. "Yes, we did. You sat there and listened to the story of my son's family. If you had any compassion in you, you'd have learned something from it. I was wrong to think your scum had a heart."

"You're wrong." Her trembling voice made her sound like a scared little girl. "I felt for you. I felt for your family. I felt sick about what happened to them."

He shot his hand out and grabbed her arm. "Here's something you'll remember for what's left of your pointless life. I didn't take my eyes off you since that first attack on the queen. And every step of the way, you revealed more of yourself. You exposed your friend. If it weren't for you, I would have never considered that palace guard was a rebel."

Hilia remembered Parviz's last comment. *Everyone who's talked to you more than twice is already dead.*

The irony hurt almost physically.

"No," she rasped. A futile attempt at denial.

"If you don't give me Windhammer, I'll show you pain you've never imagined."

She unstoppered the vial. It was time. This was how she was going to die. Alone, drowning in her own blood and spittle. But this, as Windhammer liked to say, was a necessity. If she lived, more people would suffer or die.

Hilia was about to take the poison when Kadder said, "I'll break that librarian you're so fond of."

She stopped. Her crushing guilt, her cold fear, her dark despair, they all fused into one emotion. Rage. She found her hand clenched around the vial so tightly she thought she'd break it soon.

Kadder didn't stop there. "I'm going to bring your father in, and I'll tear him apart limb by limb until you . . ."

Hilia heard nothing after that. Roaring, she attacked the Inquisitor, shoved the poison in his mouth, and punched it in together with his teeth. As Kadder went down, she jumped over him, straddling his midsection, growling, "Now, here's the last thing you'll remember before you die. My friends are coming to kill the queen. The same friends who killed your stupid son and his worthless family. I was there. And I enjoyed it." Even uttering those words filled her with disgust. But something had snapped in her.

Kadder thundered as his hands squeezed Hilia's neck, throttling her. She tried to get his hands off her. She clawed at his face, tried to scratch his eyes out. But he was too strong. Her eyes felt as if they would pop out. Fighting became more and more difficult as her head grew heavier. Darkness blotted her vision. Her eyes flickered.

Just as she finally gave up the fight, the grip loosened.

Hilia dropped beside Kadder. Her chest burned. Her throat throbbed as though his hands were still around her neck. With what energy she had left, she forced some measure of air through her locked windpipe, which brought her to coughing and gagging. It took a long time before she could breathe properly, and even then, the pain and the constricted feeling in her throat did not go away.

When air flowed through her chest and some of her energy came back, she got up. Kadder lay motionless, bloody foam pouring out of his mouth. The fury and hatred in his eyes had lived past his own death.

All vials but one had shattered under both their weights. She picked it up, then got to her feet, almost falling. She had little authority over her limbs. Still gasping, she stumbled to the wall and leaned against it.

As more of her presence returned, the frightening reality sank in. *Fuck.* She had killed the chief Inquisitor of Delavaran. "It's fine. I can salvage this."

Diva would rise in a few hours, and no one would look for Kadder until then. Once the operation was over, Hilia would run away with her friends. "It'll work," she said, rubbing her mouth. She was now talking to herself like a maniac. "Keep it together, girl. You've got this." A few raspy breaths. "You've got this."

30

I watched as her life tumbled, as everyone she knew betrayed her. I only watched, for I was not destined to interfere. I was—we were—the master of all elements, and our destiny was to find the savior. And after centuries, we found her, reborn from the ashes of whom she used to be.

HILIA'S BREATH MADE a plume even inside the chambers. She hated the Dark Fusion. Everything was cold and red and demoralizing. Back in Livid, she would spend these days in her bed. Winehouses were closed, and so would be her father's.

She glanced at the queen over her shoulder, whose hand, like all else, had a crimson tint. Dark Fusion suited the otherwise colorless witch. The queen's tea glass was empty, which meant she'd ingested the entire dose of sapping potion. The Erkenblood of Saba could now kill the queen if a fight broke out.

Hilia turned back to her counter as she put the cutlery away. That was when her gaze dropped to the steak knife. The sharp point, the serrated edge, formed a thought in her head. Why wait for the Erkenblood? It was pointless to risk her life if Hilia could end this right here. It would not be the first time she killed someone. Not the first time she killed an official.

The knife was not exactly a weapon, but it was enough to get the job done. One stab to the side of the neck or a quick slice across the throat. The queen's neck was surely more tender than the steaks they cooked in the kitchens. And physically, Hilia was taller and fitter if a struggle ensued. Back in her winehouse days, she'd grappled with drunkards twice her size, and working in the palace had not made her muscles any thinner.

She picked up the knife, gingerly approaching the queen from behind. She could hear her own heart beating.

Suddenly, a soldier entered. Hilia slid the knife up her sleeve to hide it, then rushed to collect the queen's empty glass, pacing her breathing not to give her anxiety away.

"Your Highness," the soldier announced. "Inquisitor Yoltan requests an audience."

The queen finished chewing, dabbed her lips with the napkin, then gracefully got out of her seat. "I'll be heading to the throne room shortly. Tell him to await me there. Dismissed."

Hilia collected the plate and cutlery and took them to her maid's nook. She dropped the fork and spoon in the bowl of dirty dishes to mask the sound of dropping the steak knife back in place. Only then did she let out a relieved sigh. What had she been thinking?

"Come here, Hilia," the queen said. "There is something I need to talk to you about."

Hilia frowned as she turned, unsure what it was about. Despite her hesitation, she complied.

The queen picked up the Dark Scepter upon Hilia's approach. "Things are happening in this palace," she said once they were both standing at the table. "Things I cannot explain . . . unless you have touched the scepter."

The statement was like a cold punch to Hilia's chest. "P-pardon me, Highness?"

"The day after the Reunion ceremony. You were in my chambers when I returned, and my drawer was a crack open. You touched the scepter that day, did you not?"

"Highness," Hilia tried, "I've never touched—"

The queen cut that lie short by grabbing her arm and slamming her on the table. She then lowered the scepter as Hilia pleaded, "No. No, please!"

But it was too late. "Now, you have." The Dark Scepter pressed on the back of Hilia's neck.

The whispers came crashing down, but all Hilia could think about was the much darker fate that awaited her. The last time Queen Artenus had done this to someone, the victim had died by her own hand.

The woman disconnected the scepter from Hilia's skin and let her go, muttering under her breath, "I was right."

"Am I going to die?" Hilia said tentatively.

The queen almost rolled her eyes. "I don't know. Why don't you pick up a knife and disembowel yourself?"

Hilia's legs wobbled, but she had no intention of killing herself. She gawked at the queen, flustered. No. Petrified was a better word.

"I did not think you would." The corner of the queen's lips turned up into a sardonic smile. She ambled away from Hilia, mumbling to herself, "It makes sense now. That's why it never works. You are touched by First Arcane, and you are there when it happens."

When what happens? The woman was not making sense. "Why didn't I kill myself like everyone else you touch with the scepter? Why let me live?"

The queen shook her head as if Hilia had asked the most stupid question. "I do not command the Dark Scepter, nor do I have any authority over what happens to those who come in contact with it. You have heard the whispers, have you not?"

Hilia nodded. There was no sense in denying it at this point.

That response brought a dim smile of understanding to the queen. Her gaze brushed over the length of the scepter as she spoke. "Then you already have your answer. The Dark Scepter has a will of its own. Few can survive its temptations. That you have touched it twice and still stand shows a connection between it and you."

Three times, to be exact. "What kind of connection?"

"That is for the scepter to know," the queen said, stroking the ruby, "and for you to find out."

The woman's evasive answers created more questions, and there were already so many in Hilia's head. "The ruby," slipped out of her mouth.

The queen removed her hand from the gem, the earlier softness leaving her expression.

"I saw it glow the day the Erkenblood attacked," Hilia pushed. "And it drove her powerless. Was it not you who controlled it?"

"You are observant," the queen said, "but I cannot trust you with that knowledge. You've already caused damage I can only hope to rectify, and I cannot have you interfere with these forces more than you already have."

"What forces? I need to know if I'm to steer clear of them."

The queen scoffed. "If you are still alive, have your wits intact, and must ask that question, it means you are far enough from First Arcane."

DEEP WITHIN THE LINGERING morning mist and under the crimson light of Diva, the imposing walls of Delavaran looked like the gateway of death. Panthea's teeth chattered. Either because of the stabbing cold penetrating all her layers, or the fear of having no roof above her head but the violet and red sky.

It was bad luck to be outside on a Dark Fusion. Angelian temples held vigils during this time. Of course, attending one had never been an option for Panthea, thanks to Rassus's strict rules. Instead, every Dark Fusion she filled her room with candles and spent the night and day praying in solitude. She had never imagined even that becoming a luxury.

Last night, the nightmare potion had kept her asleep for hours, and although Arvin had bought her candles, they refused to remain lit. Now, she faced northward and whispered prayers to ward off as much of the bad luck as she could while her breaths made plumes of vapor in the frigid air. The saddest excuse for a vigil. It would be a miracle if nothing went wrong today.

Footsteps approached, and a moment later, Arvin was at her side, holding a book. "Check this one out." He pointed at a specific line. "There will be those of you who make the ultimate sacrifice."

Her scalp bristled. Arvin was reading from the Book of Creation—a strange yet endearing image to behold. She knew these verses by heart, so she recited along with him, "Not of life, but soul. They cleanse the world with their taint. They erase shadows with their darkness. And with every soul they surrender to Angra, they do so tenfold for Annahid."

By the end of the verse, her eyes were cold with tears. She'd been repeating these verses throughout the trip, hoping she was one of those souls who, by surrendering themselves to Angra, saved hundreds more. She hadn't expected Arvin to read the holy book of the Angelian religion, the religion he hated, to find her solace. And for him to land on these exact verses . . . "I can't believe you read the Book of Creation. I hope you know how much this means to me."

Arvin closed the book and rubbed her shoulder. "I told you if someone could ever sell your religion to me, it'd be you."

The compassion in his eyes sent a tingle through her chest. She knew he cared. But after everything that had happened, she no longer trusted her own judgment. She didn't trust the goosebumps she got when he was close, her flushing cheeks when he gave her that look. If Evian could break Panthea's heart, there was no one who couldn't. Besides, she had already seen too much from Arvin.

"By the way," he said, "is there really no concept of an afterlife in your religion?"

A welcome break from the whirlwind of her thoughts.

"Well," she answered, "not in the same sense as you have in yours. Annahid and Angra are in a constant battle. Depending on how virtuous you are, depending on the lives you touch while you're alive, you merge with one of the two when you die."

"And becoming part of something else motivates you to do good?"

She narrowed her eyes. "I . . . suppose?"

"It's fascinating." Arvin looked toward the city. "We're promised riches and gardens and lovers in the afterlife, and people still do unspeakable things. But you? You do good for the sake of doing good."

She shrugged. "I thought that was what any religion was about."

"Maybe." His smile turned rueful. "You know, in my religion, Ahura forgives sins against himself, but sins against his creations are only theirs to forgive." He paused for a moment. "I know this is a lot to ask after everything I've done. But do you think you can find it in yourself to forgive me?"

She had tried. After Arvin had come to save her, after her conversation with Mart. But she could not silence the voice inside her that said he was part of the reason Ash was gone. Then again, Panthea herself was not free of guilt. Ash would still be alive if Panthea had not gone back to Saba, if she'd not gone to the meeting alone, if she hadn't been so scared of her power.

She looked down. "Arvin. You know I rarely flatter people, so you know I mean it when I say you're the closest thing I have to a friend. It's just . . ." Her next words came painfully. "I want to forgive you. I really do. But right now, I can't even forgive myself. I hate feeling like this."

"Hey," Arvin cooed as his hand slid to her back. "It's your choice, and I understand." He stepped in front of her and leveled his head with hers. "But promise me you'll forgive yourself. Grief has a way of getting into your head. There's always one thing you could have done differently, one thing you could have done to prevent it. But trust me, you'd feel this way even if you'd done everything right."

Panthea wiped the cold tears around her eyes as she nodded.

Mart joined them. "You've lost your touch, Arvin. You used to make girls laugh. Nowadays, you only make them cry." He regarded Panthea. "It's time to go."

As Mart went to get ready, Arvin squeezed Panthea's shoulder and said, "Whatever happens today, I'm sure you're right up there with Annahid. You're the kindest person I know." His eyes dropped to her chest. "By the way, remove your pendant. It's best if you don't have it on you when you enter the palace. We'll keep it in one of our safehouses in Delavaran until after the operation."

As he joined Mart and Gvosh, she removed the pendant. She was going to take it to Arvin when something gave her pause: Ash had died because of Panthea's failure to bring the Bond to the meeting.

Panthea would not repeat the same mistake. She would not lose Rassus too. She would try her best to keep the stone safe, but if all else failed, if Rassus's life was on the line, she would give it away. After everything she'd suffered, she had earned this much.

She looked back to make sure the others were still busy. Then she opened the pendant and took out the marble box. Taking another glance over her shoulder, she removed the Bond from the box and dropped it directly inside the pendant, closing the lid over it.

"Dazzle-eyes," said Mart as he approached. Panthea quickly shut the empty marble box in her hand and hung the pendant around her neck. "You stay here with Cousin. He'll take you to the bureau when it's time. I've told him to stay with you for as long as he can, but don't get scared if you end up alone in the interrogation room."

Worry swirling in her chest, she nodded.

Mart then clapped her shoulder. "Say hi to your old man for me when you see him. Tell him his apprentice is a badass."

She offered a smile, which she hoped looked genuine enough.

Arvin came to her next. "All right, this is it."

"I suppose so," she said.

"The pendant?"

She put the empty marble box in the hand he was holding out, looking into his eyes for any sign of suspicion. He shot a glance at the pendant, but she tried to staunch his curiosity with, "I would like to keep the pendant for when I see Rassus."

It took him a second, but he bought it. "I understand."

Mart gave Gvosh a last wink, then, together with Arvin, they headed toward the city. Gvosh stood tall, arms crossed. Panthea sat down on the grit and shifted the blanket around herself as she watched Arvin and Mart go. Their footfalls made the only sound in the hills, and even that faded as the two sank deeper into the red mist. Then there was only silence and the unforgiving cold.

31

A world that cannot keep its balance for more than a decade shall break into war.

HILIA PACED ACROSS the main hallway like a caged lion. She didn't know if she should escort her friends from the gates or if they were coming here on their own. She knew nothing about the logistics of this mission. *Damn it.* It was almost noon. People trickled out of the library, and her worry grew with every one of them.

She went back to the shelves to spend some time there before everyone would get suspicious.

"Psst. Grumpy," said a voice from her side, making her jump.

When she turned, Mart was standing there. Seeing her friend after six years was surreal. She took a deep breath to recover from the start he had given her. "Well, if it isn't my favorite asshole." She cocked her head. "You still have that stupid mustache?"

She reached for it, but Mart slapped the back of her hand. "Not the mustache."

"Are you alone?" she asked.

Mart smirked as he stepped aside, and a rush passed through her when she saw Arvin standing there in the shadows, smiling. A warm feeling emanated from her chest and radiated through her body. She felt like a stupid twenty-year-old again.

Arvin had gained a little weight. His beard was thicker than before. But those intense and thoughtful eyes had not changed one bit. Only this man could make the Sapphire plates look heroic.

"Hi, Hilia."

"Arvin." She realized she was wearing the silliest grin. She collected it and turned to Mart. "Is the Erkenblood here?"

"Yes," Mart said. "She'll be at the Inquisition bureau soon."

Hilia winced. "About that. I don't think the Inquisitor is the only person she's going to meet. The queen herself wants to pay her a visit at the bureau."

Arvin's features tensed. "Are the others aware?"

"I don't know," she said, her own concern amplified.

"Are they in their posts?"

"I don't know."

"What *do* you know?" Mart stepped in. "Did your handler tell you nothing?"

"My handler's dead. He was made."

Mart's expression sobered.

"Panthea's walking into a trap," Arvin rasped.

"P . . ." It took Hilia a moment to gather why Arvin was using the name of the goddess. "Wait, the girl's name is Panthea?" She grimaced. "Who names their child that?"

"That's what I told him," Mart said. "Anyway, the mission is compromised."

"Not necessarily." She glanced between her stupefied friends, bracing herself for their response. "This morning, I spiked the queen's tea with sapping potion."

"You did what?" Arvin exclaimed before he lowered his voice. "Do you have any idea how dangerous that is? What if you were found out?"

"I, uh," she mumbled, avoiding his gaze. "I was. That's the other thing

I have to tell you. The chief Inquisitor of Delavaran is dead. I . . . kind of . . . killed him."

Arvin's dubious stare said he was trying to discern a sign of a non-existent joke.

"Say again?" said Mart.

She rolled her eyes. "You heard what I said."

"I did. Let me see if I'm hearing it right. You, Grumpy, killed the chief Inquisitor."

She nodded, and Mart reflected the movement of her head. "I'm not sure if I should burst out laughing, or cry, or yell at you."

"For starters, don't rub it in. Tell me. Does the Erkenblood know to kill the queen if she gets the chance?"

"Ah, this again." Mart clicked his tongue. "Grumpy. I like you, but you're a pain in the ass. The queen. Cannot. Die."

"That's where you're wrong." Hilia turned to face Arvin. "That's where you're all wrong. I've proven my theory, and my handler was going to relay the news when he died. On the day of the Reunion ceremony, they shot the queen with three arrows. I watched her bleed. She almost died."

"Bleed?" Arvin asked, but Mart spoke over him.

"Almost is the key word here. She didn't die."

Hilia sighed. "That's because she disappeared. The queen is a space-wielder. That means she can—"

"I know what a space-wielder is," Arvin cut her off, impatient. He seemed much more interested in the conversation than his companion was. "Get to the point."

Hilia wondered how Arvin knew about it when she herself had learned it only this year. But she shelved that thought and continued, "She disappeared for the entire night, then returned good as new. Wherever she went, whatever happened to her, that's the key to her survival. But one thing I'm sure of is that if she can't go there, she can't heal."

Mart twirled his mustache. "So," he said, sticking one finger out, "the queen goes somewhere and does something to heal. Now, here are my questions. Where does she go? And what does she do?"

"I don't know."

He swept a finger in the air. "Exactly. There's a lot of 'I don't know' going on, and I'm not risking our lives and the fate of the rebellion on that." He turned to Arvin to say, "We've not prepared the girl for this," and then back to Hilia. "What happens if the Erkenblood attacks the queen and fails? Logistically speaking. And don't tell me you don't know."

Hilia was no longer able to keep the sting out of her voice. "As a matter of fact, I do. If the girl survives the fight—which I doubt—the blackhoods will arrest her. The queen will then be escorted back to . . ." She paused. If the girl failed, they were going to bring the queen to where she would be the safest. "The chambers," trickled out of Hilia's mouth as a plan formed in her head. A dangerous plan. Much more so than what she had tried at breakfast.

They would take the queen to the bedchamber, where she would lock the door from the inside so nobody could touch her. Unless . . . someone was already there when she arrived.

Someone like Hilia.

"We have to call it quits," Mart interrupted Hilia's thoughts. "We extract Grumpy and hope Cousin can handle the situation at the bureau."

"No," Arvin and Hilia said simultaneously, but perhaps for different reasons. Arvin gave Hilia a slight frown before he explained his. "Our people won't make a move without us, and Gvosh can only save himself. There's no way Panthea can get out of there without our help."

Mart grabbed Arvin by both shoulders. "Varina's cunt, forget the girl. We expose ourselves now, we compromise the whole rebellion. It's not worth it. She'll understand."

"No, she won't," Arvin said, removing Mart's hands. "I've betrayed her twice. I'm not going to betray her again. Even if I have to fight the queen herself, I will extract Panthea."

Hilia's skin prickled with pride. This was not the Arvin of four years ago. That Arvin always put his mission first.

"Fuck," Mart said. "You two will be the death of me. Lead the way then, *milady*."

Hilia gestured for them to follow as she headed toward the empty hallway in the middle. Hiding behind the last shelf, she barred her friends with her arm. "Let's wait here. They'll soon close the public entrance. The guards are now searching the place for anyone who might have overstayed their welcome."

"Like the queen?" Mart quipped.

"Hush," Hilia whispered. "The guards on the other side of the royal entrance know me, and they won't be surprised to see me with two soldiers, given everything that's been going on. If they ask, you say you escorted me into the city. Then we came to the library through the public entrance. And here we are."

They both nodded. The three of them hid there until the public doors were closed. This was a moment she had never seen in this library. An enormous, fortified prison, sealed on both ends, cut off from the rest of the city.

"Let's go," she said, and they all went toward the royal doors.

A guard emerged from between the shelves. At their sight, his face turned hostile, and he called as he approached them, "What are you doing here?"

She rushed to stand between the guard and her friends. "I'm Hilia. Handmaid to the queen. I was here when the bells rang, and I thought it easier to enter through the library than go all the way around the palace."

The man spent some time scrutinizing Hilia, Arvin, and Mart. "All right, soldiers. Let's see your Fusion Mandate certificate."

Arvin stood silent, eyeballing the guard. Mart looked at Hilia, but she had no idea what the guard was talking about.

"What is it?" said the guard. "Didn't get your slip yesterday?"

Her chest constricted. Why had they changed the rules the day before the Dark Fusion?

"Here's my identification," Mart said as he shoved Hilia aside. The guard went for his sword, but Mart stabbed his neck with a dagger and withdrew it.

The soldier grabbed his neck, gurgling and sputtering blood as he went down. Hilia closed her eyes. *Does this game ever end?*

Another voice echoed, "You are trespassing." Hilia hoped she was wrong about the owner of that voice. But there he was. Her former friend, Parviz, marching to them, the vein in his neck bulging. "This is sacred ground."

Arvin and Mart exchanged looks, and it was clear what they had in mind. To alleviate the situation, she began, "Parviz, whatever you think this is—"

"I know what this is," the librarian snarled. "Here's what's going to happen. I'm going to knock on that door"—he pointed at the public entrance—"and you three turn yourselves in."

Without hesitation, Mart charged at the librarian.

"No," Hilia yelped.

Mart grabbed Parviz and held the edge of his dagger in front of his neck. "I didn't get it, smart guy. Would you be so kind as to repeat what we're supposed to do? I'm a little thick."

"Mart, stop," she pleaded. "He won't turn us in."

Mart brought the man back to them, and Arvin, too, drew his sword. Hilia blocked his way to the librarian. "Both of you. Stop this madness. This man intends no harm. I can talk to him." She fully turned to the poor librarian and looked down into his eyes. "Parviz, what are you doing?"

"Protecting what matters to me."

"At what cost? No one will hold you accountable for our actions. Please stand out of our way. Please think before you choose your next words because I can only protect you so much."

He gave her a scornful smile. "So, this is Hilia. The real Hilia."

"You're in no position to judge me," she threatened.

"I say we kill him," Mart suggested.

"Shut up, Mart," she shot. "No one's killing anyone. Parviz is just confused." She held Parviz's gaze. "Please. Think about your sons. You're making me look like the monster here."

Arvin pressed a hand on her shoulder from behind and whispered in her ear, "How important is he to you? Because right now, he's a liability."

Her stomach churning, she implored, "What's it going to be, Parviz?"

His stare didn't leave her eyes. Even when he finally put both his hands up in surrender, those eyes still pierced through her, peering into her darkened soul. "You don't need my help to look like a monster."

Hilia swallowed the sting in those words and focused on the one person left to pacify. "Let go, Mart. It's fine. I'll tie him up. He won't tell."

"You know I can't let this go," Mart said. "He made a serious threat."

If she had learned one thing, it was that Windhammer's people left nothing to chance. There was no version of this where the librarian would walk. Hilia looked away. She knew it had to be done, but that didn't mean she had to watch.

"Stop." That single, unexpected word from Arvin brought her new hope. "If she says he won't tell, he won't tell. We're not here to kill librarians."

Hilia locked her gaze with Mart's, wondering if Arvin's words would work. She strove to keep anything provocative out of her expression while Parviz's fate hung by a thread.

After an excruciating moment, Mart let go. Parviz shook his robe and straightened it, too unfazed for someone whose life had almost ended.

Hilia exhaled in relief, glaring at Mart the way she'd wanted to all along. "You can sheathe your knife now."

Mart jutted his head toward the librarian. "Go tie him up." It was an order. Nothing less.

Arvin gently grabbed her arm, whispering, "You're not a monster."

"Yeah, well." She took a moment to steady herself. "You two hide the body and cover the blood while I restrain Parviz. Mart's made a mess."

PANTHEA'S HEART WAS in her mouth. It was bad enough that she had entered Delavaran—the palace no less. Now, they were in front of the Inquisition bureau itself. The polished marble of the walls reflected the light of Diva almost perfectly, giving off a bloody hue that well suited what was inside. Two arrays of giant braziers lined the pathway to the entrance, putting the cold of the Dark Fusion to shame even from this distance.

Eight soldiers and a few blackhoods guarded the building. Those dark uniforms still gave her chills. They were reminiscent of everything she'd lost.

She realized she was rooted in place when Gvosh grabbed her arm. "Remember. Don't show any resistance before Yoltan arrives." He then pushed her forward for the act. "Move."

Panthea played along. It wasn't difficult to look scared. All she had to do was think about every part of this that was not a lie. She *was* entering the Inquisition bureau, and there was a real chance she wouldn't make it out.

As they approached, the two blackhoods who guarded the door stopped them, one of them looking up at Gvosh. "Hold it. Who are you? And who is she?"

Gvosh produced a piece of parchment. "I'm here to deliver the Erkenblood of Saba on the order of Inquisitor Yoltan."

The blackhood's eyes widened under the cloak's shadow. "She sapped?"

"This morning. But feel free to sap her again."

He handed Panthea over. The sentry grabbed under her shoulder and pulled her inside the building. The interior was made of the same marble. Though, because of the hanging sconces and the absence of windows, the walls flaunted their natural milky white, tinged with the glitters of the decorative shields and weapons hung all around them.

Her captor took her to the only wall that was different. Along this one stood a medium-sized statue of the Great Annahid, a little taller than Panthea. What a sacrilege. A symbol of kindness erected in a place where the teachings of the Book of Creation were trampled upon.

On the other side of the room, Gvosh spoke to a few fellow blackhoods, pointing at Panthea in between.

Her captor held out a dose of sapping potion. "Hey, witch. Take this. You're in for a rough ride."

She took the vial and drank. As the bitterness coursed down, she hoped her power would remain intact. With how scared she was, it was easy enough to know it had gone nowhere.

After a while, Gvosh came to Panthea and received her again. "I'll take her downstairs."

With as much aggression as the other blackhoods, he took her toward the only door that was made of steel. As he opened it, she found herself on top of a long, dark stairway. There was no sign of shiny marble here. Only rigid stones, smell of damp, and the cold of the Dark Fusion.

They went down the stairs onto a narrow hallway lined by old metallic doors. Was this where they tortured prisoners?

Gvosh stopped in front of one of the doors, then used a key to open it. "I made a little arrangement for you. Don't make me regret it."

When the door opened, her breath froze as she saw before her the man she'd sacrificed everything to rescue. Her words escaped her. Rassus sat there on the floor. His face had a nasty bruise. His eyelids were swollen, his robe tattered. But it was him.

"Go," Gvosh whispered. "You have until Yoltan shows up."

Panthea did not need his permission. She rushed to Rassus and dropped to her knees, failing to hold her tears back. "Master. What did they do to you?"

The door locked behind her with a clank, the sound of her last destination before her fate would be decided. She would either kill Yoltan and escape this place or die trying.

None of it mattered at this moment.

Rassus's eyelids opened wide. "What are you doing here?"

"I'm here to save you, Master," she whispered. "I'm working with the rebellion."

Rassus lifted one arm, his hand quaking as he held her chin up, inspecting the sutures on her cheek. "Little one. I wasn't worth your sacrifice."

Those words shattered her heart. The tame and apologetic look in his eyes was something she'd never seen in them before. She wished he would chastise her like he used to; tell her what a fool she had been to have come here.

She sniffled, bobbing her head while she gathered herself. She attempted a smile as she said, "You said you'd come back for the pendant.

I thought I'd save you the hassle."

Rassus frowned. "Did you bring the pendant with you? That pendant contains—"

"I know. I know . . . everything. I just couldn't take any chances."

The old man's brows drew further together. "You know how to use it?"

Before she could answer, the door clanked and swung open. Inquisitor Yoltan walked in with a smug smile, accompanied by a few blackhoods. "I see you found your way back to me, witch. Have you come to your senses and brought what we want?"

She pressed Rassus's hand between both of hers before she shot up, glaring into Yoltan's eyes. "I have the stone somewhere safe. You let him go, and I'll give it to you."

"You don't learn, do you?" Yoltan took something out of his pocket and flourished it. "You know what this is?" It was a gleamstone, but that was probably not the answer he sought. "Here's a hint. We found it on your friend when we arrested her." He chuckled. "Damn, did I give it away?"

Panthea's grief resurfaced, quickly turning to rage. She would kill him right now, but one thing she'd learned was that rushing into action could have severe consequences. After all, was it not what this gleamstone represented? "The Bond is my only leverage. As soon as I give it to you, you'll kill both of us."

"Leverage?" He raised an amused eyebrow. "I'm not bargaining with you, witch. The Inquisition bureau is where the world ends. For you, anyway. Now, I'm in the mood for turning a few of your bones to mush, but luckily for you, the queen wants to talk. So, you go up there, you listen to her, and you behave." He motioned to his men. "Take her."

"No," Rassus said from her side before turning to the Inquisitor. "Leave her be. I am the protector of the Bond. I am the one you want."

"Master!" Panthea said. "Please."

"Fine, fine," Yoltan said. "Don't fight over it. I'll take you both. After all, I need to teach the girl the true meaning of leverage." He gave Panthea a self-satisfied wink.

Before the blackhoods got to them, she whispered in Rassus's ear, "I'm not sapped."

The old man's reaction to that statement was the complete opposite of what Panthea had expected. As they got them both to their feet, Rassus's eyes widened. "What have you done? Artenus has the Bond of Second Arcane. She will kill you."

"Keep them separated," Yoltan commanded.

Her captors shoved her forward, putting distance between her and the old man.

"I'll take her," offered Gvosh once they were outside the cell.

The blackhoods handed Panthea to him, and he almost dragged her until they were out of earshot. "Wait for the queen to leave," he whispered. "Do not engage. You hear me? Do not engage." He then muttered curses under his breath.

The party went up the stairs and back to the ground floor, where they met a flock of Sapphires surrounding a woman who was impossible to mistake for anyone else. The golden Mehrian crown stood on top of her crow-black hair, adorned by brilliant pieces of ruby and amethyst. Her emerald eyes stared through Panthea, the color in them unhindered by the Dark Fusion. Arvin had been right. She looked frighteningly youthful.

Once everyone was there, Yoltan stepped forward and bowed. "Your Highness." He threw his shoulders back and pointed at Panthea. "I'm afraid I was right. The girl is making demands."

The queen left the cocoon of soldiers and sauntered toward Panthea, the bottom of her crimson gown sweeping the floor, its golden embroidery glittering in the lamplight. She held an intricate scepter in her right hand, the top of which was formed as three snakeheads with a single piece of ruby in one of their mouths.

Stopping at a safe distance from Panthea, the queen waited until enough of the soldiers caught up. "And what would be those demands?" she asked, only glancing at Panthea. Her voice was calm. A perfect lullaby if one didn't know who she was. Panthea did, and that voice scared her to the marrow.

The Inquisitor answered, "She wants the old man freed."

The queen glanced over at Rassus before she addressed Panthea directly. "That man is not worth your protection." She regarded Rassus. "Have you told her how you took my family from me?"

How did the woman dare utter those words? "He didn't take your family," Panthea defended Rassus. "You killed them yourself, even your infant daughter."

The queen's features tensed. Panthea seemed to have hit a sore spot. Strangely, this brought her some satisfaction.

"Mind your words when you speak of my Hita," said the queen. "Child, you have been caught amid something much greater than you. Power greater than you can fathom. Your guardian knows it, and he has accepted the risks involved. But you don't seem to have the slightest idea. So, I suggest you step aside and let the adults deal with politics."

"My friend died because of your politics. You destroyed my life."

The queen exchanged a glance with Yoltan before she raised an eyebrow. "Did I destroy your life? Or was it the law that keeps us all safe? The law that does not allow a wielder to run rampant and kill everyone she so desires. You southerners were eating each other before me. I turned your centuries-long enemies to allies. I cut the expensive import of arcane artifacts from the north and used the money to save our economy.

"Now, tell me, child. Who destroyed your life? Was it the queen who picked up the falling pieces of this kingdom"—her voice took an edge of disdain—"or was it the impulsive girl who stumbled upon something dangerous and wasn't wise enough to stand clear of it?"

To accept this nonsense was to accept Ash had died for nothing. For Panthea's blind ambition. "The laws don't keep us safe. You have killed my kind—your kind—for years. Your laws have brought us to the verge of extinction."

"No. Human fear brought us to extinction." The queen gave a mirthless smile. "That, and our own hubris." She continued toward Panthea with slow steps. "My religion praises the arcane. Denouncing it was the hardest decision I've ever made. I would not have taken such extreme measures if there was another choice." She stopped right in front of Panthea, raising her hand to pacify the guard who had become uneasy at the pair's proximity.

The woman leaned forward and whispered in Panthea's ear, "These lesser humans have always wanted us gone. I merely showed them what they wanted to see. The Erkenbloods of the Southern Kingdom who know their worth are still alive. They're waiting for you beyond the seas. All you have to do is accept my calling. Together, we can cleanse this world."

She patted Panthea's shoulder as she stepped back, smiling. "The time to decide is now," she said with a voice audible to the others.

An army of Erkenbloods. That was what the queen was creating. It was why captured Erkenbloods disappeared instead of being publicly executed. Through her shock, Panthea managed, "You want to bring back the Dark Ages."

The queen left Panthea's side as she said mockingly, "What would you know about the Dark Ages?"

Panthea followed her as the pieces of her past came together. "So that's why you killed my mother. She wouldn't stand by and let you do it."

The soldiers stopped Panthea before she could get close.

"Vetrieca was a fool," the queen said. "She died not knowing any of this."

"Vetrieca wasn't my mother."

The queen turned to face Panthea, her eyes narrowed.

"I'm the daughter of Lady Sana."

Confusion took over the queen's countenance. "Impossible." After a brief pause, her frown dissipated, and she gave a slight pout. "You know, Sana and I were close once. Like sisters, if you will. Before she, like everyone else in this palace, betrayed me."

The queen tapped the red stone on her scepter. "These Bonds of Arcane are the key to bringing balance back to this world. You know loss. You know grief. You have seen the cruelty of this world. I intend to correct the mistakes humanity has made over centuries, and to do that, I need. These. Stones. And I'll give everything I have, I'll kill everyone I must, to acquire them. Can you understand this, Panthea?"

Panthea didn't respond, but her glare was enough to kill the queen's humor.

"All right, daughter of Lady Sana. You know the choice you must make, and I have explained myself to you far more than anyone can expect from the ruler of this land. I *will* have the Bond of Third Arcane, but what happens to you by then is determined by your actions. Tell me where the stone is, or I will leave you to the mercy of these men."

Panthea swept a look around at the array of guards, the blackhoods, the Inquisitor, and the expectant queen. It was frightening, but this was no longer about her life or Rassus's. It was no longer about the Southern Realm. With the second coming of the Dark Ages, the fate of Sessara—and possibly the entire world—was at stake. Panthea took a shuddering breath and braced herself. "No."

HILIA TIED THE LAST KNOT around Parviz's wrists behind the chair. He hadn't spoken a single word throughout.

"This was your own fault," she muttered, trying to elicit a response from him. "What were you thinking, standing up to two armed rebels?"

She went and stood in front of him, but it seemed like the cluttered desk was far more worthy of his attention. Leveling her head with his, she looked directly into his eyes. "You're lucky to be alive. That man out there?" She pointed outside the study. "He doesn't believe in loose ends. I'm the reason you're still breathing. I hope you understand that."

There was not even a blink or the slightest twitch in his jaw. His unmoving, listless expression was like a concrete mask.

Tendrils of anger crawling inside her skull, Hilia sighed. "Fine." She shoved one of the two remaining pieces of rag into his mouth, for which she faced no resistance from him. Finally, she secured the gag with the last piece and tied it behind his head. She drew herself up, giving him one final chance to relent. "Goodbye, Parviz."

Parviz's eyes shifted to her for one moment with a look riddled with pity. And it was all he had to offer before his gaze returned to his desk.

Hilia was numb. She wasn't mad at him. It was hard to describe how she felt. One thing was certain. She had no time to think about it. This mission had to succeed at any cost. Nothing was less heroic than dying nameless on the palace grounds, having achieved absolutely nothing.

She closed the door to the study, then returned to the hallway, where Mart and Arvin waited for her by the royal entrance. They'd already taken care of the corpse.

"Are you ready?" Arvin whispered, and she answered with a curt nod.

He knocked on the steel doors, the sound vibrating through Hilia's body. *Moment of truth.*

A scrape came from behind the door. Then another. And a third. Then a click, before the door swung away from the library, revealing two palace guards Hilia had seen before. One of them put on a dubious frown when he saw her. "What are you doing here?"

She told him her made-up story, and it took all her energy to act innocent. The guard studied her for a moment before he moved out of the way and let them through.

She sighed in relief as she entered the hallway with her friends.

The other guard began to close the door when the first one called, "Wait. Is that blood on the floor?"

Fear pulsed in her chest as she turned around. She saw a flash from the corner of her eyes, and before her mind could catch up, Mart's blade cut across the guard's exposed neck.

"Hey," burst out of her mouth involuntarily as blood spattered her face.

Mart and Arvin crowded the other guard and struck him down as he reached for his weapon.

"Hey," she repeated, this time of her own volition. "What under fuck! This is Delavaran Palace, for gods' sake. You can't just prance around, killing people."

Mart grabbed the still upright guard and threw him inside the library while Arvin dragged the other one there.

"In case you haven't realized yet," Mart said as he sheathed his weapon and went to close the door, "this is an incursion."

"No, it's an extraction," Hilia countered. "A stealthy one, if you'd be so kind."

Mart closed the door and, with Arvin's help, picked up the first of the three bars to put it in place. "Let me tell you a secret, Grumps. The only way we can get the girl out is to storm the bureau. So, the point here is not avoiding discovery but delaying it. And the dead tend to be slower in spreading news." He grimaced, looking her up and down. "You got a handkerchief?"

"No."

"Then use your hands. You have blood on your face."

"And whose fault is that?" She scrubbed frantically until Arvin grabbed her wrist.

"It's fine. It's gone."

She shot Mart a last glare before leading the way through the hallway. As they went into the open, soldiers were running toward the main palace entrance. Hilia stopped, frowning. One came to them. Arvin reached for his weapon, but she put her hand above his to stop him.

"You shouldn't be here," the soldier said when he noticed them. "The palace is on lockdown. Are you a resident?"

"Yes," she answered. "I'm the queen's handmaid. What's going on?"

The soldier pointed back. "There's an insurrection outside the main entrance. We're trying to keep the rebels from breaking in. But for your safety, I urge you to go to the residence building and stay there until we contain the situation." He glanced at Arvin and Mart. "Do you need further assistance, ma'am?"

She shook her head and waited for the soldier to leave before she faced Mart. "Did you plan the insurrection?"

"Nope," Mart said. "But I was afraid it would come to this. This is the sort of thing that happens when you shoot arrows through the queen and kill the chief Inquisitor. Now, everyone thinks the Sapphire Order is a joke. Every thug in the neighborhood is trying to make a name for themselves by overthrowing the queen."

She grimaced. "You look so disappointed. Isn't that what we want?"

"No, Grumpy. Just because they want the queen dead doesn't make them friendly. If you think those bastards will think twice before killing the queen's handmaid and her guards, you're mistaken. So, let's find the girl and get the fuck out of here before they breach."

This was the perfect opportunity for Hilia to kill the queen. This was the world telling her she should follow through with her plan. The soldiers were busy at the gates, and the queen would most likely be taken back to her chambers. If Mart and the rest of the rebels didn't believe the queen could die, Hilia would give them the ultimate, undeniable proof.

"Oh no," she started, making up her excuse as she went. "I left some documents in my room. Letters from the Windhammer. I need to destroy them before leaving the palace."

"Fucking shit, Grumpy," Mart chided. He had bought the ruse. "Why would you keep those letters?"

"You go ahead." She set to run to the residence building. "The Inquisition bureau's that way. You won't miss it. Look for the braziers. I'll join you outside once you're done."

Arvin followed her, leaving Mart alone on his path to the bureau. "I'm coming with you."

Mart stopped, rubbing his mouth in exasperation.

"No," she spat, almost pushing Arvin back. "You'll slow me down. I don't want to explain to everyone who you are and why you're with me. Besides, the Erkenblood needs you more." When Arvin didn't move, Hilia continued, "Please, Arvin. I've survived in this palace for four years. I promise you I'll be fine. You're wasting precious time here."

Mart grabbed Arvin's hand and said, "For once, Grumpy's right. Let's go. If we survive, I'll get you two a room."

Hilia smiled uncomfortably, shaking her head. "Asshole."

"Thank you," Mart called as he and Arvin dashed toward the bureau.

Her smile still lingering at Mart's familiar humor, she murmured, "You're welcome." She shook her head again as her smile dissipated. *Now, to live up to that promise.*

32

Book of Creation, fifth Visage, verses one to three. "The world will burn in flames of war. Kingdoms will collapse, and who among you still lives will mourn the world that used to be. So is the end of days."

THE SOLDIERS PINNED PANTHEA down, one of them twisting her arm from behind to almost the breaking point. She took short, raspy breaths through the pain in her shoulder. Rassus had a dagger held in front of his neck.

"Look familiar?" Yoltan stepped into Panthea's view and crouched before her. "Give us the stone or watch him die like you did your friend. Your choice."

The fury that overcame her at that comment made it almost worth it to kill the monster and seal her and Rassus's fates. Almost. With a voice that trembled, she said, "Back in Saba, I was afraid. I was weak. I had something to live for. I'm not afraid anymore. And if you kill that man, I'll have nothing left to lose."

Yoltan rubbed his chin. "Perhaps I should use a different tactic."

Without standing up, he produced a needle from his pocket, and before Panthea could even wonder what it was, he buried it in her arm and pulled it out in one swift motion, making her yelp. He handed the needle to one of his men and stood up, bequeathing a smile to the queen.

Turning to Rassus, he said, "There are five vials under my belt. Three are sapping potion. One is the most potent poison you can find in Sessara—a small amount of which I just administered to your apprentice. And one is the antidote." He glanced at her. "In about five minutes, she'll feel dizzy. It only gets worse from there. She'll be dead by the next bell unless we have the stone."

The queen's smile dimmed. "Panthea. Don't die for this. You are an Erkenblood. Nothing in this world is worth your life."

The idea of dying was scary, but if it could save Rassus, if it could save the world, it would be selfish and cowardly of Panthea not to embrace it. After all, wasn't that what Evian had done? Why she hated him?

Rassus bit his lip, the guilt on his face heart-wrenching. "Panthea. I realized too late that I was putting my trust in the wrong person. It should have been you. You had the strength. You had the devotion. I trust you now. There is yet another Bond of Arcane Artenus has to acquire, so if you want to save yourself and let her have this one, you can."

Panthea shook her head in disbelief. She had not lost everything for Rassus to give up like this. "Will it make a difference?" She sniffled. "Will it make a difference if I die?"

Rassus averted his eyes, mumbling, "I don't want to give you that answer. You must choose for yourself."

"Tell me, Master," she insisted. "Ash died for this stone. Tell me her death meant something."

"All right, enough," Yoltan called. "Take him out of here."

The soldiers crowded the old man, but he managed to say, "I would have died for it," before they covered his mouth and dragged him toward the steel door.

That was the answer Panthea needed. With newfound energy, she threw Rassus's two captors away with her power and then went on to her own. Once she was free, she stomped to the queen.

Queen Artenus took a step back, eyes wide in apprehension.

"Let him go," Panthea growled, her teeth clenched, preparing herself to strike if she refused.

The fleeting hint of fear left the queen's countenance, and contempt dripped from the smile that formed on her lips. "Did you think I didn't know this the moment you walked in?"

Yoltan looked around. "Which one of you geniuses was in charge of sapping her?"

"Inquisitor," blurted the one who had handled her earlier. "I swear I gave her the potion."

The queen held up her hand. "This isn't your fault. It appears our young wielder has learned a few tricks along the way." Her gaze returned to Panthea. "So, this is the rebellion's grand plan. Granted, only now did I realize that I'm sapped. That part went well for your friends. Their folly was to send an infant to kill a former High Lady of Sepead."

Sapped? If this was part of the plan, no one had mentioned it to Panthea. Regardless, it gave her the advantage she needed. "Release him, or I'll do something I'll regret."

"Oh, I don't doubt that," the queen murmured. She didn't seem to take her seriously.

To show she meant it, Panthea wielded the woman and tried to hit her against the wall. But her power vanished without warning. Her vision was bright, and even the rush of power was there. Yet she couldn't move or sense anything. *What's happening?*

The queen swept her scepter, and Panthea was lifted from her feet. The room spun around her, and she landed on her shoulder with a crack.

Queen Artenus had just wielded matter. She was a space-wielder, she was sapped, and neither of her hands held a gleamstone. There was no way she should have been able to do this.

The red gem on the scepter glowed like the Dark Fusion Diva.

Panthea's power flared without her even trying to use it, and she was thrown into a column, then flew again and landed on her chest. Gasping for air, she tried to crawl away, but an invisible force dragged her to the queen.

This was not conductive wielding. And from the pain that crept into her head, from the exhilaration that overcame her every time the queen attacked, Panthea knew exactly what it was. Rassus's earlier reaction about Panthea not being sapped made sense now. *"Artenus has the Bond of Second Arcane. She will kill you."*

This was inborn wielding. It was Panthea's inborn wielding. Using the glowing ruby, the queen was drawing from Panthea as if she was a mere arcane artifact.

Before the queen attacked her again, Panthea rolled over and tried to will the scepter out of the woman's hand. Not only did she fail, her attempt ended in a shooting pain in her head. The red gem's light intensified. No. The whole room brightened. The light became blinding, the pain numbing, until she only saw white, only heard a ringing, only felt a thousand knives stabbing her brain. Cramps curled in her muscles, twisted in her gut. Sounds dimmed until there was one moment of euphoria when it all stopped. All pain, physical or emotional, ceased to exist.

Is this death?

Voices hummed again. The whiteness faded, and the room slowly materialized. Queen Artenus's blurry image towered over her, her voice warbling. "You have sealed your fate, daughter of Lady Sana. A traitor, like your mother."

Consciousness gripped Panthea with a jolt. The pain came back tenfold, and she couldn't help a scream.

"Goodbye, Panthea." The queen pushed the top of her scepter on Panthea's wrist, making a thousand whispers swarm inside her head. She couldn't breathe amid the cacophony.

"You shall survive if you listen to the Bond of Arcane."

Panthea's gaze caught something on the ruby. An etching. The same kind as was on Rassus's Bond, but with a different letter. This one had the second letter of the Angelic alphabet, while Rassus's had the third.

The scepter disconnected from Panthea's skin, and she inhaled as the whispers fizzled out. The queen dropped a knife in front of her. Panthea glanced at the knife, then the queen, wondering why she had done it.

After a few moments, the queen sighed. "Of course." She then retrieved the knife as she addressed Yoltan. "She's weakened. Don't kill her before she gives up the stone."

The woman headed out again, and Panthea was in no shape to stop her this time. Her body trembled, her head spun, her breaths were unrelenting. She watched as the queen left the room with the guards.

Soon after, the guards hoisted Panthea to her feet as Yoltan approached and struck her face. "You're in for a lot of pain, witch."

She spat at him. Another strike severed her from her captors, and she took another blow from the hard floor. This time, Yoltan himself grabbed her by the collar and got her to her feet. "Now you watch your old man die."

Panthea channeled all her anger into a scream and used her power to throw Yoltan back.

Everyone in the room charged at her. She ran toward the door to the stairway, but before she reached, a soldier kicked her from behind, dropping her onto the floor. He went to grab her. She tried to push him back, but with no time to focus, his head turned backwards with a nasty crunch. Panthea yelped, rolling away before his body fell. Watching someone die, no matter how many times she saw it—or did it—didn't get any easier.

Her nose burned. Whatever the queen had done to her had drained her power, and she had to be sparing with it if she was to make it, which proved decidedly difficult. As more blackhoods attacked, she became more reactive and used more power. And every moment that passed intensified her headache.

By the time the last of them fell, Panthea's breath had become short. Her head throbbed, and she felt dizzy.

The sound of clapping hands came from the far side of the room. She turned to find Yoltan slowly walking toward her.

"Well done. You just used the little power the queen had spared you."

Panthea shattered the floor under him. He space-jumped, grabbed her from behind, and hurled her away, sending her falling on her face. She scrambled up and spun around. He had disappeared again. This game was getting old, and Panthea would not stand here and play into it. Besides, fighting would only drain her further.

She rushed to the steel door to the cells and even reached for the handle before something hit the back of her head, the blow reverberating in her skull as her face smacked against the metal. Yoltan grabbed her hair and pulled her to himself. "Going somewhere?"

She tried to tear him apart, but as soon as she began to focus, she lost her support and fell on all fours as Yoltan disappeared again. Getting up, she roared in frustration, "Come out, you coward. Come out and fight."

Yoltan appeared in front of her and smacked her in the chest, knocking the wind out of her. She fell on her back, sliding on the slippery floor, gasping. She tried to crawl away, but he caught up and kicked her in the gut. As the taste of blood filled her mouth, all she could think of was how useless she was. Panthea, an Erkenblood, was unable to defeat an ordinary human, while said human had the competence to break the boundaries of the arcane. He could space-jump with a cursed piece of northern marble.

And that was when it occurred to her. Could his gleamstone be made of a different material?

Yoltan rolled her over and punched her in the face, and in the time it took her to recover from the blow, he poured something into her mouth. She coughed and gagged as she swallowed at least half of what she then realized was sapping potion. *No, no.*

Her power was still there, though weaker now after two doses. She still had her matter-sensing, so she focused on Yoltan's gleamstone. And there it was. As intimate, as vivid as the rest of the surrounding matter. This was not northern marble, which meant she could destroy it.

She stumbled away from his grasp and tried to shatter the gleamstone when Yoltan grabbed her by the ankle. A moment later, she was falling, with everything around her displaced. Yoltan had space-jumped along with her. She hit the floor on her back and her elbows, with Yoltan's entire weight landing on her chest.

Groaning in pain, she willed him off herself, but only managed a slight push before he regained his grip on her. Using her state of confusion, he shoved another vial into her mouth. "How much more of this do I have to feed you?"

She could feel his gleamstone's fragility, which meant she still had some power. She used what was left to pull the stone out of his hand, but what was left was no longer enough. Yoltan noticed the gentle tug and responded by prying her mouth open and pouring his third vial of sapping potion in it despite her hopeless resistance.

Panthea spat out as much of the liquid as she could, but what she ingested was enough to chase the last of her power away. She felt no hint of matter around her anymore. Not Yoltan, not the floor ... not the gleamstone. Yoltan got up, regarding her with pity.

It was over.

His eyes narrowed as he looked down at her chest. "You know what? I think I found the stone."

The pendant had gotten out of her shirt during the fight, and the lid had cracked. Yoltan shot his hand and ripped it off her.

"No," she moaned as she crawled after him, a mix of blood and tears streaming down her face. What a foolish mistake she had made. She should have listened to Arvin and left it in his safehouse. She had failed Rassus. She had failed Ash. She had failed the rebellion. She had failed the world.

"You got yourself killed," Yoltan murmured as he inserted his knife into the slit of the pendant.

Panthea used her remaining energy to get up. She would not surrender.

Yoltan continued, "You got your old man killed." The pendant split into four pieces that dropped, along with the Bond of Third Arcane. Wearing a complacent smile, Yoltan bent to pick it up. "And you gave us the stone, anyway."

She ran as best she could and threw herself at him. The stone flew from his hand as he peeled her off himself. Panthea didn't hesitate. She jumped over the stone and took it in her fist. She would not unfold those fingers. Not while she lived.

She felt the power of the Bond of Third Arcane again. This time, she understood what Ash had said when she'd first held it. It did feel like a gleamstone. But not like a gleamstone she held in her hand. The power came from behind her, where Yoltan stood.

"Give it up," Yoltan growled as he sat on her. "You have no power; you have nowhere to go. You're done." He pressed his knee on her back as he tried to prise her fingers open. "What's your plan, witch? I'll cut off your hand if I have to." He even pulled his knife with his free hand to do it.

She cried out as she struggled to get away, "Get off of me!"

A rush of exhilaration passed through her, and a moment later, she found herself unrestrained. Not only that. She was on the opposite side of the room. Yoltan's gleamstone was glowing in his hand, and so was the Bond of Third Arcane in Panthea's.

Did I just space-jump?

Yoltan seemed as transfixed as she was. The source of power had shifted. Panthea now felt two distinct, though weaker, sources from where Yoltan stood. It suddenly made sense. Yoltan had two gleamstones on him. His own, in his hand, and Ash's, in his pocket. It had to be those Panthea was feeling. And she had just used an already-bound gleamstone. *"Listen to the Bond of Arcane,"* the whisper repeated in her head.

The image of the Bond of Second Arcane on the queen's scepter came back; what it had done to Panthea. *Dear Annahid.* Ash had been right about the three kinds of power. She had just got the order wrong. The Third Arcane was conductive wielding.

Yoltan's gleamstone glowed, but Panthea convinced herself it was hers and tapped into it before he could space-jump. The air cracked, and the power of conductive wielding pulsed in her hand. It was as if Yoltan's gleamstone was bound to her. So, this was how the queen must have felt when she'd drawn from Panthea.

"What under Diva?" the Inquisitor mumbled as his eyes glanced between Panthea and the stone he couldn't use.

The energy of Yoltan's gleamstone was strange. Different. She had used it by chance, and she was not going to experiment right now. As long as she kept him from space-jumping, she could win. The Bond's white glow was so fierce it had turned her entire hand into a crimson night lamp.

Yoltan's gleamstone shone even brighter.

"Time to win this fight," a distant voice echoed in her ear. *"Use the second source."*

Panthea tapped into Ash's gleamstone, which had the familiar energy of matter-wielding. *Here's why gleamstones are not for space-wielding.* She shattered Yoltan's gleamstone like it was a piece of glass.

For the first time, Yoltan lost his composure. He drew his knife and charged at her, but she threw him back with the arcane power in Ash's gleamstone. Then she willed the knife out of his hand and let it float in front of herself as she hobbled to him.

He walked backwards. "That stone doesn't belong to you."

Repeating the image of Ash's death over and over in her head to fuel her anger, Panthea began peppering him with weapons, tables, and anything else she could find as she recited, "There will be those of you who make the ultimate sacrifice."

His eyes wide, dodging the barrage of sharp objects, he called, "Don't do something that cannot be undone! You have murdered enough people. There's still time for you to repent."

He had to be desperate to guilt her like this. To go so low as to exploit her faith. There was one thing he didn't know. She had accepted her fate as an agent of Angra. Yoltan was someone who would only strengthen Angra's soul. It was her painful duty to darken her own to help Annahid, even though she would not join her. Closing the distance, she kept reciting, "Not of life, but soul. They cleanse the world with their taint. They erase shadows with their darkness."

The Inquisitor was against the wall, with no room left to retreat. His gaze not leaving hers, he said, "You kill me, you'll never know which vial is the antidote."

At her command, Yoltan's knife shot into his chest. "I'm not bargaining with you," she said as she willed the knife out. Crimson blood poured over the leather as Yoltan dropped.

The remaining floating objects fell back to the ground as she stopped wielding. The room darkened as the light of the arcane artifacts faded.

Panthea stumbled to the lifeless Inquisitor, panting through her burning lungs. She winced as she kneeled beside him and emptied his pockets. Leaving the vials aside, she took out Ash's gleamstone. "This doesn't belong to you."

Blood dripping from every scratch in her body, she shuffled to the open door and went down the stairs, using the walls to steady her descent. Down there, Gvosh had killed a dozen blackhoods, and it had taken a great toll on him. He was pinned on the ground, covered in cuts. The two remaining blackhoods were ready to strike him down, but when they saw Panthea, they stopped the execution.

"Kill them," Gvosh growled. "Kill the bastards."

She considered the survivors. Tears filling her eyes, she held up Ash's gleamstone to end them, but through her blurry vision, she saw a faint image of her best friend standing between her and the men. Panthea couldn't breathe. Ash wouldn't approve of what she was doing. She'd already been avenged, and she wouldn't want more blood spilled in her name. No. The young wielder would not have wanted any blood spilled in her name. She hadn't hurt a soul in her life.

When Panthea blinked, the image disappeared as the tears finally found their way down. She felt empty. It was as if she had lost Ash for a second time. She lowered the gleamstone and muttered, "Leave . . . before you face the same fate as your Inquisitor."

The blackhoods dropped their daggers and ran away, leaving Panthea, Gvosh . . . and Rassus. Pain was visible in the old man's features. All kinds of pain.

As she passed by Gvosh, she looked down at him, at his wounds. "Are you all right?"

"Yeah," he said with a fatigued voice as he eased onto his buttocks and slid to the wall. "It takes more than this to kill me." He motioned toward Rassus. "Go to your old man."

Panthea wanted nothing more. She went to Rassus and sat to his right, putting both stones on the floor. Slowly, carefully, she wrapped her arm around his, then rested her temple on the rough, torn fabric covering his shoulder. He kissed her head, his breaths short and quick. Wearing a faint smile, he said, "Now, look what you got yourself into, you brat."

So, Rassus does say brat. She pulled away and leaned against the wall. The ancient, musty smell of his robe, laced with sweat, comforted her. His presence extinguished the fire she had in her moments ago, and her heart slowed with a sudden, almost inexplicable relief.

Rassus regarded her from the corner of his eyes, wincing when he tried to turn his neck. "What about the antidote?"

"I don't know which of the two to drink. It could be the poison. I could die faster than I am now."

He groaned as he shifted in place. "You must try."

"No. I just want to spend what time I have left with you."

She closed her eyes, leaned to him again, and took a soothing breath. This moment was one she would take with her.

33

I can smell the stench of burning flesh, see the smoke rising from the horizon, hear the cries of widows. I can see the war approaching.

A CLANG CAME FROM the top of the stairs. Two, no, three, no, ten pairs of footfalls echoed in the hallway. Panthea opened her eyes to find Arvin and Mart running down, along with a few soldiers. Arvin dropped in front of her. "Panthea. I'm so glad you're alive."

She smiled and said with what voice she had left, "You're always late, aren't you?"

"I'm sorry," he said with a rueful smile. He shifted to Rassus. "You must be Master Rassus. It's an honor to meet you. We are with the rebellion, and we're here to—"

"See if my apprentice," the old man croaked, "survived the death trap you made her walk into?"

Arvin winced.

"What happened to you, Cousin?" Mart said. "You look like shit."

"Fuck off."

The bells rang to announce the new hour—the bells that were

supposed to mark Panthea's end. She felt groggy, but that was to be expected, considering her thinned blood. But she was very much alive. She turned to Rassus, who seemed to be as flustered. As relieved.

A titter burst out of Panthea, and Rassus followed suit. The poison had been a lie. Inquisitor Yoltan, the formidable Inquisitor Yoltan, had pulled such a cheap trick to coerce her into cooperation.

"Am I missing something?" Arvin said, smiling. His admiring gaze had that same intensity that sent butterflies to her stomach.

Panthea shook her head. "Let's just say someone made his last bluff."

"Where's Grumpy?" Mart asked. "She should be here by now."

"Hey," Arvin said to Panthea. "Did you see a tall woman coming here?"

Panthea frowned. "I didn't see any woman . . . except the queen."

"Where is the queen now?"

She gave a slight shrug. "After I attacked, they took her away."

Arvin got up, a disconcerting realization turning his expression. "Oh, Hilia." He faced Mart. "There were no documents. It was a lie. Hilia is waiting for the queen in her chambers."

"Of course, she is," Mart said. He then turned back. "Hey, Cousin. Make yourself useful. Get your ass up and help the old man out of here. We'll regroup at the rendezvous point."

"I'll rip that mustache off your face," Gvosh said as he used the wall to get up. "*Cousin*."

Mart clapped Arvin's back. "Let's go, my man. We've got a grumpy daredevil to extract."

"I'll help," Panthea offered.

"No," Rassus said. "You stay out of this."

She looked into the old man's fatigued eyes and said, "Master, these people have saved my life multiple times. It's my turn to help them."

"You have been reckless enough for one day," Rassus said sharply. "You barely survived the fight with the Inquisitor. You cannot take on Artenus. Have you forgotten you're sapped?"

"But that's good," she argued. "It means she can't use her Bond to draw from me. Besides, she's sapped too. And I have the Bond of Third Arcane to prevent her from using a gleamstone, and I have Ash's gleamstone to use myself."

"You have the Bond?" Arvin said. "So, what did you . . ."

Panthea winced. "Sorry. I couldn't take the risk."

He pursed his lips. "And, uh, you know how to use it now?"

She nodded, turning to Rassus again, who was still struggling with his decision. "Master. You said you should have trusted me from the beginning. I want you to trust me now."

The old man sighed, and although there was no conviction in his assent, he nodded. "Be careful. I have already lost one apprentice."

She kissed his forehead before she got up with Arvin's help. As much as she wished she could reassure Rassus, she knew he would never agree to her putting her life on the line like this.

"All right, Dazzle-eyes," Mart said. "Let's kill some bastards."

"No," she rebuffed, squeezing Ash's gleamstone, her only remaining weapon. "No killing before we get to the queen. I'll knock out the guards." She remembered how Yoltan's gleamstone had felt weaker from across the room. "When we get there, keep me close to the queen. The connection of the Bond weakens with distance."

HILIA HELD HER BREATH as the steps got close, and she remained still until Queen Artenus walked in.

"Guard the room from outside," the queen commanded as she locked the door. When her gaze caught Hilia's baleful grin, a visible start passed through her. She rushed to undo the lock.

Hilia closed their distance, pointing the steak knife at her. "Uh-uh, I don't think so," she said as she chased the woman away from the door. "And don't try calling for help, or I'll cut your throat before your voice gets out."

Queen Artenus let out a short, scornful huff, shaking her head. "Save them from monsters, sacrifice everything for them, and yet, they bite like rabid dogs." There was no sign of fear in her eyes, and even the initial shock was gone. "You disappoint me, Hilia."

Hilia smirked. "Don't beat yourself up. I disappoint a lot of people. Any last words?" She removed the key from the door and flung it to the far edge of the room.

"You have it all figured out, have you not?" The smile on her face was infuriating. "I almost want to let you do it. Alas, the fate of this world is much too important for that."

"Well, lucky me, because I'm not going to need your permission. You may have fooled everyone else in the palace, but we both know you're not immortal. You won't survive if you can't space-jump. Now, tell me I'm wrong. Tell me I don't know what I'm talking about."

The queen nodded, and Hilia noticed her hand reaching for the drawer on the bedside table. "You are wiser than I gave you credit for. But there is still much you don't know. And what you don't know will be your undoing."

"Oh, well," Hilia said. "Guess those were your last words." She charged at the queen, jabbing with the knife. The woman dodged and slid away from the corner she was in.

From behind, she smacked Hilia in the back with the Dark Scepter, and by the time Hilia fully turned, it was already touching her neck. Hilia jumped back to escape the whispers. "You can't kill me with that thing. You said it yourself."

Hilia attacked again, but the queen used the scepter to deflect her swing. The knife got caught between the snakeheads and flew to the other side of the room. The queen produced her own dagger as she bellowed, "Intruder!"

The guards began ramming the door.

"You bitch." Hilia jumped on the queen. The woman tried to stab her, but Hilia was faster, and they both went down on impact.

The door heaved and cracked as the soldiers used all their might to break it, but Hilia didn't pay heed. If she was going to be executed, she would at least kill the witch. She pinned the woman down using all her weight, and the bitch did not make it easy. She was as strong as Hilia, if not more so. The blade was inches away from Hilia's skin, and she had to focus half of her strength on not being stabbed in the throat.

"You fool," the queen muttered. "I'm the savior. Your world will collapse without me."

Beads of sweat forming on her forehead, Hilia said under clenched teeth, "You're no one's savior. You're a disease that needs to be cured." She used her everything to wrench the queen's arm out of her face and more to twist it to her side. She cried out as she finally plunged that dagger into the queen.

Shock washed over the woman. Hilia withdrew the weapon and rolled away, panting. Warm blood bubbled out of the wound. The queen slowly got up, and she shuffled to the nightstand, wincing at the pain. Hilia jumped to her feet, pointing the blade in her direction. "Stay down."

"You know the difference between you and I?" the queen said on her way, a tremor noticeable in her voice. She opened the drawer and picked up a fist-sized ball of milky marble. "You improvise. I plan. That's why I'll always be one step ahead of you."

The stone glowed white, which seemed to be something the queen wasn't expecting, for her features contorted into an expression of disbelief.

The door splintered, and Hilia gasped as she shifted the point of her dagger to the intruders while squeezing herself to the corner. She could not fight all the guards. If they were the guards, that was. Instead, it was Arvin and Mart who entered the room, accompanied by a girl. Hilia's breath froze. It was not just any girl. It was the one Hilia had seen in her nightmares over and over. The dead girl. Same face, same innocence.

The girl also had a glowing stone in her hand. It was minuscule compared to any other arcane artifact Hilia had encountered—with the exception of the ruby on the Dark Scepter.

The queen chuckled mirthlessly, her forehead glistening with sweat. "Look . . . It's Panthea. The girl with the Bond of Arcane." *Well, that's one question answered.* "I suppose you're wondering whether you're fast enough to switch to your own gleamstone and kill me before I space-jump." She grunted. "I'll . . . give you the answer. You're not. Now, release your hold before you hurt yourself. That Bond is no toy."

Panthea didn't give up. "Surrender, Queen Artenus, and die with dignity. It's over."

"I understand these people." The queen's voice shook as she lost more blood. "But not you. You think they're your friends? Let me break it to you, Panthea. You're an Erkenblood. People have always feared us, and they always will."

"Shut your mouth, witch," Arvin said. "Don't try to manipulate her."

The queen didn't even pretend she heard him. She went on, as if not interrupted, "The moment you're no use to them, they won't hesitate to stab you in the back. I'm the only one in this room who can protect you."

"Protect me?" Panthea said with a pained smile. "Is that why you left me at the mercy of the Inquisitor?"

"I left him at *your* mercy. He never stood a chance against you."

Hilia hoped Panthea was not buying this ruse, though it seemed like she was. Although the stone in her hand didn't stop glowing, the hand itself lowered.

The queen's lips twitched into a self-satisfied smile as she slowly approached the girl.

Hilia gripped the handle of the knife. It wasn't hard to guess what the witch had in mind. Throw Panthea out of the window, get her stone released, and space-jump. She would succeed too. Hilia had seen it in her nightmares. The girl was always dead, sprawled under the residence building, curdled blood covering her face.

In one swift motion, the queen grabbed Panthea by the shoulders. And Hilia began running to save the girl. To her surprise, the queen didn't push Panthea out of the window, but away from it, and she used the momentum to jump out herself.

In those few moments it took Hilia to reach the window, the girl found her balance again and went after the queen, yelling, "No!"

Then she, too, dove.

Hilia dropped the knife and caught Panthea's ankle in mid-air, her heart racing. Time almost came to a halt. And before the girl's weight even took hold, Hilia knew the queen's actual plan. Save the Erkenblood, jump out of the window, fall out of range, space-jump.

Panthea still had her Bond of Arcane pointed toward the falling queen as she swung into the outer wall. This was the moment that would decide the fate of the Southern Kingdom, and Hilia had but an instant to make that decision.

And before the girl's weight even took hold, Hilia let go.

She barely registered Arvin's cry from her side as he rushed to the window. "Panthea!"

The two women went down. All the way down. And Hilia looked away as two thunks echoed. Two. Not one. The queen of the Southern Kingdom was dead. At long last, it was over.

No one breathed for the next few seconds. Grief was all over Arvin's now pallid face. "What . . ." he rasped, visibly failing to digest what had transpired. Tears tumbling down his cheeks, he dashed toward the exit. "We need to help her."

"Arvin." Hilia ran after him, catching him by the arm. "She's gone. There's nothing you can do."

"Fuck you." Arvin yanked his hand free, his face burning with rage. "This is your doing. I told you to wait for us outside. And she's not gone until I see it for myself."

Tears stung Hilia's eyes as Arvin stormed out of the chambers. He didn't know all of it. Panthea had not died because of Hilia's poor decision. Hilia had let her die. She had decided, even though for a moment, that the queen's death justified her sacrifice. And that judgment had cost an innocent life. Hilia went back to the window and looked down. The girl was just like in the dream: blood covering her face, gluing her hair together. Hilia had realized the nightmare.

Residents of the palace formed a circle around the fallen women, stunned.

Mart joined Hilia's side and clasped her shoulder. "Don't take it personally. He's just grieving. On the bright side, the queen's dead."

Hilia let out a slow huff. *Bright side.* It wasn't the words that stung. It was the part of her that agreed, that was relieved by this. If nothing else, it reminded her of the kind of person she'd become. The kind who would choose whom to sacrifice and whom to save. She had become the Arvin she'd left. She had become Mart. She had become every rebel under Windhammer's command. She had become Queen Artenus herself.

Turning away from the scene, she mumbled, "You're right."

PANTHEA COULD NOT draw breath, and the little air she could take in came at the cost of excruciating pain. Her vision was blurry, dark around the edges. Her arms were limp, her legs broken. As soon as she turned her head, the pain from her neck tore down her arms. She couldn't even scream.

Beside her lay Queen Artenus, or at least what appeared to be her. Panthea had used the Bond to prevent her from wielding space on the way down. And it had worked. This was a good death if it meant the freedom of the Southern Kingdom. Although Panthea's spirit would join Angra's, she found solace in having saved the world from the return of the Dark Ages.

Two figures towered over her. Although the image was too hazy for her to make out their faces, she could tell they wore green robes with their hoods pulled forward. One of them crouched beside her while the other went to the queen. The figure opened Panthea's hand that had fused with the Bond of Third Arcane. She would resist if she could move at all.

The stranger took the Bond before putting their hand on Panthea's chest. A glow emanated from the person's face, and what followed dwarfed any physical pain she had felt up to that moment. Her bones cracked. Her muscles twisted. Darkness grew toward the center of her vision until it was all she could see.

34

The war is nigh, but I have served my purpose. I have found our savior, the uniter of Sessara, the Wandering Queen. I have found you . . .

I NDISTINCT VOICES SPOKE from far away. Panthea could not make out whom they belonged to or what they said. It took her a while to realize she lay on a bed. She opened her eyes to a dark room. This could not be what being a god felt like. Nor could it be the Garden of Virtue Ahuraics believed in. A moment later, when all the pain came back, she knew she was not even dead.

Fighting the aching in her back, she slowly rolled to the side and slid her legs off the bed to sit on the edge. When she tried to stand, her knees screamed with pain under her weight, and she dropped to the floor.

"Arvin." Her voice was too weak for anyone to hear. Frustrated, she extended her arm toward the door and willed it to swing open.

The other room was well lit, and there, around an oblong table, stood five to six people, among whom she only recognized Arvin and Mart.

Eyes wide, Arvin rushed to her. He sat her up, then scooped her into a tight embrace. "I thought we'd lost you. Don't ever scare me like that again."

Arvin helped her stand. With him holding under her shoulder and carrying most of her weight, they exited the room.

As she fully regained her senses, the image of the moment before she had blacked out came back to her. "Did the queen die?"

Arvin exchanged a look with the others, then said, "We don't know."

"What do you mean, you don't know?"

"She disappeared. When we arrived at the bottom, she wasn't there."

Panthea felt a chill as she remembered the figure taking the Bond out of her hand. "The stone. Where's the stone?"

Arvin pursed his lips.

"No." Her voice cracked. After all this, she had lost the Bond, and the queen was not even dead. Worse. She probably already had the stone. "So, it was all for nothing?"

"Nothing?" Mart said from behind the table. "How hard did you hit your head, girl? We killed two Inquisitors, the queen is missing, and people are taken to the streets. Delavaran is on the brink of collapse. You call that nothing?"

The tall woman she'd seen in the queen's chambers entered the house. She beamed when she saw Panthea, although there was something behind her smile. Some kind of apprehension. "Hey, look who's back from the dead. Brace yourself, girl, because I want to learn everything about the famous Erkenblood of Saba."

Before the door closed, Gvosh also walked in. When he saw Panthea, his eyes widened. "There she is. Alive and awake." He let out a good-humored huff. "You're the craziest girl I know."

"Hey, Splat," Mart called. "Do you want to join us over here?"

The woman slapped her forehead.

"Splat?" Panthea wondered.

"You know," Arvin explained, almost cringing. "You jumped, you splatted. Sorry about him."

Gvosh shrugged. "I like Splat. It's far better than the other names he used for you while you were asleep."

"What did he call me?" Panthea asked, smiling.

"Um, let me think. Jumper, Undead, Immortal, Madwoman. Oh, and my favorite. Pressed Peach."

"You're an asshole, Mart," Arvin said as he and the woman shook their heads.

"I try." Mart winked. "Anyway, there are things we have to discuss. We still don't know if the rioters will take over the city. If they do, we don't want to miss out on the prize. The big guy will be pissed if his life's work is handed to some good-for-nothing cult leader or a stupid vigilante. We need a course of action."

"They won't take Delavaran," Arvin reassured, his voice confident. "They're not half as organized as we are, and Sapphires have contingencies in place for a coup. This uprising will die down, and what's left will be a thrice-fortified capital and a neglect of the Shiranian region. As we speak, our man is being sworn in as the new head of the Inquisition in Saba. We can finally take over Shiran while the army and the Inquisition are busy reclaiming Delavaran."

Mart's lips turned up in a crooked smile. "I like the sound of that. I'll write to the big guy. Meanwhile," his gaze shifted to Panthea, "Splat, there is something we need your help with. It's a document."

Arvin gave him a hard look. "Have some manners, Mart. She's just woken up. Let her rest for a few days."

"No." Panthea hobbled to the group, her eyes tearing up with the pain in her knees. "I've rested enough."

"By the way." Arvin picked up Ash's gleamstone from the table and held it out. "You dropped this when you jumped."

Panthea's heart leaped. "Thank you," she said before she took those last painful steps toward the table and retrieved it. It was no longer glimmering as brightly as it used to. With the amount of power she'd drawn from it, there would not be much left now. This little glimmer, she would preserve until the day she died.

Mart raised a finger. "Let's get something out of the way first. This girl plunged three stories. Yet, she's still here with us." He looked her up and down. "Most of her, at least." He then swept a look across his audience.

"Anyone know what this means, or do I have to spell it out?"

"That the queen has also survived," Arvin suggested.

"No, you idiot. It means we have one of them on our side. Splat here is as immortal as the queen is."

"I'm not immortal," Panthea rebutted.

Arvin turned to her, raising his eyebrows. "Few could have survived that fall, Panthea. How did you do it?"

"I don't know." She tried to make sense of those last images. "There were these figures. One of them put their hand on my chest, and all I remember from there on is pain. I believe they did something to me."

"Mm-hmm," the tall woman, Hilia, said. "To you and everyone else at the scene. Everyone was unconscious when Arvin arrived."

Arvin gave Hilia a half-smile before he turned to Panthea. "Do you think they heal you with arcane power?"

Panthea opened her mouth to say that was not how things worked, but she paused. There had been a lot of things that shouldn't be. There was still a lot, it seemed, that she needed to learn about the arcane. "I honestly don't know. What I know is that the queen is creating an army of Erkenbloods, and she wants to bring back the Dark Ages."

"Which brings us to our first point," Mart said, sliding a small stack of papers toward her. "Grumpy here found this note in the queen's drawer. Do you recognize the language?"

Panthea looked over at the writing. "It's Angelic."

"Can you read it?"

Panthea started to read and translate.

I admit she wasn't my choice at first. We had searched for centuries for the ultimate savior . . .

As Panthea read the letter, an uneasy feeling came over her. Whoever had written this knew a lot about the Angelian religion and even more about history. She kept reading until the end.

The war is nigh, but I have served my purpose. I have found
our savior, the uniter of Sessara, the Wandering Queen. I
have found you, Artenus.

Panthea's breath hitched, and the others seemed as stupefied as she was. Even Mart's smirk had staled.

"It adds up," Hilia said. "Back in the chambers, the queen said she was the savior." She grimaced. "What does that even mean? Savior of what?"

"This is far worse than I thought," Panthea exclaimed. "The Wandering Queen is an end-of-time prophecy. For it to be realized, the whole world must be at war."

The door opened, and Rassus walked in with the aid of a simple staff.

"Master!" Panthea hobbled to him and drew him into a hug. Being with him was surreal after everything that had happened. It almost felt like she didn't deserve it. Gripping the gleamstone, she wished Ash were here to share this moment with her.

The old man also wrapped his arms around her. "You should really stop getting yourself in trouble." He kissed the top of her head.

"I'm sorry, Master. I failed."

"You didn't," Rassus said. "If anyone is to blame, it is I. I should have prepared you for this. I've been a fool." He pulled away and squeezed her arm. "I'm proud of you, Matter Star."

A fuzzy feeling tingled her scalp and warmed her face. She loved hearing that name again after so many years. Especially now that she knew what it meant—everything it meant. She glanced back to find everyone watching the exchange. She wiped her tears. "Master. The rebels have found a letter in the queen's chambers. I think you should read it."

They went to the table and, with everyone's eyes upon him, Rassus read the note, stroking a shaky finger under the words. He remained quiet for long after he was finished, until he finally said, "So, this is why Artenus is after the Bonds. Whoever these people are, they have knowledge they should not have; information obscured for almost five centuries. We need to stop Artenus before she finds the Bond of First Arcane. I do not know her intentions, and I am not willing to wait to find out."

By now, Panthea knew two of the three Arcanes. "What is First Arcane, Master?"

Rassus swept a passing look through all the expectant eyes. "Pure, unbridled power. The kind that created the first Erkenbloods. The power to reshape the workings of the world. My forefathers removed its every mention from the History of the Arcane so no one other than us protectors could know. That these people do makes them dangerous."

Rassus did not seem to believe the contents of the letter, but with everything Panthea had witnessed, she couldn't ignore the possibility, as uncomfortable as it made her feel. "What if they're right? What if the master of all elements has really arisen? What if the end of time is upon us?"

"And Artenus is the Wandering Queen?" Rassus huffed. "Evidently, some people are trying to use the prophecy to further their own goals. We need to go to the Northern Realm."

Gasps rippled in the room. Even Panthea's own heart skipped a beat at the mention of the queen's birthplace, even though she had always wanted to travel there.

"I'm sorry?" Mart sneered. "Sleeping with the enemy, are we?"

"The Northern Realm is no one's enemy," Rassus said. "And they have the remaining Bond of Arcane. We need to warn the High Lady of Sepead and ask her for help."

HILIA STIFLED A SNORT at the irony. Fighting against something for six years, only to have to go back to it for help. This old man sure had not met that many northerners. He hadn't lost his whole life's work because of some pompous northern bully.

Arvin seemed to recognize the sting of those words, for he stared into her eyes sympathetically. She gave a beckoning motion with her head as she exited the house. She waited there, gazing toward the people milling about in the main square of the Upper City until Arvin joined her.

For a time, neither spoke, until Hilia opened the conversation, wearing a lopsided smile. "So, you're still in the business of saving eighteen-year-old girls."

"Still in the business of losing them." He regarded her wistfully.

She didn't want to get sentimental, but knowing he missed her just as she missed him brightened a guilty corner of her heart. She glanced back at the house. "She's sweet, by the way."

He pursed his lips. "You want to leave, don't you?"

Arvin was always this perceptive. Standing next to him, Hilia was having a hard time remembering why she had left.

It didn't matter. She knew why she had to leave now. She needed some distance from Arvin, from the rebellion. From this Hilia. The Hilia who would so easily let an innocent girl die.

Panthea's survival had been a wake-up call. There was still a chance for Hilia to redeem herself, and she would damned take it.

"This isn't my life," she confessed. "This cause is taking away the part of me I'm so desperately trying to preserve. I was too ignorant to see it before. I was blinded by revenge, by . . ." She glanced at him and mumbled as quickly as she could, "Love."

There was a pause. Long enough for her to wonder, but not long enough for her to look.

"I've been thinking for the last few days," Arvin murmured. "About what we had, what could have been. Seeing you again brought back so many memories. I'd be lying if I said that through these years, I never thought of leaving it all behind, begging for your forgiveness, and getting away with you to live the simple life. Do you think we made a mistake?"

He was not making this easy. Shouldering him playfully, she said, "Don't be corny. Doesn't suit you." She took a deep breath to shake off her emotions. Well, emotion, singular. "I don't think either of us can ever live a simple life." She looked into his beautiful eyes and gave herself a second to relish before she surrendered to pragmatism. "And I don't think we made a mistake. This is who you are, Arvin. I would have hated to see you stop being the hero I knew. You inspired me so much, I've been living your life for six years. But now, I think it's time for me to go back to who I am. Some things belong to the past."

Arvin looked away, visibly going through a few emotions himself. "Where will you go?"

"You know where I'll go."

A nod. "I think your father could use the company. I hope one day, our paths cross again."

"I'm sure they will. In the meantime, take care of Panthea for me, will you?" She smirked. "You've been doing a lousy job so far."

REBELS HAD GATHERED in Mart's home, drinking, laughing, celebrating. The only familiar faces were Mart, Arvin, Gvosh, and a few of Mart's friends Panthea had seen in Serene.

Mart clapped his hands as he went to the middle of the sitting room. "All right, everyone. A moment?"

He waited until the chatters died down before he began, "Here's a message the Windhammer wanted me to deliver to you. He thanks you for your bravery and your devotion to the cause. There was a time when hope was all we had. Together, we grew stronger, and on the Dark Fusion, we shook the foundation of the Sapphire Order."

Cheers rose from the room.

Mart then raised his cup. "And here's one from me. Raise your glasses or cups . . . or whatever that guy's holding, to the heroes we've lost. To Mehran. A great friend, a valiant hero. To . . ."

Mart said a few names, then others chimed in. Panthea's mind drifted. These people were not the only ones who had died by the bloody hands of the Sapphire Order, but they had the privilege of being known by the rebels. Those like Ash, who had been unfairly killed, would never be mentioned.

"To Ash," Arvin's voice ripped her out of her thoughts with a start. "A devoted friend with a pure heart. The young woman who gave her life to protect the Erkenblood of Saba."

Everyone cheered for Ash. Panthea's scalp prickled, her eyes warming with tears. And Arvin's reassuring nod made her feel at home. The names continued. Now that Ash was mentioned, now that everyone knew her for the hero she had been, Panthea felt so much lighter. Although there was little left of her old family, she had found a new one. For the first time in her life, she knew her destiny. She knew who she was. Panthea, the Erkenblood of Saba, the freedom fighter.

She felt about with her hand until her fingers touched Arvin's. He gave her a short glance, then a smile, then he took her hand in his.

ACKNOWLEDGEMENTS

The Erkenblood was not just a novel for me. It was my journey to becoming a writer, and I owe it to the immense help and support I received from the amazing people who made it possible.

First and foremost I would like to thank my wife, who was a pillar of patience, and whose constant encouragement drove me through a path that was not always easy. From listening to the story and discussing plot issues, to providing emotional support, to celebrating every little success with me, she was always by my side.

A shout-out goes to my critique partner, Laken Honeycutt, who was always there when I needed help, and who helped me shape the story. I've also had the honor of working with some amazing beta readers. My thanks go to Malyn Long, McKenzie L. Moos, Michele Quirke, and Charlotte Taylor for their invaluable feedback and their support.

I'd like to thank my editors, Charlie Knight and Jodi Christensen, and my proofreader, Jodie Angell, for truly caring about this story. They all went above and beyond to help me bring out its essence and turn it into what you just read.

My thanks also go to my talented cover designer, Lance Buckley, who created a cover that's on par with those of bestsellers in bookstores. And, of course, the cover wouldn't be the same without the blurb masterfully crafted by Jacob Steven Mohr.

My eternal gratitude goes to my parents for always believing in me, especially my mother, who raised us on her own, and wishes nothing but greatness for me and my brother, regardless of what endeavor we embark on.

Lastly, and most importantly, I'd like to thank you, my reader, who followed Panthea and Hilia through their joys and their tears. I hope you'll stick with the series to see how their journey continues.

About the Author

From the heart of the Black Forest in Germany, H. Ferry writes stories of broken people navigating broken worlds. When he's not writing, you can find him reading his next favorite book or building an electronic contraption or a piece of software.

www.ferryfiction.com

contact@ferryfiction.com

twitter.com/AuthorHFerry

instagram.com/ferryfiction

facebook.com/ferryfiction

Printed in Great Britain
by Amazon